A Wild Dreaming . . .

Julia saw the hungry look kindle the Scotsman's eyes. He gathered her to him, drawing her up in his arms till they both knelt in the middle of the mattress, pressed together. Before she could protest, his mouth crushed down on hers, a searing, possessive kiss.

His hand slid down her spine to the hollow of her back, holding her firmly against him. The wool of his plaid rasped her tender flesh, but through its folds she felt the hard, shocking proof of his desire.

Julia struggled to no avail as the Scotsman continued his aggression, parting her lips and invading her mouth. She started as his tongue laid siege to hers, stroking and ravishing till her blood surged beneath his seduction.

But as the heady kiss continued, the air turned heavy once more. Without warning, the Scotsman vanished from her arms, leaving her clutching thin air. Julia tumbled back onto the pillows panting for breath, while overhead the draperies dissolved from red into blue. . . .

A Slip in Time

Kathleen Kirkwood

A TOPAZ BOOK

Topaz
Published by the Penguin Group
Penguin Putnam Inc., 375 Hudson Street,
New York, New York 10014, U.S.A.
Penguin Books Ltd, 27 Wrights Lane,
London W8 5TZ, England
Penguin Books Australia Ltd,
Ringwood, Victoria, Australia
Penguin Books Canada Ltd, 10 Alcorn Avenue,
Toronto, Ontario, Canada M4V 3B2
Penguin Books (N.Z.) Ltd, 182-190 Wairau Road,
Auckland 10, New Zealand

Penguin Books Ltd, Registered Offices:
Harmondsworth, Middlesex, England

First published by Topaz, an imprint of Dutton NAL,
a member of Penguin Putnam Inc.

First Printing, October, 1998
10 9 8 7 6 5 4 3 2 1

 REGISTERED TRADEMARK—MARCA REGISTRADA

Printed in the United States of America

Chapter 1

Scotland, September, 1893

Dunraven Castle. A chill of unease spiraled through Julia at the very thought of the name. Strange it should affect her thusly, yet it did, no less now than when first she heard it, two nights past—the night Emmaline burst in upon her solitude and made her ebullient announcement. . . .

"We're off to Scotland, cousin! Lord Eaton has invited the lot of us to his Highland estate, Dunraven Castle. He leaves on the morrow, and we are to follow. Isn't it exciting?"

Emmaline whirled off in a flurry of pastels and lace, leaving Julia slack-jawed and thoroughly aghast.

Scotland? On the morrow? How could her aunts have agreed to such? Certainly, she wished to leave Braxton Hall, but she longed to return to Hampshire, not the distant wilds of the Scottish Highlands. Indeed, she had intended to broach the subject with her aunts over breakfast and remained determined to still. It was why she had retired early, forgoing the customary gathering for charades and whist. She had polished and practiced her speech till it flowed most persuasively from her lips.

But now this. How could Aunt Sybil and Aunt Rachel accept so precipitous an invitation? And from Lord Eaton. Now there was a packet of trouble. . . .

The shrill of the steam whistle pierced Julia's ears, jolting her back to the present, back to the constant rattling and shaking of the train beneath her. She huddled deeper in her thin woolen cloak, her fingers stiff with cold.

"Oh, look!" Emmaline enthused beside her, wiping the

droplets of condensation from the window with her handkerchief. "A castle. Isn't it splendidly romantic?"

As she spoke, the solid, rumbling resonance of the wheels
and rails changed to one of hollow clattering. The mountains
nearby, muted by mist and drizzle, slipped suddenly from view.

Julia leaned forward to see around Emmaline's caped and
behatted figure. Still, this proved difficult as the bench they
shared faced backward, and the scenery could only be glimpsed
as it flew past and disappeared down the line.

Closing the space between them, Julia peered out through the
mizzling rain. And regretted it instantly. The train raced along
a viaduct, high above the rolling landscape and at a fabulous
speed. Her stomach did a flip-flop, threatening to turn completely as it had so many times since leaving London early this
morn. She steeled herself and at Emmaline's insistence looked
again.

She saw now that the viaduct curved in a wide arc, following
the contours of a deep and sheltered glen. Far below, at the
heart of the glen, Julia spied the unroofed ruins of a centuries-
old tower house. Its red-sandstone keep rose from a spit of land
that projected into a silvery loch. A gauzy mist wreathed the
grounds and tower remnants, lending the scene an enchanted,
otherworldly aspect.

Lilith, Julia and Emmaline's elder cousin and the third in
their party, stirred on the cushioned bench opposite. She rose
from her reclining position and gazed out the window.

"A castle?" Lilith sniffed. "That crumbling pile?"

"Oh, but surely it was once a great fortress," Emmaline declared. "It looks to have endured a tempestuous history, does it
not? Imagine all it has witnessed throughout the centuries. If
only its stones could but whisper, such tales they would weave
of the proud Highland chieftains who once dwelled there. And
loved there," she added the last with a wistful sigh.

A smile stole through Julia. The tapestry bag at Emmaline's
feet held a cache of Scott's stirringly romantic novels—*Waverly, Rob Roy, The Fair Maid of Perth,* and more, all well
worn. Like so many of their countrymen racing north, Emma-

line had caught the "Scottish Fever." Julia began to tease her of as much, when Lilith spoke.

"Your 'proud Highland chieftains' of yesteryear were little more than coarse barbarians, dear cousin."

"Say what you will." Emmaline tossed her dark curls, smiling. "But, I'd wager they were immensely more passionate and colorful than any of the men in our company this summer."

Surprise stung Lilith's eyes, as though she had just received a personal affront. Her lips formed a response, but before she could voice it, Emmaline turned back to the window, giving a light shrug.

"Well, almost any of the men."

Julia blinked, unsure about to whom Emmaline referred. Lilith eased her rigid pose, presumably believing Emmaline included Lord Eaton in her comment. It was no secret that Lilith—and her mother, Julia's Aunt Sybil—had staked her future hopes on the exceedingly blue-blooded, exceedingly wealthy Roger Dunnington, Lord Eaton. Yet, Julia's instincts told her Emmaline held someone else in mind. Someone in their company, then? Traveling to Dunraven?

Lilith regarded Emmaline a long moment as if considering the same. She then reached across and patted her hand, concern stitching her brow.

"I do worry for your judgment, cousin. Fantasies aside, 'passion' and 'color' might offer temporary diversion, excitement even, but they cannot replace more solid, reassuring qualities in a man such as titles and privilege. Those are the things upon which you must set your heart, if you are to make an advantageous match."

"Titles are not qualities. And surely a heart must be given to more than cold fortune," Emmaline retorted, quick, defensive. A shade too quick and too defensive to Julia's mind, and she wondered how the conversation had skipped from phantom chieftains of centuries past to husband-hunting among the peerage.

"Do not dismiss their import so quickly," Lilith continued. "Passion and color fade. Then what is left a woman? You have heard our mothers speak. Choices poorly made carry a lifetime of consequences." She slid a glance to Julia, an indefinable look entering her eyes. "Do you not agree?" her tone turned candy sweet.

Julia recognized the hidden barb, directed at her own parents' marriage, but she answered anyway. "Some choices, well made, regardless of station, prove without regrets."

A thin smile unfurled over Lilith's lips. "Of course, you would think so." Drawing up the high fur collar of her pelisse, she settled back against her seat and feigned rest, yet her smile remained.

A stricken look washed over Emmaline's face and she started to speak, but Julia shook her head. She blamed herself for playing into Lilith's manipulations. Again. Soon enough, Julia promised herself, she would return to Hampshire and be no longer plagued by Lilith's ill manners. She would miss Emmaline, however.

Julia nibbled her lip, her thoughts circling back to who might have captured her cousin's affections. Julia could think of several in their company with more dash than station. She could also imagine Aunt Rachel's horror to find her daughter enamored of any one of them.

Another scream of the whistle caused Julia to jump. In the next moment, daylight disappeared and the pounding of the train amplified threefold as they entered a tunnel. Gratefully, gaslights burned continuously in the compartments on Scottish lines. She owed this to the numerous tunnels through which they passed, some miles long.

She prayed the tunnel would prove short, for every discomfort of rail travel seemed magnified in its confines—the pungent odors of the engine's discharge, soot sifting through the window margins, the deafening noise as the iron giant labored up the gradient, plus the relentless jarring and the unsettling motion of traveling backward. Julia pressed her lashes shut and tried to ignore her stomach as it roiled beneath her wretchedly tight stays.

She forced her mind to more pleasant thoughts. Stubbornly, they returned, time and again, to the prick of Lilith's comments.

Julia released a small sigh. She did not belong here, in the highborn circles of her mother's family. Not truly. The Symington ties had been severed years before, upon her parents' wedding day. And until their deaths, those ties remained broken, punishment to a daughter who dared choose her heart over the desires of her parents.

It had been a year since the tragedy. Since the ship sank off the coast of Ceylon, taking her beloved parents and all those aboard. Then, several days after the memorial services, the inconceivable happened.

Julia had spent a grueling morning with her father's former partner and their solicitor, reviewing matters of the estate's debts. No sooner did she see them out of her home, when a dark green phaeton, bearing the Symington crest, pulled before the entrance. A footman hastened to open the door and a woman emerged, diminutive in size but ramrod straight and heavily veiled in black. Julia remained fixed in place, stunned as she realized her visitor to be none other than the "old lioness" herself, Arabella Symington, her maternal grandmother.

They stared at one another for long moments before Julia recovered enough to invite her visitor inside. At first, Lady Arabella moved silently through the rooms, reaching out at times to touch some cherished object—a family photograph, her mother's lace fan and silver hair brushes. But when she discovered a china doll, once belonging to Julia's mother as a small child, Arabella's steely control crumbled. She clutched the doll to her breast and sobbed her daughter's name till her voice went raw with grief. Julia watched astounded, and in that moment she could nearly forgive her grandmother the past. Nearly.

Much later, they sat in the front parlor, sharing tea in silence. Her grandmother, composed and dry-eyed, studied Julia closely. Julia assumed it to be a trial for her to do so, for she possessed her father's golden looks and his clear green eyes.

Yet, she knew she bore a marked resemblance to her mother as well, about the nose and mouth, and in the tilt of her brows.

At length, her grandmother broke her silence, setting down her teacup, some decision made. "You will come to Gramercy with me, child," she stated with the air of one accustomed to giving orders. "There, your needs can be comfortably met while you see through the months of mourning, and we weigh the possibilities for your future."

Whatever Julia expected it was not this. Why should she accept an invitation from the family that had treated her mother so callously, or allow any of them a say in her future? She started to decline, but her grandmother raised a hand, staying her.

"I am an old woman filled with regrets. Regrets that will burn in my soul long after I die. I cannot undo the past. But let me do this much—for both your parents. For you."

Lady Arabella paused, fidgeting with the cameo at her throat as she considered her next words.

"I know that your circumstances are, shall we say, straightened, that your parents' investments—the cargo they accompanied—went down with them at sea. You have many decisions to make, and I suspect your fine home will need be let out, if not sold. Meanwhile, come to Gramcery, child. If for no other reason, it was your mother's girlhood home. She loved it dearly. And if you do not know it, she first met your father there, too. Perhaps, you can find something of them both at Gramercy still."

And so it was that Julia entered the gilded world of the aristocracy. The world her mother once forsook.

But if it pleased her grandmother to take her under wing, Julia received a frosty reception from the other members of the family—her mother's brother, Henry, now Lord Symington, Earl of Wye, and his countess, Sybil, as well as her mother's younger sister, Rachel, the Viscountess Holbrooke.

The months crawled past. While Julia secluded herself in Kent, garbed in black, her cousins, Lilith and Emmaline, sparkled through the gala court balls and bright entertainments of London society. Gossip-filled letters arrived daily from their mothers, updating Lady Arabella as to their daughters' successes and news of the most promising catches of the Season.

As it happened, the end of Julia's period of mourning coincided with the conclusion of the London gaieties and the beginning of the midsummer migrations among the stately country houses. Before the latter commenced, Lady Arabella packed Julia and herself off to her town house in London's exclusive West End. There she summoned the family and announced Julia would accompany Lilith and Emmaline on their forthcoming social rounds. This brought wails of protest from Julia's aunts. But the "old lioness" prevailed.

Within days, Julia joined her aunts and cousins on the dizzying social circuit, traveling from one grand estate to the next, staying no more than a handful of days in any one place. From the first, Emmaline welcomed Julia with sisterly affection, delighted to have gained a fresh relation. Lilith, however, like her mother, held her with disdain.

Julia refused to feel diminished by such haughtiness. Yet, she understood their reticence to her presence. While this was Emmaline's first Season, it was Lilith's third. If she did not snare a husband this time out, she risked being labeled stale goods and doomed to spinsterhood. Lilith needed no additional competition in the field.

Julia resolved to enjoy her summer wanderings, no matter her reception. She fancied she retraced her own mother's footsteps of years past. Especially of one summer, when the lovely debutante, Helen Symington, declined the proposal of a duke of royalty to marry a baronet.

Myriad diversions filled her days—recreations of every order, elegant teas and soirees, sundry sporting events, and ceremonious meals. Of an evening, there were the requisite charades and whist and sometimes a dance, lasting till midnight in a tent on the lawn beneath the stars.

Into this dazzling world came a steady stream of missives from Lady Arabella, filled with matriarchal advice and expectations. Surely, Julia would find a suitable match, she heart-

ened. Not a titled first son of course, but a second or third.
Though Julia's dowry be slim, she *was* a Symington "of the
blood" after all, her lineage ancient and illustrious.

The days slipped past. Despite the legion of guests passing
through the great houses, Julia became well acquainted with
many, their paths crisscrossing throughout July and August.
She first believed this to be coincidence. But it soon became ap-
parent that a steadily swelling group arranged their itinerary to
"drift in tandem." The smooth-spoken Lord Eaton seemed at
the core of this merry band.

By summer's close, the excitement and glamour of elite society began to pale. The pleasure-seeking nobles were an indo-
lent lot, Julia found. Their most pressing concerns centered on
staving off their perpetual boredom.

Such aimlessness wore on Julia. She longed to gain focus to
her life. Direction and purpose. In truth, she longed to return to
Hampshire and continue the endeavors of her parents in assisting the less fortunate.

Her decision made, she prepared to approach her aunts. But
that very night Lord Eaton had issued his impulsive invitation.
Next morning, amidst a flurry of packing, Julia appealed to her
aunts. They dismissed her request out of hand, declaring they
would not risk another of the "old lioness's" verbal maulings.

Without further discussion, they set off for London, excepting Aunt Rachel, who chose to stay behind. Now with each
mile Julia journeyed farther from her goal. She refused defeat,
however. Tomorrow morning, she purposed to pen a letter to
her grandmother and make her plea directly. Surely there would
be a means at Dunraven to post it.

Dunraven Castle. There it was again. That prickly feeling
that tingled across the back of her neck and shoulders and down
her spine.

Perhaps it was just her aversion to being in the same company as Lord Eaton once more, she reasoned. She didn't trust
him. Oh, he was charming and mannerly and tolerable enough
in looks. But there had been discomforting instances when he

seemed to shadow her, once trailing her on the winding paths at Asridge and then again at Saltram.

Rumors reached her ears, too, of his fondness for the gaming dens and for certain actresses in Regent Street. The very hastiness of his invitation northward, coupled with his disappearance from Braxton, puzzled Julia. He caught the overnight Express, she was informed, ostensibly to open Dunraven and ready it for the expected entourage, the guests and their servants numbering some thirty-odd.

Julia pulled her thoughts from Lord Eaton, disquieting sensations still eddying through her. The sooner she could leave Dunraven Castle the better.

The train emerged from the tunnel to bruised but brighter skies. The rain fell faster now, in sheets, splattering the windows. Mountains thrust upward all around, their drama masked by the drenching downpour. Wooded glens soon gave way to softly rolling hills which, in turn, flattened out as the train reached the coast. Here, masts of fishing vessels crowded the shoreline. In short order a whistle blast was heard, announcing their arrival at Dunbar, one of the rare but brief stops on the line.

Julia looked up as Aunt Sybil hastily rejoined them, having left them at the previous stop to move several compartments forward to the saloon car. As the train rolled out of Dunbar and headed inland, Aunt Sybil settled herself.

"We shall reach Edinburgh within the hour, I am told," she announced crisply, her gaze compassing Lilith and Emmaline but never touching Julia. "There, we shall change trains and be on our way to Perth, our final stop. Lady Bigsby informs me Lord Eaton's carriage shall be waiting. It shan't hold us all, of course." She bent her gaze meaningfully to Julia. "But we may hire what transport is available for the remainder of the journey. Being Scottish, though, it will no doubt prove outmoded."

At that, she fell to sharing the gossip she had gleaned in the saloon car and spoke of possible excursions to the spa at Strath-

peffer and to Royal Deeside. The Prince, she confirmed, was in
residence at Albergeldie.

Within the hour, the train smoked into Waverly Station, sit-
uated in a deep and open ravine in the heart of Scotland's cap-
ital. The city towered all around, its crow-stepped gables,
multilevel tenements and soaring spires adding to its height.
Edinburgh Castle dominated all, frowning down from its
craggy perch.

Julia disembarked on wobbly legs, immensely grateful to
gain solid ground. Joining the others in their group, she moved
swiftly along the concourse, beneath the station's vast glass
dome.

The sky above appeared darkly battered now, its wind-tossed
rains buffeting the glass with considerable vigor. On she
pressed through the mad rush that mobbed the station. It would
seem half of Britain had emptied itself, come for the hunt and
recreation.

Julia hoped for a brief respite from the strains of their travels, but with a scant fifteen minutes to switch trains, luggage
and all, it was not to be. Renovations in the station complicated
the transition, making for detours up, down, and through numerous steps and passageways.

Boarding the train destined for Perth, Julia found herself and
Emmaline under the watchful eyes of Nettie, her aunt's personal maid. Meanwhile, Aunt Sybil sought out the saloon car,
taking Lilith with her.

Leaving Edinburgh and the Pentland Hills behind, the train
headed north and climbed through Dalmeny. The majestic Forth
Bridge came into view, with its cantilever trusses and diamond-
shaped towers shooting upward to a phenomenal height. In minutes, they traversed a massive stone viaduct, then entered onto
the bridge proper with its surpassing views.

On the other side, the train followed the shore to Kircaldy.
Veering inland, it passed over the richly wooded Leven valley
before it swung north, climbing ever upward, into the Central
Highlands.

With each passing hour, the weather continued to deteriorate.

The temperature inside the compartment plummeted. Numbed with cold, her stomach knotted and mutinous, Julia sought relief in sleep. She managed to doze lightly for a time, stirring to see their arrival in Perth, where it stretched along the Tay.

As promised, Lord Eaton's private coach awaited. In preemptive fashion, Sybil appropriated seats for herself, Lilith, and Emmaline, abandoning Julia to the care of acquaintances from Braxton.

"Won't you join us, my dear?" invited Lady Charles, sympathy touching her features. The plumes on her bonnet bobbled as she gestured to an aged equipage that stood before them. "There is ample room. Do come."

Julia stepped quickly through the downfall and climbed into the traveling carriage. Two gentlemen in their company followed, Lord Cuthburt Withrington and Sir Robert Longford. Within moments the horses set off.

Tracking the other conveyances in the entourage, they journeyed deep into the mountains, passing through cloistered glens and narrow gorges. One valley led into another and, at times, the other coaches slipped out of sight.

Every ten to twelve miles, they would come across a little post house where the horses could be changed or rested. Here, they could briefly rejoin their friends and refresh themselves with thin hot soup and oatcakes, though more often than not, whiskey proved the sole staple.

Julia's stomach would tolerate naught. She felt dizzy and bruised to her bones from all the tossing about. Still, she welcomed each respite, noting with some concern their coach lagged increasingly behind the others.

What had been soaking rains now became a brawling storm. Fierce winds pummeled the carriage, causing it to sway. Darkness closed in, requiring the coach lanterns to be lit early. Julia wondered if she'd survive this wild and empty land.

A fit of shivering suddenly took hold of Julia, owing more to her fatigue than the icy drafts breezing over her. She drew up her lap rug but it aided her little.

"Allow me." Sir Robert leaned forward, offering his own

blanket. He tucked the plaid about her so she was well layered in its thick, woolen folds.

"Bound to improve, you know. The weather that is." Sir Robert smiled easily, causing ray lines to appear at the corners of his eyes. "If one thing is predictable about Scottish weather, Miss Hargrove, it is that it is thoroughly *unpredictable*. And as it has been devilish since we crossed the border, I'd say we are due for a change any time now."

"Devilish?" piped in Lady Charles, resituating herself beside Julia after another jolt. "The weather has been positively diabolical. How you men think to hunt in it, I cannot conceive."

Lord Withrington, who shared the bench opposite with Sir Robert, peered over the top of his steel-rimmed glasses.

"Longford is quite right. Bound to improve. But I, for one, don't intend to allow a patch of bad weather to deter me in the least. Some of the finest sport is to be found in this portion of Scotland."

"But how will you manage it, let alone find the creatures in such a broil?" Lady Charles persisted.

"My dear lady, I've sported throughout the Highlands for many a season and in considerably wetter climes."

Lady Charles looked to Julia, mouthing Lord Withrington's last words in disbelief.

"All that as it is," he continued, ignoring her look, "I wouldn't miss this opportunity. To my memory, this is the first time Dunraven has opened its doors to guests in two decades. I don't know how young Eaton convinced his uncle to agree to it, but I am supremely gratified he did. Mark my words. The forests will be thick with game."

"Lord Eaton's *uncle*?" Julia puzzled. "I thought Dunraven was Lord Eaton's estate."

"Oh no, my child." Lady Charles wagged her head. "Roger Dunnington has yet to come into his titles. No, 'Lord Eaton' is only his courtesy title. Lord Muir, his uncle, is quite alive, though a tad ancient, seventy if he is a day. It is he who bears the prestigious title of marquis. He holds numerous lesser titles and estates in England and Scotland, as well, including that of Twenty-seventh Laird of Dunraven Castle."

"But, you say Lord Muir has invited no guests these twenty years past?" Sir Robert injected, looking to Lord Withrington. "Is there a reason?"

Lord Withrington dragged on his chin in thought. "It's all rather mysterious, actually. There was a day when the castle hosted numerous hunts. But Lord Muir closed it up quite abruptly one Season and without explanation."

"True," Lady Charles concurred. "My late husband attended several hunts at Dunraven in his younger years. He knew Lord Muir personally and praised him as a superb marksman and a genial host."

A line pleated her brow as she reached for some thread of memory.

"I believe Nigel attended that last autumn. The hunting was prime, the men of good cheer; then, on the final night of their stay, Lord Muir retired early as he was wont to do. Something occurred in the night. Or so one presumes. The next morning, he did not appear to bid his guests farewell. He became somewhat of a recluse after that and closed Dunraven to visitors."

"Rumor holds it possesses some murky secret," Lord Withrington added.

"'Possesses'?" Sir Robert's brows rose. "As in '*possessed*'? Heads floating in the castle halls, glowing 'Green' ladies, phantom pipers?"

"No, no, man. Nothing like that. But there is something peculiar about the place. Something . . ." Lord Withrington groped for the word. "Something *hidden*. Why else shut up the castle for so long? Should make for an interesting stay, eh what?"

Julia could not believe her ears. After the rigors of the day, must she now sleep in a castle harboring dark secrets?

"Well, I do hope we shall be soon to Dunraven," Lady Charles opined. "Nights are obsidian in the Highlands, and tonight there will be no moon."

"No moon?" Julia wrapped her plaid more tightly about her.

"Ah, you mean it is the night of the New Moon." Instinctively, she glanced to the window.

"Careful." Sir Robert's comment drew her gaze back. "There are mysterious forces surrounding the moon. Or so the Scots believe. They have a rich lore dealing with lunar cycles—when to cut one's hair, dig ditches, plant crops, marry—all based upon whether the moon is waxing or waning, rising or setting. On the night of the New Moon, it is courting bad luck to gaze at it through glass."

"Preposterous," Lord Withrington protested. "You mean to say, if I should even look through my spectacles, or out this window here, ill would befall us?" Putting his bewhiskered face to the window, he purposely stared out. "See. No harm done."

At that, lightning fissured the sky, followed by peals of thunder. The coach lurched hard to a stop, as if a giant hand reached out of the ground and seized the back wheel, pulling it down into the mire.

With the other carriages far in advance and unaware of their plight, the little group was left to rely upon themselves. The men gallantly assisted the driver, while the ladies took refuge under umbrellas, wrapping themselves in plaids.

An hour later, dislodged from its muddy trap, the coach lumbered on. Next to the loss of her parents, Julia thought, surely, Scotland was her worst nightmare.

At Devils Elbow they left the main route and proceeded slowly through ponderous mountains, into the teeth of a galloping squall. The skies clashed and roared all about, and they feared the horses would bolt. Cautiously, they traversed narrow passages, climbing and plunging with sometimes no more leeway to the precipice than a hand's stretch.

Spectacular flashes of lightning filled the sky as they arrived long last at Dunraven Castle. Despite Sir Robert's warnings, Julia looked out and caught sight of the castle. Another flash of lightning revealed a massive, truncated tower rising on one end, while a Jacobean extension crowned with corbels, turrets, gables, and pepper-pots sprawled eastward in a haunting but pleasingly proportioned array.

The carriage ground to a halt, and the gentlemen climbed out quickly, in turn, aiding the ladies.

The wind and rain whipped wildly about Julia as she emerged from the carriage. A sharp crack of lightning drew her attention, once more, to the massive tower.

In her fatigue, she imagined it watched her, contemplated her. Cold—or was it apprehension?—shivered along her spine. Lord, but what she would give to be in Hampshire now, or even Braxton Hall for that matter. As she gazed on the brooding tower, she wondered what secrets its ancient stones held.

At that, the sky fired with dramatic display—a spidery hand reaching down to earth as if it would snatch both her and the tower right up. Julia gasped, the air catching in her lungs.

As the spectacle dissolved into ebony darkness, the castle door pulled open. Grim-faced servants appeared, dimly illumined in torchlight, bidding them enter Dunraven Castle.

Chapter 2

Julia stood dripping onto the flagstone floor and took in the cavernous hall with its high vaulted ceiling and walls bristling with antlers.

To her left, a peat fire blazed in a great, yawning fireplace, its light crowding back the darkness that swamped the chamber. Half-spent torches flickered in iron brackets affixed to the wall. These created pockets of illumination down the length of the hall—wavering, ruddy gold pools, tilting against the gloom.

Opposite the entrance, to the chamber's far end, rose a magnificient stone staircase. A dozen broad steps reached up to a spacious landing. There, as below, ornate candelabra crowned the newels—rearing bronze stags, sprouting heads full of antlers, the points spiked with tapers. From the landing, twin flights swept to an upper gallery, the whole of it swallowed in shadows.

Julia's gaze drew downward. At ground level, right and left of the staircase, and then again behind it, to either side on the back wall, passages led off, each vanishing into an Egyptian darkness.

The torches and tapers proved a feeble match for the vast expanse of the hall, Julia observed as she continued to glance about, noticing for the first time an immense tapestry covering the wall to her right, its hunting theme barely discernible in the dimness.

Truly these were the lodgings of a gamesman, a man unrelievedly passionate for the sport. And yet, Dunraven had welcomed no hunters for nigh on to twenty years. How was it their group should be allowed here now, she wondered? Did Lord Eaton hold such sway with his uncle? Julia decided she very much looked forward to meeting the "ancient" laird of Dunraven Castle.

The storm rumbled without, as if in response to her thoughts. The fine hairs lifted on the nape of her neck, and she clutched her sodden cloak closer, over her chest.

"Yer wrap, miss." The butler's voice sounded behind her, scabbed with impatience.

Julia turned and met his dour gaze. He stared at her from beneath a bramble of brows, a gruff-looking little man, no taller than she. Squarish in build and kilted in red, he possessed a receding crop of coppery hair and full side whiskers, threaded liberally with gray.

Julia fumbled with the fastener at her throat as he continued to wait and glare.

"We've created a small lake, I fear," she offered conversationally, spying the puddles that mottled the floor where she and her companions had tread.

"So ye have," he agreed sourly.

Without further comment, he accepted her mantle and moved off to aid Sir Robert. At the same time, a tall, needle-thin woman came forward. Dressed in an unadorned dress of gun metal gray, her hair skinned back into a knot, the woman presented a stark contrast to the colorful, bandy-legged Scotsman.

"The floor will clean up tidily enough," the woman informed, her voice as expressionless as her narrow face. "I am Mrs. McGinty, the housekeeper. You have met Mr. McNab." She gestured to where the butler now retreated from the hall, his arms laden with a mound of sopping coats and cloaks.

"The fires in the parlor were extinguished several hours past when the ladies retired for the night. I must ask that you remain here. The hearth will afford you sufficient warmth while you await Lord Eaton."

The housekeeper withdrew, gliding over the flagstones with

an eerie grace, her spine arrow-straight, shoulders level with the floor, head never bobbing.

"I do believe the woman's face would crack if she attempted a smile." Lord Withrington echoed Julia's thoughts as she joined him and Lady Charles before the expansive fireplace.

"Such a gloomy twosome," Lady Charles declared. "Let us hope the rest of the staff is more cheerful."

Dull thunderings sounded without. Julia wrapped her arms about her and looked to where Sir Robert paced the length of the hall, examining varied trophies of the hunt. As he neared the far end, light spilled from an unseen door, illuminating the passage to the left of the stairs. In the next breath, Lord Eaton appeared, accompanied by a half dozen or more men, all of whom Julia recognized as having traveled from Braxton.

"We'd quite given up on you!" Lord Eaton greeted brightly, relief evident in his voice.

Tall and mustached, he cut a dashing figure in his costly smoking jacket of quilted satin and velvet. His hair waved from a fashionable center part and gleamed of Macassar oil which made it several shades darker than its true russet color.

Julia considered Lord Eaton to be passable in looks but not truly handsome. His was a meticulously fostered image, both in style and manners, one that engendered an aura of attractiveness and a certain magnetism. Yet at times, behind the polish and charm, Julia thought to glimpse . . . something. She could not quite lay a finger to it, but she sensed it to be somehow disingenuous.

Lord Eaton clasped hands in welcome with Sir Robert then moved toward Lord Withrington, repeating the same, and finally bowed to the ladies.

"We were just now discussing forming a search party and who should go. Jove, but the lot of you are sopped to the gills!"

Julia smoothed a self-conscious hand over her traveling dress, knowing the lower portion of her skirt to be saturated. The bows and lace on her bonnet drooped as did Lady Charles's feathers, a rather soggy mess that draggled over the brim of her chipped-straw hat. The men's trousers fared worse, not only drenched but mud-splattered, attesting to their labors.

"Confounded piece of luck, don't you know." Lord Withrington adjusted his glasses. "Roads went to pudding and sucked in our carriage right up to the axle. Took an eternity in the bloody downpour to liberate it."

Lord Eaton's dark eyes whisked to Julia, sweeping over her none too discreetly before shifting to Lady Charles.

"What a wretched welcome to the Highlands. But here, we must see you all into some dry clothes and put some heat back into your bones."

Catching sight of the housekeeper reentering the hall, Lord Eaton turned to her.

"Mrs. McGinty, bring plaids for our guests before they catch their death in this drafty hall, and see what McNab is doing about the luggage. We'll need a fire built in the parlor and some hot tea."

The potent odors of cigar smoke and whiskey assailed Julia's nostrils as Lord Eaton and his companions crowded about them, inquiring further of their mishap. Julia lifted a hand to cover a sudden cough. Obviously, the men had come directly from that venerable male sanctum, the "smoking room." She coughed again, then cleared her throat.

"My dear Julia, are you well?" Lord Eaton closed the space between them, catching her hands in his. A look of intense concern charged his features. "You haven't a jot of color and your fingers are freezing."

Julia repossessed herself of her hands, nettled that he took the liberty of addressing her by her first name when she had never given him license. Again the brawny odors of tobacco and liquor assaulted her.

"Thank you, Lord Eaton." She cleared her throat once more. "But I would much prefer to join my aunt and cousins now and turn in for the night."

She half expected him to instruct her to call him "Roger" as he ever did when she used his title. Instead, he paused, his lids dropping to hood his eyes. He raised a long forefinger to his chin then tapped it in thought.

"Actually, Lady Symington felt her accommodations to be somewhat cramped, what with herself and your two cousins."

A discernible "harumph" issued from Mr. McNab, who, to Julia's surprise, had silently rematerialized and now stood just behind Lord Eaton's left shoulder.

"But have no fear." Lord Eaton ignored the butler. "Dunraven boasts many agreeable rooms. Isn't that so, Angus?" He glanced over his shoulder, giving the Scotsman a hard eye.

"I'd say they're gettin' scarcer by the minute, m'lord." He returned the look.

Julia took scant note of the butler's impudence, so shocked was she that her aunt had barred her from her room. It should come as no surprise, Julia reasoned. Had not Aunt Sybil methodically removed her from the mainstream of activity throughout the entire day? Had she not relegated her to the least comfortable accommodations and excluded her socially from the others in their company, both on the train and again in the coach, when she virtually had abandoned her at Perth's station? Now this.

Julia fought down a tide of anger welling inside her. Perhaps it would be preferable to be lodged apart, where she did not have to suffer such slights or insults. Yes, she would welcome a measure of solitude after months of being surrounded by strangers.

Julia looked to Lord Eaton and masked her agitation with a smile. "I shall be happy with any provision that can be made for me. If someone will only direct me to a chamber and send for Nettie . . ."

"Ah, there is another slight problem. Your aunt requested that our staff provide someone to assist you. Her maid, Nettie, is understandably overworked attending the three of them."

"Yes, of course." Julia floundered, stung yet again by her aunt's wiles.

In fairness, Aunt Rachel's maid, Dorrie, had remained behind with her at Braxton. It was Dorrie who had attended Julia throughout the summer along with Emmaline. Aunt Rachel, though certainly not elated by Julia's presence, had been generous with her in numerous small ways. But then Aunt Rachel was her mother's sister by birth. Sybil had married into the family and was no blood relation.

"Mrs. McGinty, what of that girl, Betty?" Lord Eaton's voice drew back her attention.

"She's readying the rooms in the east wing, my lord."

"Then fetch her, fetch her!"

Julia dropped her gaze, embarrassed she had brought no lady's maid of her own and must rely on Dunraven's staff. It could not be helped. The servants who so faithfully had served her family had had to be dismissed and her home let out.

Returning her attention to Lord Eaton, she found him deep in discussion with Mr. McNab, determining which rooms were to be made available for the new arrivals. Lady Charles quickly requested a room in the east apartments, specifically the one once occupied by her husband. Two rooms on the floor above it were agreed upon for Lord Withrington and Sir Robert.

"What of the Gold Room for Miss Hargrove?"

"Lady Reynolds and her twin daughters are settled there, m'lord."

"The north wing, then? There are two rooms still unoccupied, I believe."

"One is without furniture, and the fireplace in the other is unusable, m'lord."

"Well, what of that chamber in the south tower? That would do nicely. Yes, put Miss Hargrove there."

"The *south* tower, m'lord?" The butler's thicket of brows raised a full inch.

"It *is* furnished, is it not?" Lord Eaton's tone held a note of irritation at being questioned by the servant.

"But no one sleeps in the south tower," the butler argued, resisting the notion.

"And why would that be?" Lord Eaton snapped, his face reddening at the butler's continued mulishness.

Mr. McNab shrugged. "Just is, m'lord. Has been since the day I took service with Lord Muir here at Dunraven."

"Did my uncle expressly forbid using the south tower?"

"No, m'lord."

"Then I see no reason to allow the room to stand empty when we are in need of it." He began to turn away then halted. "Or does my uncle reserve those quarters for his personal use, when he is in residence?"

Julia's ears pricked at the comment, realizing Lord Muir was not present, as she had assumed.

"M'lord is occupying m'lord's chamber," Mr. McNab informed him somewhat crustily.

Lord Eaton tossed up his hands in exasperation. "Well then, ready the Tower Room. I want Miss Hargrove settled there directly."

Julia did not miss how the butler and housekeeper exchanged swift glances, nor the darkling looks they now sent her way. She rubbed her forehead, too exhausted to worry over it.

"Very well, m'lord," Mr. McNab conceded, his voice brusque. "I'll send young Tom to lay in a fire straightway." At that, he quit the hall, walking at a brisk pace, his kilt switching.

Lord Eaton cinched the belt of his jacket, visibly composing himself. "My apologies. These Highland Scots make testy servants. Far less refined than our English ones."

From the corner of her eye, Julia glimpsed Mrs. McGinty lift her chin and glide from the hall.

In short order, several servants appeared, two proving to be Lord Withrington's and Sir Robert's personal valets. They helped fetch in the luggage, dribbling in additional rain to pool on the flagstones.

Mrs. McGinty returned with a young woman, plump and dark-haired, of an age with Julia. She introduced the maid as Betty Shaw then instructed her to escort Julia to the south tower.

Betty's eyes widened, shifting to Julia. She dropped away her gaze, shielding her surprise, and gave a quick nod.

"Dunraven maintains only a skeletal staff when Lord Muir is

not in residence, Miss Hargrove," Mrs. McGinty informed. "Betty will assist you as best she can manage; however, she must also attend to her other chores. I would ask your patience if she is unable to respond promptly to your summons."

"Yes, of course," Julia replied, aware of Betty staring at her once more.

Mrs. McGinty turned to confer with Lady Charles while, at the same time, Lord Withrington and Sir Robert decided to join the other gentlemen in the smoking parlor.

En masse, the group migrated toward the end of the hall. Mrs. McGinty and Lady Charles ascended the grand staircase, the luggage-weighed servants trailing behind. Meantime, the men drifted toward the side corridor after wishing the ladies a pleasant sleep.

Betty lit a small oil lamp and led Julia left of the staircase and toward the back wall. "This way, miss," she enjoined, continuing to the door gaping there like a black, open maw.

A biting chill enveloped Julia as she entered the passage. She rubbed her arms briskly and followed close to Betty, whose lamp was now throwing shadows onto the walls, huge and misshapen. Tables and chairs lined the way, while scores of stuffed birds peered down from shelves, their eyes gleaming beads of jet.

Diverse corridors led off the main passage, but the maid conducted Julia the full distance to its end. There it opened onto a dark-paneled vestibule with a shell-headed alcove. Turning right, they progressed less than a hundred feet when they came upon a richly carved staircase.

The women's footsteps sounded sharply on the bare wood as they climbed the many stairs. Reaching the top, they bore to the left and entered another passage, this one containing an elaborate display of antiquated pistols and rapiers, glinting menacingly from the walls.

Weary and cold to the marrow, her every bone aching, Julia relished the thought of sinking into the comfort of a bed, any bed, even one in the abandoned tower chamber.

But why the butler's protests, she wondered? And what of

the look he traded with the housekeeper? Betty, too, showed surprise that Julia was to be quartered in the tower. What might she know? Julia studied the back of the maid's dark head, debating whether to raise the matter.

"Betty, there is something that is unclear to me," Julia began in an informal tone. "Mr. McNab indicated the tower chamber is furnished but never used. Is there a reason?"

"Rare it is for Dunraven to have guests, miss," Betty answered obliquely as she directed Julia into another corridor. "Though, several times a year, Lord Muir is in residence with his 'Society' friends."

Julia wondered what society the Scots could possibly enjoy in this isolated region. But Lord Muir was an English aristocrat with Scots ties, according to Lady Charles. Likely, his friends trekked north across the border for their gatherings, as those from Braxton did this day. Still shivering with cold, she sympathized with them most sincerely.

"Even when Himself is present, no one sleeps in the tower," Betty chattered on in her musical voice. "'Tis the original and most ancient part of Dunraven. Forgive me to say so, miss, but you must be very special to Lord Eaton for him to lodge you there."

"Lord Eaton?" Julia nearly choked on the notion. "You misunderstand, Betty. There were simply no other rooms available."

Unable to see the maid's face, Julia could not read her reaction. Julia's thoughts returned to the chamber. Perhaps, Lord Muir preserved the room untouched due its great age and history. Whatever his reason, she knew she must be careful to disturb nothing there unduly. Only the bed, which she intended to sink into for at least an aeon or two.

Julia continued to rub warmth into her arms while she took note of their surroundings and attempted to commit their route to mind. At times, she could hear the roar of the storm without. At others, when she and Betty turned back into the bosom of the castle, she could scarce hear any rumblings at all. They now began to climb yet another stairway, this one more ornate than the last.

Gaining the top of the stairs, Betty led Julia through a lavishly embellished portal. Just inside she halted.

"This is the 'Long Gallery,'" Betty spoke in a hushed, almost reverent tone. " 'Twas once what was called a 'communicating gallery,' something like a cloistered walk, opened but still protected from the elements. It connected the south wing to the tower. In time, the gallery was enclosed and became part of the castle complex. Sometimes, I fancy the people of yesterday walk here still, bustling back and forth with messages for their laird."

Julia lifted a brow at Betty's fanciful imagination, then looked to the wide gallery stretching before them. Gloom devoured the greater portion of it, though windows lined the full length of the right wall.

As the storm bellowed outside, lightning flashed in sporadic intervals, illuminating the sky and flooding the gallery with an eerie blue light. In those piercingly bright moments, Julia could view the expanse before her, filled with overstuffed chairs, small ornate tables, vases and statuary on pedestals. But most startling of all, a vast collection of ancestral portraits covered the wall to her left, rising three tiers high.

Julia stepped closer to Betty as lightning continued to brighten the hall in fits, transmuting the faces of its unsmiling inhabitants, conferring on them sinister aspects. True to the illusion of portraits, every painted eye followed the women as they continued along the gallery amid flashes of blue.

At the gallery's end, Betty veered right. In the soft glow of lamplight, Julia saw that the wall to her left was comprised of large, rough-hewn stones.

Again they turned, and Julia began to despair of finding a bed this night. The maze of corridors seemed without end. Curiously, this one led through thick rock, ten feet or more in length. It ended at a planked oaken door where golden light flowed around its edges and escaped beneath its bottom.

Betty pushed open the door fully and crossed the threshold, pausing there as she waited for Julia to follow.

"Here we are, miss. Please come in."

"The south tower?"

"Yes, miss. 'Tis the ancient heart of Dunraven."

Julia hesitated at the portal. It struck her that she stood in no corridor at all, but within the stout defense walls of the keep itself, the entryway cut through its stone.

The heart of Dunraven. The words flowed pleasantly through her. Stepping inside the chamber, she found it handsomely appointed and inviting.

To her right, an expansive fireplace filled the wall, columned and deeply hooded, no less than six feet wide. A cheery fire burned there, filling the room with its distinctive, peaty odor.

A round, gate-legged table stood centered before the hearth, flanked by chairs covered and fringed in pale green velvet, the arm supports and legs gleaming of dark, polished wood. To Julia's left loomed a monstrously large armoire, again of dark wood, paneled and carved, with blue-and-white china jars perched on top.

The room's showpiece, a magnificent canopied bed, occupied the left corner of the far wall. Its solid headboard rose to meet a high, deep crown, the whole of it carved with elaborate foliage and hung with blue trappings.

Persian carpets warmed the floor in blues and cream, while narrow windows with hand-thrown glass and the timbered ceiling overhead added to the chamber's atmosphere.

"Of all the grand rooms in the castle, this is my favorite," declared Betty as she placed the lamp on a side table near the bed and moved to free the window curtains from their ties.

Julia could easily understand her attachment as she continued to glance about, discovering a curious mirror hanging left of the fireplace, small and octagonal, encased in a deep, boxy frame of rosewood.

"The keep itself might be aged, but the furnishings do not appear to be so," Julia observed.

"They are from many different periods, I am told." Betty

crossed to the bed and folded back the counterpane. "The chairs are from the last century, the armoire from even earlier—Queen Mary Stewart's time—and the bed, it dates to the fifteenth century."

Betty ran a hand lovingly over one of the poster's carved acanthus leaves.

"The piece is original to the room. According to Mr. McNab, who has it on authority from Lord Muir himself, one of the early lairds took a Flemish noblewoman to wife, a widow. She brought the bed with her at the time of her marriage. She liked her fineries, that is known. Some of her personal belongings survive—several gowns, jewelry, and a silver perfume bottle."

Betty fluffed the pillows. "Of course the trappings are fairly new. Lord Muir refurbished the chamber when he bought Dunraven Castle, so proud he was to bring it back into the family."

"How is that?" Julia prompted as she moved closer to the toasty warmth of the fire, recalling Lady Charles's mention of the matter.

"His Scots blood flows through the female line, his maternal grandmother. After the Great Rising of Forty-five, the castle passed out of clan hands. It wasn't until this century, after the wicked Highland clearances when so many were cast off the land, that Dunraven came available and Lord Muir made its purchase."

"And he used it as a hunting seat?" Julia pressed.

"So I'm told, but no more." Betty looked about the room wistfully. "He cares very much for Dunraven and is partial to the keep in particular. Bless him. By his direction, 'tis my personal duty to care for the tower chamber—see it clean and dusted, the linens kept fresh and all."

Julia inclined her head, puzzled. "No one stays here, yet the laird instructs you to keep the linens changed?"

"A fine, dear man, our laird, but a bit dottled," Betty confided.

A shuffling sound drew their attention to the door, where a young man appeared, tall, and sandy-haired, lugging Julia's trunk.

"Thank you, Tom. Put it there, by the wardrobe." Betty pointed to the exact place.

While Betty unpacked Julia's clothes and hung them in the armoire, Tom brought heated water for the washbasin then transferred the empty traveling chest to the corner nearest the door.

After his departure, Betty helped Julia from her wet clothes and freed her from her stays, a most welcome relief. After seeing to her face and teeth, she slipped into a snowy white nightgown trimmed with violet ribbons and cascades of lace down the front and at the sleeves.

Julia waited by the fire while Betty readied the sheets, sliding a brass warming pan between them, chasing away the chill. Yawning hugely, Julia turned in place to heat her opposite side. Her gaze fell to the hood of the fireplace, and she noticed for the first time an engraved crest bearing a boar's head—a rather ugly boar's head—holding the shank of an animal in its mouth. At the same time, the wind and rain battered the windows violently, shaking them in their casements.

Julia shuddered and hugged her arms about her. The Highlands were indeed a wild, inhospitable land.

"The sheets are ready, miss," Betty advised as she carried the pan to the hearth and emptied its hot contents.

The maid's words filled Julia's heart with joy. Climbing into the high bed, she melted into its downy warmth. It felt so-o-o-o good. Utterly delicious.

"Thank you, Betty." She smiled at the young woman.

Turning down the lamp, Betty bid Julia a good night and left.

Julia lay quiet a moment and gazed out into the darkened room, listening to the wind and rain lash the windows. The redgold of the fire provided the room's only source of light, still it was enough to illuminate the furniture directly before it, a portion of the walls, and the timbers overhead.

What was it Emmaline had said? "If only the stones could whisper their secrets, such tales they would tell." She imagined the stones of this room could tell many tales. Now, in a way, she, too, was a part of its history.

She smiled groggily at the thought, then dismissed it, turning into her pillow. She had caught a touch of Emmalines's "fever." Too much talk of ancient keeps and chieftains.

She nestled into the mattress, her eyes drifting shut, and sank into blissful oblivion.

Dunraven Castle, September, 1437

Rae Mackinnon, Third Laird of Dunraven Castle, quit the hall and climbed the spiraling stairwell to his bedchamber. It had been a devil of a night, and his mood was black—black as the moonless sky and as turbulent as the storm that raged without.

'Twas vexing enough that Dunraven burgeoned with contentious guests, and new arrivals were expected on the morrow, but now cattle had been reived from beneath the clan's nose on this most wretched of nights.

Rae had led his men out to assess the loss and reinforce the guard. The deed had the markings of more than simple thieving. It reeked of a trap, he swore it. But his brother, Iain, would not be convinced. Despite the fiendish weather, Iain had insisted they give pursuit, then quarreled with him openly before the others when Rae ordered the men back to Dunraven.

Rae vented a few choice expletives as he managed the narrow steps. Pushing open his chamber door, he strode past the ornate bed and halted before the great fireplace that consumed much of the wall to his left. The weariness and disgust escaped him in a sigh as he stared into the flames.

His gaze lifted to the engraving on the deep fireplace hood— the head of a surly boar with a sheep shank in its jaws. Rae's lips drew into a grim smile. He felt as snarly as the animal looked.

An ear-splitting crack of thunder wrenched his attention to the shuttered windows. What a night to be out chasing down reivers. Did Iain really think they could find the thieves in this brawl?

Rae scrubbed a hand over his face, then worked the kinks from his shoulder muscles. Pulling over a chair, he braced his foot on the seat and unlaced his brogues then set them aside. He next removed his dirk and scabbard from his belt, then the wide leather belt itself. Unfastening his shoulder pin, he let his plaid drop to the floor and drew off his shirt. Folding it and the many yards of plaid, he placed them on the nearby trunk and stood naked before the fire. Naked except for the charm stone suspended on a silver chain about his neck.

Och, but the fire felt good. He tilted his head back and savored the intense, dry heat of the flames. Let the others continue their arguments below, guttered in their cups, he thought. He longed for the comfort of bed and a decent night's sleep.

His mind bent once more to the squall without. *Dhia,* but the weather had turned savage this night, bolts of lightning dropping all around as he and his men returned. As they rode for the safety of the castle, the sky suddenly exploded in a spectacle of light, a great withered hand streaking earthward from the sky, clutching for the great tower itself. Clutching for him, or so it seemed.

Rae touched the charm stone that lay on his chest, recalling the *cailleach*'s warning to not remove its protective power from his neck. The old woman's warnings still unsettled him, not that he understood her ramblings, but had she foreseen this night? Had the stone guarded him in some wise?

On entering the hall, Rae had hoped to retire straight to his room but Malcom MacChlerich and several other of Dunraven's guests delayed him. He joined them in several rounds of *uisge beatha* as they thrashed out the particulars of the night's raid, postulating who might be the culprits. Thankfully, Iain saw fit to keep his tongue in his head and not challenge his authority as laird again.

The discussion moved on to other matters such as the recent gathering of Highland chiefs, and the "detainment" of the Dowager Queen and the wee king at Stirling Castle. Rae saw dire portents there, but his companions expressed only moderate interest in the current drama of the crown.

Rae left the lot of them deep in their cups and arguments and sought his chamber. Thankfully, Moira, Malcolm MacChlerich's daughter, had retired earlier to her chamber, and Rae escaped her fawning attentions. Moira's interest in him was unmistakable, as was that of her father in seeing their clans joined. The statuesque blonde had accompanied her father to Dunraven a week past, and since then, endeavored to impress Rae, being ever near, ever solicitous. If that were not enough, Malcolm embroiled Iain with his own fiery views, agitating his brother's passions which ever sought the answer to all ills in cold steel.

Ah, Iain. Would they ne'er see eye to eye? And Donald, a keen young man but easily swayed. This youngest brother, so soon to marry, must learn to trust his instincts where others would bend him to their narrow cause.

Rae rubbed his eyes, bone weary. The Macphersons would arrive early in the day to finalize the details of Donald's marriage to their sister, Mairi, and the terms of her *tocher*. Rae had agreed to meet with Donald at dawn to make their own preparations.

Though Rae held some concern over an alliance between their clans, he believed Donald to be a lucky man. He'd not only won himself a bonnie bride, but the two were quite genuinely and deeply in love.

Aware he could now catch only a precious few hours of sleep, Rae headed for the bed, a luxurious piece, skillfully carved with acanthus leaves and draped with scarlet trappings.

As he approached the bed, he felt a weightiness to the air and a slight wave of dizziness crest through him. 'Twas as if the room had suddenly moved and he did not. He thrust a hand through his dark hair. Surely, he hadn't imbibed that much of the potent *uisge beatha*.

Rae reached for the covers and began to climb abed when he spied a shapely feminine contour outlined by the blankets, and a woman's bright hair flowing over the pillow like a river of gold.

He snatched back his hand and stared, startled to find a woman there, one who apparently awaited his companionship. His eyes narrowed over the sleeping figure as he gleaned the deception that passed here.

"Moira," he growled.

So this was her scheme to trap him into marriage. Likely her father was part to the ruse, making his way up the steps this very moment for an unannounced, late-night "chat." Och, but the two were of a kind, plotting to ensnare him well.

Not wasting a moment, Rae seized hold of the woman and yanked her from his bed. Sly lass. She'd not play him for a fool.

Slipping an arm beneath her legs, he caught her up and held her firm against his chest. She came fully awake at that, if ever truly she slept. The lass yelped and writhed, but he gripped her all the tighter and strode with her straight to the door, harboring not a drop of sympathy.

"Oot wi' ye, hoor," he snarled.

Yanking open the door, he took a single step outside the chamber, deposited the lass on the stairwell, then fell back a pace across the threshold and slammed the door.

"Fashious wench," he muttered, heading back to the bed. It dimly registered that the lass wore a long shapeless gown, frilled with ribbons and lace.

"Damn odd," he muttered again, flipping back the blankets and climbing abed.

Why would she wear such finery? And since when did a body wear clothes to bed? Of course, if she purposed only to entrap him, she might have plotted to do so without losing her virginity. Her father's timely appearance would have forestalled that.

Rae turned into the pillow and breathed the floral scent that clung to the linen casing. 'Twas the lass's fragrance. He'd breathed its sweetness in her hair as he carried her across the room. Strange, but it wasn't a scent he recognized as Moira's. And was it his imagination, or did the lass seem to stand of a shorter height, and her hair seemed brighter than Moira's and without its reddish cast?

Rae rolled over and faced the wall, dismissing the lass and the incident from his mind. He'd not trouble himself to rise and take a closer look. No female would get away with such underhanded trickery. If a lass warmed his bed, 'twould be because he himself invited her there.

With that, he burrowed into the pillow and mattress, aware of the lingering warmth and floral scent pervading the linens. Grumbling, he flipped the pillow over, punched it into shape, and burrowed in once more. Surely, it had been the very devil of a day.

Julia tottered on the stone landing, its icy cold stinging the soles of her bare feet. Stunned and disoriented, she gaped through the tangled curtain of her hair.

Julia's eyes rounded to saucers as she caught sight of a tall, barbarous-looking man, shockingly naked, his dark sable hair flowing to his shoulders and his piercing blue eyes hardened with anger.

Julia stared speechless, too startled to withdraw her gaze from the sight of such raw masculinity. The man spoke not a word, but withdrew into the bedchamber and slammed shut the door.

Cheeks flaming and utterly aghast, Julia gasped rapid breaths, her heart pounding. Her gaze remained riveted to the door, and she questioned whether she saw what she thought she saw.

Her brows bunched together. Did her eyes play her a trick? The door was arched and its planks scored and studded with nails creating a diamond pattern.

Julia dragged her hair from her face and looked about her, turning in place. She found herself standing in the confines of a stone stairwell. A torch blazed in its bracket several steps below, its pitch popping and hissing as the flames' shadows danced upon the wall.

From belowstairs rose the sound of boisterous male voices— voices that spoke a strange melodic tongue and sounded suspiciously sottish. Julia wondered if they, too, were guests of Lord Eaton, local inhabitants, perhaps. Possibly, the intruder mistook her chamber for his own or presumed it empty. Still, why the rude eviction?

An unsettling feeling twined through Julia as she realized she stood enclosed in the thick wall of the keep. But where?

Dash it all, think, Julia commanded herself, her nerves fraying. She had been fast asleep when she heard the roar of a deep male voice. Hands like bands of steel clamped about her arms and hauled her from the bed. In the next instant, strong arms caught her up, and she found her cheek pressed against warm flesh—the very solid and well-muscled chest of the intruder.

But there was something amiss about the direction. He carried her toward the wall to the right of the bed and passed through it! No, she corrected, he passed through a door, *this* door with its arch and nail studs. But, from where did it come?

Her feet smarting with cold, Julia shifted from one to the other and hugged herself against the chill air. Plainly, she could not remain in the stairwell the rest of the night catching her death. Dare she descend the steps, garbed in her thin nightgown, and risk discovery and possible violation by the men gathered below? Or should she reenter the chamber and brave the one?

Plucking up her courage, she shoved open the door and stepped inside the chamber, braced to confront the naked stranger and if necessary make a dash for the opposite door.

Julia halted, her jaw dropping wide as her gaze fastened on the bed, its trappings scarlet red. Hesitantly, she forced her gaze around the room. An iron-bound trunk occupied the wall where the massive armoire should have been, and the gateleg table and velvet chairs had disappeared from sight.

Of a sudden, an oppressive heaviness filled the air. Julia lowered her head to her hands, pain shooting through her temples. A moment later, the sensation passsed.

Julia looked up, searching for sign of the intruder. Astonishingly, all in the room appeared as before—the bed trappings blue instead of red, the armoire in its place, and carpet soft beneath her toes. The fire that burned brightly moments before was now glowing coals.

Julia twisted around. The door through which she just passed had vanished without a trace!

Chapter 3

Julia stirred from the depths of her slumber, coming slowly aware of the toasty warmth that enveloped her. She smiled at the delicious sensation and stretched out, feeling liquid as honey on a hot summer's day.

Julia's lashes flew open and she bolted upright. Scrambling back, she pressed against the ornate headboard and yanked the blankets with her, covering her chest. Frantically, she scanned the bed for the naked intruder of the night past, fearing he was the source of her warmth!

The bedcovers lay flat though rumpled before her. Not wholly reassured, Julia leaned forward and swatted down the fabric, then jerked the sheets upward and peered beneath. Dropping them, she crawled to the end of the bed, flicked aside the bed hangings, and darted a glance around the room.

The chamber appeared vacant, save for herself. Still, Julia's heart beat an erratic tattoo. What of the stranger? How had he gained entrance? And where was he now?

Alarm struck Julia. Swinging her legs to the floor, she dropped to her knees and made a hasty inspection beneath the bed. She found herself staring at bare floorboards, unmasking not even a ball of dust.

Rising to her feet, she turned a full circle, her gaze skimming over the walls and furniture. Had she dreamt the whole bizarre episode? Yet the details were so vivid, so palpable.

Even now, her senses tingled with the memories—the strength and heat of the man's body as he held her fast, the pounding of his heart beneath her ear, his manly scent, the furious look in his eyes as he cast her from the room and she glimpsed his unclad form.

Julia's face burned at the memory, his hard-muscled body shockingly magnificent and thoroughly illuminated in the fire's glow. She took a long swallow, struggling to suppress the image. What hidden, shameless part of her could have conjured such a man?

A wave of fatigue crested through Julia, overcoming her. She sank onto the nearest chair, feeling suddenly and inexplicably sapped of all energy. Smoothing a hand over her face, she drew back her tumble of hair. The arduous journey and disrupted night's sleep were exacting their toll, she told herself. Yet, a lassitude spread through her bones, unlike anything she had known before.

A dream. It had only been a *dream,* she insisted silently. No doubt, the unfamiliar surroundings and the violent storm had brought it on. Then, too, her head had been filled with talk of shadowy secrets enshrouding Dunraven, and of Emmaline's castles and chieftains of time gone by. Clearly, the day's excitements had fired her imagination, only to emerge later, during her sleep, in the form of a graphic dream.

Julia's spirits lifted at her swift and logical deduction. She shut the incident from her mind, holding no wish to examine it closer or consider why her subconscious would bring a wild and naked Scotsman to life in her bedchamber.

Her gaze traveled over the antiquated room and furnishings. Sleeping alone in a chamber such as this would dispose anyone to dreams, she assured herself. And yet . . .

What if the man *had* been real? What if, during Lord Muir's prolonged absences, someone else resided in Dunraven— whether beknown or unbeknown to the laird? Someone who occupied this very room and accessed it by means of a hidden passage. As far-fetched as it seemed, it would explain the butler's protests last night and the maid's instructions to keep the chamber in readiness for guests who never arrived.

Fresh energy swirled through Julia's veins. Rising on unsteady feet, she crossed to the wall opposite, right of the bed.

She studied the stones for evidence of a seam, a secret door. With walls ten or more feet thick, they could easily conceal passageways, even small rooms.

Finding nothing of note, she moved to the fireplace and searched the bricks and sculptured mantel. Pushing, pulling, prodding, and twisting, she sought a mechanism to trigger a false panel. Even should the entire wall somehow open before her, she realized it would not explain the appearance or disappearance of the furniture last night, or how the bed hangings changed their color from blue to red.

Meeting no more success with the fireplace than with the wall, Julia directed her attention to the massive armoire. Standing before it, she flung open the doors and shoved aside the clothes.

The back panels stared out at her. Cautiously, Julia climbed inside the wardrobe, anticipation shivering along her spine. She rapped on the boards and listened for a telling, hollow sound. Methodically, she continued to knock across the panels, bending closer, her ear intent on every note and vibration.

"Might I be of assistance, miss?"

Julia shot upright, a cry escaping her as she stumbled backward and nearly fell out of the wardrobe. Regaining herself, she managed to step out with a modicum of decorum and without further mishap. Heat blossomed in her cheeks.

"Good morning, Betty." Her voice wavered with forced brightness.

Betty quirked her head and peered inside the armoire at the disarray of clothes.

"I, er, dropped something . . . in the armoire . . . My ring." Julia offered quickly, holding up her hand to display the elegant band and its unusual quartz stone. "But I found it. See?"

Julia winced at the lie which sprang so easily to her lips. Yet, how could she confess to the object of her quest—a hidden panel through which a naked stranger had materialized in her chamber?

"The ring was my mother's," she added truthfully, seeing Betty's perplexed look.

Comprehension touched the young woman's eyes, followed by a melting look of compassion. "And she's gone now, is she?" Julia nodded. "Poor lamb, of course you would be fetching the ring from the closet. I would have torn it apart myself. Do not worry over the gowns. I'll see to them straightway."

Betty moved off, taking up the pitcher of heated water and towels she had left on the table and filling a flowered porcelain bowl in the washstand. Wordlessly, she set out scented soap, then bustled to the windows and drew back the curtains. Buttery light spilled in.

Julia stared at the mullioned windows. Had there been shutters there last night, rattling against the wind?

"'Tis a fine, bonnie day," Betty cheered, moving off to fluff the pillows and tidy the bed.

"Yes. Yes it is," Julia said absently, culling her memory for images of the shutters, but could find none. She looked again to the windows and noted the height of the sun. "It is much later than I expected," she sighed, discovering the morning to be half spent. She turned toward the bed, but the maid was not in sight.

"The sleep did you good, for certain." Betty's muffled voice came from the armoire, the front half of her lost in its depths as she neatened the gowns.

Julia wrapped her arms about herself, uncertain any good had come from the unsettling night.

After cleansing herself at the basin, Julia began the ritual of dressing, donning her silk "combination"—a snug-fitting union of chemise and drawers. Betty next cinched her into her corset, over which flowed a camisole and two petticoats, all lavished with embroidery, tucks, ribbons, and lace. Cotton stockings completed the requisite undergarments.

At Betty's insistence, she slipped into a dressing sacque to ward off the room's chill, then allowed the maid to dress her hair. As Julia sat under Betty's ministrations, she turned vexing questions over in her mind, wondering if she might pose any of them to Betty without revealing too much or rousing her suspicions.

"I am curious, Betty," she began with a collectedness she did not feel. "Are there any stories that survive about the keep? Or this room, perhaps? Anything unusual?"

"Unusual, miss? In what way?" Betty drew the brush through her hair in long, rhythmic strokes.

"The tower is centuries old. Do you think, for instance, it might conceal a hidden passageway?"

Betty's hand stilled, then she chuckled and resumed her brushing. "Not likely, miss, though Dunraven does lend itself to such notions on stormy nights."

Julia smiled at her gentle teasing.

"But no," Betty continued. "I've not heard tales of the like. The tower is a simple block affair, massive stones, piled straight up. If hidden stairs and hallways exist in Dunraven, they are more likely located in the newer additions—designed into the wings at the time of their constructions, do you see?"

Betty worked Julia's hair into a thick chignon at the back of her head and secured it with pins and a decorative comb, topped with a line of faux pearls.

"Dunraven is the result of centuries of amendments and improvements, miss. But passages in the tower?" Betty shrugged. "I'd think it unlikely, but Mr. McNab might know. He has been in service here the longest of any of us."

Betty moved to stand in front of Julia as she styled the soft fringe of curls framing her face.

Julia opened her mouth to reply then closed it. She held little desire to speak with the irascible Scotsman. And after all, there was no need. What she experienced during the night was a bad dream, that and no more. Secret passages, indeed. She must be balmy to consider it.

Choosing a morning dress of striped changeable silk, she rid herself of the dressing sacque and drew it on. Betty gushed over the gown's details—the multicolored stripes of rose, green, and brown, and the lacy "Vandykes," long V-shaped points of snowy Irish lace running in double rows down the bodice and edging the cuffs.

In truth, the style was a year out of date, the skirt being somewhat narrower than this season's and the upper sleeves not as full above the elbow. Such vanities mattered little anymore, Julia reflected with a heavy sigh. The darkness of her loss unexpectedly loomed, twining icy fingers about her heart.

Julia consulted her pocket watch for the time, then slipped it inside her belt. If she accomplished nothing more this day, she must pen her letter to her grandmother and post it. She needed to be away from this place. Away in Hampshire where she might do something of use with her life. Away from Dunraven Castle and its provocative, heart-stopping dreams.

Departing the chamber, Julia followed Betty, impressing their route to mind so she might later find her way back without becoming hopelessly lost.

Entering the Long Gallery, she found it to be quite handsome in daylight and the portraits not nearly so sinister. Julia slowed her steps, perusing the faces there. None resembled the man in her bedchamber, leastwise, not with their clothes on.

Julia went rigid, shocked by the wayward turn of her thoughts. Suddenly his memory surrounded her—the feel of his hard torso as he held her in his arms, the warmth of his bare flesh, the piercing blue of his eyes. Julia shook away her wanton imaginings, ignoring the shimmer of heat that passed through her.

"Are you all right, miss?" Concern filled Betty's voice.

"Yes, perfectly. But I could really do with a strong cup of tea."

Long minutes later, retracing their steps of the previous night, they arrived in the entrance hall. Betty quickly conducted Julia to the breakfast room, then disappeared to inform Cook of her presence.

Julia found the room to be snug and welcoming, warmed with rich oak paneling. Paintings hung all around, depicting popular sporting themes—salmon fishing in the icy lochs, still lifes of game birds, and hunters bringing home stags on sturdy Highland ponies.

Julia turned her gaze upward and was surprised to see elaborate plasterwork embellished the ceiling overhead, so in contrast with the room's solid, masculine furnishings.

Despite the coziness of the room, there was an unnatural

quiet. Though their party from Braxton had descended upon Dunraven the night before, no one seemed to be about this morning. Indeed the castle seemed strangely empty.

Julia drifted her gaze over the fine oils as she moved around the confines of the room, then stopped before a series of etchings grouped near the fireplace. Each portrayed Dunraven Castle from one of eight different vantages. Julia examined them closely, striving to comprehend the layout of the castle.

Hearing a soft footfall and the rustle of material, Julia turned to find Mrs. McGinty entering the room with a porcelain tea service.

"Good morning, miss," the housekeeper greeted crisply, a slight chill to her tone. She placed the service on the sideboard, made several small but precise adjustments, then faced Julia, unsmiling. "Our breakfast hour is past, but Cook will prepare fresh porridge if it pleases you."

Julia perceived the trace of disapproval in Mrs. McGinty's eyes but could not account for it.

"Please tell Cook not to trouble. The tea will be quite satisfactory."

Mrs. McGinty turned to leave but Julia delayed her.

"Is Mr. McNab nearby? I should like to ask him some questions about Dunraven's history."

Mrs. McGinty gave an indelicate snort, at odds with her taciturn manner. "Mr. McNab led the gentlemen out early this morning for deerstalking. I'd not be expecting them back for many an hour."

Julia's brows creased in confusion. "I thought he was the butler, not a gillie."

"Mr. McNab is many things."

An awkward silence followed.

"Can you tell me if my aunt, Lady Symington, is about? Or my cousins? I have yet to see any of the ladies from Braxton. The castle appears quite abandoned."

"The ladies departed a short time ago for an afternoon's outing and picnic. They are not journeying far, only a few miles to visit the Falls of Glendar."

A brief pause hung between them as Julia absorbed this news. Mrs. McGinty clasped her hands before her with a shade of impatience. "Will that be all, miss?"

"Yes, thank you." Julia watched Mrs. McGinty's stiff withdrawal, wondering whether the animosity she sensed in the woman was real or imagined.

Julia poured herself a steaming cup of tea at the sideboard then carried it to the double door that opened onto an adjoining room. There she found a cheerful parlor with sunlight spilling in through tall, full-length bay windows. Bright patterned chintz enlivened the furniture and draperies while book-lined shelves climbed the far wall.

Julia crossed to the handsome mahogany desk that stood before the nearest bay. She should have thought to ask the housekeeper for pen and stationery, she chided herself, feeling the need to begin her letter to Lady Arabella.

Julia set her saucer and cup on the desk and reached for the top drawer, hoping to find writing materials. Her hand stilled as she glanced out the window, her thoughts diverting to the ladies down the road, in particular to her aunt.

Had she misunderstood Aunt Sybil's intentions last night? Did her aunt truly mean to separate her from herself and her cousins for the duration of their stay at Dunraven, or for just the one night?

Julia sipped her tea as she recalled fragments of her conversation with Lord Eaton. Did she misread his explanation for lodging her apart of the others? Were the sentiments he conveyed truly her aunt's, or his own perhaps? And what of Lord Eaton's insistence on billeting her in the tower over Mr. McNab's protests? Julia cared not at all for the look the butler sent her before quitting the hall.

Pulling herself from her thoughts, Julia gazed out at the rain-rinsed skies and imposing mountains. They beckoned to her. Too distracted to write and seized by an urgent need to find her aunt and settle these questions, she decided to ride out. An adept horsewoman, Julia felt confident she could easily catch up with the group, provided a mount was available.

Julia rang for Mrs. McGinty, pulling the silken cord that hung by the door. No doubt, the woman would be unhappy with the interruption. So be it, Julia set her jaw and rang again.

Mrs. McGinty appeared directly. Julia's request brought a look of surprise to her carefully controlled features, but she stated she would send young Tom, Cook's son, to ready a horse. He could also be spared to serve as her guide.

"I shall need Betty's assistance just long enough to change," Julia called over her shoulder as she quickened past the housekeeper and left the breakfast room.

Julia hastened to her room, and despite a few wrong turns, arrived there presently, her determination overriding her hesitation to return alone.

Still, Julia paused on the threshold and ran a glance around the room before entering. Assured it stood vacant, she directed her footsteps toward the armoire, and ignored a keen urge to drop to her knees and peer underneath the bed.

Drawing open the wardrobe doors, she located her riding costume. No sooner did she lay out the articles than Betty arrived, much to Julia's relief.

Betty's eyes widened at the sight of Julia's garments spread on the bed. "How very grand a riding habit," Betty exclaimed, slightly out of breath for having hurried. "Do you ride to the hounds then?"

Julia shook her head. "Only for pleasure. Rather, I *used* to ride in Hampshire." *With my parents,* she added silently. She rode at Gramercy as well, trying to escape her pain. But today she would ride for pleasure once more, this time in the wild Highlands.

Betty assisted Julia out of her gown then into her habit, beginning with the trousers of chamois leather. The skirt followed, the cloth being a deep, ultramarine blue. Next came the basque, a close-fitting jacket of the same color, waist-length, with a single row of buttons, long tight sleeves, and a short tail at the back. High-topped boots added polish to the outfit.

"Ah, 'tis very smart, miss. Very smart indeed." Betty beamed as she handed Julia her high-crowned beaver hat.

Julia fixed the hat in place, then accepted her gloves from the maid and accompanied her out of the chamber. As they reached the gallery, Julia halted.

"Oh, bother. I've forgotten my riding crop. Do go on, Betty. I've delayed you from your duties long enough. I'll pop back and fetch it."

"Very good, miss, if you're sure."

Julia nodded and returned to the bedchamber. Reentering, she moved briskly to the armoire and rummaged inside for her riding crop. In the process, she dislodged her hat and mussed her hair.

"Drat," Julia muttered, abandoning the wardrobe for the room's small, octagonal mirror.

She fingered the wayward strands of hair back in place then repositioned her hat over her coiffure.

Suddenly, the air altered, growing weighty and pressing down on her. The hat toppled from her fingers, and she cupped her forehead in her palms.

Julia's heart raced. She straightened slowly and rounded in place, then sucked in her breath. The space was bare before her, devoid of table, chairs, and carpeting. An iron-bound trunk lined the wall, the armoire having vanished once more. To her dismay, shutters now bracketed the windows—windows no longer fitted with glass.

Julia started toward the door through which she had just entered, thinking to escape. But it, too, had disappeared. Spinning around, her gaze fell across the room. To the right of the bed waited the studded arched door, partially opened.

A chill shivered over her skin.

"A dream. This is a dream," Julia uttered aloud, failing to convince herself.

She took a shaky step toward the bed and caught the draperies between her fingers. Her heart dipped as she stroked their texture. They were real, tangible, but God help her, the cloth was red instead of blue.

Julia stepped apart of the bed and swept her hand through the space the table had occupied moments ago. She gave a small cry, catching nothing in her palm but air.

Julia clamped down on her fears and moved toward the arched door with an overpowering need to know what lay on the other side. Her hand shaking violently, she dragged the door fully open and passed through the portal.

Julia found herself on the remembered stairwell, all appearing exactly as it had in her "dream." The low murmur of voices rose from below. But this time they sounded neither loud nor boisterous. In truth, she distinguished female voices among them, and children's as well.

Wary, but immensely curious, Julia started down the narrow spiral of stairs, forcing her feet down one step, then another, her heart beating high in her throat.

Narrow slits pierced the thick wall at intervals, admitting in light to softly wash the stairs. The acrid smell of spent torches assaulted her nostrils, but as she neared the bottom, it mixed with the peaty odors of cooking fires and that of broth and meat.

The steps ended in a sheltered alcove which, in turn, opened directly into an expansive hall. Julia's thoughts scrambled to recall the castle etchings, unable to place this extension.

Shoring up her courage, Julia stepped from the shadows of the alcove, moving just inside the long hall. There, people bustled and scurried about, engaged in various tasks. Their clothing struck her as somehow out of place, out of time—the men garbed in voluminous kilts of an era long past, the colors muted. The women, for the most part, wore skirts to their ankles over plain blouses, some with plaid shawls. One woman, tall and blond, wore a surprisingly elegant gown, moss green in color with contrasting sleeves of gold. But it, too, seemed sorely out of date.

As Julia puzzled the scene, her gaze came to rest on a tall figure across the hall—a man with sable locks flowing to his shoulders and with piercing blue eyes. He stood in conversation, his leg cocked on a bench, his arm braced there, a cup in his hand. He, too, wore the old-style kilt. And he wore it well, she observed, warmth sliding through her.

Someone shouted to Julia's right. The man across the room looked up and flashed a smile, tossing back a rejoinder in his

Gaelic tongue at what was evidently a jest. As he drew his gaze
from the other man, it settled on Julia. His features froze, his
eyes locking with hers.

Fear and fire swarmed through Julia. Slowly, the man
straightened, setting aside his cup and lowering his leg to the
floor. His gaze swept downward over her breasts and clear to
her toes, taking in the details of her attire. As his eyes returned
to hers, a frown creased his forehead as if in troubled thought.

He abandoned his companions and began toward her, rivet-
ing her with his piercing blue gaze. His companions fell silent
around him and turned to see what so captured his interest.
They stared in Julia's direction but finding nothing remarkable,
returned to their cups.

The tall Scotsman continued across the hall, his long strides
rapidly closing the space. A movement caught the corner of
Julia's vision and the blonde in the moss green gown stepped
into view. She raised her hand toward the man, but he paid her
no heed, continuing straight toward Julia.

Julia's pulses spun. How strikingly handsome he was, his
features regular and pleasing—the nose straight, the lips well
defined, the jaw square-cut. His shoulders were broader than
she first had realized and as he strode forward, she could well
envision his powerful body moving beneath his garments.

Julia felt boneless under the intensity of his gaze. He closed
the distance between them and reached for her. In that same instant, a wave of dizziness assaulted her, the air compressing
and crushing down on her. The room, and the Scotsman, swam
before her eyes and she feared she would faint.

As her knees dissolved beneath her, Julia put out her hand to
break her fall. The stone floor rushed up in a blur. But, seconds
later, as she crumpled completely, it was not stone that met her
hands, but grass.

Opening her eyes, Julia discovered herself sprawled on the
grounds outside the castle, looking back up at the ancient keep.

Chapter 4

Julia rose on quivery legs. What madness was this? Some demented dream? A hallucination? Yet here she stood, outside Dunraven's ancient keep.

She eyed the tower's solid stone face. Was she to believe she had passed through rock?

Julia examined the ground about her, a tangle of weeds where the hall and the Scotsman had stood moments before. Still she could feel the touch of his hand, his fingers encircling her arm even as he disappeared.

Julia massaged her forehead. Perhaps she *was* deranged, the strain of this past year snapping her sanity. Certainly, should she tell anyone of these occurrences, they would believe it to be so and commit her straight off.

Julia paced the ground, her nerves in a boil. Spying fragments of a low wall nearby, she went to examine it. The ruin ran in a straight line, perpendicular to one side of the tower, sheltering a small explosion of rich pink primroses.

A shiver tingled through Julia as she realized the wall's location approximated that of the chimerical hall. Crouching down, she traced her hand over the stonework, the surfaces dressed and regular, the stones of a size similar to those in the tower. A foundation perhaps, or remnants of a larger structure?

Julia drew back the border of dainty primroses and yellow-green foliage to better examine the wall. Curiously, the lower, more protected surfaces appeared blackened in areas.

Julia rose to her feet with more questions than before. She took several steps toward the tower and tipped back her head,

her gaze scaling its height. Narrow slit-like windows punctu-
ated the wall, rising in a pattern that would match the remembered stairwell.

Roaming the keep's southward side, she spied the windows
to her room, their glass flashing with sunlight. But another pair
likewise glinted some yards higher, betraying a room directly
above her own. Had the stairwell spiraled upward, she wondered uneasily? She could not remember, though it seemed
likely, and the slitted windows indicated as much, reaching
nearly to the roof.

Julia continued to inspect the tower grounds until young
Tom appeared, leading a sturdy Scots pony, saddled and ready
for her to ride. When she informed him she no longer wished to
join the other ladies but requested sketching materials instead,
he looked visibly disappointed. It could not be helped, and she
apologized for his troubles. Good fellow that he was, Tom uttered no complaint but led the pony away, fetched the requested
supplies, and returned to his chores.

Plucking up her nerve and her spirit, Julia set out. The same
insatiable curiosity that first had prompted her to investigate the
tower stairwell now drove her over Dunraven's grounds to find
the answers she required. She'd make her own sketches, she decided. She'd record her findings and compare them with the
etchings in the breakfast parlor.

For hours, Julia explored the surrounding property, rendering
views of the castle, primarily those nearest the keep. On one,
she roughed in the placement of the alcove's portal where it had
opened onto the hall. She also sketched the hall's interior as she
remembered it, detailing the people at their activities and capturing the essence of their dated garments. Though Julia considered herself less than gifted at rendering people, there could
be no mistaking the tall Scotsman staring out from the heart of
her drawing.

The hours slipped past. Even when the women returned from
their excursion, and later still when Betty appeared and announced tea, Julia remained out-of-doors with her papers and
pencil. She made her excuses and lingered for a time, walking

restlessly over the grounds, having little desire to enter a castle which might cough her back out at any given moment.

"Little wonder no one has hunted here for twenty years," Julia mumbled to herself as she trod on. Had not Lord Withrington claimed there to be something "hidden" about Dunraven?

" 'Hidden' indeed." She blew a wisp of pale hair from her eyes. "Hidden in my bedchamber!"

Julia's thoughts turned to Lord Eaton and the querulous butler, Angus McNab. Where the one had insisted on lodging her in the tower, the other had opposed it, each with matching vigor.

Whatever their motives—whatever they knew or did not know of the tower's irregularities—they'd best agree upon other quarters for her, preferably on the furthermost end of the castle complex. She simply could not, *would* not stay another night in the ancient keep!

The sun slung low over the mountains. As the temperature dropped, Julia's constant motion warmed her but marginally. The cold nipped her nose, stiffened her cheeks, and numbed her fingers and toes. Still, she found the clean Highland air marvelously invigorating.

Julia tarried as long as she might, intent on intercepting Lord Eaton on his arrival. But when dusk gathered and still the men did not return, she relented. Teeth chattering, she headed for the front of the castle and its main entrance, unable to endure the falling temperatures a moment longer.

No sooner did she round the west end, than the hunting party appeared amid a frenzy of excitement. Shouts rang out, clamoring for the servants to fetch a physician. Julia rushed forward as several men lifted Lord Eaton down from his horse, his face grimaced in pain. A commotion surrounded Lord Withrington as well, and she spied blood smearing his jacket.

Julia followed the troupe into the entrance hall where Lord Eaton's bearers eased him onto a knobbly chair. Simultaneously, the ladies poured forth from a side parlor and besieged the men with their attentions and concern.

When one of the men attempted to remove Lord Eaton's boot, he bellowed in pain. Lilith, Aunt Sybil, and a half dozen other ladies moved immediately to consol him.

"Don't worry overmuch," Julia heard Sir Robert to say as she joined Emmaline. "It's no more than a twisted ankle. He'll recover after a hot soak and a night's rest."

Was there a tinge of annoyance in his tone? Julia looked again to where the women hovered over Lord Eaton. He groaned full-throated as Mr. McNab now pried the boot from his foot. The ladies sent up small gasps, fluttering about him like a cloud of anxious butterflies. His mask of pain slackened ever so briefly as he slid an appreciative glance over the swell of bosoms poised above him.

Julia's sympathies withered. "What of Lord Withrington, is he hurt?" she asked of Sir Robert, turning toward the older man and noting that he garnered far less concern though his clothes were blooded.

"Quite sound, quite sound," chirped Mr. Sampson Dilcox at her elbow, one of their company from Braxton, an energetic little man of great charm and little hair. "But he and Sir Robert are quite the heroes of the day. They captured the day's take after it ran off, don't you know? The ponies, that is—they ran off with the deer carcasses strapped to them." He stopped himself with a twittery laugh. "Forgive me, Miss Hargrove. I do get ahead of myself."

"Damned bloody fool!" Lord Withrington grumbled to Lady Charles as Julia and her companions joined them. "Eaton nearly took off my head."

Julia and Emmaline turned rounded eyes to Sir Robert, who nodded grimly.

"Our host was handing his gun off . . ."

"Handed it off pointed and loaded, without a gnat's sense of safety," groused Lord Withrington.

"Yes, well . . ." Sir Robert cleared his throat. "As he handed it off, he tripped over an outcropping of rock."

"The lead shot right over my shoulder, grazed my whiskers!"

Lord Withrington declared while Lady Charles patted him with a calming hand.

"Thankfully, no one was hurt." Sampson picked up the story. "But the blast startled the garrons—that's the Scots ponies— and they ran off, stags and all."

"But what of the blood on your jacket?" Julia looked to Lord Withrington.

"Deer blood. When we caught up with the garrons, some of the stags had come loose. Had to retie them. Fine job of catching the beasts—the garrons, that is." He gave an appreciative nod to Sir Robert. "And you, Sampson. Obliged for what you did pacifying them and leading them back."

He gave the smaller man's back an open-handed clout. Sampson flushed with pride and stole a nervous glance toward Julia.

Lady Charles turned her attentions to Julia. "My dear, you are positively waxen." She felt Julia's cheeks and took her hands in her own. "You stayed out far too long, dear. You're like an icicle. Come along, we must thaw you out before you catch your death. Perhaps Cook can prepare a Highland remedy to ward off your chills."

Mr. McNab, rather than Cook, prepared his "antidote for all ills" before the fire, a steaming mixture of sugar, lemon juice, boiling water and a double measure of whiskey from Dunraven's private stock. The "Highland toddy" instantly diffused heat to Julia's nether parts, warming her blood and radiating a decided glow through her very being.

Cook held supper while the belated hunters completed the day's rituals, downing a bracing shot of whiskey, full-strength, followed by a long, soaking bath. The women likewise retired to their rooms to dress and ornament themselves for dinner.

Julia, unable to avoid the moment, accompanied Betty to her bedchamber to exchange her riding frock for more appropriate attire. Impatient to leave, her nerves knotting up, she asked Betty to select something for her.

The maid chose a gown of pale peach China satin trimmed with white lace and emerald green ribbons. Julia recognized the dress to be one her Aunt Rachel had given her before her departure, a castoff but truly lovely. Drawing it on, she found its square neckline fell a trifle low, though not objectionably so.

Julia tugged up the bodice, refusing to be detained one second longer than required. Once cinched, hooked, and buttoned, Julia whisked from the room, putting distance between herself and the tower as rapidly as possible.

Dinner proved a wearisome affair, the conversation revolving about the day's near-tragic hunt, the details recounted ad nauseam. Lord Eaton's gaze strayed periodically to Julia's neckline as did those of several other gentlemen including Mr. Dilcox, who had skillfully maneuvered himself into the seat beside her. With the men's added height, Julia realized too late, they could glimpse a tantalizing hint of cleavage.

A pox on you, Aunt Rachel, Julia fumed silently as the servants cleared away the soiled plates, replacing them with small crystal bowls.

". . . I mean, do these Scots eat nothing besides oats?" Lady Henrietta Downs complained several seats away, drawing Julia's attention back to the conversation which had blessedly taken a new turn. "Cook has served little else since our arrival—for breakfast, lunch, tea, *or* dinner."

Lord Eaton turned to the butler, who stood beside him, holding a silver bowl. "Lady Henrietta is quite right, Angus. Cook even sent us into the field with cold bars of porridge in our pockets instead of sandwiches."

"Most tradition, m'lord."

"And what of dinner just now? Oats in the soup, the stuffing, the pud, even the fish was coated with oats."

"A tasty way it is to prepare fresh fish, m'lord."

"Hmm, yes. What is that you have in the bowl there?"

Everyone's eyes turned to the silver bowl and its fluffy contents.

"'Cranachan,' m' lord, a traditional sweet."

"And what, precisely, is 'cranachan'?"

"A delightful creation—lightly whipped cream served with raspberries."

Lord Eaton frowned. "What are those flecks in the cream?"

"Toasted oats, of course, m'lord."

A moan echoed around the table.

Later, retiring to the salon, the guests broke into small groups, some playing at whist and varied parlor games, most sinking into overstuffed chairs and sofas simply to continue their dinner discourse or read.

Julia saw that Lord Eaton continued to be surrounded with constant attentions. She could not possibly speak to him of her room openly. Making matters worse, Lilith perched on the arm of his chair and Aunt Sybil stood behind, both with the vigilant looks of watchdogs.

Julia fidgeted with her ring. Somehow, she must make arrangements for another room. And there were still questions she would have answered. She scanned the salon for Mr. McNab and spied him delivering the last of the drinks from his tray and heading toward the door. Julia quickened across the room, catching him just outside, in the hall.

"Mr. McNab, I would speak with you. I must know your objections to my staying in the tower room. What is wrong with it?"

"Wrong, miss?" His brows rumpled. "There is nothing wrong with the room. 'Tis simply my employer's—Lord Muir's—practice not to billet guests in the tower, that and no more."

"Yet, the room is kept in readiness, the linens fresh and the furniture dusted. Betty told me as much." The Scotsman only shrugged. "Why then did Lord Eaton ignore his uncle's desires and place me there after all?"

The Scotsman shifted his weight, avoiding her gaze. "It would be indelicate of me to point out the obvious, miss."

Oh, but the man was annoying. "And just what is the 'obvious,' Mr. McNab?"

"Why the proximity of m'lord's room in the adjoining corridor, of course." He tucked his tray under his arm and set off down the hallway.

Shock rooted her in place. Several minutes passed before she collected herself enough to return to the salon. She leveled a murderous gaze at their insufferable host, who sprawled in a deep cushioned chair, his leg outstretched on an ottoman, surrounded by half the females in the room.

One thing was clear to her. Aunt Sybil may well have contrived to situate her in a room far distant from the others, but certainly not near at hand to Lord Eaton's. Julia also now understood the disapproving looks of Mrs. McGinty and Mr. McNab.

Julia moved woodenly toward the fireplace. She *must* speak with the butler yet again. In her surprise, she had forgotten to request new lodgings.

"You are still so pale, dear Julia." Lady Charles clucked her tongue, coming to stand beside her. "I fear your humors have yet to revive. Here, a sherry is what you need. That and the warmth of the fire."

Julia settled into a comfortable chair and sipped the drink as she waited for Mr. McNab to reappear. Several others joined her, including an attentive Mr. Dilcox. She listened to the surrounding conversation, her gaze wandering from time to time to where Emmaline stood surrounded by admirers.

An inordinate fatigue overtook her. She laid it to the toddy and sherry and her long wanderings out-of-doors in the sharp Highland air. Yet, this lethargy seemed disturbingly familiar . . . a bone-deep tiredness that dogged her since morning . . . when she first awoke . . . and again, when she found herself on the lawn . . . outside the keep . . .

Her thoughts trailed off into sweet oblivion.

Julia came hazily aware of someone lifting her. She caught a whiff of men's cologne and thought of Sir Robert. Nice man. Emmaline seemed to think so, too, she thought fuzzily. Julia drifted off again, then felt the softness of a mattress beneath her, and Betty's voice as she helped her from her clothes. Through the groggy mist of fatigue and drink she felt the silky fabric of her nightgown whisper over her skin, then the weight of sheets and covers piled atop her. She mumbled her thanks to Betty and asked her to find Emmaline to come share the room.

"Whatever you say, miss." Betty's footsteps faded across the floor.

Julia burrowed into the downy bed, confident Betty understood her, despite a few slurred words.

Julia floated on a thin layer of sleep, dreaming of the poetic little cottage gardens of Hampshire. She admired one in particular abounding with hollyhocks, sweet Williams, mignonette, and roses hemming the cottage door.

The air stirred and she lifted her face to the sun, anticipating a light breeze to feather her cheek. Instead, the atmosphere grew heavy as iron, weighting her down and choking off her breath.

Panicked, Julia fought her way to consciousness. Hauling open her lids, she lay gulping the air. Awareness unfolded through her in increments as she focused on the shadowy canopy overhead. She lay abed in the tower chamber once more.

Julia groaned and turned her head to glance at the hearth. A lively fire crackled in its confines, bathing the room in shades of golds. She watched a moment, then dragged her gaze from the flames and settled it inadvertently on the bed hangings. Red.

Julia stiffened, her gaze skipping to the foot of bed. There in the shadows stood the elusive Scotsman, fully dressed, his eyes boring into her.

Julia squealed, her arms flailing gracelessly as she bolted upright and threw herself back against the headboard.

"W-who are you?" she gasped out, snatching for the coverlet and yanking it to her throat. "What are you doing in my chamber?"

A swift shadow of surprise swept across the man's features. *"Sassenach!"* The word escaped his lips, the sound deep and rich, mixed with incredulity and disapproval. He stepped from

the end of the bed and rounded the side, his movements
smooth, purposeful, dangerous.

"'Tis my bed ye are warmin', lass, and I didna invite ye
there. I know no' wha' mischief ye are aboot, or who sent ye.
But I dinna take kindly t' trickery."

Rae Mackinnon gazed down on the girl, wholly mystified.
How did a *sassenach* come to be in his bed? Or in his castle for
that matter? Was this someone's sorry idea of a jest, knowing
of his long imprisonment in London's Tower?

Yet something set ill here. Three times now, the golden-
haired lass had appeared, seemingly out of nowhere. And what
of her clothes?—odd to be sure, especially the figure-hugging
gown she had worn this afternoon, flaunting her bewitching
curves. It surprised him that his men did not line up to win her
favors or do worse.

Yet therein lay another puzzle. 'Twas perturbing enough the
girl had vanished before his eyes, but 'twould seem he was the
only one in the hall to see her. *Dhia,* there was much to explain
here.

"I repeat. Who are ye, lass? Who sent ye?"

"I—I am Julia Hargrove," Julia stammered beneath the
Scotsman's penetrating stare. "I—I am a guest of . . . of the
Laird of Dunraven Castle."

Let him challenge that, she thought, her confidence returning. She might be Lord Eaton's guest, but she was indirectly
Lord Muir's as well.

The Scotsman leaned forward, bracing his arms on either
side of Julia and trapping her against the headboard. "Tell me
how tha' can be, lass, when *I* am Laird o' Dunraven and hae
ne'er set eyes on ye afore?"

Julia's eyes widened. "*You* are Lord Muir? But, I—I understood you to be aged—seventy years or more."

"I know no' this 'Lord Muir' and as ye can see I am far from
aged—nine-and-twenty years t' be exact. Now explain yersel'.
D'ye think t' plant yersel' in my bed and seduce me t' some
end?"

"*Seduce?*" Julia's voice vaulted several notches higher. Her temper flamed at such gall, overriding her shock. "That is out-rageous!"

The Scotsman's lips pulled into a hard smile. "And yet here ye be, waitin' in yer finery." He ripped the covers from her fingers, exposing her nightgown and her bare legs where the fabric bunched at her knees. "I am wonderin' why ye bother wi' it a'tall for 'tis plain ye wear no' a stitch beneath." His gaze fell to where the soft roundness of her breasts rose and fell against the thin fabric of her gown.

Julia's mouth opened and closed several times before she could speak. "This, sir, is my *nightgown*. I was *sleeping*," she grit out, yanking the covers from his hands to shield her breasts. She rose on her knees, her anger multiplying. "I *told* you. I am a guest here, in particular of Roger Dunnington, Lord Eaton, and, in turn, of his uncle, Lord Muir, the Twenty-seventh laird of Dunraven Castle."

The Scotsman's eyes narrowed dangerously. "The de'il ye are."

"You call me a liar?"

"Aye, tha' I do. For how can ye be the guest o' the 'twenty-seventh' laird when I mysel' am the *third*."

"The third?"

"Aye, the third."

"Laird? Of Dunraven Castle?"

"So I said. Are ye deaf or daff? I am Rae Mackinnon, Third Laird o' Dunraven Castle in the year o' Our Lord, fourteen hundred and thirty-seven."

Julia's jaw dropped, her breath fully deserting her. She struggled to regain herself and snapped her mouth shut.

"You, sir, are the liar. Or a lunatic. What game do you play, stealing into my chamber in the midst of the night, compromising my reputation? Do you play me for a fool? Fourteen hundred and thirty-seven indeed," she huffed. "The year is eighteen hundred and ninety-three!"

"Enough!" He grabbed her arms and pulled her against his chest. "Who are ye, *sassenach*? Who d'ye serve and for wha' gain? Did the English send ye? Or another clan, holdin' hands across the border, or mayhap here at home wi' those who would control the king?"

"King? What are you talking about? Victoria is Queen."

The Scotsman scoffed outright. "James is but a bairn o' six. He has no queen."

"James?"

"Aye, James, Scotland's wee king."

Julia began to declare Scotland had no king of any size or age. But the look in the Scotsman's eyes gave her pause, a look that told her he believed every word he spoke. She felt the heat drain from her face. What was happening here?

"Victoria is queen of the British Empire. She is seventy-four and a widow," Julia voiced in a bare whisper. "Who . . . *what* are you?" she asked breathlessly, her gaze fixed on his seemingly solid features. "Are you a ghost?"

Irritation flickered in his eyes. "Flesh and bluid I am, lass, o' tha' ye can be sure. But mayhap 'tis ye who is the *hant* for ye disappeared beneath my verra hands this day."

He went rock still then pulled back from her, as though his last words struck some fresh thought deep in his heart. The Scotsman's expression darkened, his eyes scouring her with such a black look, it set Julia's heart to pounding.

"Mayhap 'tis no ghost ye are, but a witch," he said with a growl, his blue eyes cleaving her. "A witch, bearin' a witch's mark!"

Lightning swift, he raked the bed covers from between them, then stripped Julia's nightgown straight off, over her head in a single motion. Flinging her down on the mattress, he pinned her with his weight and began to examine her inch by naked inch, muttering he'd have his proof.

Julia's sensibilities reeled under the Scotsman's assault. She struggled against him, the prickly wool of his kilt sending up an instant rash wherever it grazed her bare skin. His strength held her fast though she squirmed and fought him as best she could. Fear stole her voice though she managed a strangled cry.

To Julia's mortification, his hands moved over her, seemingly everywhere at once—skimming her breasts, stomach, thighs, and backside. He turned her this way and that, from front to back to front again. He even now inspected the soles of her feet and ankles for the cursed mark.

Julia started as his hands slipped upward over her calves and thighs, sending shivers of fire to some hidden core between her legs. But when one hand came to rest low on her abdomen, the fingers splaying and brushing her most private part, she began to thrash wildly, unsure of his intention.

Rae Mackinnon caught the girl's wrists as she clouted his chest, entangling one hand in the chain about his neck. As he drew away her hand, the chain and its talisman followed, dragging from his shirt, snared by the lass's ring.

Working quickly, he freed the two, lest the chain break and he lost the "healing stone" which protected against evil spirits and witches. He then pressed the golden lass back against the mattress, his stone dangling between them.

He studied her, uncertain what to believe as their gazes locked, blue burning into green. The lass beneath his hands was as warm and real as any he'd ever known—certainly not a ghost and seemingly no witch either, for he found no condemning mark.

She still panted for breath from their exertions, glaring up at him with a mingling of anger and fear in her eyes. Her hair spilled over the pillows and about her in glorious disarray, gilded bright by the fire's light.

Och, but she was a beauty, Rae thought. Mayhap, she was an enchantress after all, holding him in thrall with her wide green eyes and temptress body. He knew not what wiles or power brought her to his bed, but for that trespass he'd require one kiss from her. One kiss in recompense, giving her reason to flee or to stay.

Julia saw the hungry look kindle the Scotsman's eyes. He gathered her to him, drawing her up in his arms till they both knelt in the middle of the mattress, pressed together. Before she could protest, his mouth crushed down on hers, a searing, possessive kiss.

His hand slid down her spine to the hollow of her back, then over her backside, kneading her flesh and holding her firmly against him. The wool of is plaid rasped her tender flesh, but through its folds she felt the hard, shocking proof of his desire.

Julia struggled to no avail as the Scotsman continued his aggression, parting her lips, and invading her mouth. She started as his tongue laid siege to hers, stroking, fencing, and ravishing till her blood surged beneath his seduction. Her voice abandoned her as did her strength, so undone was she by his virile Highland possession.

But as the heady kiss continued, the air turned heavy once more. Without warning, the Scotsman vanished from her arms, leaving her clutching thin air.

Julia tumbled back onto the pillows, panting for breath, while overhead the canopy and draperies dissolved from red into blue.

Chapter 5

Pale light threaded past the window curtains and into the chamber, tickling Julia's eyelids.

She awoke with a gasp. Castigating herself for nodding off, she slid from the bed and made a swift search of the room. Rae Mackinnon lurked nowhere in sight. Leastwise not in the nineteenth century!

What was she saying? Did she really believe him to be from the past—a ghost, or whatever? She didn't want to think about it. It didn't matter. She was leaving. The ghost, the room, the castle, Scotland, everything. She was leaving. Now. Forever. She had endured quite enough.

Julia retrieved her traveling trunk from the far corner, hauled it in front of the armoire and shoved open its lid. Yanking wide the armoire doors, she seized an armful of clothes and stuffed them into the trunk.

Julia grabbed a second armful and jammed them in as well, then halted abruptly. She would need a gown in which to travel. The serviceable brown wool she had worn from London was still being cleaned, and she certainly couldn't be seen in the rumpled mess she now wore.

After the Scotsman's disappearance, she had rushed to dress herself, trembling fiercely as she pulled on layer upon layer of mismatched clothing in the dark. She'd then rummaged in the bottom of the armoire for her riding crop. Finding it, she kept vigil through the night, crop in hand, lest the lusty "Third Laird of Dunraven" return and attempt to ravish her with more than his kiss.

Julia's cheeks flooded with warmth at the memory of that kiss, the sensation of his mouth on hers, the strength of his arms, his hands caressing . . .

She jerked her thoughts back, her flesh tingling with his re-membered touch. "Hampshire." She swallowed hard. "I must get home to Hampshire."

Shoving back her disheveled mass of hair, she snatched out the remaining gown that hung in the wardrobe, an almond green silk day dress. Too fine for travel, she would have to risk spoiling it. Besides, the boned bodice would help amend her bungled attempts with her corset and laces.

Julia began peeling off the protective layers of garments—jacket, two shirtwaists, three skirts, more petticoats, several chemises. . . .

She should have vacated the chamber during the night, she admonished herself as she slipped into the green dress. But where would she have gone? She was loath to wake the servants and didn't know where her aunt and cousins slept that she might join them. Nor did she desire to linger in the inky corridors with all the dead, stuffed animals, or await daybreak in the Long Gallery with the grim-faced portraits watching her.

She worked the buttons on her gown, thankful it opened down the front, allowing her to dress without assistance.

In the face of all that had befallen her the past two days, she supposed it unwise to have remained in the room through the night. Still, she had. Could there be some part of her that se-cretly hoped Rae Mackinnon *would* return and possess her with another potent kiss?

"Certainly not!" Julia cried aloud, appalled at herself for even considering so scandalous a notion!

She finished securing her dress, fingers shaking, then brushed back her hair and tied it with a bottle green ribbon. She looked a fright, no doubt, but she had no time for vanities. She must leave Dunraven Castle. At once!

Julia bundled the last of her clothes into the trunk and locked it. Someone, perhaps young Tom, could fetch it down to the coach after she made her arrangements with Lord Eaton and

Aunt Sybil. She didn't intend to return or to put so much as one toe back in the room if she could avoid it.

Nerves spinning, Julia departed the chamber. Traversing the gallery, stairways, and corridors at a rapid pace, she arrived long minutes later in the entrance hall.

She braced herself to speak with Aunt Sybil and Lord Eaton. Predictably, there would be objections, but she would not allow anything they might say to override her determination to leave. She would also need to dispatch a note to her grandmother and one to Mr. Lawson, her solicitor in Hampshire, informing him of her imminent return.

Julia tumbled words through her mind, unsure how to broach the subject with her aunt and host. But did it matter if she blundered her way through as long as a coach could be provided to see her to the station at Perth? If Dunraven held secrets, as Lord Withrington had suggested, then surely they had found her. She must escape this place and the Highland lord who haunted her nights and days.

As Julia approached the breakfast room, she observed the others assembled inside through the open double doors. Their interest appeared fixed toward the head of the table. Good, she thought. Lord Eaton was present, most likely with his foot propped high and the ladies twittering about him. Well, they could twitter off or stay, but she'd have her talk with him now.

Julia whisked through the portal then halted in her footsteps. At the head of the table stood a distinguished-looking man, attired in full Highland dress, his tartan of red in vivid contrast with his snow white hair.

Lord Muir, she realized in utter amazement. It could be none other.

Though advanced in years, he appeared fit and hale. His most striking feature was his luxurious mustache and a longish beard that reached to the top button of his tweed jacket. A plank of snowy brows bridged a strong nose and deep-set eyes, these pale blue in color and underscored with heavy pouches.

The guests from Braxton sat tense in their chairs, apparently having swallowed their tongues. Lord Muir glowered down the length of the table to where Lady Henrietta Downs poised a heaping spoonful of sugar over her porridge. His frown deepened.

Lord Muir himself stood before his own bowl of porridge, unadulterated and steaming, a frosty glass of milk beside it. As he continued to glare his disapproval, Lady Downs yielded, the corner of her mouth twitching as she deposited the sweetener back into the sugar bowl.

Lord Muir's features eased. Giving his attention to his own bowl, he spooned up the piping hot porridge, dipped it into the cold milk, then walked to the window and consumed the fare as he gazed out.

Julia slipped quietly down the right side of the room to the sideboard, where she poured herself a cup of tea. As she added a splash of cream, she caught snatches of muffled conversation behind her. If she understood aright, the marquis had arrived no more than an hour past and was far from pleased by their presence. Some expressed concern he would turn them out.

Julia stirred her tea in thought. Surely Lord Eaton had approached his uncle on the matter of billeting guests at Dunraven. On the other hand, Lord Eaton's invitation at Braxton had been impulsive. Not impulsive, she corrected, abrupt—as was his disappearance northward overnight.

Julia stole a glance over her shoulder to the marquis and found him at the table dipping another spoonful of porridge in the glass of milk. He then walked slowly along the far side of the room eating the porridge as he surveyed the hunting oils that lined the wall.

Would he pack them off? That would certainly solve her dilemma. Still, from the little she knew of Highland hospitality—mostly from Emmaline and what she'd gleaned from her readings—Scots hospitality was renowned, even when entertaining one's foes. Of course, Lord Muir was only part Scots, Julia reminded herself, though by the look of him, his Scots blood ran strong.

Turning, she cast about for Aunt Sybil and found her sitting beside a gentleman known to her only as "Rokeby." Lilith and

Emmaline sat further down, side by side with the Reynolds twins, Ava and Ada, the four of them attended by a clutch of young swains. At the head of the table, Lady Charles conversed with Sir Robert and Lord Withrington while Sampson Dilcox listened intently from his place opposite them. Notably, Lord Eaton was absent.

Tea in hand, Julia started from the sideboard, thinking to approach her aunt.

"Miss Hargrove, here is a place." Mr. Dilcox sprang to his feet and pulled out the chair beside his own.

"Yes, do join us," heartened Lord Withrington, adjusting his spectacles.

Julia glanced to where her aunt bent in conversation with Rokeby, their heads nearly touching. Releasing a small, frustrated sigh, Julia lifted her lips in a smile and joined the others.

Lady Charles's eyes rounded wide as Julia settled herself in her chair.

"My dear, are you ill?" she blurted, drawing the attention of those nearby. "You are positively ashen. I do not mean to be unkind, but there are huge dark smudges beneath your eyes."

Julia cringed as she fell under the scrutiny of a dozen pairs of eyes. She touched a hand to her hair, silently upbraiding herself for not checking her appearance before coming down to the dining room.

"I am only little tired. Truly."

"We should send for a doctor at once," Mr. Dilcox's voice rang with anxious concern. "I shall ride out myself if someone will direct me where to go."

"No, please, Mr. Dilcox . . ."

"Sampson."

"Sampson. I only lack sleep . . ."

"Don't tell me you had *another* restless night in the tower chamber." Lady Charles clucked.

Lord Muir, who had seemed to be purposely ignoring the conversation, abandoned his attention to a painting of game birds and pivoted in place. His eyes veered to Julia then to Mr. McNab, who was just entering the door.

"You lodged this young woman in the south tower?" he barked.

Every head in the room swiveled to the marquis then to the butler. Mr. McNab began to stumble out an explanation, but Julia rose from her chair and intervened.

"Lord Eaton insisted over Mr. McNab's protests, your lordship. Mr. McNab had no choice." She blinked. Now why did she take up for the cantankerous Scotsman, she wondered, astonishing herself? "I am quite prepared to vacate the room," she added quickly. "In truth, my belongings are already packed."

Across from her, Sir Robert leaned forward, his expression perplexed. "You couldn't sleep so you packed—before breakfast?"

Julia caught her lower lip with the edge of her teeth. She couldn't openly reveal her decision to leave when she had yet to mention the matter to her aunt.

"The tower room is very fine and I am most appreciative for its use. But my sleep there has been, shall we say, disturbed."

"Disturbed, Miss Hargrove?" Sampson quirked his head.

"D-dreams, that is all."

Blank stares confronted her.

"Disturbing recurrent dreams." She reseated herself and took a small sip of tea. "Nightmares, actually. Most distressing."

Julia fought to control the tremor that overtook her hands as she replaced the cup on the saucer. Lord Muir returned to stand before his porridge, but he neither ate nor spoke. Julia could not meet his eyes but felt his scowl.

"Perhaps a doctor *is* in order, dear," Mrs. Charles broke the silence. "You haven't been well since you arrived. Obviously, it is your state of health, not your room, that is the cause of your distress. I'm sure the marquis would be amenable to sending for a physician."

Julia thought to hear Lord Muir issue a grunt of assent. Her head began to throb. If she didn't leave soon, she would truly need a doctor to treat her for a splitting headache.

Julia took another swallow of tea, noticing Lady Charles had engaged Lord Muir in conversation, though in truth, it was entirely one-sided. Julia continued to sip her tea, listening as Lady Charles spoke of her late husband once hunting at Dunraven.

"Lord Muir, what a handsome tartan," Lady Charles said, changing subjects with ease. "Nigel told me you claim descent from Clan . . . Oh dear, was it Mackenzie? Macintosh? Macpherson . . ?"

"Mackinnon," he said gruffly.

Julia shot to her feet, the tea spilling down the front of her gown. "How clumsy of me." She snatched up the napkin from Mr. Dilcox's place and wiped furiously at her skirt.

Mackinnon. Lord Muir was a *Mackinnon.* Julia's mind reeled. What had Betty said—the marquis "brought Dunraven back into the family," that it had been lost in the previous century? But Betty had neglected to mention the clan by name. Even when Rae Mackinnon had identified himself, it hadn't occurred to her that he and Lord Muir might claim a common lineage. Regardless that both bore the title of "laird," the land and castle could easily have changed owners any number of times throughout the centuries.

And yet, if Dunraven had remained in the clan's possession until the time of the Jacobite Rebellion, that would mean the portraits in the gallery would be overwhelmingly . . . Mackinnons. Julia groaned. Did Rae Mackinnon's likeness watch from the wall there, too?

"Your beautiful silk will be ruined if you don't set it to soaking," Lady Charles fretted.

"No need." Julia forced a smile. "It is only a little tea and see, it is coming clean."

"But it must dry," Lady Charles persisted. "You might even lie down for a time in your room and . . ."

"No! I mean, no. The fabric will dry quickly enough, and, besides, I must begin a letter to my grandmother. It is long overdue."

Julia lowered herself to her chair, fearing she had made a spectacle and had further affronted Lord Muir. But when she dared a glimpse of him, she saw his expression had changed from one of displeasure to pensive thoughtfulness.

Of a sudden, he became animated and gestured over Mrs. McGinty.

"Some hot porridge will help put this young woman to rights. See what else Cook might offer her. Some kippers, perhaps, or cold grouse and scones with marmalade."

Julia drew more than a few envious looks, in particular from Lady Downs. At the same time, Lord Muir fixed his attention on the men.

"I suppose you are all itching to get off for some sport. Can't join you myself, too old for the rigors of stalking. But I'd suggest you try the hills south and east of Dunraven. Angus knows the spot and will lead you out. Oh, Mrs. McGinty, see Cook sends the men out with something other than those cold porridge bars of hers. I'm sure they'll find a sandwich more agreeable after hiking and crawling about the day long."

Jaws sagged around the table as Lord Muir excused himself and, after another penetrating look to Julia, left the dining room.

"Extraordinary!" muttered Lady Charles.

The next hour saw Julia in the breakfast parlor, sitting before the bay window, penning a brief note to Lady Arabella on thistle-embossed stationery.

Frustratingly, Aunt Sybil had slipped away with Rokeby before she could speak with her. Lilith, too, had disappeared, but with the Reynolds twins. Presumably they searched for Lord Eaton. Emmaline, bless the girl, kept her company, relaxing on one of the chintz-covered sofas, reading Scott's *Bride of Lammermour*.

Despite the marquis's arrival, Julia remained undeterred in her course. She would leave Dunraven and flee the rugged Highlander who continued to invade her life. Ghost or fantasy, Rae Mackinnon stirred in her feelings that were disconcertingly physical and seemingly beyond her control. Yes, she must leave before he returned.

"Pardon me, Miss Hargrove."

Julia started, then looked up to find Mrs. McGinty, unsmiling as ever.

"His lordship, the marquis, requests your presence in the library. He is waiting there now."

Mrs. McGinty ushered Julia into a handsome room with a high, barrel-vaulted ceiling and book-lined walls. Marble busts topped the bookcases while a large painting of a lady and her two tartan-clad children hung above the fireplace.

Lord Muir sat at his desk, rapidly scratching out a missive on cream-colored paper. At Julia's entrance, he set aside his pen and rose.

"You may leave Mrs. McGinty. See we are left undisturbed."

Julia tensed, uncertain what the marquis was about, and further flustered that he should put her reputation at risk. Was he so angered by her occupancy in the tower? She watched with dismay as the housekeeper withdrew, stone-faced.

"Your lordship, this is far from proper." She stood her place at the door.

"At seventy-three years of age, I am done with 'proper,' Miss Hargrove. Please, be seated."

Wary, Julia crossed to the tapestry-covered chair facing his desk and lowered herself onto its edge. With hands folded, she worried her ring around her finger and braced herself for a scathing reprimand.

"I shall be direct, Miss Hargrove." Lord Muir fixed her with an incisive gaze as he reseated himself. "Do you know why my nephew chose to lodge you in the tower?"

Julia's heart sank. Had Mr. McNab apprised the marquis of his own conjectures on that subject? Did Lord Muir now seek to wrest some sordid confession of midnight trysts with Lord Eaton? She lifted her chin and strove to meet the marquis's eyes with a clear, unfaltering gaze.

"I was among the last of the guests to arrive at Dunraven, indeed the lattermost to be accommodated. To my understanding, the other rooms were already occupied or somehow unusable. Lord Eaton recalled the tower chamber and thought it would be suitable."

"I see." Lord Muir fell silent though his eyes remained boring into hers. He drummed his fingers lightly on the arm of his chair. "Your sleep, you say, has been 'disturbed'? Is there a problem with the room?"

Julia found it curious that, unlike Lady Charles, he should suggest the room, rather than her health, to be the source of her troubles.

"D-dreams, your lordship, I only suffer dreams."

" 'Nightmares,' I believe you called them."

" 'Nightmares,' 'dreams,' they have robbed me of my sleep since my arrival."

Lord Muir studied her a long moment. Self-conscious, Julia shifted in her seat. Did she appear so ghastly with the smudges darkening her eyes?

"Would you characterize these as 'sleeping' dreams or 'waking' dreams?" he asked after another moment.

"I—I don't understand . . ."

"The keep is ancient and has certain 'peculiarities.' Is it possible, Miss Hargrove, what you experienced was no dream at all, but something of a wholly different nature?"

"Different nature?" Her hand floated to her throat. "H-how do you mean?"

He leaned forward, his eyes afire beneath his snowy brows. "Is it possible the room changed before your eyes? That you found yourself suddenly looking in upon another age, though you felt certain you had never moved from your own?"

Julia rose on unsteady feet, her breath wedged in her throat. "You know. You know about the room. It is why you closed Dunraven to visitors so many years ago, is it not? You met him, too."

"Him?"

"Rae Mackinnon, the Third Laird of Dunraven Castle."

"The *Third* Laird. How do you know his name and title?"

"He told me so himself."

Shock cleaved Lord Muir's features. His mouth dropped open and he fell back in his chair.

"Your lordship! Are you all right?" Julia quickened around the desk, fearing her bluntness had caused him some harm. She reached to test his forehead and cheek, but he seized her hand tightly in his.

"The laird spoke with you? The two of you *conversed*?"

Julia nodded and the marquis looked even more astonished. She feared he would suffer a stroke if he did not calm himself. Instead, his beard split wide with a grin. Leaping spryly to his feet, he grabbed Julia by the waist and whirled her around.

"Do you know what this means? I have waited *twenty* years for this!"

"For what?" Julia panted as he set her down.

"For time to 'slip.'"

Julia wavered. She didn't care for the sound of that.

"We must celebrate. Yes, a 'wee dram,' that will do nicely. Then I must hear your account."

Julia followed him across the room to a walnut cabinet which he opened and retrieved two small glasses and a crystal decanter.

"Your lordship? Lord Muir?"

"It is still morning, I know, but just a drop. Or would you prefer sherry?"

Julia shook her head, having no desire to emerge from the library smelling of alcohol. She followed him back to the desk.

"About the room's being haunted . . ."

"No, not haunted. You saw no ghosts. What you experienced is a most rare phenomenon but very real. How shall I explain it?"

He pulled at his beard. "It is like a window opening between two times, a 'doorway' if you will. Those on both sides are able to observe the other, sometimes even interact. Yet, neither one feels they have left their own time, nor does the 'window' remain open for long. In scientific circles—those devoted to the study of psychic occurrences—we call the phenomenon a 'slip in time.'"

"I think I should sit down." Julia groped for the arm of the chair and sank into its support.

"Perhaps, a 'wee dram' is in order after all?"

Julia nodded but couldn't find her voice. She knew Rae Mackinnon was somehow real, or at least solid. But she had not imagined, never conceived, that he had stepped across time—a living, breathing Scotsman straight out of the fifteenth century!

Or had she crossed into his—a woman of the future stepping into the past?

"How unsettling for you. Poor girl, you must have thought you were going mad." Lord Muir furnished her with a small glass of amber liquid, then sat down with his own. "It might help if I tell you of my own experience."

Julia took a swallow of the whiskey then grimaced, her throat burning. "Yes," she rasped. "I would like that."

He smiled and took a sip of his glass. "Thirty-five years ago, I purchased Dunraven Castle, restoring it to Mackinnon hands. Being an admirer of all that is historic and old, I claimed the ancient tower chamber for my own use. Thereafter, over fifteen years, Dunraven hosted annual hunts. Then, on one night seemingly no different from the rest, I experienced the most amazing event of my life."

Lord Muir's eyes grew misty with memory. "I went to bed at my normal hour but couldn't sleep. Above the fireplace hung a ceremonial sword. It had recently come into my hands and once belonged to a Mackinnon ancestor, a Jacobite intriguer of some renown. Taking the sword down from its place of honor, I sat polishing it when the sound of weeping came to my ears.

"When I looked up, I discovered the room inexplicably filled with people—right and left, front and back of me—the men all dressed in old-style kilts. The furnishings in the room had changed as well, and there was a woman lying abed, apparently dying. A lordly looking man, tall and red-haired, held her hand, grief lashing his eyes, while three young boys crowded beside him.

"As I watched, the woman took a chain from her neck, bearing a pendant of some manner, and placed it over the head of her eldest child. He was trying to be a brave lad and not cry, but he couldn't help himself. He was wiping away the tears when he looked up and saw me. I turned to see if anyone else noticed me as well, lest they not be a friendly sort and bare their blades. But in that fraction of a second, the scene disassembled and I found myself alone once more, the room returned to normal. Since then, I have endeavored to learn all I can about what happened that night and how to transcend time."

"And so you closed Dunraven and preserved the room as it was?" Julia guessed aloud.

Lord Muir nodded, then sighed heavily. "But I must have disturbed or altered something when I moved my personal belongings from the room. Either that, or other conditions were at work that I have yet to understand. I kept watch night after night, I and my colleagues of the 'Society.' Disappointingly, there have been no further 'time-slips.' Until now."

He lifted his eyes to hers. "So you see, my dear Miss Hargrove, I am quite desperate to know what you have witnessed and to know all the details, however trivial they might seem."

The marquis poured her another "drop" of whiskey, which Julia accepted but left untouched. At his gentle but persuasive insistence, she yielded and began to recount her strange experiences of the past two days, omitting the more intimate points. Lord Muir sat spellbound as she detailed each of the three "time-slips."

"By your description of Rae Mackinnon, he must be someone other than the man I saw. Scant information survives on the early lairds, none on the third. At least now we have a name to put to him. My dear, do you realize your experience far exceeds any other on record? And to think *thrice* you slipped time and conversed with the laird directly."

And touched him, and kissed him, and now bore a rash all over her body from his scratchy plaid, Julia mused.

"So, Rae Mackinnon's not a ghost after all."

"No, my dear," Lord Muir exclaimed, eyes sparkling. "He is perfectly real."

Julia was trying to decide whether that was good or bad when the marquis caught her hands in hers, tears of joy brimming his eyes.

"You don't know how I've waited these long years for this moment, Miss Hargrove. Tonight, we shall watch in the tower chamber *together*!"

Chapter 6

How did she let herself agree to this, Julia reproached herself
for the thousandth time? Bad enough she must endure another
night in the tower, but that she should allow a man into the bedchamber with her, regardless of his age?

Julia glanced from her place on the bed to where Lord Muir
busily removed an assortment of instruments from a deep, velvet-
lined case and arranged them on the table before him. Despite the
belated hour, he brimmed with energy.

Could she have done otherwise, she wondered? She had insisted she must leave. He had implored her to stay, appearing
stricken by the possibility she might not. He reminded her of a
small child who had been tantalized with the most resplendent
of gifts only to see it snatched away.

Julia sighed. How does one say no to an overly excited young-
ster of seventy-three, one who happened to own the castle, not to
mention the horses and carriage needed to see her away? In the
face of his earnest, urgent pleas, her resistance crumbled. The
phenomenon might be connected to her personally somehow, he
had stressed. It was not enough for him to watch in the chamber
alone, but vital she be present as well.

Settling back against the pillows, Julia twined a strand of
pale hair around her forefinger. Now that she understood something of the occurrences in the tower, she admitted she was intrigued. But if she must face Rae Mackinnon once more, she
much preferred to be chaperoned, however improper the
arrangements. She only hoped no one had observed the marquis
enter her bedchamber.

Julia loosed the coil from her finger and looked again to the elderly lord. He bent over a small, worn book now, making notations, oblivious to her ruminations.

He wouldn't heedlessly jeopardize her reputation, of that she felt certain. Indeed, earlier he had shown himself to be most considerate.

After their encounter in the library, he had directed Mrs. McGinty to release Betty from her routine duties, that she might solely attend to Julia's needs. He further had instructed that additional help be hired from the village to assist Dunraven's overworked staff with its many guests. This Julia learned from a very excited and chatty Betty, thrilled by her elevation to the status of lady's maid.

To Julia's relief, Betty remained ever present whenever it became necessary to return to the chamber, as when she changed gowns for afternoon tea and later again for supper.

The evening meal proved a grand affair and Lord Muir a genial host. Course after course flowed from the kitchen beginning with a thick, creamy crab soup called *Partan Bree*, followed by smoked salmon terrine, haunch of venison with tart rowan jelly, pheasant and mushroom pie, a selection of fruits and cheeses, and a delectable plum charlotte, all accompanied with a fine claret and followed with port.

Julia assumed the sumptuous menu to be the marquis's doing—or Cook's, demonstrating her approval of the lord's return to all. In any event, the guests indulged themselves to excess, Lady Henrietta to embarrassment.

Lord Eaton ate little by comparison. Usurped from the head of the table by his uncle, he occupied a place at its opposite end, though not at its foot as one might expect. Julia detected a thread of tension between the two lords, and could only guess at its cause. At tea, Emmaline had divulged that Lord Eaton had relinquished his room to the marquis, though Lilith maintained he had done so of his own accord. In all frankness, Julia cared not at all where Roger Dunnington resided as long as it was far distant from her own lodgings.

After dinner, Angus played the pipes outside the parlor win-

dow, to everyone's diversion and delight. Julia then partici-
pated in several games of whist to pass the time, Mr. Dilcox
roosting ever near.

Lord Muir, accustomed to early hours and being of advanced
age, retired early without ruffling a feather of suspicion. Julia,
however, prudently waited to withdraw with the other ladies.
When at long last the hour arrived, the men escorted them to the
bottom of the hall's grand staircase, lit their candles, and
wished them good night. As the women ascended the steps—
and Julia headed for the corridor behind the stairs—the men retreated to the smoking parlor for their whiskey and cigars.

In the tower chamber, Julia readied for bed with Betty's assistance. But as soon as her new maid departed, Julia doffed her
nightclothes, laced herself loosely back into her corset, and
slipped into a roomy morning dress. Comfortable and decently
attired, she awaited the lairds of Dunraven Castle.

At the appointed hour, well past midnight, Lord Muir arrived, exercising the greatest of caution to enter unseen. Julia
wondered if her reputation could possibly survive with so many
eyes and ears about. Secrets did not remain so for long in such
places as this.

Julia diverted her gaze once more to the marquis and found
him sitting motionless, his pen poised over his notebook, his
face clouded with thought.

"Your lordship, is something the matter?"

Lord Muir heaved a sigh and rested back in his chair. "The
instruments, I almost fear to use them. Their very presence
could disrupt conditions. My own, as well."

"And if you are not present, how ever will you be able to witness your 'time-slip' again?" She smiled gently.

He returned her smile, sending her a nod of agreement.

"What are the instruments you have there?" Julia rose from
the bed and went to stand beside him.

"Compass, barometer, thermometer, and chronometer." Lord
Muir pointed out each one. "They will register any changes in
the atmosphere that occur during the actual time shift. The
compass is sensitive to the electromagnetic field, the barometer

reads air pressure, and the thermometer temperature. The chronometer, of course, is the most accurate device available to track the precise time. We will compare its reading with the other timepieces both inside and outside the chamber after the time-slip occurs. We may find discrepancies."

Julia considered the items, a sudden thought striking her. "It is possible you might not have the opportunity to make use of the instruments."

"How is that, Miss Hargrove?"

"During each of the time alterations I witnessed, the furniture in the chamber vanished. The furniture in our own time, that is. It stands to reason, should the table disappear tonight, so will your instruments. Even your chair could evaporate beneath you, spilling you onto the floor."

Lord Muir looked to the piece with mild surprise. "I hadn't thought of that. Years ago, when I sat polishing my sword, I did so there on the floor." He gestured to a place right of the fireplace. "When the time-slip occurred, I remained there, undisturbed. But what of the bed? Are you not in the same danger?"

Julia shook her head. "The bed exists in the past, though the mattress is lumpier." She smiled.

Lord Muir stroked his beard. "It was not present in my own experience, which might indicate an earlier date. I will make a notation and ponder it later. For now, you are quite right. I best claim a space on the floor."

Julia pointed out where the medieval-style trunk would appear as well as a rough table and three-legged stool. They decided to relocate him to the corner nearest the door—the door in the current century. After transferring the instruments to the floor there, Julia brought pillows from the bed and helped the marquis settle himself. Whatever discomfort he suffered, he made no complaints.

As the night deepened they fell to a companionable silence. Julia immersed herself in Tennyson's *Idylls of the King,* reading by lamplight. When her head suddenly jerked forward, she realized she had dozed off.

Julia drew a deep, freshening breath of air, then massaged

her neck and shoulder where the muscles bunched. Looking to the corner, she found Lord Muir awake but rubbing his legs, which she guessed to have fallen asleep.

"Would you care for a glass of water, your lordship?" she asked, rising and crossing to the narrow table that stood against the wall.

"Hmm, what?" Lord Muir looked up from his book, where he browsed his notes. "No, Miss Hargrove. Thank you." He returned his interest to his book, thumbing a page.

Julia reached for the pitcher, but as she did the air grew weighty.

"Do you feel that—the air, pressing down?" She lifted her hand to her head.

"I feel nothing." Lord Muir straightened, glancing to Julia, then his instruments.

Before Julia's eyes, the pitcher, tray, and glasses dissolved to air. Julia gasped and sprang back a pace.

"Miss Hargrove? What is it? Do you see something?"

"No, I don't. What I mean is, the table is gone and everything on it. So are the chairs. I can't see them." She scanned the room. "So is the armoire and my traveling trunk, the little mirror on the wall . . . all the furniture is gone, excepting the bed."

She lifted her arm and pointed to the space where roughly the armoire had been. "There, against the wall, the trunk is back. It's bound with thick, iron strips and looks very old, weather-worn. Can you not see it yourself?"

"I see nothing, Miss Hargrove. But can you see me?"

Julia looked to where Lord Muir sat. "Yes, yes, but not your instruments. They are gone, too."

"No, they are all here in front of me, but the needle on the compass is fluctuating wildly."

"I don't understand . . ."

"Do not worry over it, Miss Hargrove. Such is known in other cases. Tell me what else you see."

"The implements by the hearth are different, but the carving on the fireplace hood is the same—a rather homely boar's head, with a bone in its mouth."

"Yes, the Mackinnon crest."

"I'm sorry, I didn't know."

"Please, go on."

Julia moved toward the bed. "The hangings are no longer blue, but a deep, rich scarlet." She fingered their texture then looked to the wall. "There is a door on the wall here now, but the one beside you has disappeared."

"Is the laird present?" Lord Muir asked, his tone hopeful.

"No. However, the door is open to the stairwell. There are voices."

She stepped closer, then leapt back as a bent figure entered, nearly colliding with her.

"What, Miss Hargrove?"

"A servant. He's carrying thick bars of peat. He just deposited them before the hearth and is squatting down. He's beginning to build a fire."

"Can you describe him?"

"He looks to be in his early twenties, clean-shaven, his hair a medium brown. He wears a bulky kilt and the colors are muted."

"Mmm. The *feileadh-mor,* the 'great wrap.' The dyes would be made from vegetable matter, whatever is available here abouts. Have you seen the man before?" She shook her head. "Does he see you? Can you talk to him?"

Julia attempted to speak to the servant, joining him at the fireplace, but he continued at his task, taking no notice.

"He doesn't see me, but it was the same in the hall. No one but the laird could see me."

A certain dread gripped Julia that Lord Muir might think she merely fantasized what she claimed. She could offer no proof.

"Rae Mackinnon and I did speak, truly. And I can assure you, he was quite solid to the touch."

"You touched him?" Lord Muir's snowy brows shot upward.

"Actually, he touched me. We touched each other." Julia wished to kick herself for opening the subject. "He no more understood my appearances and disappearances than I his. In one instant, he feared me to be supernatural and trapped me by the arms. When he held me against him, I felt his breath."

"Felt his breath? You didn't mention this before." Lord Muir scratched furiously in his book, but seemed far from scandalized. "The phenomenon has many singularities. There must be something in particular that enables the two of you to directly interact. We'll speculate on that later. Is there anything happening in the room now?"

Julia looked back to find the servant, but another man now entered the room.

"There is a second servant. He is carrying a bucket of water. He's pouring its contents into a deep, footed pot and positioning it before the fire."

"You said earlier you actually passed through the door." Lord Muir pressed on. "That would mean you went through stone. Can you step out on the stairwell now?"

Julia hesitated, then crossed the room to do so. She had twice done so before, why did she pause? Hearing the voices again, she stopped before the portal.

"Someone is standing not far down the steps. I hear them speaking—a man and a woman. For the most part, I hear the woman. Her voice is very sharp and loud."

Lord Muir struggled to his feet, watching Julia closely. "Try at least to put your hand through the door, so I might witness what happens."

Julia looked to the door, bit her lip, then stepped directly before it and started to reach her hand through the open archway. As she did she felt the air begin to change, she snatched back her arm.

"Time is shifting again. I feel it."

Disappointment lanced through Julia as she realized she would not see her Scots laird tonight. But as she looked up, Rae Mackinnon suddenly appeared, filling the doorway and gazing down on her.

They stood scant inches apart, the tips of her breasts nearly brushing his broad chest. Their gazes locked and held, blue melding with green, and despite herself, Julia smiled at the splendid sight of him.

"He's here," she whispered, barely able to force the words past her lips.

As Rae Mackinnon disappeared, he returned her smile, a slash of white splitting his face. The force of it sent heat rushing to her toes. Julia instantly reprimanded herself, fearing he interpreted her smile as open encouragement. Lord, the man needed no encouragement!

She turned back to the room, her heart thudding madly and strived to appear calm. It took a full moment to realize all was as before—the armoire, carpet, table, and chairs back in their respective places, the bed hangings blue.

Lord Muir came forward and helped Julia to a chair.

"Are you all right, my dear? I fear this has overtaxed you."

He brought her water and sat with her at the table, patting her hand. She assured him she was fine.

"He saw me—Rae Mackinnon—just before he vanished."

"Are you sure?"

"Yes, he smiled at me." Julia felt herself flush, remembering the potency of that smile.

Lord Muir chuckled. "The laird must be as taken with you, as you are with him. Not that I blame him one whit."

"Oh, but no . . . He, I . . . we're not taken with anybody," Julia said.

"I might not have been able to see Rae Mackinnon, but I could easily see the intensity of the smile you sent him." Lord Muir gave her a conspiratorial wink.

Julia rubbed at the pain in her temples, knowing she blushed from head to toe.

"You must be exhausted. We can finish this tomorrow. You should rest for now."

Lord Muir rose and packed his instruments into his case. "Do not fear to remain in the room tonight. From what you have told me of the other incidents, there should be no more time-slips until tomorrow. But I can send Betty to stay with you, if you are fearful of being alone."

"No, that isn't necessary, really. I suddenly feel so drained, I'm certain I shall sleep through anything, even another time-slip."

Julia saw Lord Muir to the door. Checking outside in the corridor, she determined the way was clear. She stepped aside as he emerged from the chamber.

"Thank you, my dear." He smiled and gave her a small peck on the cheek. "You have made me a most happy man."

With that, the Twenty-seventh Laird of Dunraven took his leave.

Roger Dunnington, Lord Eaton, traveled silently along the gallery, his slippers in hand. Who would have guessed Lady Downs to be such a talented woman?

A grin tipped his mustache.

Reaching the far end of the gallery, he turned left, into the narrow servants' passage which connected the south tower to the west end, ever so useful for nocturnal visitations.

He stopped a moment and looked back toward the short neck of a hall that led to Julia's tower room. He gave a brief, courteous bow. There awaited another conquest. He sighed through his liquored haze. He hadn't forgotten her, not beautiful, golden Julia. Pity she had so meager a dowry, or he would snatch her right up for his bride.

He began to turn and head off when light knifed the darkness, Julia's door pulling open. He pressed into the shadows, concealing himself behind a pedestal and bit of statuary. Julia appeared and scanned the passage.

What could she be about at this hour, Roger wondered, intrigued.

To his astonishment his uncle emerged from the chamber to stand beside Julia. Kissing her cheek, he spoke words of gratitude, something about being a "happy man." The marquis then hastened away, passing just a few feet from Roger as he turned and proceeded down the length of the gallery, moving in the direction of his room.

Roger bristled, confounded that his ancient relative should

be tupping the much younger and exquisite blonde. His thoughts then turned to Julia, blackening indignantly.

"The sly little cat."

So she played him a game, rejecting his own advances throughout the summer, biding her time to gain just such an invitation as he had issued her to Dunraven, all the while waiting to sport for bigger game. Well, she'd have her "sport," he vowed. His discovery this night would not be without profit.

Roger still stung from his uncle's sharp words of this morning. Upon his arrival, the marquis had roundly bawled him out over the matter of his gambling debts. The old man refused to advance him a shilling more, though he knew Roger's allowance to be exhausted for the year.

"Profligate," his uncle had called him. Roger admitted his debts to be the reason for his hasty flight north, his creditors at his heels. Still, he simmered at the rebuke.

Marriage to Lilith would solve the strains of his finances until he came into his titles. Her dowry was quite generous, significantly improved from last Season, he noted.

But now, if he played his cards shrewdly, his dottering uncle would not only cover his existing debts, but fund his "habit" without grievance to protect Julia.

His thoughts went to the beauty. If his uncle would subsidize him, the two could continue their romp. But Julia Hargrove would have to satisfy his own desires as well, Roger Dunnington promised himself. That or she'd see herself ruined in society. He swore it.

Chapter 7

Julia stifled a yawn.

"Shall I send for more tea, Miss Hargrove?"

"Thank you, no."

Julia sent an appreciative smile to Lord Muir, sitting opposite her behind his expansive mahogany desk. She centered herself further back in her chair, then fought down another yawn.

"Forgive me, your lordship. I've been excessively tired of
late. I never fully recovered from the trip north, then with the
nights being so disturbed . . ." She gave a little shrug, smiling.
"I was late to breakfast again this morning. Everyone must
think me a terrible slug-a-bed."

Lord Muir templed his fingers in thought. "Fatigue could be
a side-effect of the time-slips. You say the air grows heavy
when the actual shift occurs?"

"Yes, it seems to compress and push down all at once."

Lord Muir entered a note in the red, leather-bound journal
that lay open before him. Finishing, he leafed back through several pages, skimming each one, then swiveled the book around
and scooted it toward Julia.

"I have detailed the accounts of each of the time-slips as you
have described them. Each occurrence appears with a number
and heading, followed by the date, time of day, and duration of
the shift—the first three being approximate, the fourth, last
night's, being an actual measurement. The particulars of each
episode follow. Please, read over the entries carefully. If you
find them to be accurate and complete, then give them your initial."

As Julia lifted the book to her lap, Lord Muir sank back into his chair and stroked his beard.

"The shifts appear to be opening sequentially onto Rae Mackinnon's past, their manifestation and duration correspondent to those in our present," he ruminated aloud. "You'll remember, during the third 'slip,' when you awoke to find the laird in the chamber, he mentioned seeing you that afternoon. He referred to his own time, but you had seen him that same afternoon in *your* time as well."

Julia quirked a brow, not wholly understanding.

"My guess is that the two timelines, past and present, are somehow connected, running parallel, so that when the 'window' opens between them, both you and the laird have progressed forward the same number of hours and minutes. We do not know what 'laws' govern the phenomena." He splayed his hands in the air. "Theoretically, time could slip randomly to any point in the past, but that doesn't seem to be the case."

Julia hadn't considered that. In one instant, Rae Mackinnon would be a virile young man, and in the next, aged or an infant, or not even be born at all.

Lord Muir sighed heavily and rubbed his forehead. "There is much still to learn. We shall need to maintain precise records as we witness more of the phenomena."

"More?" Julia straightened, placing the book back on the desk. "Your lordship, I agreed to watch in the chamber last night but to nothing 'more.' "

The marquis cocked his snowy head to one side. "Miss Hargrove, you surprise me. You are party to one of the most exciting, unimaginable, implausible events of our century—the breaching of time. You yourself have touched the past. Literally! And it doesn't seem the time-slips are about to cease. Can you walk away from it so easily? Or him?"

"Him?"

"The Third Laird of Dunraven."

Julia dropped her gaze to her hands, unable to form an answer.

"Do you fear him?"

"No! Yes. Somewhat. He is a fifteenth-century Highlander, after all. Lilith warned they were barbarians."

Lord Muir snorted. "And did she tell you Highlandmen honored their women and treated them well, the children, too, of both sexes? They did, much more so than the 'civilized' English of the day. Rae Mackinnon must be as confused as you about the incidents he is experiencing, but I doubt he would deal you a harm."

"Unless he believes me to be a witch and decides to burn me at a stake." Julia looked at the marquis squarely.

"Is that what you saw in his eyes when he smiled at you last night?" Julia diverted her gaze. "Perhaps, it is not the Third Laird of Dunraven you fear, Miss Hargrove," the marquis added softly.

Julia's pulse quickened at the thought of Rae Mackinnon. Yes, she feared him. Feared what he did to her senses, emotionally, physically. Feared that part of her which had responded to his kiss and now craved more.

Julia cleared her throat. "As I expressed yesterday, I wish to return home to Hampshire . . ."

"What awaits you in Hampshire, Miss Hargrove?" Lord Muir interrupted, catching and holding her gaze. "Your estate is let out, your parents tragically gone, God rest them. Yes, I know of your sorrow and misfortune. I make it a habit to know something of those in my nephew's company and made a few discreet inquiries, forgive me. But what is so important in Hampshire that it cannot wait?"

Taken aback, Julia couldn't piece her thoughts together for a moment.

"My father's works," she said at last. "Perhaps you've heard of his programs in Fareham which benefit the poor. They are quite innovative and successful. Mr. Twyford, my father's former partner, carries on the works as I wish to do on returning to Hampshire. I've been far too idle of late."

"But if Mr. Twyford is overseeing them satisfactorily, they will continue with or without your presence."

"Yes, that is true," she conceded reluctantly.

Lord Muir rose from his chair and came around the desk to sit on its edge. "You can find any number of causes to support here in Scotland, Miss Hargrove, if you wish to engage in benevolent works. And I am prepared to help you to that end with an offer of my own. But first, there is something I wish you to see."

At Lord Muir's encouragement, Julia accompanied him from the library and next found herself traveling familiar corridors and stairways. At first, she thought he led her to her tower room and began to object. But they continued to climb higher in the castle before turning down a lengthy hallway, paneled but devoid of paintings or furniture.

Julia realized they now walked above the Long Gallery and that the hall ended at the outer wall of the ancient keep, one level above her bedchamber. Lord Muir produced a heavy key from his pocket and opened the door there.

"Please come in Miss Hargrove. This is my private study. I believe you know where we are."

Julia entered and found the room to be spacious yet snug, the ceiling low-vaulted and the walls crowded with bookshelves and file cabinets. A large table surrounded by chairs sat at the center and a high-topped desk to one side. Not surprisingly, the room also contained a large hooded fireplace, engraved with the choleric boar's head.

"Have a seat, Miss Hargrove." Lord Muir ushered her to one of the leather-upholstered chairs then began to pace, tugging thoughtfully on his beard.

"Where should I begin? Twenty years ago, after I found myself momentarily surrounded by the past, I committed myself to learning all I could of the phenomena and of Dunraven's history. What you see here is the result of that quest."

He gestured to the book-crammed shelves and partially opened cabinets where an assortment of papers peeked out.

"At the risk of my reputation and of being considered demented, I actively sought out every scrap of information, every theory that existed on the possibility of transversing time. Some with whom I spoke argued that I saw a ghostly scene from the past, no more. I might have agreed had it not been for the child in the past seeing me during the time shift. In fact, he pointed me out to his lordly father, which is why I turned to see if the other men in the room might be unsheathing their blades to protect him against my intrusion."

Lord Muir stopped his pacing and turned to Julia. "Of course, science holds that time is absolute, that we are trapped in it, unable to travel forward or backward. That is the core of Newton's law. But I knew what I had seen that night, just as you know what you have experienced, Miss Hargrove. Time *can* be traversed."

He resumed his pacing. "At first, I did not understand the concept of 'time-slips,' of windows or portals opening between past and present. I debated the possibility of transgressing time with countless learned men—physicists, cosmologists, astronomers among them. I also gathered with those who seriously and scientifically undertook the study of unexplained phenomena.

"Eleven years ago, we founded the Society for Psychical Research. My colleagues and I have since investigated, recorded, and studied a variety of phenomena. I found I am not alone in my experience. What we in the Society refer to as 'time-slips' are among the more rare phenomena. Indeed our deliberations on them leave them still in the realm of 'theory.' But even Newton's law is theory, is it not?

"My dear Miss Hargrove, do you understand the vast importance of what is happening here at Dunraven? All other reported instances of time-slips are singular, nonrepeating. What you are experiencing is unique, a resounding breakthrough for science.

"I understand your desire to leave, but I invite, nay, I encourage you to stay and join me in my work. I can offer you an official position as my assistant and pay you handsomely, enough to grant you a measure of independence and sustain your good works."

Julia found Lord Muir's offer quite remarkable. And tantalizing.

"For how long do you propose I assist you?"

"For as long as you like, Miss Hargrove. May I call you Julia?" At her nod, he continued. "Certainly, I would like you to remain at Dunraven while the phenomenon continues. We will need to compile our findings and travel to London at some future date to address the Society. Meanwhile, it is my intent to invite several of my closest associates to Dunraven to watch with us and to corroborate our methods and findings."

More men in her bedchamber? Julia's heart sank at the thought. It would be challenge enough to keep Rae Mackinnon's hands off her and her clothes on. But was she to have an audience while she accomplished the feat?

"What of my aunt and the others? Surely they will consider it strange if I suddenly accept employment."

"For now, they need know only that you have agreed to assist me in cataloging my library and setting it to rights. We can use your state of health as an excuse for you to stay close to Dunraven and indoors. But be assured, I will speak to your aunt and convince her it is all very proper."

Lord Muir stopped in front of her and looked down.

"Before you make a decision, why don't you inspect the collection here for yourself. There are volumes of correspondence, books on theories of time, clan histories, castle history, case descriptions of other time-slips, and more. I am sure you will find it fascinating."

For the next hour, while the marquis sat at his high-topped desk drafting letters, Julia examined a sampling of the tomes and letters in his private library. As he promised, she found herself enthralled.

Lifting down a volume on Clan Mackinnon, she searched for reference to the illusive Third Laird of Dunraven Castle. Knowing nothing of Highland clans, it came as a surprise to learn the Mackinnon lands were based in the Western Isles.

Reading further, she found that a certain daughter of a Mackinnon lord married a Cameron chief of Lochiel. A bodyguard of clansmen accompanied her to her wedding. These men, in turn, were granted lands in Moy and remained in service to the bride as her personal guards.

But years later, an altercation broke out, over what it was unclear. The result was that two sons of the original Mackinnon settlers parted ways with the Camerons and migrated east to the Grampians where they established a new branch of the family in Glendar and built Dunraven Castle. Only the founder's name survived—Donald, the First Laird of Dunraven. Nothing more was known of the early lairds until the fourth in the line, another Donald, and his deeds were many.

But Rae Mackinnon and his accomplishments were lost to the pages of history, as were those of his sires.

A sudden melancholy swept through Julia. But just as suddenly, it struck her that it was within her power to restore history where it had been lost forever. She could speak with the Third Laird face-to-face.

A smile spread through her, the thought taking root, exciting her through and through. Lord Muir was right. The opportunity to experience the time-slip phenomena was unmatched. She must stay.

Yet, if she was to continue to meet with Rae Mackinnon, she'd best find a way to keep him at arm's length and her clothes in place.

Chapter 8

"We could hae o'ertaken them, I tell ye." Iain quaffed down the last of his ale and wiped his mouth on his sleeve.

Rae halted his steps partway across the hall and held his silence, those gathered round the table unaware of his presence.

Dugal, his large burly cousin with a reddish gold mane and florid face, barked a derisive laugh at Iain's contention.

"Oh, aye, a guid piece o' sense tha', Iain. Chase the reivers o'er the mountain passes in tha' de'il's brew when we couldna see our hands afore our faces."

The other men rumbled their agreement and drew on their cups.

"Whelps, that's wha' ye are," Iain spat hotly. "They couldna hae ridden far. They were plagued by the storm, same as us, and the cattle would hae slowed them. Likely they sheltered in a cave near aboot. We could hae caught them, I tell ye, the whole thievin' lot and our cattle, too."

Dugal crossed his arms over his thick barrel chest.

"And wha' direction should we hae followed, tell me tha'? The storm washed away the trail. Wi' so few cattle lifted, 'twas best tae bear the loss than blindly ride oot and lose clansmen down a ravine. Rae had the right o' it—wait oot the storm and gae after the reivers next morn, just as we did."

Iain swept a black, censuring glare over these men, who now nodded in concurrence with Dugal.

"'Twas the principle o' the thing, no' the number o' cattle tha' mattered, and any Mackinnon worth the name knows these parts wi' his eyes closed. By now the Camerons are back in Lochiel feastin' on Mackinnon cattle."

"Och, Iain, we dinna know 'twas Camerons for sure," Donald declared.

Iain rounded on his younger brother, giving him a clout on the back of the head.

"Are ye forgettin' the sprig of crowberry Ewen found? 'Tis the plant favored by the Camerons, their badge." Iain's narrowed gaze traveled over his kinsmen. "I tell ye, they reived the cattle and left the crowberry apurpose as a sign o' their displeasure o'er Donald marryin' a Macpherson."

"Ye'll no' insult ma Mairi nor her clan." Donald shot to his feet, reddening with anger. "The Cameron's feud is wi' the Macintoshes, no' the Macphersons."

"Aye, but the Macphersons are part o' Clan Chattan and the Macintosh its chief. They've crossed blades wi' Camerons afore in the name o' Chattan, at Inverhaven, if ye'll remember. And dinna be forgettin' our own bonds through marriage tae the Cameron of Lochiel. He'd hae rather seen ye strengthen those ties again by marryin' a Cameron lass. Wi' Bishop Cameron as chancellor and influential o'er the regency o' little James, such a match would hae its advantages."

Rae crossed the distance to the table, a muscle leaping in his jaw. He wished to throttle Iain for taking issue with his decision of two nights past, yet *again*, and for stirring trouble amongst his men. Ever moody and quarrelsome, Iain continually overstepped his bounds.

In part 'twas to be expected. Iain, indeed the whole clan, had despaired that Rae, or any of the other hostages held in England, would e'er gain their freedom. But the death of Scotland's king, James I, negated the reason for their captivity—surety against their king's ransom, the better part still due. With James's English queen expected to take part in the regency of their little son, James II, the captives were released, the English crown no longer wishing to bear the expense of keeping them.

Rae had returned north to find his father on his deathbed, just when Iain would have been confirmed to lead the clan in his stead. But at Rae's arrival, his father had died with tears in his eyes and a smile and Rae's name on his lips, sanctioning him as laird. Rae had sought to be patient with his brother since. Iain was a man ruled by his passions, quick of temper, with his faith in his sword. But enough was enough.

Rae stepped to the end of the table and slammed his hand down flat, seizing the attention of all. He gave his brother a quelling look. The murmurings ceased and those who had risen from their seats retook them. Iain alone remained standing to Rae's right, his posture challenging.

Rae straightened to his full height, giving him the added advantage of at least three inches over his brother. A childish ploy, he admitted, but it kept his men's attention riveted on himself.

" 'Tis true there be ties wi' the Camerons, but I'd remind ye our grandsire, Donald, and his brother, William, parted company wi' Lochiel for their own sound reasons. When our own Donald and his Mairi wed, the Mackinnons o' Glendar will nae more be part tae the deadly rivalries between Cameron and Mackintosh, than those between Macpherson and Davidson tha' was spawned tha' same day at Inverhaven. Those quarrels are no' our own and we hae no need to make enemies."

Rae slowly scanned the faces at the table. "Times grow troubled. Wi' the king murdered in Perth this winter past, and little James and his mother now all but prisoners in Stirling Castle, we may face more lawless times. The king's guardian, Douglas, does naught while Livingstone and Crichton plot over custody of the monarch's wee person. Already, the King's Law unravels and the barons replace it wi' their own. The Boyds and Stewarts and the Keiths and Mackays are murderin' each other again and our auld enemy the MacLeans have come out o' the west to harrow the Stirling plain."

With saddened resolve, Rae released a long sigh.

" 'Tis only the beginnin', I fear. We'll soon be back to the disorder tha' gripped Scotland under Albany afore our late king gained his release from captivity to take his crown. We are no' a large clan, the Mackinnons ne'er hae been, and most o' our

strength is in the Isles. 'Twill be important that we make our alliances carefully and for mutual defense and that we no' become embroiled in the deadly feuds o' others."

Rae reached into the folds of his plaid and produced a sprig
of evergreen. He held it forth for all to see.

" 'Tis the crowberry Ewen found this morn. Pass it round. Iain
believes 'tis a token o' the Camerons. Ye'll hae t' decide for yer-
selves. But take a guid look a' it. Ye'll remember two nights
past, the storm raged fierce. Yet, no' a speck o' mud clings tae
its spines and the sprig is near perfect. One would think, in such
a storm, 'twould hae been battered tae ruin and trampled into the
mire beneath the hooves o' the cattle and horses."

Dugal scrunched his brows. "Sae wha' are ye sayin'?"

"Tha' the crowberry is too convenient a find. Someone
wishes us tae think 'twas Camerons."

Iain took a step toward Rae. "Ye've been lang from the
Highlands, *brathair.* Pretty words, but yer instincts hae gone
soft."

Iain snatched the crowberry from black-haired Lachlan's
grasp and waved it in Rae's face.

" 'Twas Camerons all right, and they left their token in plain
sight." He flung the sprig down on the table.

"Bluid o' Christ, Iain! Hae some respect," Dugal barked, rising from his bench.

Rae stayed his cousin with a hand.

"Wha' would ye hae me believe, Iain? The shrub grows in
the high areas near aboot. The cut is fresh and unsoiled. No
matter who left the piece, they did so after the storm. Am I tae
think one o' Dunraven's own did the deed?"

Iain glared at him, silent, his eyes burning. Meanwhile, a
murmur rose among the men.

Ewen spoke up. "Perhaps, the MacLeans swung through
after raidin' Stirling and lifted a few cattle, just a little 'hallo'
and 'good-bye' afore they returned tae the Isles."

Thoughtful, Donald added, "It might hae been no more than
a *creach*—some young men goin' through the rite o' manhood,

perhaps from the Murrays nearby." The others gave him skeptical looks.

Rae considered the possibility, thinking it made as much sense as anything else. A *creach* would have been carried out on an impulse, the men taking just a few head to prove they could.

"Bah! 'Twill be the day a Murray lifts a heifer from beneath my nose," swore Lachlan.

"Well, someone did!" Ewen grinned wide at Lachlan. "Ye were standin' guard if I remember rightly."

With that, Lachlan floored Ewen with a single punch, while the others roared with laughter.

Hours later, Rae presided over the evening meal, eating roast haunch of venison while steeped in conversation with various kinsmen and Dunraven's guests. As the evening wore on, to Rae's surprise many approached him individually, offering their suggestions and views on which clans the Mackinnons might align themselves with, and which they should not.

Malcolm MacChlerich, having earlier listened to Rae from the threshold of the hall, seized the opportunity to press for a match with his comely daughter, Moira.

"Join wi' me, lad," he had said. "Our lands run together. 'Twill double our strength t'form a strong defense. In time, they'll come t'ye through Moira, ma only *bairn*. 'Twill be hard t'find a bonnier lass t'warm yer bed and ease yer needs." He elbowed Rae in the ribs.

Julia flooded his mind while MacChlerich continued to rattle in his ear. Rae's heart quickened as he savored the memory of her beauty and her warmth beneath his hands.

He reined his thoughts back to his guest, who once more spoke of joining their lands and now of bedeviling neighbors. Rae reminded himself Malcolm MacChlerich was not without enemies.

Iain was right. He had been long from the Highlands, thirteen years long. He did not fully know what rivalries had deepened or sprung up anew in his absence. He would need to speak with his kinsmen in greater detail on the matter.

To his knowledge, there were branches of Clan MacChlerich attached to the Camerons and others to Clan Chattan. He would need know of the alliances of those of Glen Dol. Donald's bride brought with her *tocher-land* of the Macphersons, land his clan would now be committed to defend. Iain's earlier words spurred his concerns for 'twas easy to imagine a Cameron raid on the land, spiting their brother's marriage.

Marriage. Rae had entertained few thoughts on that possibility for himself. Scarce returned from his captivity, he savored each moment of his freedom. For four short months, he'd awakened the mornings to the sweetness of Dunraven's clean, free air. Having immediately assumed the responsibilities of lairdship on his arrival, he was committed to the needs of his people with little time for aught else. But a wife? He would need consider it sooner or later, he knew. And, in truth, 'twas not an unappealing thought with the right woman.

At dinner's end, the tables were disassembled and the cups replenished. Moira, encouraged by the others, seated herself behind the harp and filled the hall with music. Tormod, the clan's *seanachaidh,* soon joined her, and against her softened notes, sang of the Mackinnon's royal ancestry, of the valorous deeds of King Alpin and of his noble, if tragic, end.

Rae watched Moira's long fingers caress the strings and lost himself to the beauty of the music and the bard's tale. Lifting his eyes he found she watched. Their gazes brushed and she sent a warm smile.

Rae settled back and sipped his ale, the *seanachaidh* now singing of his kinsmen in the western isles, who hid the Bruce on Arran and later stood with him at Bannockburn.

His thoughts drifted to Julia, then back to Moira. Mentally, he compared the two women. There was something about Moira that reminded him of his late stepmother, an extravagant woman who never could be satisfied.

Rae's gaze skimmed over Moira's blond tresses. He wondered, when first he found Julia in his bed and mistook her for Moira, why he hadn't recognized the difference between the color of their hair.

Julia. Now there was a woman to get under a man's skin, *sassenach* though she may be.

Was Julia Hargrove real, he wondered. Or was *he* delusional? Still, this business of being from a future time, how could such be possible?

He pictured her delicate features, her heart-shaped face, the slim nose and large green eyes. However she appeared in his chamber, Rae could not deny his strong attraction to her.

Och, but she was a fair maid to fill a man's bed in any age. He should have been less hasty in tossing her out of his. He smiled at his folly, wishing she lay there awaiting him now.

His mood dipped.

If Julia indeed was from another time, there could be no future for them. Even now, he could not be sure he would ever see her again.

Chapter 9

Rae entered his bedchamber, instinctively looked to the bed, then ran a searching glance around the room. The chamber stood vacant. As it should.

Disappointment blossomed in his chest, a part of him hoping to find the mysterious, captivating Julia.

Rae jerked his thoughts into line and crossed to the fireplace. What was he thinking? 'Twas not healthful to dwell on a phantom woman with a quirky tendency to pop in and out of his life. Had he not concerns enough with reivers and weddings and the daily cares of his people?

He expelled a pent breath, shoving his fingers through his dark hair. The golden *sassenach* was a part of a waking dream somehow, real to the touch, yet as lasting and vaporous as the morning mists.

Rae propped his foot on the stool by the hearth and began to unlace his brogues. As he bent forward, the charm stone about his neck came free of his shirt, and dangled on its silver chain, glinting with firelight.

Catching the charm in his fingers, Rae pondered its rose-hued crystal as he straightened, his mother's gift of long ago, given for healing and protection.

Rae's thoughts skipped to more recent times, to a day in early May when he journeyed homeward from captivity. Rae's father, having received word of Rae's release, sent Donald and a small escort to meet him at the border and see him safely to Dunraven.

Och, how the lad had grown, Rae recalled scarce recognizing his brother, now a man in his own right, five-and-twenty years of age.

At the River Forth, they stopped to bathe, the day bonnie and warm. Rae disrobed, removing his clothes and talisman and placing them on the bank. After enjoying a good soaking, he started for the shore, but as he strode from the water, a *cailleach,* an old woman, appeared shrilling anxiously, waving his charm stone and chain in her clawed fingers.

He didn't ken her fuss or why the sight of men bathing in the river should agitate her so. She rushed forward, unheeding of the water or his nakedness and thrust the stone and chain into his hands.

"Ne'er remove the charm. Ne'er!" she scolded. "No blade o' steel can save ye, only the stone, the stone alone."

Wary of the woman, Rae drew the chain over his neck then moved to take up his clothes and don his shirt. The *cailleach* followed. She squinted up at him, tilting her head from side to side, seeming to read something in his face or bearing.

"Ye future doesna lie here, son."

Donald joined them hastily, dripping from the river and clutching his plaid loosely about his waist.

"Ye hae the right o' it, old mother," he called, breathless, an edginess in his voice. "My brother's future lies north in Glendar." He cast a quick glance to Rae. "'Tis time we be away."

The *cailleach* peered at Donald, a needle-sharp gaze. "Glendar holds yer future," she said, pointing a gnarled finger at Donald, then turned her yellowed gaze to Rae. "But for ye, it holds shadows. Dark shadows. Dangerous shadows," she hissed. "But wait, something more."

She screwed her wrinkled face, eyeing him more closely.

"'Tisna clear." Her voice crackled like dry parchment. "A veil . . . it covers the future . . . a rip . . . a tear . . . e-e-e-ah."

She gave a keening wail, losing the vision, then focused once more on Rae.

"Forces gather aboot ye. Beware. Cross the Forth, and like the king, ye shall no' return. Yet something besides clings tae ye . . ." She stared at him, glimpsing the illusion once more then clawed at the air, as if to grasp it. "*Now* holds the future. *Future* holds the past," she chanted. "A rip, there is a rip in the veil o' time."

The *cailleach* sank to the ground and held her head, swaying back and forth. "Seek the stone's protection. Dinna be withoot it. 'Twill deliver ye from harm when naught else can."

Rae set aside his brogues, mulling the old woman's words. He would have given no credence to her bletherings had it not been for Donald who had gone ashen.

Later by the campfire, Donald told him how at Christmastide past, King James was heading north to keep Christmas with the Dominican friars at Perth. At the Forth, he reputedly encountered a *cailleach*, such as this one, who warned should he cross the Forth he would ne'er return alive.

"James ignored her warnings and rode on," Donald continued the tale. " 'Twas said the old woman followed and the night James Graham and his conspirators slipped into the friary and murdered the king, the old woman sat withoot in the cold, still echoing her warnings." Donald locked gazes with Rae. "Dinna ye see, *brathair*? 'Tis she, the *cailleach* who foretold the king's death, one and the same. She has the 'second sight.' Do as she says. Keep our *mathair*'s stone aboot yer neck. Even she gave it t'ye for a reason. 'Tis said *maithair* hersel' had the 'sight.' "

"A 'rip in time,' " Rae repeated the *cailleach*'s words, now staring at the rose-tinted stone wrapped in bands of silver. Had she foreseen Julia in his life? But what of the "dark" and "dangerous" shadows? Was he to believe Julia was part to that? He rejected the notion. He sensed no deception in Julia. Confusion, mayhaps, but no evil.

He continued to turn the matter in his mind as he undressed. Laying his dirk aside, he unbelted and unpinned his plaid, letting it fall to the floor as was his custom. Gathering it up, he folded its great length into a neat, thick square and stored it atop the iron-bound trunk that stood against the wall. He stretched a moment and worked a kink from his back.

"Ah, lass, where in time are ye?" he murmured, expelling a long, wearied breath. Drawing up the bottom of his shirt, he turned round, the fabric hiked waist-high, and came face-to-face with Julia.

Rae's heart near leapt from its cage, while his hands froze in place. He gaped at her, round-eyed, then remembering himself, he yanked down his shirt, covering his vital parts.

"Lass," he gulped a breath, pulse pounding. "I dinna expect ye. I mean, I hoped ye would come, but . . ."

Rae halted his stream of words and darted a glance over the chamber. He returned his full attention to Julia and canted his head to one side.

"How d'ye do tha', lass? Yer comin' and goin', tha' is."

Julia felt a rush of shock, embarrassment, and tingling excitement. Were she and Rae Mackinnon destined to ever meet thusly, one or the other of them unclothed? She struggled to find her voice, mindful Lord Muir watched from his place in the corner.

"In my time, it is you, sir, who is the one 'coming and going.' Your furniture, as well."

"My furniture? In *yer* time?"

"Yes, in the year eighteen hundred and ninety-three."

He said nothing for a moment, his gaze fixed on her, trapping her in its brilliant blue sea. Slowly, the side of his mouth lifted in a crooked, and thoroughly sensuous, smile.

"Whose ever time we be in, lass, 'twould seem fate hae conspired tha' we share the same bedchamber." His rich voice grazed her senses, as did his gaze as it roved over her, from the top of her upswept hair, down to her slippered toes. "Ye are a verra fetchin' sight tonight." His smile grew.

Julia's heart beat light and rapid, her throat gone dry as ever it did in the Scotsman's presence. She held herself primly erect, glad she had the foresight to wear a high-collared gown and her best corset underneath, a longer style than her others, with decidedly more stays, all double-stitched. Dunraven's Third Laird wouldn't win past such modern armor so easily, she thought with a measure of confidence. He'd not be stripping her naked this night.

"Verra fetchin'," Rae Mackinnon repeated, his gaze lingering over her bodice in a most disconcerting way. "Though I like yer hair best flowing free like a golden rainfall, and yer gown"—his brows creased in a frown—" 'tis a bit . . ."

"Concealing?" Julia raised her chin, full of self-assurance.

"Revealin', is more the word." Julia's chin dropped, her brows winging high. "The fabric molds ye like a second skin and displays yer charmin' curves to distraction."

"Sir!" Julia gasped. Oh, but the man was nothing if not blunt. Julia took a swift step forward, dropping her voice to a hushed tone. "I should advise you we are not alone."

"Truly now?" The Scotsman scanned the room then inclined his head toward Julia's. "Ye are sure aboot tha' now are ye?"

"Do you not see him?" Julia felt a bite of disappointment. Was she alone able to observe both men while neither of them could view the other from their respective times? "Lord Muir is present with us this very moment."

"Ah, the 'ancient' laird o' Dunraven. I remember yer mention o' him."

Julia blinked at the incongruity of his statement. Who was calling who ancient here, she thought ruefully.

"I assure you Lord Muir *is* present. He is sitting there, in the corner." She pointed to his precise location.

"I am sorry tae disappoint ye, lass, but I dinna see yer Lord Muir. Only yersel'."

Julia shook her head with a sigh. "He cannot see or hear you either. The 'time-slip' is unpredictable and there is much about it we have yet to understand."

Rae Mackinnon slanted her a puzzled look. " 'Time-slip?' "

"It is a phenomenon that is somehow causing a portal to open between our two times."

"The 'rip in the veil o' time,' " he murmured.

"Julia," Lord Muir called from his place on the floor. "Time may be brief. Give the laird my greetings."

Julia turned once more to the Scotsman. "Lord Muir bids you good evening. He wishes you to know, he is your descendant, the Twenty-seventh Laird of Dunraven Castle. He traces his ancestry through his mother's line, back to Donald, the Fourth

Laird." She dropped her lashes, her voice softening. "Presumably, Donald is your son."

"Nay. I hae no sons, legitimate or otherwise. I am no' married and I dinna make a habit o' wenching."

"Oh! I see." His directness took her aback. Secretly pleased by his answer, Julia bit her lip and repressed the urge to smile. Looking up, she found his blue eyes penetrating her.

She reminded herself to breathe, then turned and repeated his words to Lord Muir, stumbling over the "legitimate or otherwise" portion.

"Ah, no bastards," declared Lord Muir, unabashed. Julia rolled her eyes. "Then I suspect he will sire a son and name the child after his forefather, the First Laird, Donald. I suppose there is no harm in his knowing that."

Julia felt her cheeks warming as she conveyed Lord Muir's message to the all too virile Highlander.

"A son, I like the sound o' tha'." His gaze remained on Julia, causing her pulse to flutter erratically. "And Donald is a fine name. 'Twas my grandsire's, true. My youngest brother bears his name."

"And was your father named Donald, too?"

"Nay, Alasdair was his name. Alasdair Mackinnon, Second Laird o' Dunraven."

"But you were not named after him?" Julia found this curious.

"I take my name from my mother's clan, the MacRaes."

"MacRae, excellent!" Lord Muir beamed on gaining this nugget of information from Julia then scratched furiously in his notebook. "The name comes from the Gaelic *Mac Rath* and means 'Son of Grace,' though some would argue it means 'Son of the Fortunate One.' Let us hope luck follows Rae Mackinnon in his lifetime."

Julia turned back to the Scotsman. "Regrettably, many records have been lost through the centuries, your father's and your own among them. We are hoping . . ."

"We?"

"Lord Muir and I hope you will agree to answer a few questions so the Mackinnon histories can be recovered for future generations."

A look of pain flickered across his eyes. "Ye wish to pry into my life, d'ye?"

"Well, not pry exactly . . ."

"I'll be wanting proof ye are who ye say and tha' yer friend, yer 'Lord Muir,' is perched there in the corner. From my vantage, we stand in my time, lass, furniture and all, no' the other way round. I hae questions o' my own."

"Questions?"

"To begin wi', I would know more o' ye, my golden *sassenach,* and how ye came here." He shifted his stance and waited expectantly.

"There is not much to tell." She moistened her lips, her thoughts scrambling. What did the man wish to learn?

"My name is Julia Elizabeth Hargrove. I was born in Hampshire and schooled there as well." She saw no reason to mention her parentage, which would lead unavoidably to the matter of her recent loss.

"Schooled? A woman?" Incredulity tinged his voice.

Julia leashed her thoughts and looked Rae Mackinnon square in the eyes. "It *is* the nineteenth century."

"Sae ye claim. Gae on."

"I lived in Hampshire until this summer and have been traveling throughout the English countryside with my aunts and cousins, visiting various estates. It is through a summer acquaintance that I have traveled to Dunraven. Not alone, of course, but with a group of friends," Julia nodded quickly, but deemed it best not to mention Roger Dunnington.

"How many *sassenachs* be there in Dunraven?" His look turned thunderous. "Hae they taken o'er the entire keep?"

"Of course not." She stiffened, defensive. "There is much more to the keep these days. Besides, the English and the Scots have been at peace for well over a hundred years. You musn't say *sassenach* as if it were a curse."

"In my century, 'tis, lass. 'Tis."

Julia upbraided herself for her thoughtless comments. Of

course, his people had suffered much beneath the heel of the English and would continue to do so, she knew, in the blood-stained time that lay between Rae Mackinnon's century and her own.

She cleared her throat. "If it would please you to know, I do have a strain of Scottish blood."

He lifted a brow at that. "Truly now? And which clan d'ye claim? Yer people aren't weak-kneed Lowlanders are they?" he teased, the set of his shoulders relaxing, though there was a brittleness to his smile.

"No, they were hairy-kneed Highlanders!" she shot back, bringing a rich chuckle to the Mackinnon's lips and a tip of his head as if to say *touché*. She found herself smiling with him, an easy, warm camaraderie that she found much to her liking.

"I am related to the Gordons of Huntly," Julia revealed, then remembering the blood feuds that once had gripped the Highlands, prayed the Mackinnons and Gordons weren't deadly enemies.

Rae Mackinnon crossed his arms over his chest, then slowly nodded. "The Gordons stood wi' the Bruce, I'll gi' them tha'. They increase in power, though none rival the Douglases these days."

Lord Muir pressed Julia to know what his ancestor had said.

"He is right about the Black Douglases," the marquis commented a moment later. "Though their fortunes are soon to change and your Gordons will have a hand in that. But we cannot reveal this and risk his knowledge of it changing history." Lord Muir rose, stretching his legs. "See if he will answer another question, something simple. Ask if he has other siblings."

"There be three o' us," Dunraven's Third Laird replied at Julia's request. "Myself, Iain, and Donald. Our mother died when we were lads."

Receiving his response, Lord Muir came forward, visibly shaken. "My 'vision,' the three boys . . . Julia, quick, does he wear a stone and chain about his neck?"

Julia knew the answer even before she glanced to the talisman. She had seen it before but taken no special note of it, for

she had either been shocked by the Scotsman's state of undress
or was being undressed herself!

"Yes," she acknowledged, realizing at once that the rose-
hued stone Rae Mackinnon wore matched the one in her
mother's ring.

"It is he," Lord Muir exclaimed softly, tears of emotion
welling in his eyes. "He was the child I saw twenty years ago
at his mother's deathbed."

All humor left Rae Mackinnon's face as Julia recounted Lord
Muir's story of two decades past. He moved to the fireplace,
and braced an arm against the wall.

"In all these years, I hae ne'er spoken o' tha' night. I dinna
think even my brothers were aware o' wha' passed. I saw a
stranger sitting in our midst, an older mon polishing a slender
sword. I pointed oot the mon tae my father, but as I did, the
mon vanished from sight. In truth, only I had seen him. Ye can
be sure I received harsh words from my father for playing
pranks at so grievous a time."

The Scotsman turned back to Julia, the intense blue of his
eyes darkened, sober. "Ask yer questions then, though I will
match ye wi' my own, one for one."

Julia found herself speechless for a moment, then remembered her lady's watch, pinned over her breast. She unfastened
and opened it.

"Perhaps this is a more tangible proof. It was a gift from my
parents on my last birthday. There is an engraving inside and a
date."

He seemed lost in thought and did not take the watch immediately. Not wishing to disturb him, Julia moved to the bed and
laid it upon the mattress. Instantly the watch disappeared.

"Where is it?" Julia gasped, drawing the attention of both
men.

Lord Muir came to stand beside her. "The watch is exactly
where you placed it, child. I am looking at it now."

Julia patted her hand over the mattress but failed to locate the
piece.

"Of course, the mattress you see is entirely different from the one in our century," Lord Muir said with a start.

Retrieving the watch, he placed it in Julia's hand. At once, it reappeared in her palm.

Julia exchanged glances with Lord Muir, then turned to Rae Mackinnon, who had moved behind her.

"Here, give me your hand."

Not waiting, she took his large, warm hand in hers and slipped the watch into his palm. The piece remained solid and visible. As he examined the engraving, she heard Lord Muir exclaim the watch had once more evaporated from sight. Julia smiled, assuring him it was quite perceptible to herself and Rae Mackinnon.

"Do you know what this means, child?" Lord Muir cried, elated. "This is the first evidence we have that the time shifts are connected directly to both your and my ancestor's persons." Ecstatic, Lord Muir scurried back to make fresh notations in his book.

Dunraven's Third Laird spoke not a word but quietly closed the watch case and handed it back to Julia. She wondered if he could read the script and whether he accepted her proof.

"Perhaps you would like to begin with a question," she prodded gently when he continued to keep his silence.

His eyes lifted to hers and he nodded. "Verra well, I hae questions. Many o' them." His gaze slipped downward and centered on her clothing. He rubbed his jaw in thought. "Yer garments are sore peculiar. Let us begin wi' them."

"With my gown?" her voice rose in surprise.

"Aye, yer gown. It fits ye like a glove, but I dinna ken how 'tis done."

Julia's surprise faded as she recalled the simple, loose-fitting garments she had seen in the great hall of the past, during the second time-slip. And what of the Highlanders' voluminous kilts, which were essentially long, belted blankets? Perhaps, his interest in her gown, and in nineteenth-century apparel in general, was not so unusual.

She glanced down at her dress and wondered where to begin.

"We use a lot of seams, yes that is it, and tucks and darts. My gown is actually two pieces, a bodice and a skirt, made in the same material so, together, they appear all of one piece."

The Scotsman gave a grunt of acknowledgment as he caught up the side of her skirt and began rubbing the fabric between his fingers.

"Ah yes, the skirt . . . all right, we'll talk about that. It is 'gored' so it hugs the hips and flares into a bell . . ."

" 'Tis stiff," he commented dryly, flipping up the hem and examining the band of buckram there.

"Y-yes, of course, the fabric must be lined and stiffened for the skirt to keep its shape."

Seeing his attention shift to the lace of her pantaloons, she yanked the skirt from his grasp and adjusted it before he could begin an inspection. He straightened and began to finger the braiding and pleating that trimmed her basque and sleeves.

"As I was saying, many long, vertical seams are used to fit the dress to the contours of the . . . ah-h-h-h!"

Unexpectedly, his hands spanned her waist.

"Ye hae a bewitchingly small waist, lass, but why are ye so rigid? It feels like ye hae a shell."

"A shell?"

His fingers inched upward. "Aye, like a crab."

"A crab?" Her eyes widened.

"Or an insect." He felt about her ribs.

"Insect?" She wished to swat him but lost the thread of her thoughts as his hands came to rest at the top of the corset, stilling beneath her breasts.

"Aye, hard on the outside, all softness on the inside."

She swallowed a long breath, daring not to look at him.

"What you feel is not a shell, sir, but a corset."

"Rae is my name, lass." He smiled but did not remove his hands. " 'Twould please me to hear it on yer lips."

"Sir, Rae, this is most improper!"

"A 'corset' ye say?" His fingers resumed their exploration, moving downward and across her stomach.

"Yes, a corset. Oh! It is somewhat like a cage, made of fabric and bone stays."

"The de'il, ye say. Why would a woman wish tae wear a cage?" He frowned, discovering the wide, wooden busk at the front of the corset and busily felt its outline through the layers of cloth.

"We need the extra support of the stays." This brought a disbelieving look from the Scotsman. "Of course, we do use them to lace our waists to a smaller size, but our feminine bone structure is much more delicate than a man's and requires the additional reinforcement of . . ."

"Who taught ye such drivel?"

"Drivel?"

"Aye, drivel. And here ye, a lass wi' schoolin'."

Julia narrowed her eyes. "I'll have you know, some of the finest medical minds have concluded . . ."

"I wish tae see it."

"See what? My corset? Certainly not!"

"Humor him," Lord Muir called from his corner, appearing more than a little amused by the one-sided conversation he was privy to. "If the watch did not convince my ancestor you are from the future, what better way to persuade him? There is nothing like our English women's corset in his own time."

Julia stared at Lord Muir, dumbfounded that he should encourage such a thing.

"I *will* see the corset, Julia." Rae's voice drew her attention back. "Wi' or wi'oot yer help."

She met his gaze and saw the determination in his eyes.

"All right!" she grit out, cheeks flaming. "But not one word of this outside this chamber, either of you, ever!"

Both men swore themselves to silence, simultaneously, which Julia thought she might find amusing were she not so maddened.

Lord Muir allowed her a dram of privacy, turning his attention to the readings on his instruments.

Julia unfastened the hooks hidden beneath the braiding that ran down the front of the basque. Rae started to assist her but she slapped his hands away. He waited patiently, a smile tipping the corner of his mouth, his eyes fixed on her bodice.

Julia pressed her lashes shut as she opened the top of her basque and exposed her camisole that overlay her corset. In a heartbeat, Rae Mackinnon's hands were upon her, peeling away the basque entirely, followed by the camisole, then turning her round and round. Gasping, her eyes flew open. She found the Scotsman glaring at the corset's multitude of stays, and the excessive tight lacing that allowed her an ideal waist of twenty inches.

"Och, 'tis an evil piece," he declared before she could utter so much as a sound.

"Evil?" Julia finally found her voice.

"What is evil, child?" Lord Muir piped from his corner.

"My corset," she ground out.

Rae bent to examine the corset's busk, tracing its length to below her skirt-covered waist and over her abdomen. His warm breath caressed the swell of Julia's breasts, where they rose above the top of her chemise. She felt a tingling sensation spread to the tips of her nipples and an unaccountable, almost painful, tightening there.

Rae straightened in the next instant, a dark look slashing his face.

" 'Tis an evil piece o' torture, Julia. 'Tis unnatural and canna be healthy. How can ye even breathe? And how d'ye expect tae carry a babe? 'Twill harm the wee bairnie."

"I-I am unmarried and chaste," Julia sputtered, still shaken by her wanton response to the Scotsman the moment before.

Rae cocked a brow. "Aye, tha' I believe."

Julia ignored the comment, unsure whether she should be irritated or complimented.

"When the day comes when I am married and am with child, I will still need the support of a corset and will wear one especially designed for my . . . my . . . condition!"

"The de'il, ye will," Rae swore through his teeth. "I'll no' allow it. Take it off now," he ordered. "No woman in my castle will wear such an instrument o' torture or e'er endanger a wee bairnie in her belly."

Julia gaped at Rae Mackinnon, scandalized by his demand, and yet moved by his protectiveness toward women and babes, however misguided.

Quickly, she appealed to Lord Muir for his aid but found him thoroughly entertained by the entire episode and in agreement with Rae's position.

"Indulge him, child. It is all for a greater good."

"A greater good?" she squeaked. "I can't give him my corset!" Betty had been right. Lord Muir *was* "dottled."

"Come wi' me," Rae instructed, suddenly filled with impatience. He pulled her along with him toward the iron-bound trunk and caught something up, a scabbard, Julia realized with a start. He unsheathed a wicked-looking blade and spun her around.

"Dinna move," he commanded. In the next instant, he set the point to the seam of the skirt, sending the cloth to pool at her feet. As she watched aghast, he sliced through her laces and her corset fell away.

Julia squealed, her hands flying across her chest, then her abdomen, then one returned to her chest again. Thank heavens she wore her combination. She only wished she had worn her woolen one, not the lacy silken thing she had chosen.

Rae Mackinnon stood before her, gripping her undergarment and looking pleased with himself as he resheathed his blade.

"I'll thank you to return my corset." Her temper claimed her as she stood in the pool of her skirt, her hands fisted on her hips, arms akimbo.

Rae's gaze traveled to her breasts and their silken barrier then slowly down the length of her, taking in her lace-trimmed pantaloons. His lips parted. As he lifted his eyes, she read an unmistakable hunger there.

The air left Julia's lungs at that look. As she drew a shaky breath, she felt the air close in.

"I willna have ye harm yerself, lass." Rae said, his blue eyes raking her boldly as he began to dissolve. "Besides, I like ye just as God intended, soft and natural and womanly . . ."

Time shifted and Rae Mackinnon disappeared, holding Julia's corset in his hand!

Hours later, Julia lay abed awake, the chamber darkened excepting the glow of the fire, and Lord Muir long retired.

Julia's earlier shock had dissipated, but her emotions remained a swirl of conflict and confusion. Rae Mackinnon possessed a magnetism that devastated her senses and set all prudent, good reason to flight. Even when the man was infuriating, he fired her blood in a way that had nothing to do with anger.

She had seen the burning look in his eyes as she stood before him in her flimsy underclothes—a look of undisguised passion. God help her, deep down, some wanton part of her savored the look, savored being desired as a woman, savored the thought of Rae Mackinnon coveting her for himself.

Julia smoothed her hands upward over her waist and ribs, tracing the path his fingers had taken. Closing her eyes, she brought them to rest beneath her breasts as he had done and remembered the seductive feel of his strong hands pressing there.

Remembered his warm breath kissing the swell of her breasts.

Julia opened her eyes, her pulses quickened, a shimmer of heat tingling through her, down to her feminine core.

She yanked the sheets to her chin, fearing this ungovernable side. Fearing that part of her that craved the virile Scotsman. This was madness. She must set her mind to other men, of her own time, cultured and educated and with shorter hair.

But her heart did not listen, and as she drifted to sleep, she dreamed of her wild Highland laird.

Rae sat on the end of his bed, Julia's corset clasped in his hand. He envisioned her sleeping before him, centuries ahead in time.

'Twas true then. She came from a future age.

He leaned forward and touched the pillow, then trailed his hand over the covers where he imagined she lay. He could not deny his deepening desire for Julia, or its utter futility.

Far better he felt lust, pure and simple, a craving that would pass or could be sated with another who would not disappear in his arms. But he knew he felt more than mere physical longing for Julia. He found her as fascinating as she was beautiful, and for whatever reason, fate had brought her to him across time.

He pictured Julia as last he saw her, standing arrow straight, her high round breasts beaded against the thin cloth of her chemise, her look ready to flay him alive for taking away her cursed boned cage of a corset.

A smile spread over his lips. Julia possessed a passionate nature, whether she realized so or not. *Dhia*, what he would do to be the man to awaken her to that promise. Yet, what could they e'er hope to share but brief moments scattered in time?

His smile faded to a grim line. The cold reality of it all was that now, back in her own time, he was already dead.

Chapter 10

Julia excused herself from the breakfast parlor, finally able to extricate herself from the overly chatty Lady Charles. Julia deemed she'd been delayed long enough and now must hurry to her room and prepare for her coming session with Lord Muir.

Hopefully, the next time-slip would occur mid-morning, as did the one three days past when she found herself sprawled on the lawn outside the tower. If additional daytime shifts had transpired since then, she had not been present to witness them. Of course, therein lay a difficulty, secreting Lord Muir into her chamber during sunlight hours without the staff or guests any the wiser.

Fortunately, most of the men, those with indefatigable constitutions as Lord Withrington and Sir Robert, had left early with Angus McNab. Even Mr. Dilcox joined them as a matter of pride, to show his stamina and ability to endure the rigors of the hunt.

Fortunate, too, that despite the fine drizzle, the ladies decided to fetch their waterproofs and head out to enjoy the surrounding sights, those gentlemen not hunting joining them. Only Lady Charles remained within Dunraven's walls, she and the invisible, but ever-present, servants.

Julia sighed. She and Lord Muir must risk discovery. It was essential they keep watch. Last night's time portal had remained "open" for the longest period yet. The duration of the slips seemed to be increasing by noticeable amounts. Exactly why, neither she nor the marquis could begin to guess, but it was imperative they maintain complete and accurate records, meticulously recording measurements with Lord Muir's equipment. Perhaps they could discover the key that opened the door to the past—and to Rae Mackinnon.

Approaching the end of the corridor where it opened onto the entrance hall, Julia spied a blemish on her dress and brushed at it, her eyes cast down. As she lifted her gaze, a form melted from the shadows and stepped into her path.

Julia halted abruptly, pitching onto her toes. Hands caught her shoulders, arresting her forward plunge, and steadied her. Julia next found herself staring at a man's chest, clothed with a woolly tweed jacket that smelled faintly of mosses but also of whiskey.

The hands continued to grip her, and she cut her gaze upward, only to discover the smiling face of Lord Eaton.

"Julia, my dear. I hope I didn't afright you."

"L-lord E . . ."

"Roger. You really must call me Roger."

A spark kindled in his eyes and Julia realized for the first time there were red flecks in their amber depths.

"There is no need for formality between us, when we've known one another for so long," he persisted, his sugared words ringing falsely sweet.

"Two and a half months is hardly 'long.'" She attempted to shrug his hands away, but the pressure of his fingers increased.

"Long enough."

His liquid gaze flowed over her. Julia recoiled, feeling somehow contaminated.

"I must say, sweet Julia, the bloom is back in your cheeks, though you still appear a trifle fatigued. Are you not sleeping well in the tower?" One side of his mustache pulled upward, over a knowing smile. "Or could you just be keeping late hours?"

Julia took a sharp step backward, freeing herself of his grasp and putting a space between them. What was the man about?

"I am quite comfortable in the tower and am sleeping satisfactorily," she allowed, her tone crisp.

Lord Eaton's smile remained. "Then might I presume your stay at Dunraven is agreeable to you in every way?"

"Y-yes. Very much so." Whatever did he want? "Again, I must thank you for inviting me here. My time in Scotland has been very . . . diverting."

Julia started to step around him, but he matched her movements, blocking her path.

"Diverting? *Diverting*." He rolled the word on his tongue as if a delectable morsel. "A most interesting choice of words."

The gleam intensified in his eyes and Julia felt her nerves knot straight down to her toes.

"Lord E . . ."

"Roger," he insisted.

"Sir, I really must . . ."

"Roger." Lilith's voice sliced the air as she called out from the hall.

Lord Eaton quickly turned and stepped aside, allowing Julia a full view of her cousin, where she stood on the grand staircase.

Attired in a forest green riding habit and high-crowned hat, a riding crop caught firmly beneath her arm, Lilith tugged on long yellow kid gloves. Seeing Julia, she stilled, her gaze flicking to Lord Eaton then back again to Julia. Her eyes flared then narrowed to jade slits.

Lilith grasped hold of her riding crop and descended to the bottom of the steps, switching the crop against her skirt. As she approached the two, she grasped the crop before her in both hands.

Lord Eaton strode forward and met her partway. "Ah, Lilith, I was just telling your dear cousin how recovered she is looking. I do believe the Scottish air agrees with her."

Lilith tapped the crop against her gloved palm as she regarded him, then Julia, with a studied look. "Roger, she's scarcely poked her head out of the castle since she arrived. And now I understand she is helping your uncle set rights to his dusty books."

"Something like that." He stole a glance to Julia.

"Poor Julia." Lilith bestowed a condescending smile. "She has such a weak constitution." She rolled her eyes up to Lord Eaton. "But then it is a challenge to keep up with you vigorous men."

He began to open his mouth in response but Lilith tucked her hand through the crook of his arm and drew him with her toward the front door, her hips swaying, the crop switching her skirts anew. "Where did you say we are riding today?"

Roger turned to her, stilling her crop, and covering her hands with his own. "There is a splendid lake, black as a mirror, about a half hour's ride from here."

As Lord Eaton opened the massive door, Lilith twisted around and shot a glance back to Julia.

"Oh. Good-bye, cousin." She smiled thinly. "Do try to get outside on the grounds today. You are wretchedly pale. Positively cadaverous."

Julia clenched her hands at her sides as the door swung closed. Perhaps during their outing, the two could sort out whether she possessed a "bloom" to her cheeks or was bloodless, she mused darkly, irked with Lilith but disturbed by Lord Eaton.

Her mood fermenting, Julia turned past the great staircase and headed for the corridor at the back wall. She gave a shudder, physically and mentally sloughing off the whole grotesque encounter and continued on to her room.

She would need to take caution not to find herself alone with Lord Eaton in the future, she decided. As to Lilith, if she could not see the obvious—that she entertained not a whit of interest in Roger Dunnington—well, Lilith could just stew in her petty jealousy.

As Julia climbed the aged stairways to the upper levels, she let her thoughts run ahead. She and Lord Muir risked discovery, meeting like this, during the day, when the servants would be busy about the castle with their chores. Yet, she knew she could depend on him to divert them to the other wings and away from the tower. She herself would need to deal with an ever-attentive Betty.

Passing down Long Hall, Julia swept a glance over the portraits. Lord Muir assured her none dated to before the sixteenth
century, still she found herself searching their faces for a likeness of Rae Mackinnon. Either owing to the subjects' qualities
or the artists' level of skill, she could find no resemblances
there.

Entering the chamber, she checked her pocket watch and
deemed she still had time before Lord Muir agreed to arrive and
set up his devices.

She paced the room, biting the end of her thumbnail, concerned about the corset she presently wore and whether to risk
the Scotsman's relieving her of it. She owned but one more.

Betty chose that moment to appear, obviously having come
by way of the servants' passage which Julia had discovered
herself but yesterday.

"Is there anything you are needin', miss?"

"Yes, Betty. I'm glad you are here. I've decided to spend the
rest of the morning writing out a few letters and then I should
like to lie down for a time."

"Very well, miss. Shall I lay out your nightgown?"

"No!" Julia declared a trifle hastily, visions of Rae Mackinnon stripping the garment from her with ease. "If you could just
help me from my corset, I'll put on my dressing sacque for
now."

"As you wish, miss."

With Betty's assistance, Julia stepped from her morning
gown and gained freedom from her corset. As she slipped into
the billowy sacque she dismissed the maid.

"Thank you, Betty, I'll not need you until later, when it is
time to dress for tea."

Giving a nod and smile, Betty departed.

Julia immediately removed the sacque and moved to the armoire. She donned a pretty but simple silk shirtwaist, softly
shirred and trimmed with camellia pink ribbon and lace. This
she coupled with a brocade skirt of slate blue. Without her
corset, the skirt's waistband proved more than a little snug. She
sucked in her breath to fasten it, accepting the discomfort

which, in truth, wasn't nearly as uncomfortable as the corset itself.

Pulling at the wide upper sleeves of her shirtwaist, she puffed their fullness.

Such an incredible adventure she was part to, and such scandalous deception, she reflected, twisting the ring on her finger out of habit. She glanced down at its rosy stone. Last night's events so stunned her, she'd forgotten to tell Lord Muir of her suspicions about hers and Rae's matching stones.

Of her ring's history, she knew it to be an heirloom, passed down to her mother from the Gordon ties of long ago. Its blushing quartz reputedly came from the Cairngorms here in the Grampian region, yet it was wholly unlike the peaty stones typically found there. Could the stone Rae wore about his neck also have originated from the Cairngorms as well?

Julia consulted her watch once more and saw she still had a quarter of an hour to spare before Lord Muir would arrive. She rested in one of the velvet chairs at the table, fidgeting with its fringed arms and tapping her foot. She rose, filled with restive energy, and began to pace. She contemplated the homely engraving on the fireplace hood, then paused before the little octagonal mirror hanging to its left.

She considered her hair, coiled into a high chignon. She was tempted to release the pins and let it spill down, knowing Rae preferred it that way. She resisted, reprimanding herself for being tempted to such vanities as primping. Her sole objective was to gather information on the Scotsman's past, not to entice him, to allure or seduce him. As if she knew how, she laughed at the ludicrousness of the thought.

With that acknowledged, she peered back into the mirror, examined the fringe of curls framing her face, bit her lips to heighten their color, and pinched her cheeks, assuring they held some "bloom."

As she started to adjust a wayward curl at her temple, the mirror evaporated before her eyes, the air charging with its familiar weightiness. She straightened and looked past her shoulder to the left. The studded, arched door awaited her.

Julia worried the ring on her finger and chewed her lip. Each moment was precious. She couldn't afford to wait for the marquis.

Her decision made, she checked her pocket watch and noted the precise time. Then, bracing herself, Julia crossed the chamber and passed through the door.

Light filtered through the tower's narrow, slitted windows, softly lighting the steps. Torches, guttered in their brackets, had yet to be replaced. As she neared the bottom of the steps and the alcove, voices reached her, mostly feminine, speaking rapidly in their airy Gaelic tongue.

Julia paused, the mingled scents of venison and smoke enwrapping her as she gazed on the ancient hall. There the women, girls, and children of both sexes bustled about, all barefooted, the young girls wearing their hair flowing free.

A knot of men stood across the hall by the door, arguing, she believed. One, with reddish brown hair and a scar severing one brow, turned on another and gave him a rash of his mind. The second man was younger and taller than the first, dark-haired and smooth-faced. In truth, both favored Rae in looks—his brothers, she guessed, Iain and Donald.

As the older man, Iain, continued to berate the younger Donald, a prickly feeling spread through Julia. Iain seemed argumentative to the extreme, bullish and pugnacious. How she wished to know what they were saying.

After a moment longer, Donald quit the hall, his look black but his emotions held in check. Iain snorted a laugh and turned back to the other men, hard-looking even for Highlanders, she thought. But what did she really know of the wild men of these parts? Except of Rae Mackinnon.

She must find him, before time ran dry.

Ignoring the tremors passing through her, she stepped into the open hall and began to traverse its length. If what Rae told her was true, and her previous experience of the hall was any indication, none could see her.

Julia continued on, holding her breath and gratified no one took note of her as she crossed the expanse, stepping around several servants and passing near the men, who proved much more fearsome close up. She stepped outside the hall and into the open.

Julia squinted, the sunlight cutting her eyes. She glimpsed people at various tasks, but did not see Rae. There were more trees, she noted, scanning the grounds, and less castle. A lot less.

Julia's ears pricked at the sound of Rae's rich voice. She spied him at a distance, mounted on a stout Highland horse, speaking with several other riders. He clasped hands with them one by one, bidding each farewell. At that, the brawny-looking men departed Dunraven, riding southward without road or path to guide them.

Rae turned his mount toward the castle, exchanging words here and there with his people, busy at varied tasks. Looking toward the keep, his eyes discovered Julia and he reined his horse.

He stared at her a long moment as if debating something inwardly, then pressed his heels to the flank of his garron and rode forward. His gaze remained fixed on Julia as he brought the beast to a halt beside her.

"Come ride wi' me, lass," he invited, his eyes devouring her, his voice holding a sharp need.

Julia saw that he drew looks from others in the castle yard as he awaited her answer, leaning from his mount, his hand outstretched.

Quickly, she stepped forward and reached up, allowing him to take her up before him. His arm encircled her waist at once. Holding her fast, he urged the horse away and rode out a distance, to where none could disturb them.

Dismounting, Rae lifted Julia down, their bodies grazing one another as she slid down the hard length of him. He continued to hold her, setting her pulses to pounding, but unlike her encounter with Lord Eaton, Julia possessed no wish for Rae Mackinnon to release her.

Without the barrier of her corset, she could feel the heat of his hands through her silken shirtwaist. And by the gentle squeeze and caress of his fingers, she knew he was fully aware of the lack of her garment, too, though he mentioned it not at all.

"There is a little burn just o'er here, a stream. Ye can still see the castle from there and find yer way back should time steal ye from me."

Grasping her hand in his, he led her to an outcropping of rock amid a stand of slender birches, where he offered her a place to sit. As he released her, she folded her fingers over her tingly palm and enclosed the lingering warmth. Distracted by his nearness, she cast a glance back toward Dunraven's massive tower and extended hall.

Mountains rose steeply all around, clothed in soft hues of brown and lavender. Firs and pines dotted the lower slopes, and to her eyes the landscape glowed.

Rae's gaze followed hers. "Dunraven, is it far different in yer time?"

Julia didn't wish to alarm him, but knew he wished honesty.

"The tower remains, just as you see it, but not the hall. Lord Muir tells me it was taken down at some point in time. No records remain as to when or why, but a portion of the walls still exist, and we do know it was used as a garden enclosure a hundred years ago." She lifted a hand and pointed right of the keep. "Great, sprawling additions were made to Dunraven over the centuries spreading east and north. The keep is now part of a much larger complex. Still, it is considered the 'heart of Dunraven.' I could sketch it on the ground if you like."

Rae considered that, then declined her offer with a shake of his head.

"'Tis enough tae know the tower remains. 'Twas o' my grandfather's makin'. The hall, now that is a recent structure, built at my stepmother's insistence."

"Your father remarried?"

"Aye, roughly three years after my *mathair's* death. His new wife, Isobel, was from Flanders."

"Ah, the great bed in the chamber . . ." Julia suddenly comprehended why she was able to see the bed during the time-slips but Lord Muir had not twenty years ago.

Rae smiled, his gaze warming hers. "Aye, the 'great bed,' an extravagant piece for a modest Scottish keep, is it no'? I canna complain, though. It accommodates my size well enough."

Julia's eyes passed over his length, lingering a moment over his long, splendidly muscled legs.

"Isobel wished tae enlarge the keep," he continued. "Many o' the lairds were doin' so at the time, though my father felt it a great waste. He gave in tae her wishes, then was glad for the extra space. Isobel died afore he raised the walls tae their intended height or slated o'er it. He timbered and thatched the roof instead, leaving it as a great, single-storied hall. He wasn't much for such projects after tha' I am told."

"Because Isobel had died?" Julia tipped her head, trying to understand.

"Tha' and because, two month afore, his firstborn son had been sent into captivity, in exchange for Scotland's King."

"You?" Stunned, she searched his face and saw the dark pain lancing his eyes.

"Aye, wi' many other noble sons, all tae London Tower. Does it surprise ye, lass?"

"I had no idea," Julia whispered.

For the past days, she had devoted herself to a slim volume in Lord Muir's library on the early Stewart kings, seeking to learn to which "child king" Rae had referred the night they had argued over monarchs in the chamber. As fate would have it, five kings named James occupied the throne in succession before the tragic Mary, most gaining their crowns as minors.

Her reading revealed the young king in fourteen hundred and thirty-seven to be James II, a piteously disfigured boy with an amethyst birthmark covering one side of his face from forehead to chin. "James of the Fiery Face," they called him.

However, she had also learned that James's father, years earlier, had been captured and imprisoned by the English as a youth of twelve. He remained a prisoner for the next eighteen years, his uncle and cousin in no hurry to see him free, having usurped power and ruled in his stead as regents. But in time, that James, James I, did gain his freedom. Still, she couldn't grasp where Rae's captivity fit into this.

"Surety," Rae explained when she questioned him. "The Black Douglas negotiated James's release for the sum o' sixty thousand merks. Ten thousand was transmuted on his marriage tae the English noblewoman, Joan Beaufort, just before he obtained his freedom. Naturally, for so great a sum—the fifty thousand merks remaining—hostages were required as surety."

"And so you were sent to the Tower?"

"Aye. And forgotten." A small muscle flexed in Rae's jaw. "James, himself forgotten in captivity, forgot those held in his stead. Most o' the moneys collected in taxes, for the purpose o' the ransom, ne'er reached London but were lavished on luxuries at James's court instead. 'Twas only wi' his death that I and the others gained our freedom, after thirteen lang years."

"Then, you were only . . ."

"Sixteen when I was taken south. I hae only returned these four months, just when my father passed away."

Rae shifted his gaze to Julia, his eyes somber. "Ye wish tae restore the Mackinnon history o' Glendar. There is naught else t' tell o' Rae Mackinnon."

"Rae, I am so sorry. I had no idea. But what of your brothers during this time?"

"They were lads o' twelve and fourteen when I left, men full grown when I returned. I am only beginnin' tae know them again. Iain, he is a warrior through and through, e'er lookin' for the next fight."

Julia frowned. "I think I saw him in the hall. Donald, too."

"Donald is a bright mon, keen instincts. He must learn tae follow them." Rae's lips spread in a smile. "He's soon tae marry—a charmin' lass by the name o' Mairi Macpherson. He's a lucky mon, Donald. 'Tis a love match."

Rae held Julia's gaze, the light in his eyes shifting.

"I dinna be supposin' wi' all yer knowledge o' the future ye can tell me who 'tis I am tae take t' wife and beget my little bairnie, Donald, wi'?" His eyes burned into hers.

"N-no. As I told you, the records are lost, and Lord Muir has warned most sternly that we must be careful in what we reveal, lest doing so alters the future and changes events. People's whole lives could be affected, many of them not even born as a result, including myself and Lord Muir."

Sadness tinged Rae's smile. "And so, we dance between Past and Future wi' only Now tae call our own."

Julia's heart leapt at his words, suddenly stricken. She started to speak, but her face must have reflected her distress for he tipped her chin with a finger and smiled softly.

"'Tis all right, lass. All any o' us e'er has is 'Now.' We each stand on the brink o' eternity, do we no'?—no' knowing if we hae another day or hour or minute."

Rae coupled Julia's hands in his own and she found herself trembling beneath the power of her emotions.

"I will be honest wi' ye, lass, I canna keep ye from my thoughts and would know ye better. Yet, we canna hope for anythin' resemblin' a future. Still, we hae Now. I am willin' tae accept whatever time the Almighty allows us. And when tha' time is done, I will hold ye in my heart and my memories for all the days tae come."

Lifting her hands to his lips, he pressed a tender kiss there.

Julia felt a tear in her heart. Already, their lives were forever entwined. Yet, as Rae said, there could be no promise of to-morrow, only the hope of it.

Chapter 11

Julia rested in the great Flemish bed, her lashes closed against the afternoon light. Closed, too, against the bed's blue trappings and their constant reminder of her return forward in time.

Time. Did it conspire *for* Rae Mackinnon and herself, or *against* them? The gravity of that question brought a pressing melancholy to her heart and left her suffused with the feeling that her whole being simply wished to weep.

Her thoughts strayed to Lord Muir, who had awaited her in her chamber when she reappeared, his expression one of amazement as she seemingly stepped from the stone wall. She detailed for him her latest encounter with Rae—the facts surrounding his imprisonment, the identification of his stepmother as the Flemish Isobel, and how, when she and Rae had ridden out a distance from the keep, the time-slip had continued undisturbed.

Julia revealed nothing of her deepening attachment to Dunraven's Third Laird, but folded her most intimate feelings close to her heart. Lord Muir made his notations and departed, leaving Julia to recover from her excursion into the past.

Shifting, Julia drew open her lids and looked to the end of the bed, hoping to find Rae standing there watching. The space stared back empty, as she expected it would. Lying back, she pressed her lashes shut again, against the threat of tears. Long moments later, she drifted asleep, the melancholy and wearing effects of the time-slip claiming the last of her energies.

Julia awoke to Betty's soft shufflings in the room.

"'Tis time to rise and dress for supper, miss." Betty roused her gently, coming to the side of the bed and lighting the lamp on the table there.

"Supper, Betty? Surely, you mean tea." Julia pushed herself to a sitting position and rubbed the sleep from her eyes.

"You slept through tea, miss, so soundly I did not have the heart to wake you. But 'twill do you good, I think. New guests arrived late this afternoon. The conversation is likely to be lively this evening and the hour to run late."

"Lord Eaton invited more guests to Dunraven?" Julia found this startling, given the marquis's initial reception to those from Braxton.

"Oh no, miss. These are Lord Muir's scientific friends, those from the 'Society.' "

As the fog of sleep cleared from Julia's brain, she remembered Lord Muir's letters to his colleagues at the SPR, the Society for Psychical Research. He had invited them to Dunraven to witness and study the time-slip. Julia swung her legs out of the bed.

"How many new guests are there, Betty?"

"Three, though I overheard his lordship inform Mrs. McGinty to expect several more."

Julia wondered how long they could hope to maintain the secret of the tower chamber with so many about. Surely, Lord Muir would advise his associates of the need for discretion and to not divulge the real purpose of their visit to the other guests at Dunraven.

Julia knew she must trust Lord Muir in this. He was the most responsible and reliable of men. Yet what had she let herself in for? Would the marquis's associates believe her? Or dismiss her? Or treat her as an oddity?

"What gown will it please you to wear this evening, miss?"

Julia bit her lip. Knowing she would be the object of much scrutiny, she thought to select something sensible and reserved. But if the hour should run late, as Betty predicted, and the time shift occur early, the dress would need to carry her to her early-morning rendezvous with Rae Mackinnon.

"The pale amethyst gown will do nicely, I think, Betty."

"A lovely choice, miss. 'Tis my most favorite of all. The gentlemen won't be able to keep their eyes from you."

The attentions of only one mattered, Julia thought to herself. And she'd just have to take a chance with her corset.

Julia drew immediate notice as she entered the parlor where the others gathered before dinner. So much notice, she wondered if she had been unwise to choose the eye-catching gown or to wear her hair down in long spiraling curls. She'd dressed unabashedly for Rae, but as Lord Eaton's and Sampson Dilcox's eyes fastened upon her, and both men started moving across the room, Julia realized her folly.

Thankfully, Lord Muir stepped into view from his place near the door. He looked particularly impressive tonight, attired in full Highland dress. He wore a black evening jacket and vest with silver buttons, and a kilt of red Mackinnon tartan, all in sharp contrast to his snowy hair and beard. Too, he wore a fur sporran, silver buckles on his belt and shoes, and even the *sgian dubh*, a small Scots knife, tucked into the top of his tartan hose. He looked every inch the Twenty-seventh Laird of Dunraven Castle.

Lord Muir guided her to the right where three unfamiliar men collected along with several other castle guests, including Lord Withrington and Lady Charles.

"Gentlemen, it pleases me to present Miss Julia Hargrove, the young woman of whom I told you. She has been indispensable in putting order to my library."

The men's eyes visibly brightened and anchored as one on Julia. It was obvious they knew far more of her and the true nature of her work with Lord Muir than the other guests.

"Miss Hargrove, allow me to introduce my colleagues from the Society," the marquis continued. "Mr. Robert Armistead, Mr. Thomas Thornsbury, and Sir Henry Boles."

" 'Society?' " Lord Withrington's brows pulled together. "Which 'society' is that precisely?"

Mr. Armistead turned his attention to the older man. "Ours is a philosophical, that is to say a *scientific,* society, relatively new and devoted to research, the SPR."

Julia's breath caught. Hadn't Lord Muir spoken with his associates, after all? Despite their scientific credentials, if they admitted to being investigators of psychic phenomena, it would bring a hail of skepticism if not scorn, and at very least, alert the others to the strange happenings in Dunraven.

Lord Muir's colleagues continued to smile, undaunted, and appeared prepared with an answer. But Lady Charles spoke first.

"*SPR* did you say? Now, let me guess. Does it stand for the 'Society for Philosophical Research'?"

"How clever you are." Mr. Thornsbury gave her a nod of approval.

"Never heard of it, myself." Lord Withrington pursed his lips, causing his mustache to twitch.

Mrs. McGinty chose that moment to appear and announce dinner.

To Julia's relief, Lord Muir offered her his arm and led the procession to Dunraven's formal dining room. The others followed, Lilith claiming Lord Eaton's arm and Mr. Dilcox flustered he could not position himself near Julia.

More than a few eyebrows rose when Lord Muir seated Julia with himself and his associates at the head of the table. Julia could not fault him. Try as Lord Muir might to conceal the extraordinary event involving them and her part to it, after twenty years of waiting, this was his shining moment among his colleagues. She imagined that was why he could not bring himself to leave her midway down the table, neglected.

Julia made a composed effort to appear no more than an interested party to his scientific endeavors, the one engaged to catalogue his vast collection of books and papers.

Over the courses of braised duckling and smoked salmon roulades, conversation revolved around the gentlemen's travels from London, the latest news, and of course, the day's hunt at Dunraven and the ladies' outing to a particularly dramatic gorge an hour's ride north. Lord Muir suggested a trip to the spa at Strathpeffer for his visitors from Braxton. He offered to see the details arranged and transportation provided at his own expense.

"You've come this far to the Highlands, you really must take the waters. I wouldn't be at all surprised if the royals themselves attended this Season."

This brought much murmuring up and down the table. Julia realized this was the marquis's canny way of emptying the castle while their studies of the time-slip progressed.

As supper continued, Lord Withrington returned to his persistent queries of Lord Muir's associates.

"Actually, we are gathering to prepare an address for the Society that is to be presented in January at the annual meeting in London," Sir Henry Boles allowed.

"The subject of our research is all very hush, hush, you understand, our data incomplete," Mr. Armistead continued. "However, we can reveal it centers on the very nature of time."

Julia smiled inwardly, for no one appeared overly impressed.

"All here will be the first to know of our conclusions," Mr. Thornsbury promised. "Should any of you have an interest," he added with a smile.

After dinner, as the guests adjourned to the parlor, Lord Muir invited Julia to join him and the others for a late evening session in his private library.

For the benefit of those in hearing range, he explained, "My associates have brought several boxes of new materials to add to my library. As you have been assisting me, I thought you might like to inspect the boxes for yourself while we convene. You will need to begin listing and shelving them tomorrow."

Seeing that Lord Eaton lingered by the door, his gaze dwelling on her, Julia was only too happy to stay in the company of the older men.

"Perhaps, I should begin this evening by making introductions anew." Lord Muir stood before the small, attentive group in the tower library. "But first, for Miss Hargrove's benefit, I would like to reiterate our commitment, as members of the Society for Psychical Research, to seek out and investigate, objectively and in a scientific spirit, the Unexplained."

A chill trickled down Julia's spine at the thought of that. Certainly, the time-slip phenomena belonged to the realm of the "unexplained."

Lord Muir directed her attention to his colleagues with a gesture of his hand.

"Mr. Armistead and Sir Henry Boles are both members of the Royal Astronomical Society and bring us their expertise in that field. Collectively, though at separate times, they spent a decade at the Royal Observatory at Greenwich mapping the heavens. Mr. Thornsbury, on the other hand, is our physicist in residence."

At Lord Muir's bidding, Julia hesitantly rose and came forward to join him.

"Gentlemen, you have met Miss Hargrove, the young woman for whom the portal of time has opened at Dunraven. As I indicated to you this afternoon, the phenomena is centered in the tower bedchamber—one floor below us—the same location it manifested itself, twenty years ago.

"What is truly astounding, however, is that Miss Hargrove has experienced not one, but multiple time-slips, six now in all, the most recent occurring only this afternoon. More, she has encountered one of the early lairds of Dunraven Castle and has actually spoken with him, touched him, and even ridden out this day with him on his fifteenth-century garron."

Murmurs erupted.

"Incredible!"

"Is it possible?"

"Astonishing!"

"Gentlemen, gentlemen. Let me emphasize that we do not know the cause or source of the phenomena, only that the shifts are continuing with regularity, increasing in duration, and there is no indication they are about to cease."

He picked up his red leather journal from the desk behind him. "I would urge you each to review my official account. You'll find all the proper annotations. I would also ask you to reserve your questions for Miss Hargrove until you have done so, and not unduly tax her with unnecessary questions. The phenomena itself is quite exhausting for her."

Lord Muir returned the book to the desk and looked to Julia. "Miss Hargrove, is there anything you wish to add?"

The room fell silent as a tomb. Self-conscious, Julia fidgeted her ring around her finger.

"As you can imagine, I was shocked to find myself confronted with the past and a Highland laird, hundreds of years old."

Chuckles echoed through the men.

"Rae Mackinnon is the Third Laird of Dunraven," she continued. "He has been lost to the annals of time until now, as has his family. We have learned more of the man himself now."

Julia thought of Rae's heartfelt words and tender kiss. She slipped one hand over the other, covering the place.

"And we hope to know more of him in time to come. I do not know whether it is significant, but Rae Mackinnon wears a talisman around his neck. It is a round stone, like a large marble, encased in silver bands and worn on a silver chain. It appears to be a rosy quartz, exactly matching the quartz in my own ring."

She lifted her hand for all to see, evoking comments and whisperings.

"I can tell you the stone in my ring is very old and comes from the Cairngorms. It is not unthinkable Rae Mackinnon's does as well."

Lord Muir stepped forward at once to examine the ring, then raised amazed eyes to hers.

"My sword bore a like stone in its pommel—the sword I sat polishing the night I witnessed the time shift. I transferred it to my residence in London after I cleared my personal belongings from the chamber."

The trio of men came forward to inspect the ring.

"It's likely what Rae Mackinnon wears is a 'charm' or a 'healing' stone," Mr. Thornsbury suggested. "The Highlanders believed such stones ensured the wearer's health and protected them against evil spirits."

Mr. Armistead eyed Julia's ring closely. "We might discover something unusual about the internal structure and density of the quartz when we examine it more closely. There is a place in Yorkshire where the local rock contains quartz that is exceedingly dense. All the houses are built with it. It is said more supernatural activities occur there than in all of Britain."

"Perhaps, the stones are drawing Miss Hargrove and Rae Mackinnon across time," Sir Henry pointed out. "Not actually causing the time-slip, you understand, only making it possible for the two to see one another and experience one another with solidity."

Julia added another observance. "Twice, the laird was not actually present in the chamber when time shifted, but nearby, once in the stairwell and today outside, in the courtyard. Evidently, the stone—or whatever is pulling us together—has a range to it."

Clearly excited, Lord Muir stepped nearer. "Is there anything more you can recall, Miss Hargrove?"

Julia began to shake her head but then remembered Donald. "There may be a Macpherson connection. Rae's youngest brother, Donald, is to marry a Mairi Macpherson."

Lord Muir considered this as he slipped his watch from his jacket pocket.

"I shall consult the clan histories tomorrow." He turned to his colleagues. "For now, gentlemen, I would suggest you refresh yourselves. We will reconvene in this room no later than one o'clock. With Miss Hargrove's permission, we will join her soon after and await the next time shift in her chamber."

Julia's jaw dropped. Three more men in her room? Her reputation would never survive her stay at Dunraven Castle!

Chapter 12

It was comical, Julia thought—four grown men sitting in a row on the bedchamber floor, their scientific instruments spread before them.

They need not do so. On the first night Lord Muir had kept watch with her, they had discovered that, while the room shifted toward the past during the time-slip, it did so only for Julia. The surroundings had remained solidly stable for Lord Muir.

Still he deemed it best to stay clear of the main path of activity in the room, lest his, and his colleagues' presence disturb any unseen forces at work or affect the sensitive equipment somehow.

Julia knew little of scientific methodology but, to her eyes, the marquis and his associates reminded her simply of rather overgrown and aged boys, tinkering with their "toys" in the corner, their faces fired with enthusiasm.

"Here, my dear." Lord Muir rose and approached her. "I wish you to keep this pocket chronometer on your person."

He offered Julia what appeared to be an ordinary watch, its case austere, without flourishes or ornamentation.

"Your own watch has a tendency to slow during the course of the shift, I've noted. The chronometer, being a marine timepiece, is designed to resist atmospheric variations. It should maintain its accuracy."

"Thank you." Julia examined the piece and noted the hour and minute.

Lord Muir stroked his beard. "By my calculations, the shifts are lengthening at both 'ends,' so to speak. The portal is opening earlier and closing later, and rather significantly, too, I might add. Tonight's shift should remain in effect a full hour and a half. Allowing for another increase in time, it will actually be closer to two."

Two hours with her rugged Highland laird and these avid and meticulous men of modern science. Now there lay a challenge! Julia bit her cheek against the impulse to smile. She slipped the small chronometer into a hidden pocket in her gown and crossed her fingers she was up to the night to come.

"Miss Hargrove." It was Mr. Thornsbury, raising his long forefinger to the air, as if asking permission to speak. "Might I suggest, you encourage the Mackinnon to light a candle in his time as we have here. The flame will reveal subtle disturbances in the air flow."

"Yes, of course." Julia thought of the unglazed, though shuttered, windows in Rae's century. A flickering candle might tell them little more than the extent to which drafts plagued the tower long ago.

Feeling slightly fatigued, Julia closed her eyes and envisioned Rae, wishing him there beside her, and soon. Just then, the air grew heavy.

"I thought I should warn ye. Yer aunt, Beitris, is sore mad, Rae." Dugal scratched at his chest. "I dinna know if ye think tae marry Moira, but ye need tae make yer decision known soon. She's runnin' yer puir auld aunt aboot as though she was already mistress o' Dunraven."

Rae drew his gaze from the hearth, where a fire danced beneath the great hood bearing the Mackinnon crest. Julia didn't like the crest, he had seen it in her eyes. She thought the boar, with the shank wedged in its mouth, repulsive. She had the right of it. The corner of his mouth twitched. 'Twas an ugly beast.

He sobered his expression as he regarded his cousin. "Beitris is in a temper? 'Tis a sorry day for us all."

Dugal nodded his wooly head. "Aye, but there's more ye

need be knowin', especially if ye be thinkin' o' takin' Moira tae wife. The lass is sore superstitious."

Rae felt the room's air press in upon him. Rounding in place, he found Julia standing before him. Her beauty stole his breath.

"Moira's taken tae plantin' rowan and elder afore and aft the keep and settin' a cogue o'milk out at night, fearin' a *glastig* haunts Dunraven." Dugal grumbled on. "She thinks 'tis the spirit o' Isobel. Can ye do naught aboot it? Next we'll all hae bars o' iron in our beds and black cocks buried in the yard."

Rae's eyes moved over Julia's golden fall of hair and her pale amethyst gown. Och, but the lass knew how to stir a man's blood. His gaze settled on her waist and he frowned, seeing her constricted dimensions.

Julia's gaze traveled to Dugal, who was still speaking in their Gaelic tongue, then back to Rae. "I see we both have guests," she said, wrapping her arms about her waist, hiding her misdeed. "There are four gentlemen with me here in the bedchamber tonight."

"I dinna like the sound o' tha'," Rae muttered in Gaelic, crossing his own arms over his chest.

"Nor do I," Dugal asserted.

Rae shot him a glance.

"Moira is comely, true," Dugal rattled on. "But ne'er hae I met a more hard or superstitious lass. D'ye know wha' she did yesterday . . . ?"

Julia took a step toward Rae, netting back his attention.

"It's all quite proper," she began to explain. "They are men of science, up from London to study the phenomena. Lord Muir, of course, is with us." She gestured toward the opposite wall. "Sir Henry Boles is beside him, then Mr. Robert Armistead, and Mr. Thomas Thornsbury."

Rae scanned the vacant space, following her movements. "I see."

Dugal brightened. "Aye, I thought ye would. I'm glad we're agreed on tha'. There must be a way tae get her and her father movin' along withoot being inhospitable. Malcolm Mac-

Chlerich does yer brother no good. He fires Iain's blood and puts ideas in his head, as if Iain didna hae enough o' his own."

Julia canted her head, and Rae realized he had spoken Gaelic again.

"Mr. Thornsbury suggests you light a candle." She gestured to the empty corner. "The flame will show any disturbances in the air flow while our two times are open to one another."

"Verra well, if tha' be his wish, though there's always a bit o' a breeze through the room." Rae spoke English for Julia's benefit.

"Och, hae a heart," Dugal complained. "Ye know I dinna ken tha' cursed tongue. The question is, wha' are ye goin' tae do and how soon?"

Rae motioned for Dugal to wait a moment, then located a candle on a side shelf and lit it. The flame shot upward, straight and unwavering. He returned to Julia.

"There. Yer friends can watch their candles while we find a more private place."

"Wha' sae ye, mon?" Dugal's face creased with frustration. "Wha's got hold o' ye? Speak yer mither tongue, will ye?"

Rae looked to Dugal. "I said, cousin, I want ye tae watch the candle for me and tell me if the flame flickers and by how much."

Dugal squinted him a look, inclining his bearish head. "Hae ye gone daft? Why would a candle need watchin'?"

"'Tis a test, cousin." Rae clapped him on the shoulder. "And while ye are doin' so, see if ye can think o' a way tae get Moira and her father tae leave Dunraven. There's someone . . . er, *somethin'*, I must see tae for now."

A grin split Dugal's red-gold beard. "Ach, sae ye do hae someone tucked away in a haystack. I've been wonderin' as much." He gave Rae a manly wink. "Tell me, is she bonnie and buxom?"

Rae smiled. "Gloriously fair and wi' a wee waist ye wouldna believe."

*   *   *

Julia wondered what Rae spoke to the bearish-looking man beside him. But in the next instant, Rae's gaze sought hers. She slipped her hand in his and accompanied him to the studded, arched door. She paused before the threshold, turned, and smiled at the men lined in a row on the floor.

"We'll be back soon. You needn't worry. I have the chronometer to gauge when I should return."

Julia transferred her gaze to Rae as they crossed through the portal. What she would give to see the looks on the men's faces as they witnessed her disappearing into the solid stone wall.

Rae paused to consider which direction to lead Julia.

Guests and castlefolk slept in the vaulted chamber above, as well as in the narrow rooms hollowed out in the tower's thick walls. Above that, guards kept watch on the roof and parapet. Below, more clansmen slept on pallets in the hall, a few still awake and in their cups.

" 'Tis my thought the only privacy we'll find this night lies withoot. Are ye up for a ramble around the grounds?"

Julia nodded, her green-eyed gaze brushing his. "I've done some of my own 'rambling' around Dunraven since my arrival. You'll find I'm already familiar with the lay of the land—at least, that surrounding the current-day castle."

"And is tha' *yer* current day, o' my current day?" He flashed her a smile.

Guiding Julia down the stairwell, they entered the darkened hall. There, shadowy shapes slept near the glowing fire, and beside them, the castle hounds. The mongrels raised their heads at their passage, sensing Julia's presence, Rae guessed. Surprisingly, none growled. Instead, they flattened back their ears and dropped their heads low, a few giving forth fretful whines.

"I think they're on tae ye." Rae grinned.

His smile faded as his gaze fell on a small group of men on the opposite side of the hall, hunched over their ale. He recognized them in the hovering torchlight, a sorry lot to be sure. Worse, his brother, Iain, kept company with them.

As Rae continued to direct Julia toward the hall's entrance

door, Iain turned a bleary eye in Rae's direction and lifted his cup, as if in a mocking toast.

Julia lifted a hand to Rae's arm. "Those men, I saw them in the hall yesterday, but they seem somehow different from the rest. Who are they?"

"Their no' Mackinnons, tha' I can tell ye, exceptin' my brother there." Rae acknowledged Iain with a nod, but did not ease the frown on his brow. "Iain tells me these be auld friends. Yet, yesterday was the first I laid eyes tae them." He vented a breath. "Iain is quick tae remind me, I hae been lang from the Highlands. Perhaps, 'tis no' so strange I've no' seen them aboot afore now. Still, I'll ask Dugal wha' he knows o' them."

"Dugal?"

"Aye. Tha' great bear tha's keepin' watch o' the candle upstairs."

Catching a plaid down from a wall peg, he ushered Julia to the door. "Come, lass, let's seek oot a place for ourselves. I must ask ye tae wait tae slip on the blanket, though. The others might no' take well tae seein' a plaid floatin' through the air o' its own accord."

Julia shared a quiet laugh with him at the image that conjured.

Outside, Rae bid the guards good evening. "Iver, Coll, the night is quiet, I take it?"

"Aye, no' even the *mappies* are oot," Iver declared cheerfully.

"'Tis quiet indeed wi'oot so much as the hares paddin' aboot. I'll be takin' a turn around the grounds, mayhap down tae the burn."

"Dinna let the water kelpies get ye . . ." Coll beamed. "Moira lectured us well on tha'."

Rae shook his head. "It doesna surprise me."

Once beyond the guards' sight, Rae wrapped Julia in the warmth of the plaid.

He scratched his jaw. "Wi' so little time, I suppose we canna gae far."

"Lord Muir assures me we will have an hour and a half, per-

haps more." Julia quickened her step, matching his. "Is there a
walled garden nearby? That would offer some seclusion and be
lovely besides."

"If ye like cabbages and *kail* wi' a bit o' barley and oats sown
in." He sent her a smile. "Tha' is the extent o' our pleasure gardens here in the Highlands, exceptin' when peas and beans are
in season."

"Where do you suggest then?"

"The burn, I think, where we rode oot yesterday. There is a
copse o' firs further downstream, beyond the birches, tha' will
shield us from the guards and block the wind."

He raised his eyes to the night sky. "The moon has swelled
enough tae light our way, I am thinkin'."

Julia drew the plaid over her head against the cutting breeze
and kept up a brisk pace at Rae's side. All around rose the dramatic silhouettes of ebony mountains against a sky of indigo
blue.

"I've been thinkin', lass." Rae's rich voice brought back her
attention. "We hae spoken much o' myself, but I would know
more o' ye. Hampshire, ye say, is yer place o' birth and
schoolin'. What o' yer home and family?"

Julia tugged the shawl tight about her, as if a shield. "My
home is Prembley Manor. It lies west of Wickham in the Meon
valley, not far from the ancient forest of Bere. It's a beautiful
corner of England. I think you'd like it, especially for the fishing. River Meon is famed for its sea trout."

"Sounds invitin'." Rae kept an arm about her, aiding her over
the uneven and sometimes rocky ground. "Yer home must be a
grand affair tae hae its own name."

"It is a fine and spacious home, but not so grand as others."

"Are ye a spoiled noblewoman, then?" he teased lightly.
"Yer father, he is titled?"

"A baronet."

"Then yer mother did well in her marriage."

Julia's footsteps faltered, causing Rae to tighten his hold on
her. She turned to him.

"Mother thought so." Her voice caught.

"Wha' is it, Julia? Hae I said somethin' tae distress ye?"

Julia shook her head, the old pain rising and engulfing her heart. "My parents loved one another beyond measure, and for that they were rich. But my mother's family ostracized her completely for marrying my father."

"I dinna understand. They love each other and ye say he is a baronet."

"It is a hereditary title with some import, but its holder is still considered a commoner. Even in Parliament, a baronet cannot sit in the House of Lords."

Julia looked away toward the burn, where moonlight glistened on its slow-moving current.

"What my mother's family truly never forgave was that she did not sacrifice herself in marriage so that the dignity and prestige of the Symingtons could be elevated. The Duke of Aransdale—a cousin to the Queen, several times removed and notably eccentric—offered for her hand. Instead, she accepted the suit of Sir David Hargrove, a commoner and a 'papist.'"

"A 'papist?'" Rae quirked his head. "Ye mean Catholic? Sae, who isn't? 'Tis guid there is but one pope again. In yer time, too, I assume."

Julia looked at Rae stricken. *One pope?* He spoke of the Great Schism, of the time two popes claimed the chair of St. Peter, one in Rome and one in Avignon.

But Rae knew nothing of the split with the Church, the Reformation, still a hundred years ahead of his time. Nor did he know of the many denominations and sects that arose from it, or the ensuing bloodletting wrought throughout Christendom.

"Let us just say that the Symingtons belong to a 'breakaway' branch of the Church, the Anglicans," she explained simply, not wishing to open the Pandora's box of Henry VIII. "The Symingtons blamed my father for my mother's conversion and for my being raised in the Faith as well."

Julia deemed it best to say no more. She'd made a muddle of things enough as it was. Feeling Rae's gaze on her, she lifted her eyes to his.

"Ye dinna speak o' brothers o' sisters."

"I have none."

"And yer parents . . ."

Julia blinked back sudden tears. "They died a year ago, in an accident at sea."

"Ach, Julia, I am sorry for tha'." He gathered her near. "I know tha' misery well."

Tears welled again, burning Julia's eyes, her tight rein on her emotions slipping.

"M-my parents never regretted their decision." She sniffled. "They loved each other always."

He hugged her close. "Love should ne'er be regretted, sweet Julia."

Their eyes met and held, blue coupling with green. The pulse at the base of Julia's throat began to throb as Rae's mouth slowly, tenderly, descended over hers.

Warm. His lips were warm, their pressure firm, yet undemanding. This was not the rough, bruising assault of his first kiss, but one of intimate exploration and gentle persuasion.

His kiss continued, resonating through her, a delicious, drugging potion that mingled with her own longings and called forth her deepest desires.

Time crystallized in that single moment, suspended in the Eternal Now. Unaccountably, from where she knew not, a thought floated through her, a verse from the poet Shelley:

"Soul meets soul on lovers' lips."

Julia trembled in Rae's arms, her emotions whelming. He pulled his lips from hers.

"Why d'ye quiver like a leaf, *mo càran*? Ye should know, ne'er will I hurt ye."

As Julia read the truth of his words in his eyes, something gave way inside her, breaking through all the walls of restraint and propriety and diffidence. She surrendered to his kiss then, rising to meet him, knowing all too soon the door of time would close between them forever more.

Their lips joined with urgent need, their kisses hungry, consuming. Julia gripped Rae's shirt and plaid as he parted her lips and invaded the recesses of her mouth, stroking her tongue with his. Timidly at first, then with growing assuredness, she met his questing parries and thrusts. Julia felt like a column of fire in Rae's arms, and she wondered if he burned as she.

Minutes later, surfacing from the heady, swirling daze of passion, Julia remembered to breathe. Dimly, she also recalled her timepiece.

"We must head back," she whispered, sharply disappointed as she saw the positions of the hands on the watchface.

Rae brushed back her hair from her cheek, then dragged his thumb lightly over her lips.

"If only time were ours, *mo càran*. There is so much I wish tae show ye—the 'Fairy Falls,' the gorge o' Reekie Linn, the Caenlochan Forest. D'ye know, the sky changes colors a hundred times as the sun rises? If time were ours, I'd take ye up Glas Maol and we'd watch the sky fire the fiercest red ye've e'er seen as the sun sank again behind the mountains. Then we'd watch the gloamin' star appear."

He dropped his gaze to his feet. "As 'tis, I must ride out from Dunraven tomorrow and I'll no' be back till the day after. 'Tis my fervent prayer the portal will continue tae open and ye shall be waitin' on my return."

"By all that is possible, I shall be." Julia stroked her fingers over his chest. Feeling the stone beneath the cloth, she drew it out on its chain.

"I didn't tell you. Lord Muir and his colleagues believe our stones are drawing us together, like a lodestone, across time."

Though the light was poor, she held up both his talisman and the ring on her finger for him to see. He studied them intently.

"Can you tell? They both are a matching rosy quartz. Lord Muir's sword contains a like stone—the sword he polished that night when . . ." Julia stopped herself, remembering the great sorrow that night held for Rae. ". . . when you saw him. Lord Muir and the others do not believe the stones cause the phenomena itself. They are still seeking the key to that."

Rae lifted his gaze to hers then glanced to the moon glowing overhead. He shrugged lightly. "Who can guess what opens the door betwixt our times? It could be the moon for all we know," he suggested offhandedly, gesturing to the misshapen orb in the sky. "Something simple as tha'."

At Julia's startled look, he gave another shrug.

"Hae you no' noticed? The moon has been waxing for as many days as we hae met, increasing in size, even as the time we hae together has increased in length."

He drew her back into the circle of his arms and kissed the end of her nose. "Mayhap we'll hae a whole day to ourselves when the moon waxes full."

"The moon?"

"Connected to its cycle?"

There was a collective pause, and Julia wondered if these learned men would pronounce Rae's idea utter nonsense—that of a man living too enmeshed in nature. Suddenly, they all began to talk at once.

"But, yes!"

"Why not?"

"There *could* be a correlation."

"We'll need to consider the magnetic variations—lunar, solar, stellar, terrestrial . . ."

"And compare them to the marquis's measurements and timetables . . ."

"There are star charts in my library," Lord Muir volunteered.

"Splendid! We'll map the moon's path for the last six days, along with the stellar bodies as the moon stalks the sky . . ."

"And then estimate their pull on one another and on the earth . . ."

"What of the mountains? Their composition might further affect the gravitational pulls."

"And the Highland's cold, thin atmosphere—it might act like the lubricants in watches under similar conditions, speeding things up, as it were . . ."

"Imagine, a door in the universal clockwork!"

Mr. Thornsbury took Julia's hands in his. "My dear, your laird may be on to something here."

"There's still time to observe the moon before it sets this morning." Sir Henry rallied the others. "Let's hurry along then."

The men scrambled to gather their equipment and head for the door.

"Your lordship?" Mr. Armistead looked to Lord Muir. "Did you say the access is blocked off to the top of the keep?"

"Quite so. But there is a corner terrace on the roof of the east wing that will serve nicely for our observations."

Julia remained speechless, both amazed and fondly amused by these intellectuals, giddy as schoolboys.

Lord Muir walked with Julia. "My dear, we will finalize your account in the journal tomorrow. But, while you were gone tonight, we all agreed—you must be cautious to not become entrapped in a wall of stone as you are passing through it, or sealed in the keep's stairwell when time shifts forward to the Present. The one would kill you outright, but the other, well, you'd have no escape from the tower stairs until the next time-slip."

Surprise stole through Julia. "Have all the original doors been sealed off?"

Lord Muir nodded. "The various additions extend east and north, leaving the tower in the 'south' corner of the complex. New doors were cut to open the chambers onto the added galleries, the old doors opening only on the tower's west face."

Julia gave a thoughtful smile. "I cannot help but wonder if others through time experienced the phenomena as well. Depending on what they saw, they might have boarded off the doors between levels, believing the stairwell to be the entry point or conveyance somehow of the phantom intruders."

"We may never know."

Julia walked with the small group to the beginning of the Long Gallery.

"Be sure to get all the rest you need, my dear." Lord Muir touched her cheek, a fatherly gesture. "These sessions leave you exhausted, I know. I worry for your health."

"Thank you." Julia gave a squeeze to his hand. "You are very kind."

She remained a moment longer as the men passed down the shadowy corridor, the eyes in the portraits following them.

The familiar lassitude took hold of Julia, as ever it did after a time-slip. She started toward her room, thinking of the beckoning bed, when she heard a noise from the direction of the servants' passage. A bootfall and rustle of cloth.

Julia peered into the inky gloom, her heart picking up its beat. Did someone watch from there? Someone made of more than pigments and oil?

Chills sledding down her spine, Julia quickened her step, withdrawing into the security of her chamber, and locked the door.

Chapter 13

"Will you take tea in your chamber today, miss, or would you prefer it served here, in the parlor?"

At the marked coolness of Mrs. McGinty's tone, Julia turned from the window.

Did the housekeeper suspect the activities afoot in her strictly ruled domain? Her steady gaze betrayed nothing, her face an emotionless mask.

"As the others are gone to Royal Deeside, Lord Muir has asked me to preside as hostess over tea for his colleagues from the Society."

Mrs. McGinty's brows rose a hair's breadth, the corners of her mouth tightening.

"Very well, miss. I shall see to the arrangements."

Mrs. McGinty withdrew with her distinctive, gliding grace, her carriage rigidly perfect.

Julia's thoughts catapulted back to the wee hours of the previous morning, when she thought to hear someone lurking in the passage near to her room. Could it have been one of the servants, stationed to watch the movements surrounding her chamber and report back to the senior staff? Young Tom, perhaps?

On the other hand, rather than a subordinate, might it have been someone of superior position? To point, Angus McNab. Had he not leveled a score of disapproving looks at her of late?

How disappointed he must have been yesterday, she mused, for no visitors frequented her chamber at any hour. There had

been no need. The doors of Time had remained firmly shut, Rae
Mackinnon having also departed Dunraven.

Julia returned her attention to the thin drizzle falling outside
the window, graying the morning skies, as it had yesterday
when the carriages rolled away from the castle. Thankfully,
Lord Eaton accompanied the group, which included her
cousins, aunt, and the rest of the merry band from Braxton.

There had been a brief moment when Julia feared Sampson
Dilcox might remain behind, but Sir Robert and Lord Withrington moved quickly to take him under wing, flanking him on
either side and insisting he come along. Lady Charles sent Julia
a smile and a wink, revealing herself party to the "abduction."

Crafty woman, Julia thought, thoroughly amused. But did
Lady Charles seek to spare her from the devoted attachments of
Mr. Dilcox, or to keep him from interfering in her friendship
with the marquis and his friends?

Julia didn't wish to know what, precisely, Lady Charles presumed their "friendship" to be, but she was grateful for Mr. Dilcox's removal. There were too many men—and too much
intrigue—in her life at the moment. And too many conflicting
emotions battling in her heart.

Julia rubbed the space between her brows. It was a relief to
regain some measure of solitude and privacy. Of course, the
better part of yesterday had been anything but solitary or private. She met with Lord Muir and the others at length as they
updated the journal, compiled their data, and debated lunar
properties and peculiarities, seeking correlations to support the
theory of a lunar connection between times.

After a late-afternoon nap—skipping high tea and apparently
piquing Mrs. McGinty—she had spent most the evening with
Mr. Armistead as he examined her ring. He declared its structure to be highly dense and compact, some of its features un-
common to quartz. He voiced aloud a desire to examine Rae's
talisman himself, but Julia could not bring herself to volunteer
her ring, even in the name of science, that he might experience
the time-slip himself.

Would time slip again? A petrifying fear took hold of Julia

whenever she thought on it. Twice yesterday, at the predicted intervals, the shifts did not occur—as expected, with Rae not in residence. But now that the shifts were halted, would they resume once Rae returned?

Julia moved from the window and paced the room. The coming hours would tell, the next time-slip anticipated at half past one that afternoon. She bit at her lower lip and fidgeted with the ring around her finger. How could she bear the wait? And yet, how could she face Rae again, after the impassioned moments they had shared?

Julia plucked a rose from the mixed arrangement gracing the desk. She breathed its fragrance, then felt herself color as she recalled the force and intensity of their kiss, and the flush of desire that had overcome her and swept away all reason.

Julia walked restlessly to the window once more, stroking the flower's velvety petals with her fingertips.

How could she have behaved so recklessly, encouraged his kisses so wantonly? What must he think of her? What would he expect of her when next they met? *If* they met.

Julia felt like a fool. She knew not at all what to do or to say. Such a novice she was at . . .

At what?

Julia's movements stilled. Certainly, not *love*. Infatuation, perhaps, but nothing so deep as love. Rae Mackinnon was admittedly handsome, disturbingly masculine, a virile Scottish Highlander who could stir a young woman's senses to a fine madness and leave her breathless for him alone.

But they belonged to different times, different worlds, she and he. And someday, they both knew, the temporal door would close forever. Perhaps it already had.

"No!" Denial leapt from Julia's lips, and she whirled in place. Not yet. Surely, not yet. God would not be so unkind.

But if not now, then when? Doubtlessly, that moment would come, even as the dawn.

Dispirited, Julia turned back and stared out the window. She stood a long while sifting her feelings, composing her thoughts, her emotions.

Sensibly, as a young woman without family, she must look with care to her future. She did not know if ever she would find true love for a man in this lifetime, or even if she would choose to marry. But of one thing she felt certain. In years to come, she would look back wistfully on her days at Dunraven Castle, when once she stepped through the mists of time, into the arms of her Highland lord, and gave herself to his kisses. And she would know, somewhere in time, he remained there still, bearing her affections.

Julia crushed the blossom in her hand, a hidden thorn tearing her flesh. The prick was as nothing compared to the sudden pain piercing her heart.

Julia paced the floorboards before the chamber's great fireplace, the long time of waiting having dwindled to less than five minutes.

Lord Muir and his colleagues prepared for the coming event, monitoring the barometric and magnetic readings of their instruments and marking the advancing minutes on their large, reliable chronometer.

Julia paused at the octagonal mirror, checking her unswept hair, a more elaborate style than she usually wore but particularly pretty, thanks to Betty's skill. Julia then fussed for an untold time with her altered morning dress, adjusting her shawl to cover the bodice of her gown.

She knew Rae had not overlooked her corset when last they met. She suspected, with there being so many men about in both times, and then with her and Rae leaving the keep for the chilly outdoors, he simply hadn't pressed the matter. Nor would she.

Julia doubted he'd changed his mind on the subject, and she'd not risk the last of her corsets. Instead, she'd forsworn the garment altogether and had removed the stays from one of her roomier morning gowns, lest he find objection with those. The woolen shawl she had borrowed from Betty concealed the impropriety of her dress.

In truth, she rather liked the soft-shell feeling, that of being unconstricted, uncompressed. Of course, without her corset, she had lost the support it had given to her breasts. The silky, chemise-like top of her combination certainly offered none and left her feeling wickedly uninhibited.

"We are at two minutes," Lord Muir's voice interrupted her thoughts. "Are you ready, Julia?"

She nodded, her pulse quickening as she faced the great fireplace where Rae so often lingered when the door of time opened. She still didn't know what she should say, how she should greet him. She decided simply to smile and let him do the speaking.

Julia slipped the pocket chronometer from her waistband and watched the minute hand as it slipped forward. A sepulchral silence descended over the room as they all waited, fixed on their timepieces.

The hand on the watchface traveled the last increment, pointing straight downward, aligned over the half-hour mark. Julia held her breath and waited for the air to press down on her and the objects in the room to disappear.

Nothing happened.

Fear clutched at her heart. Julia's gaze fastened on the watchface as the seconds ticked off one by one by one. Still nothing happened. Tears sprang to her eyes. This could not be.

Dashing away the moisture, she wheeled in place and looked to the men, who were muttering amongst themselves, bent over their maps and papers, furiously checking and rechecking their calculations.

"Examine those figures for the two shifts that should have occurred yesterday."

"And the times for moonrise and moonset and the daily progression."

"Yesterday was the first quarter phase, there was no moonset."

"Gentlemen, we have not considered the astronomical data for the Mackinnons' time and how, or even if, it correlates to our own."

"With time shifting backward, it might have the greater influence."

"We simply don't have that information."

"Can we attempt to construct it?"

"Doubtful, but there is a copy of Hansen's lunar tables in the upper library that might be of help," Lord Muir interjected. "There are also writings of Clairaut and Euler that will take us back a hundred years."

"I'll fetch them." Mr. Armistead shuffled to his feet and hastened out the door while the others scrambled to find an answer.

Julia closed her eyes and lowered her head. She couldn't bear this. Anguish tore at her heart. Still she clung to hope. Her head throbbed and she rubbed her temples as it worsened.

The voices faded in her hearing and in the same moment she felt a warm breath spilling over the nape of her neck.

"Ach, Julia. I thought ye'd ne'er come."

Lips pressed warmly against the curve of her neck, lighting a fire beneath her skin.

Julia whirled round and found herself encompassed in Rae's arms. She smiled wide, great tears spilling down her cheeks. She started to embrace him, but halted, remembering that others watched.

"We're not alone."

"Then we must remedy tha'. How long do yer learned friends say we hae today?"

Julia quickly consulted with Lord Muir, at the same time noting the others' fervid activities, their instruments obviously registering wild fluctuations. They themselves looked ready to cry for joy.

"Three hours, child. Perhaps, a little more," Lord Muir replied. "The time durations should be increasing at the same rate as before."

Rae grinned as Julia relayed the news. "Then let us no' waste a minute o' it."

As Rae lead her toward the arched door, Julia bid the men a brief farewell. Passing through the portal, she heard Mr. Thornsbury and Sir Henry exclaim they'd race outside to see if they could observe Julia when she emerged from the tower wall below.

"I hope you have a swift horse to see us away." She smiled up at Rae.

"Tha' I do, *mo càran*. Tha' I do."

Rae crossed the castle yard with Julia to where Dugal's son, Eamonn, waited with two horses, one saddled for riding, the other laden with blankets and packs.

"*Go raith maith agat.* Thank ye, lad." He tousled the boy's shaggy hair.

Rae strapped his *claidheamh mor,* his "great sword," to the lead beast, then moved aside for Julia to mount. He swung up behind her.

"Can I gae wi' ye?" Eamonn handed up the reins, his face shining with eagerness.

Julia chose that moment to settle herself back in the saddle, wiggling her backside against Rae and sending a bolt of heat straight to his loins. He caught her hips as she continued to squirm, and swallowed hard.

"Another day, lad. My time will be sore tested today." Seeing the boy's disappointment, Rae reached down and rumpled the boy's mop once more. "Beitris has a treat for ye inside. Best get it while 'tis hot."

Eamonn brightened at that and dashed for the hall.

Julia twisted in the saddle, rubbing against Rae once more as she glanced over her shoulder. "You like children, I see." She smiled.

"Aye. Tha' I do." He grit his teeth as she faced front again. Why must she speak of bairns while stoking a fire in his private parts?

Pressing his heels to the garron's flanks, he urged the steed away from Dunraven.

Once they had put a little distance between themselves and the castle, Rae freed the excess cloth of his belted plaid. Drawing it up from the back and sides, he draped it over his shoulders and front, forming a cloak that covered him down to his knees and blanketed Julia in the process.

"Are ye comfortable and warm, *mo càran?*"

Clasping the enveloping tartan closed before her, she leaned back against him. "Mmm, very."

Beneath the layers of plaid and Julia's shawl, Rae slipped his free hand around her waist, securing her against him. Instantly, he discovered she wore no corset, her flesh yielding to the pressure of his fingers. The heat of her body flowed through the thin barrier of her gown and warmed his palm.

"Ah, Dhia, help me," he muttered in Gaelic as they rode on.

"What did you say?"

"Just a wee prayer for our journey, *mo càran.*"

Following a well-trod path, they soon entered a valley of heather hills, shingled rivers, and copses of birch and pine.

Here and there, they came upon crofts with sturdy thatched dwellings, built to withstand the unforgiving Highland weather. Ever the people poured from their fields and cottages, smiling and greeting their laird, often offering him drink and food from their humble hearths.

Their simple, heartfelt gestures touched Julia deeply, for they revealed these people's devotion to this man.

Julia and Rae pressed on until they came to yet another cottage, this one in sad repair. Rae reined the horse to a halt.

"I'll be but a moment," he said softly to her ear. Rae dismounted, tucking up the extra yardage of his kilt, then took a stack of blankets and several packs from the second horse.

A gaunt woman and three gaunt children appeared in the doorway. Rae spoke with them quietly, giving over the items, which the children promptly opened. Their small, smudged faces glowed, and Julia could see, aside from the blankets, Rae's gifts were ones of food—sacks of grains and a large haunch of venison.

The woman kissed Rae's hands, tears spilling from her eyes, wetting his skin. A lump clogged Julia's throat, the scene blearing through her own teary vision.

Rae rejoined Julia, mounting behind her and wrapping them both in his plaid once more. They rode on in silence.

"She is a widow?" Julia guessed at last when still he said nothing.

"Una's husband died suddenly last spring," he replied somberly. "The crops failed, too, though many o' our kinsmen gave o' their time tae work them. Una needs come tae the castle wi' her bairns afore winter sets in. I told her so, but still she stays here at the croft wi' her memories, in the house her mon built her."

"I can understand her feelings," Julia offered softly.

"As can I, *mo càran.*" Rae gave her waist a little squeeze, then released a breath, warming her neck. "I'll hae Lachlan and Ewen bring peat tae see her through till next spring."

Julia folded his words in her heart, storing them with the other details of their short journey. How deep were the bonds between these people and their laird, she reflected. From what she knew of Rae Mackinnon, he was a man most deserving of the esteem his kinsmen held for him.

Circled in the strength of his arms, she felt secure and at peace as they traveled on, her blood thrumming through her, steady and strong.

In short time, they entered the head of a narrow, steep valley, mountains soaring around them, the tallest capped with snow. The sun burned off the last of the lingering mist so that the landscape glowed softly, a shimmer of mauves and soft browns in sundry shades.

Flocks of grouse darted through the heather, and the roars of two stags echoed in the glen as they issued challenge. Nearby, a doe grazed idly, indifferent to the bucks' posturing. Rae pointed out a short-eared owl, napping in a fir tree, and a peregrine falcon soaring overhead.

The winding course continued, happy little waterfalls springing out of the rocks all along the way. Julia found herself utterly enchanted.

"Where are we?" she whispered.

"Glendar. 'Tis magical, is it no'?"

Moments later, Rae brought the horses to a halt at a stand of slender birches and dismounted.

He lifted Julia down, then offered her one of the spare blankets for use as a mantle.

"Ye'll need tae hitch up yer skirts. We'll be climbing a ways. There is a place I wish tae show ye, a special place I used tae visit when a lad. 'Tisna far, but ye'll be needin' this."

He handed her a large stick, more a staff actually. He took another from the mount along with the last blanket, a leather pack, and his sword which he strapped to his side. Leaving the garrons fastened to the trees, they began their climb with Rae in the lead.

Julia was thankful to be wearing boots. She had donned them in hopes she and Rae might escape the tower chamber and their ever-present audience. Climbing a mountainside, however, wasn't exactly what she had in mind.

The terrain proved steep and rocky, and the air grew thin and chill. But the exertion heated Julia, and soon she felt hot, as on a summer's day.

"Here we be." Rae aided her up the last distance.

The mountain was not high as mountains go, and in truth qualified as no more than a large, boulder-strewn hill, buttressing loftier elevations. But at its summit lay a lake, and to the far end, a magnificent waterfall.

It spilled from a great height, tumbling noisily down a series of rocky steps and outcroppings, the water frothing white so it looked like pearls, tossed upon the spray.

"I named it the 'Fairy Falls o' Glendar,' " Rae called above the din as he led Julia further around the lake, then set aside their sticks and the blanket and pack.

"It's a fitting name," Julia called back, entranced by the water's spectacle. "Truly, this is an enchanted place."

Rae drew her to him, enfolding her in his arms.

"If ye can feel the magic o' this place, then ye must make a wish, *mo càran*, so tha' it may come true." He continued to hold her, his hand caressing her back with long, even strokes.

As Julia gazed up into his beautiful eyes, her heart rushed

forth with a wish of its own, leaping past the logic of her mind. A fire flamed to life in her breast, and Julia knew in that instant she wished to remain with Rae always, here in his arms.

Julia's mouth dropped open at the candidness of her own admission. Quickly, Rae lifted a finger to her lips, barring any words she might speak.

"Yer wish is for ye alone tae know and tae carry in yer heart, 'til it comes true." Withdrawing his finger, he brushed a kiss over her lips. "Come, *mo càran,* there is more."

"More?" Her voice broke as she sought to regain it.

Taking her by the hand, he led her away from the lake, guiding her through a path of boulders and up an incline of several yards, to the brow of the mountain.

He held her before him, wrapping her in the safety of both his arms. "I want tae show ye a wee corner o' my homeland, as I see it. If there is a place in all the world tae hang yer heart, then I believe 'tis here, in the Highlands."

Julia gazed out on the scene before her. It stretched endlessly, surpassing all that was imaginable—a sea of receding mountains, wave upon wave, dramatic, austere, majestic. The very grandeur of it all struck her to silence.

As a girl, Julia had been taught that the Highlands of long past were a dangerous place, one of ceaseless conflicts and stunning brutalities. Perhaps it was an illusion, but here, resting in Rae's arms, gazing out over the vastness of the Grampians, she felt enveloped in a timeless peace.

Suddenly, a shrilling cry fractured the serenity of the moment. Glancing up, Rae and Julia saw a great, golden eagle wheeling overhead.

"'Tis good fortune, *mo càran.*" He smiled. "Perhaps yer wish has already been granted."

"Would that it could be," she whispered, a familiar pain pricking her heart. Turning in his arms, she lifted her face and fastened her eyes on his.

A stiff, freshening breeze blew off the mountains, stirring his dark hair about his handsome features. How striking he was, she thought as long golden strands of her own hair whipped

about her, streaming over her eyes and nose and chin. Her carefully styled hair had wilted long ago, the pins barely holding it
in place.

As their gazes remained locked, Rae's smile faded, his eyes
darkening. He threaded his fingers through her hair, sending the
pins flying and freeing its wealth to spill about her shoulders.

He gathered her to his chest then, his mouth closing over
hers, coaxing her to meet his kiss, savoring her when she did.
Desire swept through Julia as their lips merged, and parted,
their tongues coupling in a passionate dance.

She ached fiercely for more and pressed against him, her
softness yielding against his muscle-hardened frame. Dazedly,
deliciously, she felt his hand sweep up her side and over her
breast, his thumb grazing her nipple as if a light kiss.

She craved he'd continue, but his hand slipped to her back
and he withdrew from her mouth, spreading kisses over her
cheek and jaw and ear, then he buried his face in her neck and
held her tight. Julia felt his heart drubbing solidly beneath her
hand as they panted in each other's arms for breath. At length,
Rae straightened, his eyes dark as the sea.

"Och, *mo càran,* I could gae on kissing ye forever and forget
all else. But no matter my will, Time will turn and snatch ye
from me in the blink o' an eye. Then ye'll be stranded here,
alone in the future, wi' oot my protection."

Julia pressed her lips together, nodding her understanding.
Secretly, she wished to cry. She fumbled the chronometer from
her waistband, her mouth still burning with his kisses, her
breast throbbing for his touch.

"There is still time. More than an hour."

"And we'll need most of tha' tae return tae Dunraven." He
kissed her forehead, his voice sober with resignation.

Her gaze dropped to the sword at his side, realizing his reason for bringing it now. His century *was* a dangerous time in
which to live. She touched his cheek with her fingertips and offered a wavering smile.

"You needn't worry overly much. Scotland is at peace in my
century." She'd not mention that the clan system no longer ex-

isted or that the Highlands were largely empty, having been cleared of people for sheep and sportsmen. She held her smile steady. "It would be a long walk, but no one would harm me."

He grunted his disbelief. "And are the animals at peace, too?" he asked as he led her back toward the lake and the goods he had brought with them.

"Well, the wolves are gone, if that's what you mean."

He raised a surprised brow at that news. "'Tisna the only worry ye'd have."

The boar on the Mackinnons' crest sprang to Julia's mind— obviously not a domesticated variety, destined as rashers on the breakfast sideboard. She thought them to be extinct, too, but was unsure what wild animals inhabited the land to prey on her.

"Here, take a nip o' this. 'Twill warm ye." Rae offered her a small leathern flask, holding it for her as she took a taste.

Fire rolled down Julia's throat, and she began to choke.

Rae chuckled. "I said a 'nip,' no' a gulp. 'Tis potent stuff, *uisge beatha,* the 'water o' life.'"

"It was a 'nip,'" she insisted, clearing her throat. Already, the liquid warmed her pleasantly, and she felt aglow in all her extremities.

Rae spread the blanket and took out a wedge of cheese, meat, and cold oatcakes, which reminded Julia of Cook's porridge bars. She settled herself on the blanket with Rae, watching his gestures and movements, watching the man. All the while, some indefinable emotion churned deep within her heart. Though she couldn't put a name to it, it felt to be expanding, multiplying, as if it refused to be contained.

"You came to this place, as a boy, you said?" She redirected her thoughts.

"Aye, especially after my *mathair* died and when I was no' wi' the Cistercians o' Coupar Angus in Glenn Shee."

"You studied to become a monk?" Her voice stuck in her throat.

"Studied, aye." He sent her a smile and a wink. "But no' tae become a monk. 'Tis the churchmen who school the youths in

their letters, hereaboot. My father expected me tae follow him
as laird and wished me tae hae a bit o' learnin'."

"Y-yes, of course." She sat back on her heels, still somewhat
struck with surprise. "What did you study?"

He shrugged lightly, taking a bite of oatcake. "The usual—
religion, philosophy, ciphering, reckoning, the languages—
Latin, French, Gaelic, English."

Julia's jaw sagged, but he didn't seem to notice. She hadn't
expected this. Rae was an obviously intelligent man, but she
hadn't guessed him to be formally educated. Or so thoroughly.

"And did you complete your education?"

"In the Tower o' London."

Bitterness tinged his tone, and Julia did not press to know
more. But after a moment, he straightened and, gazing into the
distance, began to speak.

"'Twas no' so grim as ye might suspect, though no' verra
grand either. My companions and I were fortunate in tha' James
chose an Englishwoman for his queen and tha' he loved and
cared for her well. The English themselves were beset wi' the
problems o' another regency, and their energies sapped by their
war wi' France. They had no' time tae war on Scotland as well,
nor reason tae abuse their Scots hostages."

He dragged a hand over his face. "I and the others were
granted some freedoms. I myself took an interest in matters o'
English law, as King James had done during his long imprisonment. If there was one thing he did good for Scotland, 'twas
with Parliament and the courts. The chieftains dinna take advantage o' it though. 'Twould be to our advantage, for too often
we hae been plagued by enfeebled monarchs or infant kings, as
now. Tha' leads tae men grasping for power and a lawlessness
throughout the land. 'Tis the people who suffer in the end."

By his look, Julia saw his thoughts weighed heavily on him,
like a man who could see a solution to a grave issue that others
could not begin to grasp. She dared not reveal to him that the
Scottish crown would continue to pass to a steady stream of
child kings and be weakened by regencies for over another hundred and fifty years to the Union of the Crowns. The ill-fated

Mary was but six days old when she became queen, and her son still a babe when she abdicated.

Rae rose and walked toward the brow of the mountain once more. He looked out over the land for a moment, lost in thought, then turned once more to Julia.

"I will admit, sometimes I wished I knew what ye do o' the future and what is tae come, and at others I gi' thanks I dinna. These hours today, I wished tae be ours, *mo càran*. Tonight, I must be away again. It canna be helped. Reivers hae been liftin' our cattle and must be dealt wi'."

Her heart plummeted. "Yes, I understand. You are the *laird*, the 'lord,' and must lead out your men."

The side of his mouth slanted in a smile. "Tae a Highlander, the laird is 'father' tae his people. He must watch o'er and care for them, as well as protect them wi' arms. Though I am loath tae no' be wi' ye this night, I must resolve this problem. In truth, I suspect 'tis more than a simple raid, rather a challenge o' some sort."

"You're not in danger?" she gasped, rising to her feet.

"Nay, I shall be safe," he assured her, but his hand moved instinctively to the hilt of his sword, belying his words.

She took several steps toward him, tentacles of fear coiling through her.

"You *will* be careful? You'll not take chances?"

Suddenly the currents of emotion that had been bubbling in her heart swelled and surged upward, bursting forth.

Julia saw him then, perhaps for the first time, truly saw him—Rae Mackinnon, master of Dunraven, a rugged Highlander, kilted and girt with sword and dirk that were no mere ornaments, his sable hair flowing free and untamed to his shoulders.

Yet for all that might seem unpolished about Rae Mackinnon, he radiated dignity and unflinching courage, qualities that sprang from the man himself and that were so lacking in the men Julia knew of her own time. Rae Mackinnon wore them like a badge and commanded respect. He was a man of his word, who lived by his convictions. But above all this, he was a man of compassion who cared for his people both in heart and action.

Alarm seized her heart. She could not lose him. Not now. Not ever. Not in any time.

She rushed to him, panic screaming through her.

"Promise me you will be careful, that you'll take no risks." She clasped hold of his arms, bringing his gaze to hers. "You do not know what agony I endured waiting this day, wondering if the door of time would open or not. But now, not only must I wait and worry again, but wonder whether you've survived the treacheries of this night."

She began shaking uncontrollably. "Promise me, Rae. I cannot bear to keep losing those I love most in life."

Rae's arms surrounded her instantly, his hands soothing and stroking her arms and back. "*Mo càran,* sh-h, 'tis all right." He tipped her chin upward so that she was forced to look at him. He smiled tenderly. "Those are the sweetest words ye've e'er spoken tae me."

Her hand slipped up to cover his hand. "Promise me, *please.*"

He pressed a kiss to her hair and her temple. "Aye, I promise." He grazed her lips with a kiss then paused, pulling back. "Ye do know wha' ye've said just now, d'ye no'?"

Julia's thoughts scrambled to recall her exact words. As she did, her eyes grew wide.

"I'll no' let ye recant a syllable o' it." His lips moved over hers with tender hunger. Again he paused and squinted an eye at her. "Ye weren't thinkin' tae deny ye love me?"

Julia swallowed, her throat gone dry, her heart afire. She shook her head.

He claimed her lips once more, but this time it was she who pulled back moments later.

"And you? Do you love me?"

"Hae ye no' guessed wha' *mo càran* means?"

"My love?"

"Smart lass." He lavished kisses along her jaw and neck. "Aye, I love ye, if a heart can contain the immensity o' tha' emotion."

"I'm afraid, so afraid," she whispered against his mouth as he sought to reclaim hers.

"Afraid o' wha', *mo càran?* O' lovin' me?"

"Afraid of loving you, only to lose you."

"Our love is a blessin' we've both been given, a blessin' tae be treasured, no' feared. Time canna take tha' from us, in any century. No matter wha' may come, our love will remain."

He kissed her deeply then, a thick, full kiss, extravagant and timeless. Julia gave herself completely to that pleasure, loving him with her lips. And as that sweet joining continued, Julia felt a part of her flow out to him, even as a part of him flowed to her.

Chapter 14

Julia strolled beside the burn that burbled cheerfully in Dunraven's view. Iron gray clouds planked the sky overhead, while the wind blew high and bitter, whipping crystals of ice into her cheeks. Still, Julia glowed with an inner warmth, a warmth fueled by the fire of Rae's love.

She felt expansive, radiant, gloriously alive. Even the bleakness of the day could not dampen her joy. She had only to think of her handsome Scots lord, of his rich, opulent kisses, and that soon, very soon now, the doors of time would open and she'd be able to step into his arms.

A small, mirthful laugh escaped her as she moved among a thin band of birches and pointy firs. Such plans she'd once entertained, such grand designs. Quite sensibly, she'd proposed, on attaining marriageable age, to choose a proper gentleman on whom she'd lavish her heart. He'd be cultured, of course, well educated and traveled, striking in every way and fashionably attired. Most importantly, he would own those qualities her father bore, compassion, selflessness, and a genuine care for others.

Julia smiled to herself, deeply pleased. She *had* found such a man, had she not, despite the time and place? Oh, there were unfinished edges about Rae Mackinnon, and his tailor left something to be desired, but she harbored no complaints. Did he not possess the most splendid pair of legs to gaze upon?

She emerged from the screen of the trees and picked her way around some overly large rocks, still following the stream. Her wait through the night, without seeing Rae, had proved long and trying. "Faith," he'd told her in parting and faith did she cleave to. Surely, in his own time, Rae should now be returned to the keep and present for the coming time shift.

Julia glanced down at her pale green dress, where it peeked from beneath her mantle. She, too, must begin back and ready herself, before Lord Muir and his colleagues invaded her chamber with their equipment. She had reworked another of her morning dresses, removing the stays—a pretty frock, patterned in rose and aquamarine that would set off her eyes. Touching her hand to her corseted waist, she looked forward to being free of it again.

Above the rushing of the water, the steady clump of a horse's hooves sounded the approach of a rider. Julia turned to see who rode out to join her, then gasped to discover Lord Eaton bearing down on her.

He reined his horse before her to a showy halt, a smile spreading his lips and tilting his mustache. He dismounted, fastening his amber gaze on her as he closed the distance between them and removed his top hat. Though he continued to smile, his eyes gleamed oddly, their flecks of red appearing as miniature coals, burning hotly in their depths.

Julia drew back several steps, her senses sharpened. "L-lord Eaton. This is a surprise. I thought you were at Deeside with the others, enjoying the Scottish wilds and looking for royals."

He advanced on her one step, then another. "That we did, exhausting ourselves on both counts. The others decided to take the train on to Strathpeffer. I found myself craving the comforts of Dunraven, and rode straight back."

"What possible comforts could you miss at Dunraven that could not be found at Strathpeffer?" Again, Julia retreated a couple of steps toward the burn. "It is a spa town, after all, quite modern and filled with diversions, I am told."

"Ah, but there is one diversion it does not possess."

Once more, he close the space between them, stepping so close his frock coat brushed the front of her mantle, and his breath fell on her temple and cheek. Julia found she could back no further without stepping directly into the stream. Panic crested through her as Lord Eaton reached out and stroked a finger along her jaw and into her hair, then twined a lock around his forefinger.

"The town lacks brightness without your presence," he uttered in a low, velvet-sheathed tone. "I could not stop thinking of you, Julia, left here, alone, with my aged uncle and his friends."

She dismissed his flatteries, so typical of those he showered on anything female. She freed her hair from his grasp and moved along the edge of the stream.

"Such blandishments," she chided, hoping to lighten the moment. "You knew I remained to assist his lordship and his guests on their current work for the Society."

"*Assist,* in the middle of the night?"

Julia froze in her footsteps, then turned to face him.

"That is what truly preyed on my mind." His eyes glittered now, beneath half-hooded lids. "Yes, I know your little secret. I've seen Uncle and his friends leaving your room just before dawn, each one of them beaming with gratitude."

"You! You were the one lurking in the passage," Julia choked out with a mixture of shock and anger.

"Righteous indignation? Tsk, tsk." He traced a finger over her cheek, but she slapped his hand away. "Come now, you led me a merry chase all summer, tantalizing me, teasing me— Miss Julia Hargrove, so prim, so proper, so reticent."

He smoothed the end of his mustache, his gaze sliding over her from head to toe and back again. "I underestimated you, my dear. Oh, it is clear now you were waiting for someone with more to offer, larger titles, a fatter purse. But I had no idea your appetites were so, how should I say, *healthy.*"

"How dare you!" Julia's cheeks blazed. "Your assumptions are entirely mistaken, sir. There is nothing untoward in my relationship with . . ."

"Nothing untoward?" He barked a laugh, cutting off her protests of innocence. "Night after night, you allow four aging men into your bedchamber and see them out again hours later, and this is not untoward or scandalous?"

His smile disappeared and the gleam in his eyes hardened to

a glassy shine. "Let us drop the pretense shall we, Julia? No matter what has been transpiring in your chamber, the mere exposure of it will ruin you in polite society forever." He paused, allowing his words to hang between them, then dropped his voice, his tone turned silken. "Your secret need not be revealed, however."

Julia's breath congealed in her chest as he moved closer.

"I am superb at keeping secrets." He lifted a hand and toyed with the jeweled clasp of her mantle. "But, I will have a boon for my silence." His finger drifted to the hollow of her neck, tracing it, then returned to fondle the clasp once more. "As I see it, if your desires are so 'exceptional,' what is one more? There is no reason I shouldn't partake of your pleasures."

"Never," Julia hissed. She tried to step away, but his fingers closed about the clasp and cloth at her neck and drew her against him.

"You might enjoy a man closer to your own age, one who is more energetic, and dare I say, more experienced. It's a small price to keep your name untarnished. Call it 'gratitude' on your part, if you'd rather."

Julia fought his hold, jerking back. She felt the clasp give way but he fisted the cloth of the mantle, catching his fingers in the neckline of her gown as he did.

"You know I've desired you since the moment I met you. You stir a man's fantasies, Julia." His breath spilled hotly over her face, and he brushed his lips against her hair.

"Let me go!" She shook with rage. "I told you, you are wrong in every way, now free me, or . . ."

"Or what? Do you think my uncle can protect you? He cannot save you from the petty minds or malicious tongues of others. Would you choose ruination over what I can give you, long past when my uncle is gone? These codgers trifle with you, but I will keep you well, surrounded by every extravagance and luxury."

Julia vented a short, derisive laugh. "As what, your mistress? Surely this is no honorable proposal."

His grip tightened on her mantle and gown, while the fingers of his other hand dug into the flesh of her arm.

"I will have you, Julia. I've wanted you since the moment I saw you. You'll not deny me what you give so freely to a pack of old men."

He assaulted her with a wet, suffocating kiss. Julia recoiled under his aggression, but he held her fast, trapping her by the cloth at her neck and pinning her right arm to her side. But Julia refused to be conquered so easily. With her free hand, she struck out, striking him about the shoulder, neck, and chest, but to little effect.

Lord Eaton intensified his attack, shoving his tongue into her mouth. Julia choked, then fought fiercely, unable to breathe. He ignored her distress, twining his tongue around hers, then thrusting deeper. Julia hit at his shoulder then grabbed upward, catching him along the side of his jaw and neck. Sinking in her nails, she raked them across his flesh.

Lord Eaton lurched back with a shout, breaking the kiss and releasing his hold enough for Julia to wrench free. But as she did, she heard a tear of cloth, even as her mantle dropped to the ground.

Icy air skimmed over her chest, but there was no time to look to the damage. Julia started to run but the jumbled mantle at her feet ensnared her efforts, tripping her and sending her off balance. Lord Eaton grabbed for her, catching her about the hips. Together they pitched forward and collided with the rocky ground.

Julia's heart catapulted to her throat as she felt her legs entrapped, Lord Eaton lying atop them. But he raised up and started to move over her. Frantic, Julia scrabbled forward before he could pin her again with his weight.

Clawing from beneath him, she gained several feet but he grappled for her and caught her about the knees. Instinctively, she kicked back, heeling him solidly in the stomach and ribs. He grunted, loosing his grip, enabling Julia to scramble forward and win free. But as she started to rise and flee, his hand closed over her ankle, pulling her down again.

Panic rioted through her. Before he could secure his hold on her, Julia twisted around and slapped him full across the face, her ring laying open his lip with a slash of bright red.

Anger flared in Lord Eaton's eyes and he lurched for her. But Julia gained her feet and raced for the horse. Lord Eaton rose, too, but promptly stumbled over a rock and fell again.

Julia wasted no time in making good her escape. The horse, left untied, shied away when she first attempted to catch it and mount it. But as Lord Eaton rose, she soothed the animal with a steady flow of words and managed to slip her foot in the stirrup and mount. Urging the animal toward the castle, they galloped across the green, Lord Eaton's shouts ringing in her ears.

Julia didn't look back, couldn't look back, fearing she'd find the man still upon her. Reining the horse before the side entrance, she cast herself down from the saddle and ran for the door. Lord Eaton's voice still sounded in her hearing, growing louder. She dared a glance and found him much nearer than she hoped, her advantage shrinking.

Swiftly, she entered the servants' entrance and located the back stairs that led directly up to her room. Thank God she'd learned of it from Betty days ago and had followed it down earlier, rather than traveling the maze of corridors and stairs she normally used.

Hurriedly, Julia ran up the stairs, a catch forming in her side. Oddly, no one seemed to be about Dunraven, the servants being few and presumably elsewhere. Julia did not know whether to deem this as good or bad, but she hastened on, panting for breath, the pain in her side expanding. As she reached the last level, Lord Eaton's heavy bootfalls sounded on the wood stairs below.

Julia raced to her room, flinging open the door and slamming it shut again. The chamber stood empty, Lord Muir and the others having yet to come. She heaved for breath, deciding what next to do. She must block the door, she knew, but there was no bar for it. Then she remembered the key, kept atop the armoire.

Normally, there was no reason to lock the door, but now she seized the heavy key from its place and quickened to secure the door. Her hands shook uncontrollably as she fumbled with the key, trying to fit it into the lock mechanism, then dropped it. A cry escaped her lips as she looked for the key, at the same time hearing Lord Eaton's voice calling without.

She scrambled to retrieve the key, but as she reached for it, the piece vanished from sight.

Julia straightened, feeling the change in the air and finding the door had disappeared. Still she could hear Lord Eaton calling her name and the heavy clump of his boots.

He would appear momentarily and, no matter in which time she stood within the chamber, he would still be able to find and seize her. Her pulse beating erratically, Julia rushed across the room for the arched door and passed through its portal and onto the stairwell.

Closing the door firmly, she heaved for breath and braced herself against the wall. Time had shifted much earlier than expected. But that also meant Rae must be near in order for the phenomenon to have occurred.

Her spirit rising, she held the torn pieces of her bodice together and hastened down the stairs in search of him.

Roger Dunnington stalked into Julia's bedchamber, blood still on his lips. He swiped it away, moving deeper into the room.

The floral scent of her perfume lingered in air, yet the chamber stood empty. He prowled its confines, peering under the bed and throwing open the armoire.

"Where are you?" he growled.

Silence answered.

There could be but one explanation, something he'd suspected all along—a secret passage. Likely, it led to his uncle's bedchamber.

They'd not get away with their little deception any longer, Roger vowed to himself. Julia was probably crying in his uncle's arms this very moment. What better time to catch the two in an indisputable and scandalous situation?

Roger quit the chamber for the marquis's room, emboldened.

When he was done, he'd have his boon from both of them—
funds from his tight-fisted uncle, and from Julia . . . Roger
smiled as he envisioned her creamy flesh, naked beneath him.

Julia lingered in the alcove at the base of the stairs, debating
whether or not to leave its shelter. Lord Eaton might be able to
see her once she stepped into the hall—that is, through the wall
of the keep to the outside grounds.

During her latest outing with Rae, Sir Henry and Mr. Thornsbury had watched the keep from without, yet never saw her
emerge from the tower or pass down the road. Nor did they see
her return, though they kept vigil for hours.

It would seem, during the course of a time-slip, once Julia
passed beyond the chamber into the stairwell, she truly stepped
into the past and was no longer visible to anyone in her own
time. Similarly, it was only in her room that she could see Lord
Muir and any others present. Once beyond its walls, she perceived only those living in Rae's time.

Still, Julia feared to trust this assessment, for the phenomena
was notoriously unpredictable. It could differ from experience
to experience, witness to witness, as Lord Muir had amply
demonstrated in the many cases he had recounted. During a
single time-slip, one person might see into the past while their
companion could not. Yet, on a subsequent occasion, both
could witness the event.

No, she must not assume she would be invisible to Lord
Eaton any more than she should assume she would be able to
observe him or his approach. Clutching the ruined pieces of her
gown together over her breast, she held no wish to do battle
with Lord Eaton again this day.

Glancing out into the hall, Julia scanned the people gathered
there, assuming Rae to be near. He must be, she reasoned, or
the shift could not take place. Still, her spirits slipped when she
failed to spy him.

Perhaps, he was outside and tarried with his men, unaware
time had shifted early. She took comfort in the thought, confident he would come soon.

Julia continued to gaze into the hall, watching a grandmoth-
erly woman bestow treats from her hearth on two carrot-topped
children. As the mites ran to a corner and bit into their prizes, a
blond woman stepped into view. Julia remembered her from
before, beautiful and stately, her gown far richer than the others.

Julia could not help but wonder who she might be and what
position or relationship she enjoyed in the castle. A thought
drifted to mind, a pricking reminder. Rae would one day sire a
son named Donald who would succeed him as laird and ac-
complish great deeds for the clan. When the doors of time
slipped no more for Rae and herself, he would need to choose
a mate and fulfill that portion of his destiny. Might he choose
the blonde?

The thought rankled. Julia knew she must be unselfish and
understanding in this regard. History could not be altered, Rae
must father the child. But for now, he was hers, and she shut her
mind to the reality that he must marry, especially that he might
marry with this woman.

Julia withdrew from the alcove and climbed the stairs, brambles of jealousy sprouting in her heart. Better she wait on the
steps outside the chamber, than torture herself below.

She concentrated her thoughts on Rae. Surely, he was on his
way now and would join her in the coming minutes. Even then,
she did not intend to reenter the room until the last possible moment, lest Lord Eaton lay in wait there, with or without Lord
Muir and his associates.

As Julia completed her climb, she noticed a small niche with
a pretty porcelain pitcher tucked in it. Strange, she thought, that
these Scots would place such an object in a stairwell. Examining it closer, she saw that something lay behind the pottery,
something white. Her curiosity piqued, she lifted the vase from
its place only to find her corset where Rae had hidden it.

Triumphant, Julia reclaimed the garment. Other than needing
new lacings, it appeared in perfect condition. She pondered that
as she seated herself on the step near the chamber door.

Amazingly, the piece had traveled intact from one century to another without problem, held in Rae's grasp. Evidently, once the door between times had closed, Rae had been able to physically put down the corset without having it disappear, even though it was no longer under the influence of his stone. Julia found this fascinating. It stood to reason, if she kept hold of the corset, she could travel forward with it in time. Her greatest challenge lay in concealing her find from Rae.

But that was also the least of her problems, she sighed, glancing down to her dress. How would she explain its damage, a tear reaching a good ten inches from the neckline downward over her left breast. Thankfully, her camisole and combination had not been torn and granted her a modicum of modesty.

Thankfully, also, neither Rae nor Lord Eaton could see or confront one another. She didn't want to begin to think of what a fifteenth-century Highlander might do to vindicate his lady's honor. The image that sprang to mind was of Lord Eaton's head on a platter.

She rubbed her arms, a damp chill slipping into her bones in the unheated stairwell. Somewhere unseen, a bird twittered outside the high, slitted window. The sky appeared overcast there. How she wished she could see out and perhaps locate Rae.

Julia rooted her head against the stone wall, her thoughts drifting as her wait stretched out. The sun brightened, emerging from behind a cloud and sending shafts of light lancing through the windows, striking the wall and glancing down the steps. As Julia watched the shifting light, something sparkled on the steps below, netting her attention.

Laying the corset aside, Julia rose and moved down the stairs. Even at a distance, she suspected it to be a large gemstone. Her pulse picked up its beat as she recognized Rae's talisman, its silver chain sprawled over the steps, broken.

Julia's insides twisted to a knot. Rae was not connected to the stone. He might not even be at Dunraven. Had he returned safely last night? Without the stone, their link was severed across time.

Still, time *had* shifted, she reminded herself. She need only to retrieve the talisman and put it in a place easy and logical for him to find. She hurried down the stairwell, intent on recovering the stone. The chain must have broken and dropped from his neck. She wondered if he even realized it was gone.

As she neared the stone, a woman's voice sounded at the entrance to the alcove, seemingly giving orders. In the next instant, the blonde appeared and started up the stairs toward Julia. The woman paused, her gaze lifting in the direction of Rae's bedchamber door. She smiled then and smoothed her gown, tugging down its neckline to expose more cleavage. Julia blinked, realizing the woman was more than a little interested in Rae Mackinnon.

The blonde started up the stairs again, then halted as her gaze fell on the talisman, gleaming upon the step before her. Julia's heart leapt from its place, as the woman bent to pick it up.

Racing down the few remaining steps, Julia grabbed for the stone, colliding with the woman and propelling her against the wall. An audible "oof" left the blonde, but she managed to cling to the chain and stone. As she clutched it in her hand, her eyes widened as Julia materialized before her eyes.

Screaming, she threw her hands in the air, dropping the stone. But just as suddenly, she stopped and darted a look all around, obviously unable to see Julia anymore. Her mouth opened wide again and she ran shrieking down the stairs and into the hall.

Julia's heart beat light and fast but she collected her thoughts long enough to recover the stone and fold it safely in her palm.

"Rae, where are you?" she pleaded softly as she returned to sit by the chamber door.

Several people appeared from the hall and made a brief and nervous check of the stairwell. From below, Julia still could hear the blonde crying out a stream of Gaelic.

"He will come," Julia assured herself, leaning against the wall. And if he did not appear before time slipped, she would slip through the door at the last possible moment and leave the stone on his pillow.

The minutes passed slowly. Waiting, she watched the sky alter its mood, darkening as rain began to fall without.

Shivering, Julia hugged herself for warmth, then yawned. As she listened to the babble in the hall, her eyelids fluttered shut.

The voices melted together then faded as a grogginess overcame her, and she drifted into a light sleep.

Julia wakened with a start to pitch darkness and stale, dank air. She knew at once, time had shifted, sealing her in the ancient stairwell.

She started to rise, then remembered Rae's talisman. It was no longer in her hand nor on her lap. Quickly, she felt the stone surrounding her, thinking it must have slipped from her fingers while she slept. A part of her prayed she wouldn't find it, that it had remained in Rae's time for him to find and for time to slip again.

Her fingers closed on something smooth and sticklike in the dark, a small pile of them. She recoiled, her breath leaving her as she realized the sticks to be bones.

She scooted back, gasping the musty air. But a moment later she regained her wits, and realized what she felt were the remains of her corset, the garment having disintegrated as it came forward in time.

Her hands shaking, she reached out again and fingered the "bones." She took a swallow and calmed herself. Yes, these were corset stays, nineteen of them.

Julia began to search again for Rae's stone and had worked her way down several steps, when she heard something scuttling about in the dark, further down. She retreated back to where she had begun.

Her gaze lifted to the window where the moon shed its soft, glowing light.

"Rae," she whispered softly, her heart cleaved in two.

Please God, let the stone be with him, she prayed. For if it was not, there would be no hope of ever finding him again across time. And she would remain trapped in the stairwell of Dunraven's ancient keep forever.

Chapter 15

Rae arrived at Dunraven ahead of his men and dismounted, tossing the garron's reins to little Eamonn, who dashed forward to greet him.

Rae headed toward the keep, looking neither right nor left and certainly not back. His men's bickerings still rang in his ears. Let them have it out amongst themselves.

He had no answer for what they'd found, or insight into who was responsible. But likewise, he wanted an end to the dissensions that embroiled his men and most especially his brothers. He'd not lead them out to pick a fight with the Camerons, as Iain insisted he do. As to Donald's theories, they troubled him deeply and needed more thought.

If the past hours had not been calamitous enough, he'd been unable to return to the castle in time to meet Julia, and even worse, he'd discovered his healing stone gone from around his neck.

Rae lengthened his stride, the thought ravaging him anew. He *must* find the stone, or Julia would be lost to him forever. If he must retrace every step, turn over every rock where he'd trod this past day, he would and more.

But a black fear clutched at him, warning the stone could be anywhere, mayhaps never to be found.

Entering the hall, Rae found those within gabbling excitedly like a flock of ruffled geese. On seeing him, their movements and chatterings ceased. For all of two heartbeats. Half rushed forward while the others hung back, anxious looks scoring their faces.

Beitris, his aunt, led the charge of onrushers, her graying braids swinging madly. Suddenly, Rae found himself swamped by a sea of jabbering people. He held up his hands and called for quiet.

Beitris bustled forward, the fiery-haired twins, Calum and Caitlin, clinging to her skirts.

"They're gone, the two o' them!" Beitris exclaimed, round-eyed. "We couldna stop them, try though we did."

"Who tried, Beitris?" Calum crooked his neck to look up at her.

"We did, laddie. Shush now."

"Nay, we didna," Caitlin vowed with great certainty. At Beitris's stern look, the lassie caught her lip then shrugged. "Weel, we didna try verra hard."

Rae cleared his throat, impatient to begin his search, but swallowed a smile nonetheless. "Beitris, who is gone?"

"Moira and Malcolm MacChlerich, o' course."

Rae's brows shot upward. Here, he'd tried for weeks to get MacChlerich and his daughter to leave. Somehow, Beitris had accomplished the feat in less than a day. He tried not to look as pleased as he felt.

"And just how did tha' come aboot?" Rae pulled his brows together, exhibiting proper concern. "No one here was of-fendin' or inhospitable tae our guests, were they now?"

"On my soul, nay! 'Twas none o' us. The lass needed no help oot the door, I can tell ye tha'. She ran straight oot, leavin' her belongin's behind."

Rae drew his gaze over the faces around him and found their expressions remained uneasy.

"*Dhia.* What has happened here, Beitris?"

"A hant," Caitlin declared in her small voice. "She attacked Moira on the stairs."

"She?"

"A 'green lady,' " Calum said solemnly, darting a nervous glance back to the alcove. "Moira said 'twas Isobel."

Rae's gaze sheered to Beitris. He found her nodding in agreement as did the others.

"Is this some piece o' mischief? Wha' are ye bletherin' aboot?"

"Och, nephew, ye know wha' a superstitious lass Moira is, always fearin' there's somethin' evil lurkin' in every nook. She started up the stairwell, and no sooner left our sight when she started screechin' and screamin'. Och, 'twas a fearsome sound, turned my bluid cauld, it did. Moira came runnin' back in tae the hall. A wild-eyed creature, she was, tearin' at her hair. She said a woman dressed in green threw her against the wall—a blond woman, Isobel."

Suspicion climbed through Rae as Beitris continued.

"Malcolm went after Moira but couldna convince her tae come back. They made a hasty departure from Dunraven, Moira still raving like a madwoman, claimin' Isobel didna want her in her chamber."

"*Her* chamber?"

"Isobel's. Yer chamber, now. Moira said she was near tae yer chamber door."

"Ah, I see." Rae mulled her words, then frowned. "Nay, I dinna see. Wait, I do. I think."

Julia. 'Twas obvious Moira had seen Julia. Isobel, too, was blonde, and Moira's mistake understandable. Yet, in order for Moira to have actually seen Julia, she must have found his healing stone.

"I hope ye dinna set yer hopes on marryin' the lass," Beitris's voice broke his flow of thoughts. "Moira MacChlerich willna be back. She vowed she wouldna live in a haunted keep for any reason, or for anyone, even Dunraven's laird." Beitris cut her eyes up at him. "I hope yer no' too upset, nephew," she added dryly, looking not one crumb remorseful herself for having lost their guests.

Rae could not help himself. He grinned widely. Picking up his aunt, he whirled her around and gave her a huge, smacking kiss full on her lips. Plopping her down again, he hastened for the stairwell.

Moira must have been actually holding the stone when she encountered the "green lady," Rae reasoned. As he reached the alcove, his footsteps froze. What if Moira had kept the stone and taken it with her?

An invisible hand fisted his heart like a band of iron.

"Why are ye waitin'?" Calum spoke from behind him. "Are ye afeard o' the hant?"

Rae glanced up the stairwell then back again. "Nay, laddie, but the torches are no' lit."

'Twas truth. Rae guessed his kinsmen were almost as superstitious as Moira and feared the stairs.

Rae called for a taper then turned to Calum. "Stay wi' Beitris, now, in case Moira told ye true and there *is* a hant aboot." He gave the boy a wink.

Calum's eyes widened with alarm and he scampered back across the hall.

Taper in hand, Rae mounted the lower stairs and lit the first of the torches, mindful to watch where he trod. With the help of the light he scanned each step for sign of his stone. Slowly, he advanced up the stairs, lighting the next torch in its bracket. But as the taper burned toward his fingers, he was forced to search at a quicker pace.

Venting a frustrated breath, Rae quickened up the last of the steps, just below his chamber door, and fired the torch there. Extinguishing the taper, he laid it aside and turned. Something sparkled in the fluttering light, two steps above where he stood.

Rae's heart leapt free of its shackle at the sight of his stone gleaming there. Reaching out, he lay hold to it, and in that same instant, a form appeared before him, a woman gowned in green silk, sprawled unconscious on the steps. Julia.

Rae could scarce contain his emotions as he climbed the few steps and dropped to his knees beside her. Slipping his arms underneath her, he caught her up and stood to his feet. Her head lolled to one side, and her arm slid from where it lay, crossing her chest. Rae's gaze fell to the bodice of her gown, the cloth riven over her breast.

A blind fury swept through his soul, companioned by a galloping fear for Julia and what she might have suffered. Securing her to him, he kicked open the chamber door and carried her inside, directly to his bed.

Rae tossed back the scarlet counterpane and linens and placed Julia in the middle of the wide mattress. Removing her shoes, he covered her to her chin, then paused long enough to repair the chain of his talisman with the tip of his dirk.

Pulling the silver linkage and stone over his head, he hastened back to the stairs and seized the torch from its bracket. Swiftly, he flamed the blocks of peat in the fireplace, then returned the brand to its holder outside and barred the chamber door.

Julia looked pale as the moon, her skin translucent. 'Twas not a good sign. He considered whether his descendant, Lord Muir, and his men were present on the other side of time, and whether they could see Julia and what he need do for her.

He must take that risk, he deemed. She must be warmed thoroughly and quickly, afore she took deathly ill. As a precaution, Rae closed the curtains on three sides of the bed and partially on the fourth, where he stood. Working quickly, he flipped back the bedcovers once more and began to remove Julia's damp, clinging clothes.

A muscle leapt in his jaw as he searched for the secret that would open one of the seams to her gown. Logic told him 'twould be to the front or back. He found naught. Impatient, and judging the gown already ruined, he snatched the dirk from his belt once more and slit the fabric from bodice to hem.

A delicate wisp of a garment next confronted him. It reached no further than her waist and delayed him not at all as he dispensed with it as handily as he had the gown.

"Christ's bones," Rae muttered to discover Julia caged in another of her cursed corsets. Well, that could be dealt with readily enough, too. Rolling her onto her side, he sliced through the laces then tossed the offensive piece to the floor, along with her mangled gown and the other piece of frippery.

Julia stirred, then sank back into her sleep. He knew he'd need finish his task before she woke and could object, mistaking his intentions.

Easing Julia onto her back, Rae faced his next challenge, a peculiar garment, its scanty top joined at the waist to loose breeches, all made of a fine, thin cloth and adorned with ribbon and lace.

"Och, ye women o' the future wear too many clothes and no' a one o' them practical. Little wonder yer half frozen," he grumbled, though he felt his blood heat as he gazed on her, the dusky circles of her nipples visible through the fabric.

Rae commanded his gaze to the long row of buttons down the garment's front. Centering his attention there, he fumbled with the little knobs but made no progress. Applying his blade once more, he nipped off the buttons, sending them springing and vaulting all over the bed and floor.

Rae continued to work apace and separated the fabric, exposing Julia's full, rose-tipped breasts. His mouth went dry at the sight, but he hauled his gaze away and stripped the cloth free of her arms, peeling it past her waist and hips, continuing downward to reveal golden curls nested between milky thighs.

Och, surely he was mad to choose this course, or would be by the time he was done. Julia needed to be warmed and his own heat was the best he could offer. But *Dhia*, he was not made of rock.

Rae fought the tide of desire rising within him, as he finished drawing off the beribboned garment along with the stockings covering her lower legs. Drawing the coverlet over Julia once more, he unbelted his plaid and pulled off his shirt. Naked, except for his chain and stone, he climbed abed, slipping beneath the counterpane and linens and moving over her to cover her with his length and heat.

Dhia, but she was like ice. He grit his teeth and began rubbing warmth into her limbs. What could have befallen his beloved, he wondered. Why was she unconscious on the steps with her dress torn?

Whoever did this, he'd dispatch the two-legged jackal when he found him. The creature could count on it.

Shifting his weight to better encompass Julia, Rae dropped a kiss to her temple, achingly aware of the lush feminine contours pressing against him.

Julia awakened in a cocoon of warmth. Delicious, she thought hazily, snuggling against a surprisingly solid, yet comfortable pillow. The very core of her bones radiated with heat, and yet she remembered feeling so bitterly cold not long ago.

She began to slip again into a honeyed sleep, aware only of a steady thumping beneath her ear. Like the beat of a heart. She sighed and thought of Rae, rubbing her cheek against her pillow. It even carried his distinctive, masculine scent and felt just as she had imagined his bare, hair-roughened chest would feel. She smiled at her delectable, wanton dream and turned her face to press a kiss to her "pillow."

"Julia. *Mo càran.*"

The pillow moved beneath her head, Rae's voice rousing her. Julia's lashes flew open and Rae's lightly furred chest came into view.

"Julia. Are ye all right?"

Her voice wedged in her throat as she realized this was no sleep-induced fantasy. Their bodies were somehow wrapped together and from all she could tell, wholly unclad.

"I found ye on the stairs, *Mo càran.* Wha' befell ye? Who did ye this harm? Tell me the vermin's name and I'll deal wi' him straightway."

As Rae spoke, the day rushed back to her, Lord Eaton's assault at the burn, her being trapped in the stairwell, all of it, except this portion, lying abed with Rae, naked in each other's arms.

Julia pulled her eyes from his wide, muscled chest and shoulders and dared glance up. She dared not glance down, she knew, or move one whit.

"W-where are my clothes? Where are *your* clothes?"

"Ah, lass, tha' needs some explain' but 'tisna wha' ye be thinkin'."

"And what am I thinking?"

"Tha' I undressed ye tae take advantage of ye, but 'tisna . . ."

"*You* undressed me?"

"Aye, 'twas necessary. Yer clothes were damp wi' cauld and ye, a block o' ice. I needed tae put some heat in tae yer bones, afore ye caught yer death. I didna think ye'd mind if I shared my heat wi' ye."

"N-no, I don't, not at all. I'm quite warm now. T-thank you."

He didn't take the hint to rise or move away. Indeed, he didn't seem at all mindful that they lay chest to toes, flesh to flesh, bare as newborn babes.

"'Twas the best I could think tae do for ye, *mo càran*. But, wha' happened? I take it ye met Moira on the stairs. Yer dress was torn and ye were unconscious. Surely she didna do tha'."

"Moira, the blond woman?" At his nod she shook her head. "No. I'm the one who frightened her. She ran off."

"She hae done more than tha'. She hae left the castle for guid."

"I'm sorry."

"Dinna be. I'm grateful."

Julia's heart lifted at those two words. He wasn't interested in the woman after all.

"I was worried fierce for ye, *mo càran*."

He held her gaze, waiting for an explanation, but Julia believed it served no purpose to tell him of Lord Eaton's attack. Roger Dunnington would have to be dealt with in her own time.

Julia dropped her gaze so Rae could not read her eyes and see she told him only a partial truth.

"I was waiting on the steps for you to come and quite foolishly fell asleep. When time shifted, I became trapped. All the doors on the keep's west side have been sealed off in the future. There was no way to escape. Even the portal to the bedchamber has been blocked for centuries."

"And so ye were caught in the stairwell all the day and half the night?"

Julia lifted her hand to smooth the frown from his brow. "My dearest, I was all right, truly."

"But I wasna there tae free ye. And there ye stayed, cold and defenseless. Wha' if time hadna shifted atall?"

"But it did, and I only fell asleep in the first place because the time-slips themselves are so draining."

Suspicion perched in his keen eyes.

"And because I, er, had a rather strenuous morning."

Rae vented a long breath. "It cleaves my soul tha' I canna protect ye as I wish. If Time were ours, I would take ye tae wife and watch o'er ye every hour o' the day."

Julia's heart dilated, love flowing through her. "You would marry me?"

"Aye, and make ye mine in every way, if ye'd hae me."

In every way. His words shimmered through her, bringing a smile to her lips and a sudden, pulsing heat deep in her feminine soul.

"That I would, have you that is, and be yours 'in every way.'" She started to rise, her breasts skimming upward, along his chest. Instantly, she stilled, breathless at the erotic sensation that wrought.

Julia made no effort to move, nor did he as their gazes locked and held. Her heart pounded solidly as Time hung suspended and Rae drew his gaze slowly downward.

Again, she felt a fire kindle deep inside her as he looked upon her naked breasts. Shifting, he bent his head and placed a kiss between them.

"Ah, *mo càran,* I would hae ye now and e'ermore."

He spread a net of kisses over one breast then covered her nipple with the warmth of his mouth. Julia arched against him as he swirled his tongue over its tip then sucked gently.

He continued his seduction, and she sank her hands into his hair as he loved her breast. When he abandoned it, she started to protest, but his mouth closed instantly over her other nipple. Again he loved her thoroughly, and she found she could not hold a thought, so exquisite were the sensations he released in her.

Once more he began to move, leaving her breasts to lavish kisses downward over her stomach and navel. But suddenly, he went rock still, his hands gripping her sides.

"Forgi' me, my heart. I must stop afore I canna." He shuddered against her as he bridled his passion.

Julia's throat clogged with need, blocking the cry that would plead he continue. She ached for completion, a completion she did not wholly understand. Yet she craved it no less. Fervently did she desire to join with Rae, in body, heart, and soul.

But even now, Time was a fickle ally.

Julia wished to weep and laugh all at once. Rae would marry her honorably, but forces would deny them even the hope of sharing a future. She wished to rail against the Universe. Would that she could harness Time altogether and hold it captive to her will.

Julia reached for Rae, her hands cupping his jaw where his head pressed against her stomach, beneath her breasts. She lifted his face, a single tear spilling down her cheek.

"If Tomorrow is denied us, cannot Now be ours?" she whispered.

Rae moved upward, covering her once more with his length, and wiped away her tear.

"Ah, *mo càran*, ye dinna know wha' ye do, wha' ye ask. Time will part us, surely, and I'll no' ruin ye for another."

"There will be no other," she vowed firmly, closing her heart to that possibility. He started to argue her words but she lifted her fingers to his lips.

"One night, soon perhaps, Time will cease to shift. But this night, here, now, I would pledge you my love—my troth, if you will—and give myself to you. For if I am destined to lose you, then at least once I would be yours, and know you as mine. Love me, Rae, before Time robs me from your arms and separates us forever."

Rae gazed on Julia for what seemed an eternity, searching for the truth past their momentary passion, questing the depths of her soul. The blue of his eyes darkened and she thought to see a crack appear in his resolve, then fissure wide as his restraint buckled and gave way.

Their mouths met in a hungry, burning kiss, their passions too long denied. Julia wrapped her arms about him, moving against him, and as he shifted, she felt the astonishing proof of his desire pressing against her abdomen.

He withdrew from her mouth to rain kisses over her face and neck, showering them downward over her breasts. Julia thought she'd faint with pleasure as his tongue circled and laved her nipple in exquisite torture, then he began to gently suckle and tease the bud erect.

She threaded her fingers through his hair, holding him to her, relishing the sensations he wrought in her and the delicious warmth of his arousal. She slid her hands over the contours of his muscled shoulders, exploring them as he moved to her other breast. He cherished her anew, kissing, teasing, tantalizing her sensitive nipple till her senses stood on tiptoe, and she craved all he would give her.

Again he moved downward, trailing a path of fire over her stomach and abdomen, circling her navel with his tongue before continuing lower to sprinkle kisses over her hips, thighs, calves, and ankles. Her bones melted beneath his seduction and she wished only to open to him, like a flower blossoming to the warmth of the sun.

Shifting upward, Rae covered her once more. "Are ye sure o' this, *mo càran*? Are ye afraid?"

"Of you? Never," she whispered somewhat breathlessly, her heart beating madly.

Taking her hand, Rae drew it to his waiting masculinity. She gasped and went rigid at the feel of his firm shaft, velvet on steel.

"Maybe a little afraid." Her voice wavered.

Rae laughed richly. "Dinna be, love. A man and woman makin' love is near as old as Time itself."

He possessed her mouth in an elaborate kiss, and she rose to keep pace with him, their tongues dancing and mating in a joyous celebration of their love. When his hand cupped her breast, his thumb caressing the bud of her nipple, she moaned against his mouth, savoring his touch. When his lips left hers to feast on her other breast, she became liquid fire and prayed he'd never cease.

"D'ye trust me?"

"Yes," she said breathlessly, wondering what he could mean, at the same time aware of an intense aching between her legs.

Returning his attention to her nipple, he swept his tongue over its swollen peak and took her in his mouth. But as he distracted her with his erotic seduction, he slipped his fingers inside her feminine folds and began to gently stroke her. Julia jolted against him, but his fingers continued to caress her to a splendid madness, keeping their rhythm.

"Ah-h-h-h, what are you doing?"

"Lovin' ye, lass. Sh-h-h-h-h, now. 'Tis all right, let it happen. Let me gi' ye pleasure."

Julia seemed alive with sensation. Fiery currents crested through her feminine core as he stroked her, unrelenting, at the same time savoring her breasts. She felt a throbbing need grow between her legs, as though she climbed to some unknown precipice.

"Rae, I-I don't know what to do." Her fingers dug into his back.

"Ye will when ye are ready. Let yer instincts guide ye, love. I will show ye the rest."

He continued his torture, till she began to call his name in sweet delirium. Shifting upward, he settled between her legs. She felt his hard masculinity poised at the entrance to her womanhood.

" 'Twill hurt this once, but only this once. Are ye certain, *mo càran*? D'ye wish me tae fill ye and make ye mine?"

"I am yours already, Rae," she whispered, her pulses pounding. "For now and all time."

"In heart, now in body then, before the Almighty, we shall be joined as one. 'Tis my sacred vow tae ye."

Coupling his mouth with hers, he carried her into a deep kiss then thrust forward. Julia cried out at the sharp, searing pain as he breached her maidenhead and penetrated her with his thickness. He stilled, lying sheathed within her. Julia felt full, gloriously full of him, and exulted in this feeling of union, of being one with Rae.

He began to move against her, slowly at first, setting a rhythm. When she gave him her smile, he took her hips in his hands, showing her how to move with him and keep pace. She matched his rhythm easily, a fire kindling anew as she felt his silk move in hers.

His mouth fastened on hers as they strove as one. Again she felt as though she were climbing and, instinctively, wrapped her legs around Rae's. His breathing came heavier and regular, as did hers. Then his rhythm increased, carrying her with him on a tide of sensations. As his silken shaft rubbed against her swollen core, she felt an inexplicable sense of urgency, a burgeoning need she did not understand, as he thrust faster and deeper. Higher and higher she climbed then gasped as she spiraled upward over the top, erupting in a shuddering, pounding, convulsive release.

Rae joined her, shouting out his pleasure. Their cries joined as they reached the heavens in a fierce explosion and together became one in the timeless sea of stars.

Chapter 16

"Ee-ee-ee-ee! She's here! Someone, come quickly, I've found her!"

Betty's cries startled Julia awake. She dragged open her lids in time to see the maid fly from the room, summoning the entire castle.

The entire castle!

Julia looked to the empty space beside her, then to the bed hangings, drawn open and blue. Time had slipped, Rae was gone, and she . . . she was stark naked beneath the covers!

Julia hauled herself upright in bed, her body complaining with every movement as she made a quick search for her gown and underclothes. They lay nowhere in sight. A sinking feeling told her the clothes remained back in time with Rae. Bad enough she was stranded, nude in bed, with Dunraven's population about to descend, but drat, she'd lost another corset!

Julia eyed the armoire, debating whether she had time to make a dash to it and snatch something to wear. She began to tow back the covers to make a spring, when pain darted through her muscles.

Ah, but she was sore everywhere imaginable. Sore in the deep muscles of her arms and legs from her struggles with Lord Eaton. Sore and tender in more intimate places from making love with Rae. And drained in addition, both from her night of passion and from traveling through time itself. For all that, she felt, at some level, invigorated—tired, smarting in diverse places, yes, but also vitally alive.

Dread seized her. What if the others could simply gaze on

her and tell she'd been with a man, that she was no longer an innocent? And here she was, delivered through Time, naked to her bed, testament to her amorous ventures of the night.

Julia slid deep beneath the covers as Betty's voice grew near again, mingled with those of others. With a groan, she pleaded with Heaven that Lord Eaton would not be among them.

Betty arrived with Mrs. McGinty, followed by Angus McNab and Young Tom. Lord Muir arrived moments later along with Messrs Armistead, Thornsbury, and Sir Henry. The servants stood aside as Lord Muir hastened directly to Julia's side.

"Oh, my dear, you took years off my life. Thank God you are all right. We've been racked with distress. Tom saw you enter the keep, but then none could find you."

Julia read the anxious concern in Lord Muir's eyes and presumed he'd guessed the truth of her dilemma, that she'd been trapped in the stairwell. Young Tom, she noticed, hung back by the chamber door and would not meet her eyes. She wondered if he'd seen more of her return to the castle than he'd revealed to the others. She drew her gaze back to Lord Muir.

"I am sorry to have caused you all such worry, though it warms me to know I was missed."

She smiled at the dear man, aware that a few brows lifted in the room. The thought of Roger Dunnington came disturbingly to mind. What lies might he have spread about her?

"I went out again for a long walk and became lost. I only found my way back a few hours ago." At least, Julia guessed it was that long since she had stepped back across time.

Lord Muir's eyes remained steady upon her, and she saw now a troubled look touching their depths. Julia's pulse leapt as she realized for the first time that last night, when she and Rae made love, never once did she consider whether anyone else was present in the room.

Had the marquis and the other men watched, taken notes of her activities? The thought mortified her. Yet the look in his eyes seemed in no way censuring or accusing. What then?

Lord Muir smiled down at her. "You need your rest for now,

Julia. Later, when you regain your strength, perhaps you would take tea with us in the library."

"Regain your strength." He knew, Julia thought, her spirits tumbling.

As the room cleared of visitors Angus McNab sent her a most curious look, and Mrs. McGinty, unreadable as ever, seemed even more remote than usual, if that was possible.

Betty closed the door after the others, then hurried back to attend Julia. If she harbored any doubts of Julia or what might have transpired within and without Dunraven's walls, she revealed nothing and was only solicitous.

"You poor lamb. 'Twas bitter out last night, the wind whipping and howling. A body could die in these mountains, fall asleep, and never wake. Best we get some of Cook's broth into you and then I'll draw you a long, hot bath."

Several hours later, revived by Betty's ministrations, Julia joined Lord Muir and the other three men in the library. After Mrs. McGinty delivered tea and withdrew, Julia provided them with an amended version of the previous time-slip—how it had occurred early, and how she'd become entrapped in the stairwell, waiting for Rae.

"His talisman must have slipped from my grasp when I fell asleep, which was most fortunate."

Lord Muir nodded. "Indeed. And you say Rae Mackinnon found you during the subsequent shift?"

The question surprised Julia. Were these men absent from her chamber during the time-slip, or had they simply been unable to see her and Rae for some reason?

"Yes, he found me just outside his chamber, 'unconscious' he said. Rae, er, the laird, was quite concerned for my well-being and cared for me personally." She felt herself flush. Now why had she said that? "Of course, he was the only one who could. Care for me. In his own time, that is. No one else could see me, or warm me like . . . he, er, could."

Julia clamped her mouth shut. Lord, but she was making matters worse by the second. Next, she'd be confessing to a torrid night of lovemaking with Rae Mackinnon. She certainly didn't want *that* known or recorded in the chronicles of the Third Laird of Dunraven Castle! Julia diverted her thoughts to another matter, that of convincing these men to suspend future meetings in her bedchamber.

Just then, Lord Muir rose from his chair and asked the others to leave. Julia held her breath, anticipating why he did so and what he might say.

Lord Muir stroked his beard in thought as he resumed his chair. He lifted his pale blue gaze and she saw the same troubled look there that she had seen earlier.

"I did not wish to embarrass you in front of the others, my dear," he began.

Julia bit the inside of her cheek. He knew.

Again he stroked his beard, his lips pressed together as if he were having difficulty in choosing his next words.

"Roger returned yesterday, rather abruptly. He sought me out and seemed somewhat disappointed to find me alone, with my books, in the tower library. He bore a cut on his lip, and I do believe there were scratches on his neck, though he kept his collar raised high. All in all, he appeared as though he'd been in a scuffle."

Lord Muir rose and came around the front of his desk to stand before Julia.

"It was after I spoke with my nephew that I and the others realized you were missing. We alerted the servants and initiated a search throughout the castle and grounds. Young Tom came to me and admitted he had seen you ride from the direction of the burn on my nephew's horse, and that you appeared upset and had hurried inside the castle."

Julia shifted uncomfortably in her chair.

"He also saw Roger, coming from the same direction, running on foot. Roger, too, raced inside according to Tom, seemingly in pursuit of you. My nephew left Dunraven after he and I spoke, but there is something I must know." Again Lord Muir searched for words. "Did my nephew behave improperly toward you?"

Julia dropped her gaze to her hands, not knowing what to

say, whether she should tell the kindly Lord Muir just what a blackguard his nephew really was.

"Did he make advances, try to force his attentions upon you?" he pressed when she remained silent.

At last she nodded, but still saying nothing.

"Did he hurt you?"

"No." She cleared her throat. "Not really. We had words."

"And was it words that cut his lip?"

Julia glanced up at that. "Lord Eaton knows of our meetings in my bedchamber, at least those during the night. He's assumed the worse as to what we are about."

"And wanted to benefit from his knowledge," Lord Muir's tone was thick with disgust. "As I said, Roger came in search of me, of *us,* hoping to find us together in a compromising situation, I presume. As you said, he is aware of my, and the other men's, visitations to your room and confronted me on the matter."

Lord Muir took her hands in his. "My dear, I am as deeply concerned for your reputation as I am for your health. Perhaps it is wise to discontinue our meetings for a while. The servants already are suspicious, and I am of a mind to offer them an explanation before damaging rumors start circulating about. As to our study of the phenomenon, we have much data already, and you yourself could make notations and complete your questioning of the laird during the coming time-slips."

Julia could hardly believe her ears. Someone above must be smiling upon her and granted her wish.

"Yes, you are quite right, of course," she agreed, then moistened her dry lips. "Your lordship, I am curious. Did anyone keep watch in my chamber during the time-slip last night?"

He gave her an odd, half smile. "There was too much activity for us to set up our equipment, what with the servants in and out, and everyone in a frantic search for you. Your faithful lady's maid waited up the night, though, keeping vigil in a chair by the fire. Apparently, Betty dozed off and awoke to strange noises in the room. Though she saw nothing, she became frightened and fled the chamber."

Julia offered no comment and rose, thanking Lord Muir for his efforts in her behalf. Then, pleading fatigue, she excused herself to her chamber.

Returning to her room, Julia decided to forgo lunch and lie down. Exhaustion seemed a constant companion these days, and she wished to be fresh for Rae, whenever Time decided to slip again.

As she sank into the mattress and drew up the covers, she thought of Rae and their fervid night together. How could she face him in the light of day? He knew her most intimate secrets.

A thought followed that brought a smile to her lips, and she turned into her pillow. Did not she know a few of his secrets, too?

Sleep welcomed her quickly into its arms. As Julia drifted in that peaceful realm, she dreamt of Rae, sitting beside her, watching her as she rested. Once, he traced his finger along the side of her cheek and neck then drew it over her lips.

She stirred in her slumber and caught his hand. Warm, she thought as she pressed a kiss to his fingers, then guided his hand to her breast and held it there, cupping her. She smiled contentedly as he brushed his thumb over her nipple, sleep drawing her down, once more, into its velvety depths.

"Miss? Miss? Will you be dressing for supper?"

Julia climbed to consciousness and levered open a heavy eyelid to find Betty hovering over her. The room had grown dim, the sky dark beyond the windowpanes, and the lamp lit on the small table beside her.

As she strove to clear the cobwebs of sleep from her brain, Julia could still feel the touch of Rae's hand on her breast.

An hour later, Julia descended for supper. To her surprise, she discovered that some of the Braxton guests had returned, including her aunt and cousins, Sir Robert, Lord Withrington, and Lady Charles. With some relief, she learned that Sampson Dilcox had missed the train.

At the sight of Lord Eaton, Julia began to withdraw, but Lord Muir appeared and remained protectively at her side. As the group made their way to the dining room, Julia decided she must still be dreaming, only her dreams had turned more to the nightmarish variety.

Lord Muir seated Julia beside him as his dinner companion, while the other men of the Society formed a buffer around her, Sir Henry sitting to her right and Mr. Thornsbury and Mr. Armistead sitting opposite.

Lord Eaton, for his part, deported himself with marked coolness toward Julia, glowering at her from time to time from above a healing lip. He wore his collar high, she noted with a degree of pleasure, though she kept her gaze averted as much as possible from where he sat at the far end of the table.

Lilith, predictably, stayed at Lord Eaton's side and, if Julia did not imagine it, her cousin carried herself with an air, more haughty and self-important than ever.

Toward the end of the meal Lord Eaton rose, clanging his glass with the tines of his fork to call for quiet. Taking Lilith's hand in his, he drew her to her feet and faced the room.

"Uncle, friends, it gives me great pleasure to announce that just this day, I have taken an enormous and momentous step in my life and asked Miss Symington for her hand in marriage. She has accepted."

Cheers and well-wishes went up, toasts followed, and the wine flowed in the couple's honor.

Lilith basked in the moment as she stood smiling at Lord Eaton's side. She slid a look to Julia, one of utter triumph, then let her gaze float over those gathered before her. Lilith held herself with near regal bearing, as if all surrounding her were already hers, and she reigning as Roger's marchioness, as someday she would ultimately become.

Lord Muir said nothing, looking anything but pleased. Julia, in parting, congratulated the couple, sure the two were perfectly deserving of one another.

Taking her leave, Julia retired to her chamber. With Betty's assistance, she changed into her nightgown then excused the maid for the night and locked the door. Removing the key, Julia carried it with her to the bed and slipped it under her pillow.

Julia settled herself between the sheets and blankets, sitting up and reclining against the headboard. Brushing out her hair with long, even strokes, she willed for time to shift and Rae to come to her. She closed her eyes and imagined his hands and lips moving over her as they had last night. A fire lit deep within her. Time could not slip swiftly enough.

Julia realized she must have drifted off as she came groggily awake, her chin sagging toward her chest. Drawing open her eyes, she found Rae sitting before her, watching her in sleep.

He smiled as if she were the most precious treasure on earth. "Are ye well, *mo càran*?"

"Now that you are here." Her heart expanded with love.

Words suddenly seemed superfluous as he gathered her in his arms and kissed her long and thoroughly.

"Are we being watched, *mo càran*?" His lips pressed a warm path down the column of her neck and along her collarbone. With his tongue, he laved the pulse at the base of her throat.

"W-watched? M-m-m-m-m, no. I locked the door and hid the key."

He lifted his head, his gaze a sparkling blue sea. "Ach, then ye do love me, my Julia."

"More than Time can hold." She smiled, the utter truth of her avowal tugging upon her heart.

Their lips blended, gently at first, tasting, savoring—then more impatiently, consuming, devouring, as their hunger sharpened and desire flared bright. In moments their clothes mingled on the floor and their bodies entwined, flesh hot upon flesh.

Rae surrounded Julia with his strength as he lay her across the mattress. Their tongues mated in a frenzied, erotic dance. He rolled with her, bringing her atop him, then underneath him, drawing his lips from her mouth to feast on her breasts.

Julia gasped quick breaths, her heart beating madly at his exquisite assault. She felt her nipples pebble in his mouth as he possessed them, one by one, sending shivers of fire spilling through her to kindle an even greater fire between her legs.

Rae continued to ravish her senses, awakening the very depths of her sensuality. Julia glowed, radiantly alive. Though still new to the ways of love, she knew no embarrassment as she lay naked in his arms, only a fierce yearning to join swiftly and completely with him. But her Highland laird was intent on prolonging their pleasure this night.

Flicking his tongue over the swollen globes of her nipples, he strayed lower, trailing kisses over her rib cage, stomach, hips, and thighs, murmuring in Gaelic as he moved lower and lower. Julia sank her fingers in his hair, wishing to pleasure him somehow but scarcely able to think as his path turned upward once more, his lips moving along her inner thigh. Her heart pounded as he coaxed her legs apart and his fingers touched and caressed her.

"Ach, ye are hot and ready for me, love," he murmured, kissing her briefly, intimately, but giving her no time to think on it as he shifted upward and filled her, bringing her legs around his.

Julia exulted in the feel of him buried deep within her, though she still felt somewhat shocked at his boldness of the moment before. The very place now throbbed hotly against his taut manhood and knew no relief until he began to move against her, his strokes strong and even.

"R-Rae . . ."

"Sh, love, let me love ye well and as I will. 'Tis for ye tae enjoy."

As he increased his pace, Julia skimmed her palms over his shoulders and back, felt the play of his firm muscles flexing and rippling. He then cherished her breasts anew till she moaned his name aloud and tightened her legs about him.

Capturing her lips once more, he surged against her, bringing her to the edge of release. Julia matched his rhythm, her need near painful. Suddenly she erupted as wave upon wave of pleasure crashed through her, sweeping her to a place beyond Time itself.

"Rae!" she cried as ecstasy claimed her.

Grinning, he covered her mouth, but in the next moment Julia's name ripped from his throat as the same, powerful force claimed him. Thrusting deeply, he poured himself into her,

venting his passion and joining her in the rapturous fires of
love.

Julia sighed her content as she rested against Rae's solid,
warm chest. Was it possible to feel so splendid, so in love and
alive? Her whole being tingled with his touch, with his loving.
And she still throbbed pleasurably with the climatic force of
their joining.

Julia turned her head and pressed a kiss to his chest.

"Greedy wench." He smiled and sank his long fingers in the
silk of her hair. "Are ye wantin' more lovin' already?"

She said nothing, only smiled as she brushed her fingertips
through the crisp hair on his chest and then trailed her hand
downward beneath the sheet. He caught her hand just as a
sharp, rapid knocking sounded on the door. Julia stiffened and
looked anxiously to Rae.

"Ye are no' tha' disappointed are ye?" he teased.

"Rae, someone is pounding on the door. Do you not hear it?"

He rose quickly to a sitting position. "Nay, I dinna, *mo
càran.*"

Julia's eyes widened as the rapping continued. "It's coming
from the door in *my* time."

"D'ye think ye it needs answerin'?" He feathered kisses
along her jaw.

"Rae, I can't see the door *to* answer it."

Remembering the key beneath her pillow, she made a quick
search for it. The key was gone. Actually, it was there, in the
nineteenth century, she just couldn't locate it. Not that it would
do her much good if she could. How was she to find the door
lock, let alone the door?

"*Mo càran,* if ye can hear the knocking, mayhap ye yersel'
can be heard."

Julia agreed. Normally—well, nothing was normal about this
situation—but during the time-slips Lord Muir could converse
with her inside the chamber at least. Perhaps, whoever was outside the chamber could hear her as well.

"Who is it?" Julia called out, her voice wavering.

"Julia, let me in," Aunt Sybil's voice demanded from the other side of the door. Her pounding intensified. "I know precisely what you are about, young woman. You can't hide the truth any longer. Now open this door!"

Chapter 17

"Do you deny it? Do you deny having entertained men, here, in your bedchamber, at all hours the night?"

Sybil paced the room, her eyes roaming every corner and cranny as though she expected to find someone concealed in their shadows.

"I've 'entertained' no one." Julia lifted her chin, clutching her thin robe over her breast, knowing it was quite obvious she was naked beneath.

When her aunt had continued to demand entry to her chamber, Julia and Rae could think of no recourse but to close the door of Time between them. With a parting kiss, Julia removed her ring and the room reverted to its normal state in the future. In her race to clothe herself, she seized on the first thing she saw, her silk robe, lying at the end of the bed.

Sybil halted her pacing and rounded on Julia. Eyeing her niece's robe, she smiled thinly.

"I don't know what amusements took place within these walls, but the marquis, Lord Muir, was seen leaving your room on a number of occasions. And, on several more, he left with friends! Really, Julia, did your parents raise you wholly devoid of morals?"

Julia bristled at her aunt's slur on her parents, but Sybil paid no regard and continued to spit her venom.

"What is your game, niece? To beguile the marquis at any cost? To so enamor him with your pale beauty and acquiescence, he will keep you near, in the comfort of his great fortune?"

Sybil took a step closer, lifting an arched brow.

"Or is it something more? Perhaps, you expect the marquis to fall mindlessly in love with you, marry you, and begat a brat on you to whom his titles would then soon pass. That's it, isn't it?" Her eyes glowed menacingly. "While you are elevated to marchioness, Roger would lose his inheritance. Widowed, you would personally control Lord Muir's fortune for many years in the name of your son. Yes, you'd like besting the Symingtons, cheating Lilith out of the position and privileges to which she is entitled."

Julia stared at her aunt, stunned by her interpretation and astonished that she had slipped Lilith into the conversation. Clearly, her aunt was not distressed in the least that the family name might be tarnished by her actions, only that Lilith's shining future might be thwarted.

"Well, you shan't have a chance to spoil Lilith's, that is Roger's, inheritance," Sybil snapped. "You will pack your trunks immediately and prepare to leave. You are returning to Hampshire, where you belong. I have already dispatched a letter to Lady Arabella."

"Would that be *this* letter?"

The two women turned as one to find Lord Muir standing in the doorway. Surprisingly, though dawn was just now peeking through the windows, he was fully attired in jacket and kilt. The pouches under his eyes were pronounced, as though he'd yet to sleep that night. In his hand, he held a neat packet, sealed with a glob of red wax.

Lord Muir glared at Sybil, having obviously heard her tirade.

"Angus came to me, good man that he is, advising me of your request and asking to be excused of his morning duties in order to post your missive. I assured him I would see to it personally." Lord Muir tucked the letter into his jacket. "Have no fear. I will post your letter, along with my own to dear Arabella. I see that surprises you. Yes, I know your mother-in-law. Rather well, actually."

He stroked his snowy mustache, letting his words hang

meaningfully on the air. "I presume Arabella is as full of salt and vinegar as ever?"

Julia found herself smiling, despite her surprise at his comments. Sybil still had yet to find her tongue. When she did, a moment later, and attempted to speak, Lord Muir cut her off.

"Whatever my nephew told you of my friendship with your niece was undoutedly a lie. Her deportment is, and has been, at every moment, above reproach."

Julia dropped her gaze, wondering if he would sing her praises so quickly if he knew she'd lain with Rae Mackinnon.

"Your lordship." Sybil's voice stung the air. "Do you deny Julia permitted you and your colleagues into her chamber in the dead of night?"

"She did indeed, at my request, but you misunderstand the purpose of our gatherings. They are purely of a scientific nature. I could explain it all to you, though I doubt you'd believe any of the sensational claims I would make. Nonetheless, our investigations will soon be made public in London to the Society and your niece will, no doubt, become quite famous for it."

"No doubt," Sybil clipped.

"Believe what you will, Lady Sybil, but I do promise you this. Attempt to malign Julia's fine name or send her from Dunraven, and you'll find yourself and your daughter packed off as well, and I shall place Roger under threat of disinheritance should he ever marry Lilith."

"You wouldn't!" Sybil shrilled.

"And don't think he'll circumvent me on charges I've lost my wits. I assure you, I move in rather elite and enlightened circles, with a multitude of friends who can vouch for my soundness. Now consider my next words carefully. I believe myself still quite able to sire a son and heir, and might decide to put myself to the test if Roger, or you and your precious Lilith, vex me any further."

Sybil compressed her lips to a thin line, her nostrils flaring, and stalked from the chamber. Lord Muir watched her departure, then he directed his gaze to Julia.

"This has been a most unfortunate encounter. We realized

such might happen, still I am sorry for it. I will leave you to recover, my dear, however, there is something I need to share
with you. My colleagues and I have been working through the
night, going over the data we've accumulated. We have come
to some fresh conclusions."

He paused and stroked his beard, his brows pulling downward.

"I am sorry, Julia. My news is not good."

"Sh-h-h now, *mo càran,* we knew this moment would
come."

"But so soon?" Julia's arms tightened about Rae's waist,
tears slipping down her cheek.

"Explain tae me once more, the path o' their thoughts."

Reluctantly, Julia released her hold on Rae and sat back on
the blanket they shared, spread amidst a field of purple heather.
She glanced overhead to where the swollen moon hung in the
daylight sky, like a pale, misshapen disc. She palmed her tears
away.

"It is the men's belief that, on the night of the Full Moon, the
door between our times will close."

Her lips quivered and Rae immediately surrounded her with
his arms, drawing her against his chest. She drew a steadying
breath and continued.

"Lord Muir explained that the time-slips began with the New
Moon, when the moon's energies were at their weakest. The
time door opened—and continues to open—wider and wider.
That is, the hours and minutes it remains open are increasing.
He told me to imagine a door blowing open on a breeze which
grows stronger, holding the door open wide and for longer periods."

Julia sent Rae a small smile at the simpleness of the analogy
and found him nodding.

"I ken. Gae on."

"At the time of the Full Moon, the energies will reach their
peak. Lord Muir and the others speculate, once the moon waxes
full and begins to wane, there will be a 'reversal' effect. The

time door will slam closed, and the force of the moon's energies will work in an opposing direction, holding the door shut."

Julia moistened her lips. "None of the men have been able to determine how the phenomenon began—what activated it. There is no telling whether the door will open again, or when precisely."

Julia was keenly aware that Lord Muir had occupied the tower chamber intermittently for two decades before the first time-slip occurred. The door had then remained closed for another twenty years. True, the stone in his sword, and the one in her ring, had somehow affected the commencement of the time-slips, but there was no way of knowing how long the door would remain shut.

Julia lifted her gaze to Rae, her lashes wet with tears. "I will wait for you, my love, however long I must. I will remain at Dunraven with hope in my heart we will yet meet again."

Rae drew her tight in his arms. "I, too, shall wait for ye, *mo càran*. I vow it."

His words pierced her heart with love, bittersweet.

"You have a destiny to fulfill, my darling."

He started to object but she quickly pressed her fingers to his lips.

"You *must* fulfill your destiny, you must take a wife. Lord Muir cannot be born without your help." She offered him a shaky smile. "It is not only important to him, but also to me. It is only through Lord Muir's kindness that I shall be able to remain at Dunraven and wait for you."

Seeing the pain reflected in his eyes, Julia withdrew her fingers and pressed her lips to his. Slipping her arms about his neck, she drew him down with her onto the blanket.

As their kisses caught fire and their passions engulfed them, he freed her breasts from her shirtwaist and camisole. Brief moments later, she fully appreciated the versatility of Highland dress and its ready accommodation to any given moment, especially now as their bodies entwined and melded to one amidst the heather.

*   *   *

On Julia's return to Dunraven, she discovered that more of Lord Eaton's guests from Braxton had arrived from their sojourn to the spa at Strathpeffer.

When Julia appeared at tea, they greeted her with tacit coolness and excluded her from their conversations. Later, at dinner, Julia found her presence barely acknowledged and only then with wintry glares.

Lord Eaton smiled smugly from his place at the far end of the table. Clearly, in recompense for spurning him, he had set a buzz about the castle, intimating her involvement in a scandalous affair. Or had he used Lilith and Aunt Sybil to spread his poison? Julia slid a glance to them, but they held themselves aloof and kept their eyes averted.

To Julia's dismay, on this of all nights, the marquis and his associates chose to take their meal in the upper library as they continued to work at a feverish pitch over their books and computations. Julia faced the lions' den alone.

Many of the women—Lady Bigsby, Lady Downs, Lady Reynolds and her twin daughters, Ava and Ada, among them—regarded her with undisguised looks of disgust. Lord Withrington would not meet her eyes, while Lady Charles bore sympathy in her own.

Someone related with great relish how Sampson Dilcox had packed his belongings soon after his arrival from Strathpeffer and set off for London, stricken by some news he'd received. On the other hand, Rokeby, Aunt Sybil's ever-present and attentive admirer, sent Julia lascivious glances down the table.

Emmaline and Sir Robert, bless them, remained supportive and obviously unbelieving of the claims against her. Were it not for them, Julia did not believe she could have forborne the evening.

Lord Eaton continued to watch from his place, a superior smile slanting across his face and firing his eyes. Julia met his gaze evenly and felt his unspoken challenge. Affording him a response, she shifted her eyes to the cut that yet marred his lip and to the high collar that hid his scratches. A measure of satisfaction spread through her. Julia rose in place. Having endured more than enough for one evening, she withdrew without comment to her chamber.

"Might I walk with ye, miss?"

Julia looked with surprise to Angus McNab, who waited at the base of the great staircase in the entrance hall.

" 'Twould comfort his lordship to know ye arrived safely at yer chamber without any troubles along the way."

Julia tilted her head. "Did Lord Muir send you?"

"Aye, that he did, after he had a wee bit of a talk with the staff—McGinty, Betty, Tom, and I. Not the new help from town, of course."

"Of course."

"Some of the others fear his lordship has gone daft." He thumped his fore and middle fingers on the side of his head. "But me, I've known Himself for many a year now. A good man, he is. An honest man, and his mind is sharp as any. If he says black is white, and Highland cattle have legs shorter on one side than the other, then 'tis so."

Angus suddenly stopped, turning to Julia. "I owe ye an apology, Miss Hargrove. I canna say I understand all of what his lordship spoke on, but I was wrong about ye, and I'm sorry. McGinty, too. She'll have a hard time admittin' it, but she knows she misjudged ye sorely and 'twas without ground."

Julia found her voice clogged with emotion and her eyes stinging with tears. She wished to hug the crusty Scotsman who'd gone a "wee bit" soft. Instead, she reached out and squeezed his arm warmly.

"Thank you, Mr. McNab."

"Angus."

"Angus." She smiled.

On reaching the Long Gallery they found Mrs. McGinty and Betty waiting at the far end, near her chamber door.

They greeted Julia with a mixture of courtesy and curiosity, leaving her to wonder how extensive an explanation Lord Muir might have offered them. Mrs. McGinty still held herself with rigid composure, but the lines in her face had softened. Betty offered her a ready smile, as ever, though Julia noticed she plucked nervously at her apron and stared back at her with eyes rounded wide.

As Julia and Angus joined them, she felt the need to offer some explanations of her own.

"I understand Lord Muir has informed you of the unusual activities—that is to say, the *paranormal* activities—that have been occurring in the tower bedchamber. I can assure you there is nothing of which to be fearful. There are no ghostly manifestations for which your Scottish castles are so famous. This phenomenon is entirely different. If you have any questions, I will be pleased to answer them for you."

Betty twisted her apron in her hands. "H-his lordship has set out instruments in your chamber, M-miss. He suggested—if you have no objection that is—of course, I imagine you do . . ."

Mrs. McGinty placed a quieting hand on Betty's arm and continued for her. "Lord Muir suggested Betty and I keep company with you this evening and observe for ourselves the instruments' recordings. If that is agreeable to you, Miss Hargrove."

"Yes, I believe that is a fine idea." Julia turned to Angus. "Would you care to witness the time-slip, also?"

"Me? Oh, nay, miss. 'Twouldn't be proper." He took several steps back, fidgeting with the buttons on his jacket and scratching his whiskers. "And besides, I must be attending his lordship. Indeed, 'tis time to be checking on Himself." Slipping a glance at his pocketwatch, his brambly brows rose high. "Ach, see there. What did I tell ye? Far past time." Angus hastened swiftly down the gallery and out of sight.

Julia chuckled to herself as she turned toward her chamber and entered it. Mrs. McGinty and Betty followed with marked reserve, darting uneasy glances around the room.

As the threesome waited over the next few hours, Betty fluttered about, fussing with this and that, scarcely able to contain her emotions. Mrs. McGinty sat in a chair by the fire, calmly embroidering a fine linen handkerchief.

Sooner than Julia anticipated, the air grew heavy. She rose from her place on the bed and gestured for the other women to gather around the instruments. Amazement lit their faces as they watched the needles jump.

As the room shifted before her eyes, Julia looked to the fireplace. Rae stood there smiling, consuming her with his look.

"Would ye like tae gae for a stroll along the burn, *mo càran?*" He held out his hand for her.

Forgetting all else, Julia smiled. "Yes, I would love to."

Taking his hand, she walked by his side and passed through the arched door, onto the stairwell. Julia halted, looking with some concern to Rae.

"Is there somethin' wrong, my heart?"

"I hope not." Julia turned back to the door, concerned she'd not prepared the women for the nature of her departure. Poor Betty might not survive the shock of seeing her pass through a stone wall.

Reentering the chamber, Julia glanced to the empty space where the women had stood just seconds before. A whimper drew her gaze downward.

There on the floor she discovered Betty, kneeling beside Mrs. McGinty who had fainted dead away.

Chapter 18

Rae rode for Dunraven at the head of his men, vexed by the wasted day searching for naught, vexed to be arriving back to the keep far later than he'd hoped.

As the light fell, a number of his men continued to search the surrounding hills, avowing 'twas the best of nights to do so, for they would have the advantage of the full light of the moon.

The Full Moon. He must reach Dunraven before time slipped. He'd not lose one precious moment with Julia. Where had the last days flown? He'd spent as much of them as possible with Julia, cheering her with several brief outings, loving her thoroughly. But the duties of lairdship intruded with their demands, binding his time. Reivers had struck yet again, drawing him away early this morn.

Curse them. And curse the dissensions that continued to divide his men. Iain helped matters not at all with his harping to ride after the Camerons and blood their swords.

Och, what had come over Iain? Wild, he was—rash, unruly, and, Rae was beginning to think, a touch mad. Of equal concern, Iain possessed a fiery persuasiveness that stirred the men's blood and captured their minds, winning them to his constricted way of thinking.

Rae pressed his garron on, grim thoughts crowding.

'Twas no secret there were those amongst his clansmen who lamented he, not Iain, was laird. Iain exuded warlike characteristics that Highlanders prized so greatly in their chieftains—daring, bold, aggressive, brave. Added to this, Iain's reddish brown hair and stature reflected strongly of their esteemed fa-

ther, Alasdair. Rae was ever mindful his clansmen had expected Iain to step into their father's shoes as Third Laird of
Dunraven.

If some thought to depose him, Rae knew 'twould not be the
first time a new leader was unseated for a perceived lack of
warrior prowess. But Rae stoutly believed one needed solid
cause to spill clan blood, and certainly proof of a grievance.

The Mackinnons would risk much to recklessly attack the
Camerons of Lochiel. They were a clan of considerable size.
Iain, he knew, would argue back that Rae had gone soft as a
sassenach in London Tower and had lost his capacity for a
good brawl. Even now, his brother remained with those who
searched for the trail of the reivers, and, in Iain's case, for more
than cattle, but for a few Camerons as well.

If Rae was not quick to rise to a fight and unsheathe his
sword, 'twas with reason. A week past, he and his men had discovered carcasses in a nearby cave. One would think the
thieves, burdened with cattle, would choose to follow the old
paths that crisscrossed the fingerlike glens and which offered
an easy escape south toward Perth, or west toward Cameron
lands, or north to the Dee. Instead, the cave lay east in a place
not easily accessible.

'Twas obvious someone had feasted there, but the bones
were not new enough to belong to cattle just lifted. Nor were
they so very old.

Donald brought up the subject of James Graham and his conspirators hiding in the Highlands both before and after the
king's murder. Donald ventured that possibly not all the conspirators had been seized after all, that there were others who
had been part to the plans and aided the murderers who might
now be still hiding in the surrounding glens and mountains.

This raised many a brow and Iain was quick to ridicule Donald's assessment, which was typical enough for Iain to do. But
the theory continued to prey upon Rae's mind ever since. 'Twas
the best explanation put forth thus far. Remembering the re-
countings of the brutal tortures inflicted on Graham, Atholl,
and their followers—some administered by Queen Joan her-

self—Rae sincerely hoped none of his own clan had abetted the murderers after they fled Blackfriars in Perth.

Dunraven came into sight. Long moments later, Rae rode into the courtyard, feeling sweaty and smelling of horses for having spent his day in the saddle. On entering the hall, he ordered a hot bath to be set up in his room and drew a cup of heather ale.

Grumblings rippled round over the effort this would take, lugging the tub and water upstairs. Beitris complained 'twas late to ask such a thing.

The pressures of the day and the uncertainty of the future suddenly slammed into Rae full force. After tonight, the reivers would remain, but his Julia would not. He'd not make love to her on this, most likely their last night, smelling of horse and leather!

"I am still laird, am I no'?" he snapped, sending the others scurrying about. Rae downed the cup of ale and headed for the stairs. He arrived at the same time as the great oaken tub. In minutes, it steamed with hot water.

Bolting the door and stripping away his clothes, he sank into the tub. Ach, but the heat was heavenly. Closing his eyes, he shed his concerns and relished the moment. Reaching for the small crock of his aunt's soft heather soap, he began scrubbing himself.

He'd need soothe Beitris's ruffled feathers, but, for now, all he wanted to do was soak his aching muscles and make himself pleasing for Julia.

As Rae lathered his hair, he envisioned Julia behind his closed lids. Feeling for the small pitcher beside the tub, he grasped it then scooped up the water to rinse away the soap. At last, he rested, sinking further down in the heated water, his arms braced atop the tub's rim.

Soon, the familiar weightiness charged the air, thickening it. His pulse began to pound solidly in anticipation. Pulling open his eyes, he found Julia standing before him, returned across Time.

His mouth went dry at the sight of her, a vision of gold, her pale hair tumbling past her shoulders, reaching near to her waist. She wore a thin, flowing gown, gilded by firelight—nay, no gown, but a robe woven of a soft, clinging material from her time. A single ribbon secured it at her waist, the open neckline revealing the creamy flesh and silken swells of her breasts.

Julia sent him a smile, a tremulous smile he thought. Could she yet be shy or nervous before him at the prospect of their making love? But then her gaze turned toward the unshuttered window where the moon climbed the sky. Moisture glazed her eyes and he well understood her distress. 'Twas a blade in his own heart that Time would soon close its door between them.

But tonight would be theirs, each and every moment Time would yield, and he'd love her completely—long and well.

Rae rose, water sluicing off of him as he stepped from the tub and stood naked and unabashed before his love. He pleasured in how her eyes traveled over him, downward and back again, taking in the full sight of him. She moistened her lips then smiled as she lifted her bewitching green gaze to his. Ach, but she was a woman ready for lovin'—his lovin'. The sweetness of that thought swelled through him, quickening the beat of his heart.

He caught up the linen folded beside the tub, and began toweling himself as he crossed the short distance between them. Smiling, but still silent, Julia drew the cloth from his hand and began blotting his chest and throat and shoulders. She then followed the same path with her mouth, spreading warm kisses over his flesh, sometimes diverting to catch the droplets of water with the tip of her tongue and to trace a pattern over his skin.

"Teach me, Rae," she whispered against him, then rose on tiptoe to press a kiss beneath his jaw and outline it with her tongue. Her full, round breasts pressed against him as she did, yielding enticingly against the hardness of his chest.

"Teach ye, love?" Rae touched her bright hair, skimming his palms downward over its golden fall.

Julia caught his hands in hers and brought them to the slender ribbon at her waist.

"Teach me what I must do to pleasure you, as you do me."
She began strewing more kisses over his chest and to move
lower to his ribs.

"Ye are all pleasure, *mo càran,* the sight and feel and joy of
ye." He drew her back up to place a kiss between the valley of
her breasts.

"Truly, Rae, I want us both to remember this night always. I
want to give you the greatest joy, and I want to memorize every
inch of you to hold forever in my heart."

Rae read the love and sincerity in her eyes, and the undisguised passion there, too.

"Aye, we shall share the greatest joy together and leave no
secrets between us this night," he vowed softly.

Drawing his gaze to where his hands rested at her waist, he
tugged the ribbon free and slid the wisp of material from her
breasts and arms. His heart caught at the perfection of her
naked beauty. As he continued to drink in the sight of her, the
robe pooled at their feet then disappeared.

Lovingly, Rae smoothed his hands over her breasts, feeling
their roundness and weight, brushing his thumbs over their
peaks. He cherished Julia then, taking her in his mouth, circling, tugging, suckling her nipple. Sweet, so sweet.

Her hands strayed over his back and she arched toward him,
offering herself to him completely. He would deny neither of
them. Inhaling the floral scent that was hers alone, he trailed
kisses to her other breast and relished it with equal attention
and fervor. She moaned, pressing closer against him and cupping the back of his head.

Julia trembled slightly then, but from passion or the room's
slight chill, he could not be sure. Lifting her in his arms, Rae
carried her to the fireplace, apart of the tub. Fortunately, he had
had the foresight to lay out a fur on the chest earlier. Catching
it with one hand, he tossed it to the floor before the hearth, then
sank with Julia onto his knees.

Their tongues mated, spared and parried, their desires
mounting as they knelt before the fire. Rae urged her to follow
his lead and they began exploring one another's body, mapping

the contours with their lips, kissing, tasting, seeking one another's pleasure points.

When Rae turned her toward the fire's warmth and cradled
her from behind, she objected, saying she could not reach him
or pleasure him in any way, while his own hands could roam
freely over her breasts and torso and tantalize her most secret
places. He obliged her wish to pleasure him and slipped into her
from behind, surprising her wholly. But in the next instant, he
gritted his teeth, so hot and tight was she. Julia offered no further protest but only moans of delight as he fondled her breasts
and massaged her swelling core.

"You do not play fair, my Highland lord." Her breaths came
short and quick.

"Aye, 'tis true." He kissed the curve of her neck, chuckling,
but did not relent in his seduction. She quivered beneath his
possession and pleaded his name. Moments later he withdrew
and turned her to face him. Lowering her to the fur, he joined
himself to her once more and began to move against her hot
silk.

"Better?" He smiled and, seeing her dark, passion-glazed
eyes, did not wait an answer but savored the delicious, waiting
mounds of her breasts.

Before the warming fire, they continued their loveplay tasting, kissing, exploring. Julia suddenly bolted against him, crying out as she climaxed. Her contracting spasms triggered his
own release, and he strove with her as they rode their passions
to ecstatic heights before plummeting back to earth. For long
moments afterward, they lay panting in each other's arms.

"Rae, I'm sorry." Julia gasped huge breaths. "I couldn't wait
and it's over so soon."

"Dinna fret, love," he said on a ragged breath, smoothing
long strands of hair from her flushed cheeks. "Naught is o'er.
We hae just begun. 'Tis but a wee samplin' o' wha' is tae come,
for I intend tae love ye and treasure ye the whole night
through."

Smiling, Rae rose and drew her to her feet. Giving her a

quick kiss, he caught her up in his arms and started toward the bed. He took no more than two steps when he halted abruptly.

Seeing the look on his face, Julia followed his gaze to the bed where the bedhangings were changing their colors, flashing from red to blue to red to blue. . . . Together, they scanned the room and were stunned to find the furnishings appearing and disappearing from both centuries—the armoire, tables, and chairs from hers, the iron-bound trunk, tub, and stool from his. The oaken doors of both times winked in and out, as did the shutters and glass upon the windows.

"Can you see it all? Can you see into the future?" Julia asked, her voice filled with awe.

"Aye," Rae replied, incredulous. He glanced to her, smiling even wider now. "'Tis a most memorable night tae love ye, I am thinkin'. One ne'er tae be forgot."

Testing the bed's solidity, Rae laid Julia on the bed and stretched out beside her. With their world in flux about them, they renewed their lovemaking, sharing kisses, long and sweet, while their hands wandered the hills and valleys of their lover. Julia did not object as he introduced her to new intimacies, took her to new heights. Beneath his loving tutoring, she grew increasingly bold, surprising him, and delighting him beyond expectation.

How deeply and desperately he loved her. How he wished this night would never end, or that they had ten hundred thousand more.

Allowing no dark thoughts to intrude upon their happiness, he took Julia to the pinnacles of ecstasy again. And again. And again.

As the moon watched from on high, they loved through the night. Passionately, bittersweetly, did they love, leaving no mysteries between them as night gave way to dawn. Consumed and replete with love, they finally lay exhausted among the tousled sheets and fell asleep in one another's arms.

The twitter of birds awakened Julia. Turning on her pillow, she reached for Rae. Her hand touched the cool pillow beside her. Opening her eyes she found him gone.

Chapter 19

"Ah, Love! could thou and I with Fate conspire
To grasp this sorry Scheme of Things entire,
Would not we shatter it to bits—and then
Remould it nearer to the Heart's Desire!"

A tear slid over Julia's cheek, tumbling to the page and staining the book's fine paper. She blotted the spot with her handkerchief, then rested back against the fragment of wall where
she sat in the shadow of the keep.

Julia drew her gaze over the low tangle of growth and outbursts
of pink primroses, carpeting the ground where the fifteenth-
century hall once stood. She could imagine the castlefolk moving
there still. Imagine Rae . . .

She drew a deep breath, the chill air searing her lungs. Returning her attention to the Rubaiyat, she paged to the next
verse.

"Ah, Moon of my Delight who know'st no wane,
The Moon of Heav'n is rising once again:
How oft hereafter rising shall she look
Through this same Garden after me—in vain!"

Julia closed the book and held it against her heart. Bowing
her head, she sobbed brokenly.

At length, her tears spent for a time, Julia roamed Dunraven's grounds, then walked along the burn where Rae once
had held her in his arms and kissed her with tender passion.

Slowly, painfully, Julia made her way back to the castle and
climbed the many steps to her chamber. She lingered awhile in

the Long Gallery, studying the portraits in vain, seeking some resemblance there to Rae that she already knew did not exist.

"Cousin! I've found you at last!"

Recognizing Emmaline's voice, Julia turned to find her rushing forward from the far end of the gallery, all decorum tossed aside. Emmaline hugged Julia swiftly then grasped Julia's hands in her own.

"Please, cousin. I must speak with you."

"Yes, of course we can speak . . ."

Emmaline drew Julia down with her on a small settee that lined the gallery wall.

"I need your advice, cousin. Advice about love."

"Love? I don't know how I might advise . . ."

"You know better than anyone what it means to grow up in a house filled with love. Your parents owned a great love, and sacrificed all for it. Oh, Julia, I find myself in a like situation to your mother's."

"Emmaline, what are you saying?"

"I am in love, Julia. In love with a man of whom my parents will never approve. He holds no rank or station of import, no properties. His title is not even hereditary as was your father's. Oh, but, Julia, he is a good man, a fine, decent man, and I love him with all my heart as he does me."

Emmaline released Julia's hands and sat back, breathless by her outpouring. Julia found herself breathless as well, still trying to absorb her cousin's revelations.

"My parents will think me mad, no doubt. If they knew of him, they'd lock me away, I'm sure of it." Emmaline leaned forward again, her look sober yet animated. "But, cousin, I am not blind. I can see the way of the aristocracy and their marriages, hollow, loveless matches that lead inevitably to adulterous liaisons for both husbands and wives. Julia, I am no fool. I know my mother stayed behind in England to be with her lover, and that my father has his mistresses, several of them. And look at Aunt Sybil and Rokeby. But that is not what I wish for my life. I'd rather live simply with a man I love and with one who loves me as well."

Emmaline grasped Julia's hands once more. "What should I do, cousin? I know what my heart tells me, but I also know love has a habit of sweeping all sense aside. I do love him so. I value him above all the titles and wealth the world can hold. What shall I do?'

As Julia looked into her cousin's eyes, she saw the immensity of that love mirrored there, so like her own for Rae. Suddenly, all the anguish of Julia's own loss welled up and engulfed her heart. She could scarce find her voice to speak.

"Oh, Emmaline, if you are fortunate enough in this life to find love—*true* love—then seize it with both hands and never, ever let it go."

Tears of joy sprang to Emmaline's eyes and she threw her arms about Julia, squeezing her tightly. "Thank you, dearest cousin. Thank you. I must go now. He is waiting, and we must be discreet."

Julia watched Emmaline as she rustled down the gallery and disappeared from sight.

She sat for a moment, amazed. Remembering back to their journey to Dunraven, she recalled Emmaline's comments on the train. Julia suspected then her cousin being enamored of someone. But Emmaline had seemingly conquered many hearts among the Braxton circle and, though she could usually be found surrounded by any number of men, she never showed favoritism to any one of them in particular.

Discreet. Goodness. Emmaline was certainly that. Even now, Julia found herself wondering who had captured her cousin's heart.

Feeling her own loss, Julia rose from the settee and headed toward the chamber, heavy of heart. A dull ache began to pulse at the sides of her head. Pushing open the door, she paused on the portal as the throbbing increased and spread over her crown.

Massaging her temples, Julia crossed the room past the armoire and table, directing her steps in a straight line for the great Flemish bed. There, she cast herself upon the mattress and rested a moment. Gratefully, the pain subsided as quickly as it had arrived. Rolling onto her back, she looked up to the canopy stretched overhead. Blue. How she longed for it to transform to red.

A sound caught her ear, that of a deep voice clearing itself. Shoving upward, Julia glanced toward the fireplace. There, in one of the green velvet chairs, sat Rae Mackinnon, smiling in earnest.

Chapter 20

Languid from their lovemaking, Julia pressed a kiss to Rae's bare chest, then to his throat and jaw, moving upward until she lay partially atop him. Smiling, she traced her fingers over his lips.

"Sae ye missed me did ye, lass?" Rae levered open one eye and gazed at Julia.

"Desperately." She spread several kisses across his cheek. "Even now I fear . . ."

"Sh-h-h now. Ye mustna be thinkin' troublin' thoughts when my lovin' is still warm upon ye." He hiked his brow. "Ye are still warm are ye no'? Or d'ye need warmin' all o'er again?"

He drew her fully atop him, staying the words poised on her lips with a lavish kiss. When their mouths parted, they both seized upon the air for breath.

Julia brushed her fingertips through his dark hair. "I shall always need your loving, Rae."

"As I you." He placed a kiss between her beasts then, shifting her upward, exploring the taut bud of her nipple with his tongue.

"Of course, I was thinking . . ."

"Ye do too much thinkin', I am thinkin'." He savored her, possessing her nipple with his mouth, suckling gently and rousing her desire.

Her fingers pressed into his shoulders as her whole being surged beneath his fresh seduction.

"D-did you wish to see some new parts . . . of the castle that is? I could take you to meet Lord Muir and . . ."

"And?" His tongue worked magic on her other breast, circling, laving, tantalizing the beaded tip with his tongue, lips, and teeth.

"A-and . . . to meet . . . his friends."

Drawing her thighs apart to straddle him, he guided her hips back. Julia's eyes widened as he sheathed himself in her, a deliciously full sensation in this unfamiliar position. Her heat melted around him as he guided her once more, rocking her hips against him, moving with her, the contact exquisite, silk on silk.

"We'll see them all in guid time, *mo càran*. For now Time is ours, and we, one another's."

She caught his rhythm, matched it with her own, their bodies moving in perfect harmony. Julia relished the fiery sensations splintering through her. Rae eased her forward, maintaining their rhythm as he claimed her breasts and tormented her anew. As their passions built, they melded as one in a timeless union of body, heart, and soul.

A half an hour later, sated, they still lay entwined.

Julia smiled contentedly as she scanned the canopy overhead. Blue. How miraculous that Rae should be lying beside her with the bed hangings glowing blue. Another thought struck her, and her smile grew.

"Ach, I see yer thinkin' again." Rae lifted himself on his elbow and kissed a lock of her hair. " 'Tis no' a guid sign by yer look, for me a' least."

"Actually, it isn't." She turned her smile to him, unable to suppress the impish twinkle she felt dancing in her eyes. "I believe you'll find your clothes have disappeared."

"Disappeared?" Rae rolled from her and rose to search the floor where they had both hastily disrobed and dropped their clothes.

Julia sat up in bed. "Yes, as mine did and anything else I brought between times. They all vanished back to this century whenever I laid them down or they lost contact with me."

"I do remember yer using yer gown as a pillow on several occasions." Rae stood grinning, his shirt in hand. "Sorry tae disappoint ye, my heart, but my clothes are here, all o' them. My dirk, too. 'Twould seem the time-slip works somewhat differently, commin' forward, in tae yer future."

Surprise stole through Julia. Her smile quickly returned. "At least now you needn't leave the chamber wrapped in a sheet, or less!"

Rae tossed her a look as he pulled on his shirt and began the task of pleating his plaid.

Climbing from the bed, Julia went to the armoire and drew open the doors. She glanced back in time to see him lay his belt on the floor and position his tartan atop it, lengthwise. Stretching out atop it himself, he crossed the unpleated edges of the fabric across his middle and buckled it in place.

Julia shook her head, smiling. "Is that not a cumbersome way to dress?" She pulled on her stockings, combination, camisole, and petticoats, foregoing her corset.

"Isna tha'?" Rae nodded at her layers of undergarments, returning her smile. "The *feileadh mor* is a simple but most serviceable garment as ye might recall."

"Indeed, very serviceable." She smiled, remembering its use and versatility the times they'd lain together in the heather.

Turning back to the armoire, she choose a simple shirtwaist and skirt to wear. When she glanced at Rae, she found him fully dressed, having secured the surplus material under his belt and over his shoulders. He was just now finishing with the lacing on his brogues.

As Julia slipped into her own garments, Rae began to roam the room, clearly fascinated by all he saw.

"I dinna see the logic in laying costly tapestries on the floors instead o' rushes. 'Tis sore wasteful."

"Those are Persian carpets and they are made to cover the floor. They help keep the heat in the room, besides being beautiful to look upon."

He moved to the huge armoire, studying its dark wood and carvings. Peering inside the open doors, he plucked out something white. Her corset. Julia snatched it away, causing Rae to chuckle. He next gave his attention to the blue-and-white china jars atop the armoire.

"What guid are these for?"

"To look at. I believe they are very expensive."

He grunted, clearly unimpressed, and put them back.

He moved off, peering into the tiny octagonal mirror beside the fireplace.

"People o' the nineteenth century hae a lot o' things tha' are no' verra useful."

"There is glass in the windows. That's much more useful at keeping out the cold than mere shutters."

Rae turned his attention to the windows. Good, Julia thought, hoping that would occupy him a moment while she hunted in the armoire for her shoes.

"And wha' is this for?"

Julia straightened, one shoe in her hand, and saw he held up a hefty key, obviously having found it where she'd left it on the table.

"It's to the door, that door." She pointed across the room to the modern one. "Remember? I locked it so we wouldn't be disturbed."

Julia stuck her head back in the armoire, seeking her matching shoe. "This room doesn't have much privacy, in any time." She smiled.

Hearing metal on metal and a distinctive click, she came out of the wardrobe, grasping the found shoe. The door stood ajar with Rae nowhere in sight.

This is going to be more challenging than keeping up with a child, she thought, hurrying after him.

She found him moments later, in the long gallery, gazing at the triple row of portraits on the wall one by one as he moved slowly down the gallery.

Julia joined him, hopping as she fit her shoe onto her foot, then nearly colliding with him when he halted abruptly. He stared at the likeness of one of the sixteenth-century lairds. A flicker of recognition crossed his eyes, or so she believed. Just then, Tom appeared at the end of the gallery near her room, holding a blackened bucket.

"Afternoon, miss." He nodded respectfully to Julia, and then, if she were not imagining it, he looked to where Rae stood and then to the portraits on the wall. His gaze returned to Julia.

"I'll be cleaning the ashes from your fireplace now, if that is agreeable, miss."

"Yes. Yes, of course, Tom."

When Julia turned back to Rae, she found he'd moved further down the hall, still examining the paintings.

"That was Cook's son, Tom." She came to his side. "He's a young man of few words."

"Tom, aye."

"Rae, you could see him, could you not?"

"Aye. He's a muckle lad, though somewha' like a broomstick, spare as a pole wi' hair the color o' oats."

" 'Muckle'?"

"Large."

"Yes, large, and like a broomstick. That's Tom."

Julia read some perplexity congesting Rae's eye, unrelated to Cook's son, but something inside cautioned her not to press him.

"Perhaps, you would care to meet your descendant, Lord Muir? I suspect he and his colleagues are above in the tower library. They rarely leave it."

Rae nodded, still given to his thoughts as he accompanied her to the carved staircase just outside the gallery.

"I suppose 'meet' is not an accurate word," Julia offered conversationally as they climbed the stairs, Rae remaining silent. "It's a pity Lord Muir will be unable to see you. Perhaps, I should allow him the use of my ring so he truly can meet you at least once. It would mean so much to him, I know."

"Tha' would be verra gracious of ye," Rae spoke at last. " 'Twould mean much tae me as well."

Reaching the upper floor, they traveled the gallery and converged on the library door. They found it standing ajar, the men inside deep in their discussions.

As Julia attuned her ear to their conversation, she realized with a start they were debating, of all things, her corset!—the corset Rae had taken with him into the past, and which she'd subsequently found during a time-slip. Julia instantly regretting having disclosed how, when she'd become trapped in the stairwell, she'd found the bones and disintegrated remains of her corset, the garment having not survived the next shift through time.

The technicalities obviously bothered these men of science since, they propounded, if the corset had been touching her in the past, it should have traveled forward in time without corruption. Mr. Thornsbury currently addressed the others, theorizing the corset did not contact Julia directly but only peripherally, touching perhaps only the hem of her skirt. Thus it advanced through the years with her but without the full pretection of her stone.

Julia deemed that explanation as plausible as any, and took advantage of the men's collective pause as they considered Mr. Thornsbury's premise.

"A-hem." She cleared her throat loudly from where she stood on the threshold.

The men's gazes drew to Julia as she stepped inside the library chamber. Rae followed and came to her side.

To her astonishment, the men remained silent, their eyes shifting to the space beside her, or rather to Rae. Warmth rippled through her when still they did not speak. If she was not losing her mind, they appeared to be staring with great curiosity at Rae's ancient-style kilt, or rather his *feileadh mor,* his "great wrap."

They looked to Julia as one, but she could not fathom their awkward hesitation.

Lord Muir came forward at last. "Forgive me. You'll believe we are without a dram of hospitality. Angus didn't tell me we had another guest. Welcome to Dunraven, sir. Are you from hereabouts?" His gaze brushed over Rae's voluminous wrap. "Or further west, perhaps? Sunderland, or the Isles?"

Rae had been eyeing Lord Muir with equal curiosity, in particular his red, modern-style kilt and long snowy beard. But when Lord Muir addressed him, acknowledging his presence, a look of astonishment washed over Rae's face.

"I hail from hereabouts, though the Mackinnons are a Hebridean clan," he replied in quiet, rich tones.

"Mackinnon?" Lord Muir sent Julia a questioning look. "My dear, are you going to introduce our guest?"

Julia could scarce find her tongue.

"Oh dear." She took a deep breath. "I think you should sit down. *All* you gentlemen should sit down."

Seeing her tremble, Rae braced her elbow with a hand. She found him smiling fully, enjoying this new twist of fate.

Lord Muir eased himself into a nearby chair, canting his head. "Is something wrong, Julia?"

"No, not wrong. Just . . . extraordinary. Gentlemen, I am honored to present to you . . . oh dear . . ."

She took a deep swallow then tried to bring forth the words she must speak. Rae's hand slipped around her waist and he gave her a small, reassuring squeeze, then spoke for her.

"I am Rae Mackinnon, Third Laird o' Dunraven Castle. I bring you my greetings from the year o' our Lord, fourteen hundred and thirty-seven."

The men appeared to have gone to stone, not one eyelash did they move. Julia could not be sure if they'd ceased to breathe altogether. She found difficulty with that task herself. It was as if the air had just been sucked out of the room.

Slowly, Lord Muir rose, shaken with emotion. He came to stand before Rae, meeting Rae's intense blue gaze with his own of pale blue. Lord Muir then extended a shaky hand, his eyes rimmed with tears.

"Welcome, sir. Welcome to Dunraven in our day, eighteen hundred and ninety-three. I am James Edwin Dunnington III, your descendant and twenty-seventh laird of Dunraven. I have sought for two decades to find you again." His beard parted with a delighted smile. "You have grown since last I saw you as a boy. I imagine I have aged considerably in your eyes as well. But please come in. Come in."

The men all rose from their places now and welcomed Rae with utter awe and fascination. Introductions were quickly made. Julia saw it required enormous strength of will on their parts to withdraw intermittently to check their instruments and record the information there.

"We must celebrate this moment properly," Lord Muir proclaimed and started toward the bookshelves lining the back wall. "A drop of Glenlevit, perhaps?" He began to remove several books on the right end of the shelf.

"Or Dimple Haig," Sir Henry suggested.

"Yes, excellent." Lord Muir replaced the books and moved further down the row to the left and one shelf up. "Here we are, behind the tomes on Robert the Bruce." He withdrew two thick volumes and produced a triangular-shaped bottle filled with amber liquid. "I trust the Bruce to keep my Dimple safe from Mrs. McGinty." He winked as he set the bottle on the large table occupying the center of the vaulted chamber. "She has an irksome habit of hiding it from me."

Retrieving several small glasses from a file cabinet, he set them out and filled them to the rim. Julia politely declined as Lord Muir offered her some of the potent liquid. The men then raised their glasses in unison, toasting the moment, and Rae Mackinnon, and downed their portions in a single swallow.

" 'Dimple' d'ye call it?" Rae peered at his empty glass with a look of approval.

"Dimple Haig. It is a deluxe brand of whisky."

"*Whisky*." Rae considered the word. " 'Tis no' so strong as *usige beatha* but verra, verra smooth, is it no'?"

"Dimple is one of the more sophisticated blends. It has a mellow sweetness that is offset by a smoky, peaty flavor."

"There are others then?"

"A multitude, each with their own distinguishing characteristics. You must sample more of them while you are here in our time."

Just when Julia feared the men were going to spend the rest of their time together extolling the merits of Scotland's national drink and its many distilleries, Lord Muir invited them to sit in the large leather chairs surrounding the table.

At the marquis's request, Rae described for them how, while he waited in his bedchamber to see whether time would shift, the scene before him melted away and he next found himself in the future, surrounded by unfamiliar furnishings.

"I could do naught but wait there." He sent a smile to Julia. "The door tae the hall in my own day had disappeared."

Lord Muir sat forward, templing his fingers. His gaze traveled around the table.

"I believe we can presume the time-slips will continue for now, at least until the New Moon when the lunar energies will again be in flux. It would seem the laws that first governed the phenomenon are now working in reverse." His pale eyes drew to Rae. "Though, obviously, in new and most welcome ways. Regrettably, there is no predicting what will occur at the next New Moon, whether time will again shift to the past, or cease to shift all together."

Julia's heart sank at that pronouncement. Sensitive to her emotions, Rae reached over and squeezed her hand, a gesture that did not go unnoticed by the others.

"Time holds many mysteries, tae be sure, but also as many possibilities, I am thinkin'."

He gave her hand another squeeze of encouragement, then transferred his attention to the other men in the room.

"The moon has begun tae wane. I assume the time shifts will also shorten each day, in like measure."

"That is true, sir," Mr. Armistead spoke up. "But we will continue to investigate the phenomenon and strive to unravel its secrets before the New Moon. You may place full confidence in us, Laird Mackinnon."

"If ye please, ye may all call me by my God-given name, Rae. I am no' a man o' pretenses, and in truth, I am still unuse tae my new title."

Lord Muir nodded in understanding. "We would very much like to speak with you at greater length, during coming time-slips. Perhaps, you would consider examining the accounts that have come down to us of your ancestors, correcting or adding anything that need be."

Rae dragged on his chin in thought. " 'Tis agreeable on condition."

"Laird, Rae . . ." Mr. Thornsbury sat forward in his chair. "We are unable to divulge any information—Scottish history after your time, for example—which might result in your altering the past, even inadvertently. Your being here even now, witnessing the future, poses risks."

"Ye hae my solemn word, I willna attempt tae change the past in any wise. But wha' I would ask concerns Julia."

A look of visible relief passed around the table.

Turning to Julia, Rae covered her hands with his.

"I wish yer promise tae care for Julia when I can no longer be aboot. She has grown special tae me heart, and 'tis proud I am tae confess it. My own heart will beat easier, if I know she has others tae watch o'er her."

"Then be at peace." Lord Muir smiled kindly. "Julia is already as a daughter to me, and I believe the others fancy themselves her 'adopted' uncles as well. We shall all see to her future and well-being."

The other three rumbled their concurrence.

"Ye hae my deepest thanks." Rae released a breath. "My only other wish is tae see wha' has become o' Dunraven. Julia tells me 'tis much increased these days and my hall stands nae more."

"Easily done." Lord Muir smiled in earnest now.

"There are many guests about the castle," Sir Henry pointed out. "Since Rae is quite visible, perhaps they should be sent away."

"Or formally introduced." All eyes turned to Mr. Armistead. At their looks, his confidence visibly wavered. "We might introduce Rae as another of our colleagues, whose specialty is fifteenth-century Scotland."

"The others know we have been expecting several more of our associates from the Society," Mr. Thornsbury added.

"Rae's sudden appearance wouldn't raise undue suspicion. We could say he arrived during the night."

"Yes, I believe it could work." Lord Muir's eyes brightened as he considered the possibility. "Excepting a few meals, none of us from the Society have mingled with the visitors from Braxton. We'll do just that. With the arrival of another of our 'members,' it would be fitting to hold a small reception." Lord Muir sat back in his chair. "We'll need to hold it in late evening, during a time shift, of course. But, no matter. We men of the Society are considered a tad eccentric, are we not?"

"Is it not risky?" Julia quickly posed. "The others might ask him any manner of question or allude to simple things we take for granted but of which he has yet to learn. He would be unable to even recognize a portrait of the Queen."

Julia's fears ran far deeper than what she could reveal in Rae's presence. What if someone from Braxton should recount the more notable and distressing episodes of Scotland's history, such as the English butchery of the Scots at Culloden or the destruction of the Highland system of clanship. There was no telling how Rae might react.

"One or two of us can accompany Rae at all times, and keep the conversation directed to safe ground—hunting and fishing and Rae's own areas of expertise, the fifteenth-century Highlands. We really must attempt this, my dear. Short of keeping Rae locked in your chamber, we'll not be able to keep him a secret for long."

Julia shot Rae a warning glance lest he proclaim he'd like nothing better than to remain locked with her in her bedchamber.

"You are right of course. Tom has already seen Rae, in the Long Gallery just as we came here."

As Julia and Rae rose to leave, Lord Muir accompanied them to the door.

"I must offer a caution, Rae, the same one I gave Julia. Take extra care when time is in the course of shifting so you are not passing through stone walls or standing in parts of the castle that do not exist in your past. It would make for a long and damaging fall to the ground below. The tower library here is safe, I should think, since it stands in your own time."

Rae grinned. " 'Twill no' be safe if I appear in the women's sleepin' quarters. My aunt, Beitris, will blister my ears for that!"

Lord Muir chuckled. "So I can imagine. I had a peppery aunt of my own. Until tomorrow then, when once again, the lairds of Dunraven will entertain in style."

Chapter 21

Rae dressed with care, donning his best saffron-dyed shirt and a new plaid, woven in the soft hues of the autumn hills—brown and heather.

Bringing the plaid over his shoulder, he pinned it with a large circular brooch, ornamented with intricate silver work and bearing a central stone of rock crystal, surrounded by eight large pearls. 'Twas said to have been a gift of the Bruce to a Mackinnon ancestor, the brooch a twin to the King's own which he later lost in battle at Dalry when an attacker tore the Bruce's cloak from him.

Tonight, given the evening's event, Rae decided to wear the treasured piece, passed down from his forefathers, a symbol of his own lairdship whether the others would recognize its meaning or not.

Rae clenched his jaw, feeling a twinge of guilt. He should have taken watch tonight but sent Lachlan and Ewen in his stead. On the morrow, he would need attend to matters he'd been neglecting, especially those concerning Donald's coming marriage, which would take place in roughly two weeks' time.

But he'd not miss the opportunity of this night to visit Dunraven four centuries hence and the people assembled there to meet him. 'Twas more than mere curiosity that burned in his chest. In truth, he suspected the cur who had attacked Julia would be in attendance. Presumably, Dunraven was as isolated from the outside world in the future as it was in the past. Surely, the man guilty of the offense resided at the castle itself.

Rae's gaze drew to his *claidheamh mor* where it lay across

the bed. He debated whether he should belt it on. Instead, he picked up his long, scabbarded dirk and secured it in the front of his belt. He would need nothing more.

Stepping back beside the hearth where he could be sure no furniture would appear from the future, he waited for time to shift. When at last it did, the room livened instantly with color—blues and creams rising from the carpet, pale green warming the chairs, and rich sapphire illumining the trappings of the great Flemish bed.

Julia sat at the table in the center of the room, her maid, Betty, dressing her hair. Betty's eyes rounded wide at his sudden appearance. With a strangled squeak, she dropped the comb in her hand and fled the room.

Rae shared an amused but sympathetic chuckle with Julia as she looked at him. Her gaze then flowed over him with approval. Ach, but she was a vision herself, her gown of some frothy material all of white with shell pink blossoms cascading down one side of the skirt and her hair swept back and woven with pearls.

As he crossed to her, she rose and filled his arms. He drew a kiss from her sweet lips the nibbled at her ear.

"Mayhap, we should remain here in the chamber tonight."

"Lord Muir would be greatly disappointed," she replied, giving a delicate shudder as his lips moved to the curve of her neck. "B-but there is something I would like to show you before we leave."

Dipping from beneath his advances, Julia caught his hand and led him toward the bed. Rae's lips spread in a smile only to slacken a moment later as he spied books, open and spread over the mattress, hindering any use of it.

"We don't have much time, Rae, but you really should familiarize yourself with a picture of the Queen and a few other things that are common in our day, that is, in eighteen hundred and ninety-three. Ah, here it is," she said, leaning forward and plucking up the largest of the books.

On first sight, Rae's eyes could make little sense of what she called a "picture." He turned his head sideways.

"It's a 'photograph,' " she explained, which helped not at all.

Suddenly, the image congealed and a round, glum-faced woman stared out at him from the page. A snowy caplet topped her equally white hair, and her gown was plain and unimpressive, entirely of black. Her mouth pulled down at the corners as if weighted with iron.

"Och, now there's a sour dook."

"Rae, that is Queen Victoria."

"Queen or no', for all her royal privilege, she looks tae be a sore unhappy woman."

Julia nodded with a sigh. "She is. The queen declared her life ended the day her husband, Prince Albert, died. She adored him so. It may be of interest to you that they both loved the Highlands passionately and built Balmoral Castle on the River Dee. The queen is in residence there now as she is every autumn."

Julia's gaze returned to the picture. "Queen Victoria has worn widow's weeds since the Prince Consort's death, thirty-two years ago, and has devoted herself to preserving his memory. Sad, isn't it?"

Rae's gaze brushed over Julia, concern filling him as he reflected on these last days and their own fears of being permanently separated.

"Ye must promise, ye'll no' be mournin' me like tha' should Time close its door tae us for guid. I'll no hae ye wearin' naught but black the rest o' yer days or yer bonnie face sourin' like yer queen's."

Julia did not respond but directed his attention to another photograph which, again, made little sense to his eyes. When his vision adjusted, he realized he was looking upon a likeness of a rather grand castle.

"This is Dunraven as it stands today with its many additions. Tomorrow, we should walk the grounds so you can see it in daylight."

Rae found himself speechless, for Dunraven had not only survived the centuries but grown to princely proportions. It did his heart good to know that.

Julia next showed him something called a "magazine" which

contained many drawings of ladies whom Julia assured were fashionably gowned, elaborate carriages, and such things as rod-shaped writing instruments which ended in gold beaks. Och, such waste and extravagance when a quill could easily be had for the plucking just outside in the courtyard.

A firm knock sounded at the door and Julia opened it to the smiling face of the Twenty-seventh Laird of Dunraven.

"Are you ready to go down and meet the others?" his distant relative asked, eyes sparkling.

"Tha' I am, James Edwin. Tha' I am."

Julia accompanied the men along the corridors, at times preceding them, at others, following as Rae stopped continually to inspect whatever caught his interest. Nothing engrossed him so completely as a display of sixteenth- and seventeenth-century rapiers.

"Och, be these wha' ye call swords in yer day?" he snorted as he regarded the slender blades with their fanciful hilts, shaped into cups, shells, swirls, and loops.

"They may not look like much compared to the hefty claymores and broadswords of your own time, but they'll slice a man to ribbons," Lord Muir assured.

At Rae's dubious look, Lord Muir ushered him along, expounding on the merits of rapiers, which were meant for thrusting not slashing.

"Och, 'tis hard tae imagine such a feeble bit o' steel could do a body harm," Rae rumbled as they descended a richly carved staircase. He arched a brow. "Ye do still use steel for your blades, d'ye no', James Edwin?"

Moving into the newest sections of the castle, Rae became so fascinated by what he saw, Julia and Lord Muir had to encourage him to keep moving. He wished to stop and scrutinize everything from the lighting fixtures and furnishings to the enormous mirrors and elaborate plasterwork embellishing the ceilings.

Julia wondered if the men's decision to host a reception was a good one after all. How would Rae be able to cope with a room filled with people from a time far distant from his own, when the very surroundings themselves threatened to overwhelm him? How could he survive the night without drawing suspicion he was a man out of time? And how could they explain it?

"Ah, we are almost there." Lord Muir pointed to a wide doorway at the end of the hall through which they caught a glimpse of gowns and greenery. "I decided to hold the gathering in the conservatory. As you will see, Rae, two of the room's walls are made entirely of glass. We won't have the benefit of being able to gaze out on the mountains and scenery as we would during the day, but the conservatory is located at ground level. Should time slip unexpectedly, you will not find yourself falling some ghastly distance."

As they drew near the door, Julia and the men paused. Lord Muir gave both her and Rae a reassuring nod of his head.

"This will go fine, you will see. And do not be overly concerned the others will discern anything unusual. As a member of the Society, Rae, you are allowed a few eccentricities. Indeed, as far as our guests from Braxton know, we are holding this little affair so near to midnight because it is the only time we could allow for it in our unorthodox schedules. Which is perfectly true, is it not?" Lord Muir's beard parted with a smile. "Are you ready, then? Julia? Rae?"

Rae glanced to Julia and, reaching out, gave her hand a squeeze. Drawing himself to full height, he inhaled a long breath. "As ready as we'll e'er be, James Edwin."

Julia's confidence wavered as they neared the portal. But as her apprehensions began to crest through her, the lairds of Dunraven flanked her and swept her with them across the threshold and into the conservatory.

It seemed to Julia every eye turned as one as they entered, then riveted on Rae. Again she tensed as the room silenced.

To her elegantly dressed and meticulously groomed countrymen, she knew Rae must strike them as a most barbarous-looking man. He towered beside her, his dark hair reaching to his shoulders, his rock-hard physique making the other men in the room appear positively soft by comparison. More, Rae's Highland dress and brogues were alien to the day, their style centuries out of date even in Scotland.

But if Rae appeared slightly dangerous, even untamed, his very bearing and presence was commanding. He exuded a primal masculinity that so bespoke of the very essence of a Highlander. Julia swelled with pride and eased her concern at the astonished looks on the faces before them.

Sir Henry broke from the knot of people where he stood and came forward to greet them. The other men of the Society remained where they stood, trying to appear calm and unaffected, though Julia could read the excitement in their faces.

As she and the men proceeded deeper into the room, Lord Muir initiated the introductions, presenting Rae as a new arrival and an expert in early Highland history. He quickly explained Rae's appearance, stating Rae had worn his authentic, fifteenth-century style garments wholly for their enjoyment tonight. This seemed to both please and visibly relieve many. Gratefully, no one questioned the matter of Rae's overlong hair.

To Rae's credit, and again to Julia's own relief, he swept a single glance over the conservatory, taking in the details without lingering on any one overly long. He then gave his attention back to the discussion at hand.

There was certainly much to enthrall a man of his century, Julia thought. The very concept of indoor rooms dedicated to plants was unknown in his world, let alone the bounteous use of glass, replacing entire walls. Being night, the low-sashed windows had become reflective, functioning as gigantic mirrors.

Enhancing the glass's reflective quality, chandeliers illuminated the room's interior, not with candles, but with lamps of opalescent glass that burned with an odorless fluid. She was amazed Rae hadn't asked for one to be lowered so he might inspect it. But then the night had just begun.

Julia floated a glance over those gathered in the conservatory. Relievedly, Lord Eaton was not in evidence. Nor did she spy Lilith. Emmaline stood near the side table and punch bowl, surrounded by a number of men vying to replenish her cup. Her cousin positively glowed and chatted gaily, but she gave not the slightest hint of attachment to any one of her admirers.

Slowly, Julia, Rae, and Lord Muir made their way across the conservatory, the other guests steadily collecting about them. Julia found herself edged more and more to one side as the group swelled until, finally, she stood on the perimeter of the circle.

Lady Charles and Lord Withrington, she noted, seemed particularly eager to speak with Rae. Rokeby, decked out like a peacock in his dress tartan with a jacket of velvet, lace jabot, and shaggy fur sporran, eyed Rae warily.

Meanwhile, the Reynolds twins, Ava and Ada, were all atwitter, whispering between themselves and appearing as if they might faint away any second. Lady Reynolds kept to a distance, standing amid a group of potted ferns, her eyes bolted on Rae. She fanned herself rapidly as she trapped Lady Bigsby in conversation. The other woman likewise could hardly keep from staring at the imposing Scotsman.

Still firmly blocked out of the group, Julia drifted toward the linen-draped side table, laden with the gleaming punch bowl and an abundant offering of savories and treats provided by Cook's talented hands.

To the right of the table, a door opened onto an octagonal drawing room. From there, Angus bustled back and forth. She guessed it to be a serving area. To the left, French doors stood open to the outdoors and the darkened castle grounds.

Regrettably, by the time Julia approached the table, Emmaline had already moved off with her, following to join the crowd surrounding Rae. With a small sigh, Julia gave her attention to the food, having been unable to eat a single bite earlier and now suddenly ravenous. She surveyed platters of cold venison and woodcock, potted beef, oatcakes, crowdie olives, kipper pâte, and strips of smoked salmon with sides of cocktail sauce and lemon wedges. None of it appealed.

She moved further along the table to eye a deep, layered trifle in a footed glass bowl, plates of buttery shortbread wedges, and a rich Dundee cake, heavy with fruit and decorated with almonds. How did one decide, she wondered, reaching for a small crystal plate?

"I shall swoon, I know I shall. He is *so-o-o* handsome," Ada oozed as she and her sister converged on the table.

"He's like a Byron of a bygone age, much more rugged of course . . ."

"Raw, virile . . ." Ada giggled, snatching up a thick piece of shortbread.

Ava whirled on Julia and pressed close, practically treading upon her toes. "You work with the marquis's friends. Do you know Mr. Mackinnon well, Julia?"

"Do tell," Ada prodded anxiously, crowding her against the table.

How amazing these girls deigned to speak to her, Julia thought, she now being so "infamous" a woman, thanks to the lies Roger Dunnington had spread about the castle. His rumors had been easily forgotten in the face of her knowledge of the enrapturing Scotsman.

"Please, Julia, don't torture us. He's like a dream, stepped out of a legend." Ada sighed heavily, then shoved a chunk of Dundee cake past her lips and swiped the crumbs from her chin.

Julia lifted her gaze to Rae's reflection in the mirrorlike windows. He loomed head and shoulders above those massed around him. Unexpectedly, he looked up and met her eyes, flashing her a heart-melting smile.

"Oh he is that, most truly, a dream—straight out of the past."

Rae accepted one of the costly silver drinking cups proffered by James Edwin's butler, Angus.

Thankfully, James Edwin and the men of the Society had deftly assisted him through the trial of questions. Those concerning his own time, especially of the ill-fated James, he addressed with ease. But, more than history and long dead kings, the people seemed far more curious of his garments and ability to speak fifteenth-century Gaelic.

Rae looked down to the shiny silver cup in his hand, impressed, but next grimaced after taking a sip of its pale, pink contents.

"Och! 'Tis a bit weak, is it no', James Edwin?"

"It's a wine punch, meant more for the ladies," his relative confided then turned and whispered something in Angus's ear. The butler headed off, returning moments later with another silver cup.

"Perhaps, this will be more to your liking." Angus smiled and winked. " 'Tis Linkwood."

"Linkwood?"

"Aye, forty-three proof." He smiled and set off again.

Seeing the cup held the familiar dark amber liquid, Rae took a sip. It slipped pleasingly down his throat, leaving a warm trail. Finding it most agreeable, he cast another glance to spy Julia's image in the glass.

Just then the man named Rokeby pressed in.

"I say, the kilts of yore were ungainly were they not?" He dragged a lazy eye over Rae's plaid. "They don't make a very flattering line with which to impress the 'lassies.' "

Rae rubbed his jaw. " 'Tis far more practical than tha' sorry little scrap yer wearin' and far easier tae be rid o' should a mon find himself needin', or wishin', tae be so."

This brought laughs and titters all around. Rokeby, however, was not done.

"But your tartan, man. It's all wrong. The Mackinnons wear a bright red tartan, with green stripes and a dash of white running through it, as his lordship's here."

"Mackinnons wear what pleases them," Rae half growled, tired of the man's overweening ways. He turned to James Edwin. "Dinna be misunderstandin'. Yer kilt is verra smart and the color most handsome. I didna speak my thoughts on the matter afore now so as no' to gi' offense."

James Edwin nodded sagely. "I understand and, Rokeby, you should know the concept of clan tartans is recent to this century. Why you are strutting around in one, I cannot imagine except to show off your shanks, for you've not a drop of Scots blood in you. In the century that Mr. Mackinnon's plaid represents, the clans did not adhere to any one particular pattern."

"How disappointing." Lady Downs slipped closer, pouting prettily, and fingered the cloth of Rae's plaid. "It's a rather romantic notion—that of clan tartans." Her fingers trailed up to the brooch on his shoulder. "What of this? Is it authentic, too?"

Rae straightened before the woman could twine herself about him. "Aye. 'Twas a gift of the Bruce to a Mackinnon ancestor who fought at Bannockburn."

"It belonged to the Bruce?" Someone to the side gave an amazed gasp.

"I know you must value it, Mr. Mackinnon," said a short, pinched-faced woman who had identified herself as Lady Bigsby. "But, oh, wouldn't the Queen love to have the piece for her private collection. You'd be immensely popular with her and gain all sorts of favors. Why, she could store it with the crown jewels in the Tower of London!"

Rae's grip tightened on the cup in his hand, and he narrowed his eyes, his blood pounding thickly in his veins.

"And wha' right would she hae tae it, since the Bruce thrashed Edward's armies and won Scotland's freedom from those who shackled her sae long in chains?"

A shocked silence layered the moment 'til James Edwin cut through it.

"Well said, Mr. Mackinnon! Ah, friends, is it not splendid to have Mr. Mackinnon address us in character as a true Scotsman of the past, with all the verve and passion? It gives one fresh insight into our own history, does it not? Angus, where are you, man?"

He motioned over the butler, then dropped his voice for Angus and Rae's hearing alone.

"Perhaps Mr. Mackinnon would like his cup refreshed. Talisker this time, and bring me a cup, too."

"But, yer lordship, what we have on hand is fifty-eight proof."

"I know, Angus. Be quick about it." James Edwin drew out a snowy handkerchief and mopped his brow.

Rae had not meant to upset his aged kinsman, but he could not abide the woman's insensitive and abhorrent suggestion. Did these highborn *sassenach* in their silks and velvets and jewels know aught of true suffering? Of that borne by an entire nation?

Angus returned with cups of the "Talisker," saying someone named Robert Lewis Stevenson proclaimed it to be "The King o' drinks." It was definitely full-bodied, Rae quickly discovered—peaty in flavor with fruity overtones. Ach, but Dugal would sell his soul for a taste of this.

Rae sought Julia in the glass and found her gazing at him. They shared a smile. Ach, but he was a lucky man to own her love, even if 'twas not forever. But what was forever in this world?

Something drew Julia's attention and her gaze shifted. The smile on her lips died, and she visibly recoiled as if a snake had just slithered in from the garden.

Rae looked to where she stood across the room and followed the line of her gaze to a set of doors in the glass wall. There a man and woman paused upon entering from the outside. The woman held herself with a superior air, ignoring Julia as she moved inside to join several others. The man followed, his eyes sliding briefly to Julia. He leveled a sneering look at her, his smile matching his oiled hair.

Rae sharpened his gaze on the man. Then on his lower lip. It bore a wound, long and recently wrought.

Anger, white hot, flashed through Rae. The voices dimmed around him as he cut through the crowd and stalked toward his prey.

Julia started to move from the table before Lord Eaton and Lilith could intercept her, but failed to extricate herself from Ava and Ada who continued to gibber and fantasize over Rae.

"Well, I see Uncle's little party is quite the success," Lord Eaton commented drolly as he stepped to the punch bowl and poured a cup of wine punch.

As he handed it to Lilith, her mouth curled, her eyes narrowing to catlike slits and shifting to Julia.

"Pity Mr. Dilcox couldn't attend. He carried quite a torch for you, dear cousin. He would have made you a good match. But, then, he abandoned Dunraven so abruptly." Smugly, Lilith sipped her punch.

"Dill-cock? Is that a rooster?" Rae's deep voice sounded behind Julia.

She glanced to the reflection in the window and saw that Rae towered behind her. Oh Lord, this was not good, not good at all. Looking back, she saw Lord Eaton had paled a shade or two, and Lilith's jaw sagged most unbecomingly. Rae continued, seemingly unaware of their distress.

"Och, Julia, I canna see ye bound tae a hen yard with a plucky little Dill-cock chasin' after ye, no' when ye might soar wi' eagles. Scotland boasts the verra finest and most rare. They are golden, if ye remember."

Julia did remember—the golden eagle that had soared above them at the Falls of Glendar, the day they pledged their love to one another. As Rae stepped to stand beside her, she hoped most sincerely he would keep his sense of humor.

"Pray tell, who are you?" Lord Eaton scanned Rae's full length, taking in his outdated garments and hair. "Or, rather, *what* are you? Have we met?"

Rokeby chose that moment to join them and spoke at Lord Eaton's ear before turning to the table's fare. With a self-satisfied look, Rokeby popped an olive in his mouth and crossed his arms over his chest, waiting for the entertainment to continue.

"So, you are one of the distinguished 'Society' members." Lord Eaton continued to regard Rae as though he were some oddity, and as if not quite believing his claim. "Unusual group of men, you fellows—brilliant to the extreme, but, might I say, a trifle eccentric? But here you've gone to great lengths to play the part of a fifteenth-century Highlander."

"I dinna play parts," Rae retorted, his tone grown cold and edged with warning.

Roger did not take the hint. "No, of course not. You don't

look the sort to play games. Rokeby says your garb is authentic to the period. Not terribly impressive, is it?" He chuckled
and looked to those gathering about them, then back again.
"But, where is your claymore? Surely, you can't be a *real*
Highlander without a claymore at your hip."

"I am real, I promise ye, more than ye'd ever wish. And I
dinna wear m' *claidheamh mor* as I didna think tae hae need o'
it." His voice dropped low, deadly. "Mayhaps, I was mistaken."

"Ho! A ready wit, everyone, keen as his blade, quick for a
parry and thrust." Eaton laughed nervously and took several
steps back.

Rae matched him step for step, advancing forward.

"A Scotsman's sword doesna waste time tae 'parry' or
'thrust,' but simply slashes to its mark and cuts it straight
down."

As Rae backed Lord Eaton against the table, Eaton drew a
finger around his collar, exposing four neat rows of nail marks
there. He took a swallow in the face of Rae's menace. Julia
hoped he realized at last Rae's utter seriousness and that he
would deign to keep his tongue in his mouth.

"You know, I don't recall your arriving at Dunraven." Lord
Eaton tempered his tone. "Nor did anyone advise me of it.
What did you say your name was?"

"Mackinnon. Rae Mackinnon. Remember it."

Blessedly, Lord Muir joined them as did his colleagues of the
Society. Julia prayed they would intervene and promptly.

Lord Muir cleared his throat. "My associate arrived during
the night, Roger. I'm surprised you didn't meet him then. That
was you tiptoeing past my door early this morn was it not?"

"Roger?" Lilith cocked a hand to her hip, her look darkening.

Lord Muir turned to Rae. "Allow me to introduce you to my
nephew, Roger Dunnington."

Rae scowled, appearing not at all happy to learn of Roger's
identity as that of a blood relative to Lord Muir.

"You are a Mackinnon, you say? Surely, not from these
parts." Lord Eaton considered Rae with renewed interest.

"Aye, I grew up in these verra mountains."

"How extraordinary. I didn't know there were any Mackinnons left in Glendar. Jove, if you truly are a Mackinnon from round about, then perhaps there is blood between us."

"If no' now, there will be, I promise ye."

"What did I tell you?" Rokeby gave a laugh. "He plays the part of the brusque Highlander to perfection."

"I told ye, I dinna play parts. Especially wi' a *sassenach* wearin' a fresh cut on his lip and a woman's scratches on his neck."

The wail of bagpipes sounded that instant, causing everyone to leap in place—everyone except Rae Mackinnon, who continued to nail Lord Eaton with his fiery gaze.

To Julia's enormous relief, Angus appeared outside the conservatory, visible through the glass and drawing the attention of all as he intoned a rich lament on his pipes.

Sir Henry, Mr. Armistead, Mr. Thornsbury, and Mr. Galbraith surrounded Rae and coaxed him outside onto the grounds. Julia followed with Lord Muir, anxious that Rae and Lord Eaton be kept apart.

As she joined Rae, she saw the stark frustration in his eyes. He wished to right the offense dealt her, she knew, his sense of justice unappeased. But his was a sense of Highland justice and retribution embraced long ago, and that worried her deeply.

She laid a hand on his arm. "Please, Rae, it's over and done. Lord Muir is aware of everything and watches over me when you are not here. Please, let this lie."

Rae sighed heavily, his hands clenching and unclenching. Finally he nodded his head in agreement. "Ofttimes, a man brings his own destiny down upon his head. Roger Dunnington will no' need my help, though I'd lend it tae him in a second."

As the pipes's mournful strains filled the night, Julia looked to the star-studded sky and the glowing moon, nearly but not quite full. Gazing on its frayed and shrinking edge, her heart shrank a little, too. It reminded her all too keenly that, like the moon, her time together with Rae continued to wane with each day, dwindling to a fated and uncertain future.

Chapter 22

Julia snuggled deeper into the downy comfort of the great bed, vaguely aware of Betty tiptoeing into the chamber.

Cracking open an eye, she discovered the morning's pale light softly illumining the room.

"Sorry, miss. Didn't mean to wake you." Betty adjusted the curtains, sealing out the sun's rays. "Rest as long as you please. Most in the castle are still asleep. I doubt they'll be stirring for hours."

"Mmmm. Thank you, Betty, I think I will." Julia hugged the pillow next to her.

She drifted on a thin layer of sleep, then came hazily awake, sensing a presence. Dragging open her eyes, she found Rae gazing down on her.

He smiled his wonderful, heart-catching smile, then held up the key to the chamber door, giving her to know he had locked it. Without a word, he slipped the key under the pillow beside her. Unbelting his plaid and removing his shirt, he joined her, moving atop her as she opened her arms in welcome.

Later—much later—Julia stirred once more, having fallen asleep after a leisurely morning of loving, and making love, with Rae.

She smoothed the vacant pillow beside her, where Rae had rested not long before. The whole of their time together had been one of appearances and disappearances. Still, she could not grow accustomed to it.

He had not hurried their intimacies this morn in any way, but after they had spent their passions in exquisite ecstasy, he told her he must leave. Concerns embroiled Dunraven, he would not say what, and there were also details pertaining to his brother's upcoming marriage to which he must attend. He would "need be away" for several days, perhaps more.

He read her disappointment, gave his love to her once more, then, sometime after she'd fallen asleep beside him, took his leave.

The sting of that disappointment pricked Julia anew. Each day together had grown so precious. She could not bear to lose even one. They both knew he must go, however. Rae was laird of Dunraven with responsibilities to his own people, in his own time.

A quick, light tapping drew Julia's attention to the door. At Betty's voice, Julia realized the door to still be locked. Pulling on her gown, she searched for the key beneath the pillow, then, finding it, quickened across the room.

"Forgive me, miss." Betty huffed for breath as though she'd just run a flight of stairs. "I didn't wish to wake you, but Lord Muir asks that you come to the upper library as soon as possible. Another visitor has arrived. I think he is a 'Society' man."

"Thank you, Betty."

With her maid's assistance, Julia freshened herself, changed into a simple frock, and swept up her hair, all the while thinking it a shame their new guest had missed last night's festivities.

Feeling light and happy of heart, her skin still tingling with the touch of Rae's love, she left the chamber and turned into the Long Gallery. There, Angus waited to escort her above.

This she deemed odd, but he greeted her cordially enough, despite his grave look. But when was it not, she told herself, staving off a sudden unease. Progressing down the gallery, they mounted the stairs to the upper floor and proceeded to the library.

An inordinate silence greeted her. The men rose from their chairs around the table, excepting Lord Muir, who stood gazing out the window. At first, she thought he did not realize she'd entered, then wondered if he was simply lost in the depths of his thoughts.

Angus left her side and went to the marquis. He spoke quietly at his ear. When Lord Muir brought his gaze from the window, he appeared to have aged years overnight, his eyes rimmed with red.

Again, Julia looked to the other men and found their aspects to be equally sober. The heavy silence continued to hang over the room like a pall. Julia felt as though she'd just stepped inside a tomb.

Sir Henry broke the tension, coming forward and ushering her to a place at the table. "Miss Hargrove, allow me to introduce another of our associates, Mr. Alan Galbraith. He arrived a little over an hour ago from Inverness-shire."

Julia's gaze shifted to a man she'd not noticed till now, standing toward the back of the chamber. He was younger than the rest, perhaps in his fifties, bespeckled and of modest stature.

"I am pleased to make your acquaintance, Miss Hargrove." Mr. Galbraith nodded courteously.

"We have kept close correspondence with Mr. Galbraith and apprised him of the unfolding events here at Dunraven," Sir Henry continued. "He delayed joining us when word reached him of new information concerning the Mackinnons of Glendar. He traveled to Moidart to review it personally and comes directly to us from there now. Moidart is the ancient seat of the Clanranald chieftains. But please, my dear, please have a seat."

A knot began to form in Julia's stomach, for still the others looked long of face and solemn as the grave. "Clanranald, you say?"

"Yes. Mr. Galbraith has followed up on the information you provided, that Donald Mackinnon married a young woman named Mairi Macpherson."

Julia glanced to Lord Muir, who was now seating himself across from her with Angus's help. His hands shook as though palsied. She transferred her gaze to Sir Henry.

"But the Clanranalds are actually Clan Donald are they not— the MacDonalds? I believe I read that in one of the clan histories here in this room."

"Yes, my dear, that is true, but there is a Clanranald connection with the Macphersons. I believe Mr. Galbraith can best explain it all."

Mr. Galbraith came forward now and took the empty chair beside Julia. He spoke softly, setting his full attention on her.

"As I believe you know, Miss Hargrove, we've been short on original sources to chronicle the lives of the early lairds of Dunraven. Your information led me to a manuscript we'd overlooked till now, precisely because we hadn't realized the association. You see, the ancient Gaelic name of clan Macpherson is 'MacMhuirich,' after their name-father, Mhuirich. He was also the chief of Clan Chattan in the twelfth century, Clan Chattan being a confederation of many clans. Centuries later, one Niall MacMhuirich was bard to the MacDonald chief of Clanranald. Are you following me thus far?"

"Yes, go on."

"Niall left to us the *Red Book of Clanranalds*. Mainly, it recorded that clan's histories both of Niall's time and before. But he also entered more—other histories, snatches of poetry, genealogies and the like. It is said there existed another *Red Book*, written earlier than the one that has come down to us. It has long disappeared, but a manuscript survives named the *Black Book*, reputedly duplicating, in part, Niall's earliest work.

"Its contents are an odd collection of sundry things, but it includes bits and slices of his own clan's histories, that of the Macphersons, and tales that were passed down to him through the clan. It was in these pages that I found reference to Mairi Macpherson and her husband, and a story then well known surrounding the couple's marriage and the Mackinnons of Glendar."

Mr. Galbraith opened a large, green leather binder that occupied the center of the table. It contained loose sheaves of paper covered with small, neat writing.

"I have copied the relevant passages of the manuscript, both in the Gaelic and the English. It is a partial history of Rae Mackinnon and his brothers, the only record to come down to us." He looked to Julia, gravity weighting his eyes. "I am sorry, Miss Hargrove. The tale it bears is grim."

Julia looked to Lord Muir, who lifted a trembly hand to wipe his eyes. Meanwhile, Mr. Thornsbury came to stand at her side and placed a hand on her shoulder.

"Dear God," she whispered, dread beating upon her heart. "What does it say?"

Mr. Galbraith removed his glasses. "On the night Donald Mackinnon set out with his retinue to wed Mairi and bring her to Glendar . . . I am sorry, Miss Hargrove, there is no easy way to say this. That night, Rae Mackinnon perished in a fire that swept Dunraven's great hall."

Julia shot to her feet. "No, no! This cannot be so. Rae would have gone with Donald. Why would he remain behind while his brother rode to his wedding? Niall MacMhuirich must be mistaken."

Mr. Thornsbury and Sir Henry sought to calm her but she refused to be appeased, refused to accept the hearsay of this faceless bard.

Mr. Armistead and Angus attended Lord Muir, who had covered his eyes with his hands, tears streaming from them. Seeing this, Julia looked to Mr. Galbraith, her own eyes welling.

"Miss Hargrove, the wedding customs in the fifteenth-century Highlands were quite different from ours today. It would not be unusual, as laird, that he should await the arrival of the wedding party, to formally greet the couple to his keep and commence more celebrations there. Perhaps, in Rae Mackinnon's case, he had other reasons as well. Did you not learn that his clan is— or rather, *was*—plagued with reivers at this time?"

Julia wished to deny it, but could not. "Surely if the hall caught fire, Rae would have escaped. There is a single entrance door to the outside, true, but there is also another that leads up into the main keep. The keep still stands. We are standing in it now! Certainly, Rae could escape. He *must have* escaped."

Lord Muir spoke for the first time, his voice wavering. "Julia, there is more."

The knot in Julia's stomach grew to a massive fist, squeezing her very soul. She wished to throw her hands over her ears and shut out what they would say. Instead, she braced herself, scarcely breathing as Mr. Galbraith picked up the grievous story once more.

"Iain Mackinnon, for whatever reason, believed his brother's death to be no accident and laid the blame to Cameron treachery, contending they attacked the laird in his very hall, after Donald and his escort had departed. The Camerons vigorously denied this and claimed their innocence, insisting the remains that had been recovered were of a man too small in stature to have been Rae Mackinnon's."

"Then he didn't die," Julia cried. "Niall was mistaken, as was Iain."

"Nevertheless, Rae Mackinnon was never seen again after that night. Nor was he ever heard of, or from, again."

Julia left the table and began to pace the room, unable to remain still a moment longer. She wouldn't accept this, couldn't accept this.

"Iain Mackinnon led an attack on the Cameron stronghold." Sir Henry picked up the story. "But the Camerons anticipated Iain and armed themselves. When the fighting had finished, more Mackinnons lay dead, including Iain, though not a Cameron fell."

"So Iain died, too," Julia said, barely above a whisper. "And what of Donald?"

"Donald became Fourth Laird of Dunraven and averted a clan war. His brothers' deaths must have been a shattering blow, but curiously, Donald refused to take up arms against the Camerons, as did his new kinsmen by marriage, the Macphersons."

"Clan feuds began over much less in the Highlands," Mr. Galbraith explained further. "So, this is quite strange. The Macphersons had no love for the Camerons and had warred against them in the past, standing with Clan MacIntosh, the Camerons' foremost rival. One would have thought that, with Donald's wedding, Clan Chattan itself would have stood with the Mackinnons.

"How can I explain it? The MacIntosh held the chieftainship of the confederation and were always ready for a fray with the Camerons. The Macphersons remained a leading clan, though they no longer held the chieftainship as in Mhuirich's day. One would think both clans would have stood with Donald and called out the other clans of the confederation. The Mackinnons were too small to take on the Camerons alone, and yet the laird and his brother lay dead by Cameron hands—if Iain had the right of it to begin with.

"Without the support of the Macphersons or anyone else, Donald was probably wise to follow the course he did and avoid war. But bad blood remained between the Mackinnons of Glendar and the Camerons for decades."

Julia took a hard swallow. "Is that all?"

By their looks, she could tell it was not.

"What then?" she demanded of Mr. Galbraith. Was it not enough that he had plunged a knife through her heart with his words? Was he now to rip it out all together? "What?" she cried again, her throat aching and raw, great tears tumbling down her cheeks.

"Niall has provided us with the exact date Donald rode to his wedding—the same night Dunraven's hall burned and Rae Mackinnon lost his life. We've made the appropriate calendar adjustments to our own and . . ."

Julia began to shake her head, not wishing to hear what he would say.

"Julia."

Lord Muir's voice drew her gaze, and she found a fierce pain lancing his pale eyes.

"Julia. We are fast closing upon that date once more, both in our time and Rae's. It coincides with the night of the next New Moon. Then the door between our times will surely close forever. For on that night, Rae . . ." His voice broke, tears flooding his eyes. "Rae Mackinnon will die."

Blackness swept over Julia, swallowing her as she dropped to the floor.

Chapter 23

Something was wrong. He could sense it. More, he could see it in Julia's eyes, hear it in her voice. He could feel the tension coiled in her body even when they made love. As they had just a short while ago.

Rae gazed upon his golden love. She rested beside him in a light sleep. Even now, her cares weighed upon her brows.

What disturbed her so? Their hours together dwindled each day, in proportion to the waning of the moon. Did Julia dread the coming New Moon, fearing the uncertainty of their future and whether the door of time would reverse itself again, or remain closed?

He sensed 'twas something deeper, mayhaps, dire.

Rae scanned the blue canopy stretched above them, and sifted the past days through his mind, those since his return.

Several times, he'd caught Julia staring at him, her look cleaved with pain. If 'twas true one's eyes mirrored one's soul, then the pain he saw in hers stabbed soul-deep.

And what of Lord Muir and the others, whose cheer seemed forced of late? When first he'd met his descendant, James Edwin, he had been struck by his fitness and vigor for a man his age. Yet, Rae had been equally struck—stunned actually—to find on his return, that James Edwin's health had visibly deteriorated. Was this the source of Julia's distress? Of the other men's, as well?

Rae turned his thoughts in his mind. These last days, he spent what time could be spared with the men in the upper chamber, relating tales of his father and of his own youth. He'd also perused a book containing Mackinnon clan history—that occurring *before* his own day—and surprised them all with his ability to read. Gaelic posed no difficulty, though the later-day English offered some challenge.

Still, during those hours in the library, the men oft times found difficulty meeting his eyes directly, something shielded in their eyes. Did their concerns embrace more than James Edwin's sudden decline of health? What then? What had transpired since the night of the grand gathering?

Rae bent his thoughts to Mr. Galbraith. The man had arrived during his own absence. Might he have brought news of some import?

Rae now recalled two occasions when he'd entered the library unannounced. The men quickly assembled the papers they were discussing and closed them in a green leather binder which they hastily shelved. Had their looks contained a measure of guilt? Or something other? Had that been tears glistening in James Edwin's eyes?

What did they know that he did not? What were they keeping from him?

Rae eased from Julia's side and dressed, leaving his brogues so he could pass noiselessly through the castle, barefooted. Retrieving the key from beneath the pillow, he unlocked the door and stole silently from the room.

Faint light streamed through the tall windows of the Long Gallery, a reminder the moon was in its wane. Rae passed beneath the mindful eyes of the Mackinnons vigilant upon the wall and ascended the stairs to the upper gallery.

Proceeding to the library, he discovered the door ajar, golden light spilling into the passage. Rae edged the door open and stood framed by the portal. Lamplight bathed the chamber's interior with an unnatural yellow glow, pooling over the table in the center of the room. There, Mr. Galbraith snored softly, slumped in one of the large leather chairs. Before him lay the green binder, open with its papers lying askew.

Crossing silently to the table, Rae eased himself into a chair beside the slumbering man and slid over the binder and papers.

Putting order to the pages, he scanned their small, neat script, some of the writing being in English, some in Gaelic. Comparing them, he determined both related the same story—a story that contained his name and those of his brothers.

Choosing the pages written in Gaelic, Rae placed them before him, and began to read.

Julia awoke with a start, her dream tormenting her, the great hall ablaze and Rae not to be found.

Her heart still pounded as she glanced to the space beside her and found Rae gone. Dimly, she recalled sensing his leaving. But how could she have fallen asleep yet again? One would think she was the one still traveling across time. Rae seemed unaffected by the time shifts, confessing to no more than occasional headaches. She, on the other hand, had begun to feel enormously fatigued, more so than before, and, at times, dizzy.

Julia spied Rae's brogues on the floor near the wall. Time had not slipped back to its normal state after all. By reflex, she looked under the pillow. Not finding the key, she directed her gaze to the door and spied it in the lock.

Julia threw back the covers and swung her legs out of bed. The thought of Rae roaming the castle sent bolts of fear straight through her. What if he went in search of Lord Eaton to confront him and avenge her honor? Her gaze flew about the chamber. Not surprisingly, his dirk was not in sight.

Pulling on her nightgown and stuffing her arms into her robe, she hurried to the door and hauled it open, heading out into the Long Gallery.

She halted at once. Rae stood halfway down the gallery's length, gazing up at the triple row of Mackinnon portraits.

As she continued toward him, he caught sight of her and turned. Turmoil blackened his eyes, stealing their blue. In that single moment, Julia realized he knew of his coming fate.

As she came to his side, he directed his gaze back to a painting in the center row, the same painting of a sixteenth-century laird in which he'd taken such interest before.

"I suspected the truth when first I saw this portrait and those there and there." He pointed to several others. "See the straight brows that wing upward and the strong, clefted square chin. 'Tis Mairi Macpherson's brows and Mairi Macpherson's chin. I saw the likeness again in the painting of James Edwin's grandmother and the children at her skirts. I suspect he himself possesses the same chin beneath his beard."

Rae turned to Julia. "I know ye wished tae spare me, but yer heart is in yer eyes. The others, too. They couldna hide the secret they held inside. I hae read the words for myself just now, twice over, in Gaelic and English." He expelled a heavy breath. "These paintings bear out Niall MacMhuirich's words. Donald, Fourth Laird o' Dunraven—o' whom ye spoke, and whose deeds are renowned and many—he is no' my son. 'Tis my brother, he is. And these faces here are his descendants—his and his Mairi's. 'Tis she they favor in their looks sae strongly."

"Oh, Rae . . ."

"We must bear this, *mo càran*." He took her hands in his. "I confess I dinna expect tae find the end o' my days upon me sae soon. Still, we all stand on the edge o' time, I hae said it afore. 'Tis grateful I am for all the days given me, and for ye, *mo càran*."

Julia's heart catapulted to her throat. She freed her hands, her arms going instantly around him. "I can't accept this, I *won't* accept this, nor must you. There has to be a way to avoid this fate or alter it somehow."

"Dinna ye tell me the past mustna be changed?" His lips lifted in a sad smile. "And hae no' I given m' word tae the others tha' I wouldna change it?"

"But you cannot die!" She sobbed against his chest. "I won't let you. Not while there's a breath in me, I won't let you."

"All men die. Few know the hour. 'Tis a bitter cup, tha' I'll grant ye, but it makes each day tha' much more priceless."

Unable to contain her emotions, she wept bitterly, her body shaking violently against him. Lifting her in his arms, he carried her to their chamber and lay with her upon the bed.

Wrapped in each other's arms, they spoke no more until time slipped, stealing Rae away.

Chapter 24

"There must be a way to help him," Julia insisted. "Could we not find a way to bring Rae forward in time, permanently, somehow?"

"But, Miss Hargrove, we must not tamper with the past." Mr. Galbraith leaned forward, removing his spectacles.

"What if we are not 'tampering' with it at all? What if our intervention is part of the past? It is conceivable Rae did not die that night but escaped into the future and *that* is—or was—his true fate. We would not be changing events if we assist Rae, but fulfilling them."

The men seated around the library's expansive table exchanged glances. Despite their brilliant collective intelligence, they obviously had yet to consider what, proverbially, should be as "plain as the noses on their faces." Julia swept aside her amazement and prevailed on them once more.

"Do you not see? Niall's account states that Rae disappeared the night of his supposed death, that the body found afterwards was of a man much shorter in stature, not matching Rae's size."

"That was the Cameron claim," Mr. Thornsbury pointed out.

Julia directed her attention to him. "Even so, no counterclaim is recorded and Donald did not take up arms against the Camerons. Perhaps he held his own doubts. Please consider for a moment that Rae did escape into the future and that the body found was of another clansman who was not so fortunate to flee the fire."

"One would think the Mackinnons could easily account for a missing clansman," Mr. Armistead submitted.

"Rae's murderer, then," Sir Henry suggested. "Or the body might have been that of an accomplice."

"*If* Rae was murdered. We do not know that," Mr. Thornsbury tossed back.

"Yet, Iain Mackinnon felt sure his brother had been attacked—by Camerons." Mr. Galbraith replaced his spectacles. "His persistence in that claim cost him his own life."

Julia smiled inwardly. The men were opening to the possibility Rae had survived that tragic night. And though Lord Muir had yet to utter a word, he listened intently, a spark of light kindling to life in his eyes. She encompassed them all with her gaze.

"Gentlemen, I implore you to examine Niall's record once more. If Rae is meant to come forward in time, and we do nothing to assist him, then we *will* alter history by our neglect, by failing to do what is required of us. We must explore the possibility, at the very least. Rae's life depends on it."

Lord Muir rose, unsteadily at first, and began to pace in thought. It seemed with each step he gained fresh strength, as if the energies which had deserted him until now flowed back, invigorating him anew. When he lifted his gaze, his eyes burned bright with enthusiasm.

"Julia is right. We must not risk changing the past by our own inaction."

At Lord Muir's pronouncement the room dissolved into a rumbling discussion and thorough dissection of the situation.

"Is such a thing possible? Can we anchor Rae Mackinnon in the present and prevent him from being drawn back across time?"

"We must adhere to the details of Niall's narrative. It provides us the date and clues to the timing."

"True. Rae cannot attempt to come forward until after Donald and his retinue depart Dunraven."

"Donald will likely set out with the light of dawn. A fire could break out at any time of day—if its cause is accidental such as a kitchen mishap."

"And if not, the assassins would presumably use the cloak of night to conceal themselves."

"But if Julia is correct"—Lord Muir thumped his fore and middle fingers on the table, drawing everyone's attention— "and if Rae actually did come forward in time during one the time-slips, there will be only two windows of opportunity that day."

"We can pinpoint those closely enough," Sir Henry assured.

"It will be the day, or night, of the New Moon," Lord Muir reminded. "We'll need to secure him solidly in our time before the completion of the lunar phase. Only as the moon wanes is Rae able to enter our time. Once the cycle completes itself at the moment of the 'Dark' or 'New Moon,' the moon will begin to wax once more and his opportunity will be lost."

Julia, feeling a touch of dizziness, took a chair. "Can we not bring Rae forward before disaster befalls him? Must we wait for the fire to break out, or assassins to strike?"

"If we are to follow Niall's account, no," Mr. Thornsbury asserted. "None of the clansmen saw their laird emerge from the fiery hall. If he escaped at all—and I stress 'if'—then he must have done so by way of the tower keep and his bedchamber where the time slip is centered."

"I agree," Mr. Armistead added. "Rae must make the transition forward in time after the hall is already aflame. It will be risky in any case. If someone did make an attempt on Rae's life, they are likely the same miscreant who set the fire in order to cover the deed."

"There is still the matter of the technicalities," Sir Henry observed. "Rae Mackinnon will be able to step into the present during the time-slip, but how do we keep him from slipping back to the fifteenth century?"

Lord Muir cleared his throat. "Well, Julia's corset offers us a clue."

"Pardon me?" Mr. Galbraith's brows shot up and he snatched a quick glance of Julia.

She felt herself flush and wished to find the nearest crack in the floor and melt straight through it.

"Forgive me." Lord Muir glanced across the table to Julia as he resumed his chair. "I don't mean to embarrass you, my dear, but your garment provides valuable evidence as to what we— or rather, Rae—should and should not do."

He redirected his attention to the other men.

"Consider—Rae traveled back in time with the piece, and it remained there uncorrupted until Julia brought it forward to the present, but not fully protected. If the fate of the corset gives us an indication of the workings and risks of traveling through time, then I submit it is of utmost importance Rae remains in contact with the stone—Julia's stone—when he attempts it.

"Following this same vein of thought, it is equally important Rae rids himself of his 'healing stone' which acts as a magnet to the past. This is all theory, of course, but it is my contention, if Rae is to remain in our century, he must remove his stone at the last possible moment and cast it from him as the time portal closes. Again, he will need to maintain contact with the stone in Julia's ring which will hopefully anchor him to the present."

Lord Muir turned his gaze to Julia and she saw that their pale blue had grayed with concern.

"There could be dangers. If Rae agrees to this, he must understand it is of supreme consequence he keep contact with your ring. He should actually touch the stone itself for the best hope of success. If this attempt to bring him into the future is not executed properly, it is possible, like your unfortunate corset, Rae will instantly age four hundred years."

"And so, you must be sure to keep continual contact with the stone in my ring as the portal between times closes."

Rae listened as Julia detailed how he might broach time and avoid his fate—or fulfill it—and remain in the future with her, for good and all.

Ach, now there was the sweetest of thoughts—to not die but to live, with Julia, for the length of their days. But that he should do so four hundred and fifty-six years in the future? He could hardly compass so vast a notion. Nor was he convinced he should. There were considerations to weigh besides his own, in particular those of his brothers and clansmen.

As they strolled along the burn, Rae came to a stop and expelled a long breath, taking Julia's hands in his. Still, she continued to press her cause, reiterating Lord Muir's instructions for a third time.

"The 'healing stone' around your neck must be removed as well and thrown to a far distance so it doesn't draw you back. Rae, are you listening? Do you understand what I've been telling you?"

The anxious, pain-filled look in her eyes speared his heart. He dropped his gaze to their joined hands.

"*Mo càran*, I canna abandon my kinsmen tae save m' own skin. Ever there are people aboot the hall. Mayhaps, 'tis fate's design I deliver them from the fire whether a murderer is aboot or no'."

"Then send your kinsmen away *before* the fire!" Julia threw up her hands. "Send them to pick brambles, or cut peat, or whatever one does in the Highlands."

"Even if 'tis the depths o' night wi' no moon tae light their way?" Rae smiled though, within his chest, emotion and reason waged a fierce battle across the landscape of his heart.

"Only one body was found, Rae. Every fiber of my being tells me it wasn't yours. Please, consider what I've said." Her voice cracked. "*Please*."

Huge tears rolled down her cheeks and Rae felt a sting of guilt for having teased her. He gathered her in his arms and dropped a kiss atop her head.

"I canna make ye promises, *mo càran*. But I will think on all ye hae told me."

She gazed up at him, her fingers gripping the cloth of his plaid and shirt. "Rae, there are only a few days left to us."

"Aye, only a few and much tae do."

His thoughts went to Roger Dunnington. They need come to an understanding, the two of them. Rae would reach beyond the grave if need be, should young Dunnington ever think to harm Julia again.

Rae cast the blackguard from his thoughts. The time-slips dwindled in length with each occurrence. Even now only a few precious moments were left to him and his love. He brushed the tears from Julia's cheeks and won her smile.

Finding words insufficient, Rae caressed her lips with his—gently, reassuring, warm. Deepening the kiss, he gave her his heart until the pull of Time overcame them, drawing his lips from hers.

Rae stood alone beside the burn, robbed of Julia's presence, feeling a great void at his loss.

As he turned toward the keep, he spied his brothers arguing in the near distance, Iain jabbing the air with his hands, Donald toeing up a clod of earth as he endured another of their brother's tirades. Others collected about the two, including the rough lot that ever accompanied Iain these days.

Rae picked up a small rock and skipped it across the surface of the stream, giving himself to his thoughts. One brother was to die, the other to become laird and distinguish himself by his deeds.

He glanced again at his brothers. 'Twas easy to understand why hotheaded Iain rode out on impulse to avenge his death. Yet, why his fixation with the Camerons? And what of Donald? Why would his youngest brother not seek to avenge his and Iain's deaths?

A dark thought stabbed at the very core of Rae's soul. With the tocher lands Mairi Macpherson brought to her marriage and Dunraven added to his brother's gain, Donald would rule over substantial lands, more than any other laird of Glendar. Was it possible that his quiet, tolerant, keen-minded brother secretly lusted for such power and command? Plotted for it and the lairdship which, as a third son, he could little hope to gain?

After thirteen years in London's Tower, Rae questioned whether he truly knew his brothers anymore. Either of them. Rae had always felt he could trust Donald with his life, even before he would Iain, which was a harsh thing to say of one's brother. But, by destiny or design, Donald *would* be Fourth

Laird of Dunraven. The portraits in the gallery gave proof of
that, recording Mairi's dark, slashing brows and boxy chin.

Rae pulled his gaze from his quarreling brothers and skipped
another stone across the water. He thought on what Julia had
told him and wondered what course to take. How could he
stand by and do naught, allowing his brother and clansmen to
die in their efforts to avenge his own death? A fierce love and
loyalty to clan demanded he take measures to save them.

But how? By saving himself, so that no one need die? Or by
simply forewarning them of events to come—if they'd believe
so incredible a tale? If not directly then, he might seek to discover his murderer and a way to leave proof of his identity.

But any of those courses would change history. Even if he
himself still died, should Iain live, then he, not Donald, would
rule as laird. Rae held no doubt Iain would sire heirs. Already,
several bairns ran about Dunraven, Iain's image stamped upon
their wee faces, laddies the lot of them.

Rae inhaled a deep breath and lifted his face to the heavily
clouded sky.

Dare he play God? If he should interfere, James Edwin and
countless others might never be born. He would be depriving
them of their lives, trading theirs for those of his own people.
And if Iain lived, an entirely different line of lairds would rule
Dunraven, thoroughly altering history throughout five centuries. Och, now, that would be "tampering with history"!

Rae paused in his thoughts, another coming to mind. Weeks
ago, Donald had mentioned something that had remained a
thorn in his mind. He need seek out Dugal. 'Twas long past
time he had a full accounting of what had passed in Glendar
whilst he was caged in London's Tower.

As Rae climbed the sloping land toward the keep, slow-
moving clouds gathered over Dunraven, casting it in shadow.

The *cailleach* sprung immediately to mind and her dire
warnings at the River Forth. She spoke of shadows, dark and
dangerous, and of a "rip" in time.

She'd foretold the time-slip accurately enough, but he'd assumed the shadows to be connected to it somehow. Lately, he'd

begun to think the reference was to Roger Dunnington. Evidently, he was wrong. Both times contained their own shadows.

Rae thought back to the day at the river and grasped for the *cailleach*'s precise words.

"Yer future doesna lie here," she'd told him. "Cross the Forth . . . ye shall no' return."

Dunraven loomed before him, consumed in shadows. Would it devour him in its fire, or aid his escape? Friend or foe, 'twas the keep itself that held his fate.

Chapter 25

Julia pulled back the row of primroses along the fragment of wall to reveal the blackened stone. Her heart shrank at the sight. Fire had caused this, there could be no doubt. Why had she not recognized the markings for what they were when first she had seen them?

Standing, Julia glanced over the vacant ground where the hall once stood. She then looked to the massive keep.

Donald Mackinnon, as laird, never rebuilt over the site. Instead, according to the annals of Dunraven, he made additions to the east side of the tower.

Did Donald fear the ghosts of that dreadful night? Was it he who had sealed the stairwell and portals? Or had Rae's death been simply too painful for him and the others to bear? Did the fatal site become hallowed ground, never to be built upon again?

Had Rae died here? Julia skimmed a glance over the area then quickly withdrew from the place, suddenly unable to remain another moment.

Julia headed around the keep, toward the castle's main entrance. Wiping the moisture from her eyes, she chided herself for being so weepy of late. The uncertainty of the days to come and their tragic potential ravaged her heart and nerves. But there was more.

Slipping inside the great hall, Julia closed the door and leaned against it, her fears overwhelming without warning and engulfing her anew. Her head swam and she grabbed for something to support herself as the floor moved beneath her.

Through the blur of her vision, she saw Lord Muir appear from a side corridor, coming from the direction of Dunraven's main library.

"Julia! Oh, my dear, let me help you."

He hastened to her side and helped her to the bench positioned beneath the large hunting tapestry. Suddenly, the strain of the past days overcame her. She buried her face in her hands as a deluge of tears poured forth from her eyes.

"Julia, Julia, there now." Lord Muir held her against him, consoling her as a father would a daughter.

Julia's tears continued to flow, and she knew she was drenching his snowy beard, but he didn't seem to mind.

"Has Rae refused our plan? Is that what distresses you so?"

"H-he hasn't said," she forced out through her tears. "I think he intends to stay in his own time."

"We must have faith in Rae, my dear, and that the Almighty will guide him in the choices he must make."

A fresh torrent of tears racked Julia, so that she shook against Lord Muir.

"Julia, is there something you are not telling me?" He provided her his handkerchief then helped her to rise. "Come, my dear. We need more privacy. Let us withdraw to the little parlor."

Julia leaned against Lord Muir as he aided her to the end of the entrance hall and into the corridor to the right. A small room stood just off of it.

"Now, you must tell me what is the matter, my dear." Lord Muir prompted as he guided her to a large, comfortable-looking chair. "Unless you tell me, I cannot be of real help to you."

Julia remained standing, his arm supporting her, and looked up at him through sodden lashes. She shook her head. "You will think most ill of me, I fear."

"Julia, have a little trust in a man who's been around a considerable time and privy to a great many things. If nothing else, trust in *me* and our friendship."

Julia swallowed back her tears, dreading the disappointment that would surely replace his sympathy and favorable regard of her. When she spoke, her voice came as a whisper. "I think I might be carrying Rae's child."

Avoiding Lord Muir's gaze, she blotted her eyes and face with his handkerchief.

"I'm not sure, but there are signs—fatigue, dizziness, I confess, it is possible."

Lord Muir remained silent for no more than a heartbeat of a moment. "Julia, look at me. I'm not a man to judge you and no man should. Only the Almighty can do that. Unfathomable forces have intervened in yours and Rae's lives, drawing you across time to one another. Perhaps this, too, is fated."

Julia gazed on Lord Muir in utter amazement, first that he did not censure her, and, second, that she'd not considered this child was destined.

Lord Muir smiled kindly upon her. "My dear, consider. You might be carrying the sole child of my predecessor, a brave and courageous man who was cheated of his life at every turn—imprisoned for almost half of it in London's Tower, only to loose it, by mishap or murder, scarcely after his return to Dunraven and installation as laird. Unless, of course, he does come into the future," he added quickly, then shook his head. "Even then, he will be stripped of the life he once knew."

Lord Muir gently cupped her chin with his hand. "Lay aside your fears, at least for your child. I promise you, I'll not see the babe suffer in any way, not for food, or shelter, or even with the stigma of illegitimacy. I give you my vow. Why, I'll marry you myself to protect you!" he offered gallantly.

Roger Dunnington arrived at the bottom of the great staircase in the entrance hall and checked his pocket watch. Lilith was late. Later than he. Well, that was providential, he mused, returning the watch to his pocket. Lady Downs had delayed him somewhat today. She was becoming a rather cloying lover.

Hearing voices from just off the hall, he stepped to the side corridor. His interest spiked as he glimpsed his uncle and Julia in the parlor there, embracing. Easing closer, he listened.

Julia's voice proved too soft to hear, but his uncle's carried strong with his promise.

"I give you my vow. Why, I'll marry you myself . . ."

"Roger!" Lilith's voice overrode his uncle's words, jerking his attention from the scene.

He reeled around, looking straight through Lilith, stunned by what he'd just heard.

"Roger, where were you? I gave up and went looking for you."

She started toward him, but he quickly caught her by the elbow and steered her away from the parlor.

"What? Oh, my watch must be slow." He shot another look back at the room then conducted Lilith toward the hall's entrance and out the door.

Julia sat with Lord Muir on the settee, overwhelmed with surprise but grateful for his chivalry.

"We will see what turns fate will take in the next days, but come what may, Dunraven shall be the child's." At Julia's shocked refusal, Lord Muir argued his decision. "Though my other estates and titles are entailed, I purchased Dunraven outright, and it is mine to do with as I please. Yours and Rae's child is rightful heir to Dunraven."

Lord Muir smiled in earnest now. "It's not every day a man can bequeath his estates to his ancestral kinsman, several hundred times removed. Think of that. The babe truly is my kinsman."

"Or kinswoman," Julia amended, smiling at last.

Lilith gathered wildflowers while Roger idled beside the lake. He gazed gloomily to the distant mountains.

The doddering old fool, he thought blackly. So Uncle intended to make Julia his wife. Should he actually beget a son on her, then he himself would lose all claim to his uncle's vast lands and his titles and fortune.

The marriage could not be allowed, Roger resolved. He must do something to prevent this disaster. And quickly.

Chapter 26

"Emmaline is gone?"

"Flown!" Lady Charles declared, her voice ringing with excitement. "She ran off with Sir Robert, sometime during the night."

Joy stole through Julia, overriding her surprise. Deep in her heart, she'd hoped Sir Robert was her cousin's secret love. He was a fine man and had the capacity to make Emmaline happy. Though he'd carefully concealed his feelings, his sentiments were oft times reflected in his eyes, Julia realized now in retrospect. She warmed at the thought of the love they would share in their lives.

"Your aunt is in an absolute furor," Lady Charles confided, replacing her cup on its saucer. "She should be the first to inform you of Emmaline's disappearance, I know. But I felt I must warn you. Your aunt blames you for your young cousin's actions."

Julia's brows rose at that, but somehow the disclosure did not really surprise her.

Lady Charles continued. "I was present at breakfast when she received Emmaline's letter."

"Emmaline left a letter?"

"Sent one by a postboy, from Perth or nearer by, I presume. She and Sir Robert timed everything quite cleverly, even the arrival of the missive. By now they are who knows where."

"But you said Aunt Sybil blames me for Emmaline's running away with Sir Robert? Did my cousin mention me by name?"

"Not by name, dear." Lady Charles's hand fluttered to her

chest and she leaned forward. "According to your aunt, the letter was filled with fanciful notions of love which she insisted only you could have 'stuffed in Emmaline's head,' as she put it. At the very least, your aunt believes Emmaline followed your own mother's example."

Julia nodded. "It's true, my mother and father did elope, and theirs was a most happy marriage."

Lady Charles set her teacup and saucer aside, then looked back to Julia.

"Lord Withrington and I are quite fond of Sir Robert. But we fear he was not wise to thwart those who could make his and Emmaline's life wretched. With Viscount Holbrooke as her father, and, worse for her, her mother a Symington, they will hunt the couple down. Your aunt has already appealed to Lord Muir, and Lord Eaton has dispatched men after them and written letters ahead to London. Presumably Emmaline and Sir Robert will seek a parson before heading south to England and his father's estate in Berkshire. He's a third son, you know, though he's not without means."

"Emmaline understands her choice, Lady Charles. She also understands, in order to wed Sir Robert, elopement is the only choice she can make. I do appreciate your telling me what has transpired and forewarning me of my aunt. Emmaline and Sir Robert will be fine, I am sure. They must truly love one another to go to such lengths, and he is, I believe, an honorable man."

"They will be fine if they can elude your aunt!" Lady Charles remarked, then smiled as she rose from the settee. "Well, time will bear it out. It always does. I must be off now. Cuthburt is waiting. Men. He's quite stirred by Sir Robert's daring. I think he may be entertaining a few ideas of his own, and I intend to see that he acts on them! Take care, my dear. Your aunt has a sharp tongue. Do not let it wound too deep."

Julia watched as Lady Charles withdrew from the small parlor, passing Mrs. McGinty, who entered to retrieve the tea service. Julia wondered if the housekeeper had been listening to their conversation.

"Mrs. McGinty, I understand Lord Eaton sent men after my

cousin, Emmaline, and Sir Robert, hoping to stop them. I am curious who he might have sent as I know Dunraven's staff is still somewhat lean."

"Tom, miss, and a lad from the village. They are young but they know this portion of Scotland well."

"They won't find them, will they? I mean . . ."

For the first time Julia could remember, Mrs. McGinty smiled, a soft, reassuring smile.

"Do not worry, miss. The trains run in a number of directions, and it will take the lads a while on foot."

Julia's thoughts traveled ahead of her to Rae. She hastened down the Long Gallery, looking neither left nor right, to the portraits on the wall or out the long stretch of windows.

She'd remained overlong with Lady Charles and now it was near to the moment Rae would appear. Today, they were to meet with Lord Muir and the others to review the newly recorded accounts of Rae's father and himself. Rae would need to approve and change them if necessary.

Julia still felt conflicted, wondering whether or not to tell Rae of her possible pregnancy. She was tempted to do so, to induce him to come forward in time. But should she? Would the knowledge so distract and absorb him, that it might alter his decisions or cause him to make poor ones that ultimately would bring him to harm?

Then, too, she might not be pregnant at all. She could be overcome with exhaustion due simply to the stress she'd endured of late, or due to the continued effect of the time-slips. There certainly must be an invisible flow of energy between her ring and Rae's talisman. The objects were responsible for pulling them together across time. Perhaps that energy not only flowed between the stones, but drained her own vitality as well.

On the other hand, only she seemed to suffer this extreme lassitude. Rae always possessed an abundance of energy. She smiled to herself. Perhaps their lovemaking invigorated him, while it depleted her.

As Julia came to the end of the gallery and turned toward her room, she caught the faint odor of alcohol. Not Scotch whisky, but something else. Gin, perhaps?

Julia glanced back toward the servants' passage. A chill touched her spine as she gazed into the shadows there. Quickly, she entered the bedchamber and locked the door.

"Did your grandfather really do that?" Lord Muir laughed, wiping tears of mirth from his eyes.

"Aye. Diarmid, my mother's father, was one o' the 'wild MacRaes.' A high-spirited soul, if e'er there was one, or sae I am told. His wife, Ailis, settled him down though. Weel, a wee bit."

More chuckles rippled around the room. Julia laughed, too, then covered her mouth to hide a deep yawn. Dear Lord, she was wilting again.

"Do tell us another tale of your grandfather," Mr. Thornsbury encouraged.

"Gentlemen," Lord Muir spoke, rising from his chair. "As much as we would all love to hear more of the colorful Diarmid MacRae, I fear we have stretched our time today more than we dare." He consulted his pocket chronometer, then frowned. "Indeed, with the time shifts shortening so drastically with each occurrence, there is little time for Rae to return downstairs as it is."

As Rae prepared to take leave of the men, Julia stood to her feet, stifling another yawn. Being nearest the door, she turned and started for the open portal, knowing they must move quickly to get downstairs and into her chamber for the coming slip of time.

As she verged on the threshold, Lord Eaton suddenly appeared, blocking her way. She fell back several paces as he braced his arms and weight on either side of the thick door frame. The odor of alcohol filled her nostrils.

"Good afternoon, gentlemen." Lord Eaton inclined his head in a mock, and much abbreviated, bow. "I was passing by and decided to drop in unannounced. Oh, but don't let me interrupt your 'Society' meeting."

His gaze traveled to Rae.

"Ah, our Scots historian." He straightened and sauntered into the room several steps. "Tell me, Mackinnon. Do you ever wear trousers? These Highlanders you emulate, they really must have lived like wild animals, running about in the mountains, bare-legged, without even decent boots."

Julia sucked in her breath at Lord Eaton's rudeness, as did everyone else in the room. Save Rae. He took a step apart of the table and faced Roger Dunnington squarely. His hand moved to rest on the hilt of his dirk.

"The clansmen o' the Highland are warriors."

"'Warriors?'" Lord Eaton snorted. "Barbarians, you mean. Oh, I forgot. Barbarians *are* warriors." He chuckled at his own wittiness. "You know, all you need is a really large sword to complete your guise. Women love that. Tell me, what do you think Highland women were like? Were they wild? Did their men have to knock them about to tame them?"

Rae's eyes burned into Lord Eaton, a scorching look that, were it a blade, would slay.

"We honor our women. We dinna abuse or prey on them."

"We?" Lord Eaton's brows lifted high.

Julia felt the air press in. Before Rae could respond, he vanished before their eyes.

"Roger will be all right," Lord Muir commented to the others as he reentered the room with Sir Henry. "He is resting in his room. Angus is with him."

Mr. Galbraith pushed back the spectacles on his nose with nervous fingers. "He saw Rae disappear. He'll require an explanation."

Lord Muir whisked a glance to Julia as he seated himself. "What do you suggest?"

Mr. Armistead swiveled on his chair, staring hard at Mr. Galbraith. "Surely, you do not propose we tell him. Not with the New Moon upon us."

"We best tell him something," Mr. Galbraith persisted, pulling his gaze from Mr. Armistead and directing it around the table. "Lord Eaton heard and saw too much. He will demand, and he deserves, an explanation. I mean, he is your heir, is he not, your lordship? He is entitled to know Dunraven's secrets before he inherits it one day."

Julia could not meet Lord Muir's eyes at the comment. Her temples began to pound, and she feared where this conversation would lead.

Lord Muir drummed the tabletop with his fingertips a moment, then stilled his hand. "As my nephew has so aptly demonstrated, he does not possess the most admirable qualities one would hope for in an heir. I confess, it is not my intention to bequeath Dunraven to him. However, as you say, he has witnessed much. We will be disclosing our findings in the coming months to the Society, and there will be no way to keep it from slipping out publicly. I suppose, we need to tell Roger something, but we need not tell him everything."

Julia's heart sank to the pit of her stomach as the men further discussed what details of the time-slip could be disclosed, and which should be withheld. When the critical moment came for Rae to come forward in time—if he'd attempt it—they certainly didn't need the likes of Roger Dunnington to complicate events.

"You expect me to believe Rae Mackinnon is over four hundred years old?" Lord Eaton took another swallow of the amber liquid in his glass.

Mr. Thornsbury laced his fingers together in front of him as he explained. "Actually, Rae Mackinnon, the Third Laird of Dunraven, has stepped across time, four hundred and fifty-six years to be exact, though his own chronological age is that of twenty-nine."

"Sounds like a bit of hocus-pocus, or witchery, to me."

Julia could not help but recall Rae had thought the same when he first had found her in his bed and stripped her naked to search for a telling mark.

Lord Eaton leveled a skeptical eye at the others. "The man seems real and solid enough, flesh and blood and all that."

"Oh, he's flesh and blood, all right," Mr. Armistead agreed. "And you should be aware any blade he carries is no mere ornament but the genuine item, no doubt well seasoned according to the Highland standards of his time."

"True, take heed," Sir Henry warned. "The Mackinnon doesn't appear to have taken well to you. He'd be a dangerous man to have for an enemy."

Roger huffed a disbelieving laugh. "You all are serious, aren't you? You think this man with his coarse clothes and parlor tricks is the authentic article, right out of the past." He gave another laugh and drained his glass.

Irritable and thoroughly sick of Eaton's derision and snide remarks, Julia thrust to her feet. "The journal of notes and instrument recordings speak for themselves and are there for you to inspect. I'd suggest you do so."

"I'd much rather see the instruments while they are actually recording—whatever they record—during one of these 'time-slips.' The phenomena centers in your bedchamber, was I not told?" His gaze strayed over her, causing Julia to stiffen.

"Then do so," she snapped. "Come to my chamber tonight. Anyone here can calculate the precise time of the next shift. We shall set up the equipment so you might make your own observations."

Lord Eaton templed his fingers, a smug smile spreading over his lips. "At last, an invitation to the inner sanctum?"

"Consider it what you will. I'm sure you will find the experience most memorable."

Chapter 27

Roger could not help but smile as he traversed the darkened corridors to Julia's chamber. Tonight he would be her latest initiate. And tonight, he would learn what so enthralled the other men and kept them returning time and again.

His smile dropped moments later when he discovered Angus McNab posted outside Julia's chamber. At his approach, McNab rapped twice on the thick oaken door. At once, it drew open.

Julia stood just inside the portal, as beautiful as ever, in a flowing gown of pastel shades. She stepped to one side, motioning him to enter, which he did without hesitation.

His gaze continued to devour her as he crossed the threshold. Julia wore no corset and her breasts pressed soft and full against the silken fabric of her gown. He nearly licked his lips, his hopes for the evening rising, his loins growing warm with anticipation.

As his eyes touched Julia's green pools, she smiled and shifted her gaze, directing his attention across the room. Ready to play her game, any she might devise, he followed her line of sight with his.

Roger blanched at the sight of Rae Mackinnon, standing to the right of the bed, wearing a leather corselet, sewn with iron rings, his great claymore braced before him, pointed tip down, firelight dancing upon its naked blade. A fierce look etched Mackinnon's face and his grip remained firm upon his sword.

Julia melted from Roger's side, and he found himself face-to-face with the formidable-looking Scotsman.

"Ye can leave us now," Mackinnon rumbled.

Roger started to withdraw, then realized the words were meant for Julia. He swallowed, then took hold of himself. He was the civilized one here after all. Not this rough-looking charlatan who had so cleverly duped his uncle and colleagues.

"What is this, Mackinnon, another parlor trick?" he sneered. "You may be able to fool a group of old men who want to believe in realms beyond and time dimensions, but you don't deceive me with your Highland magic and benighted ways. If it's my uncle's fortune you are after you can . . ."

The Scotsman closed the space, a black look slashing his features. Grabbing Roger by the front of his shirt and jacket, he straight-armed him, jerking him clear off his booted heels and slamming him against the stone wall.

Roger shouted, his skull, shoulders, and spine exploding with pain. The man did not ease his hold but jammed the sword's hilt end under his jaw and forced his head back.

"*Sassenach,* I care no' wha' ye think o' me or how I came tae be here. I gi' ye this tae know—I *am* Rae Mackinnon, Third Laird o' Dunraven, and if tha' makes me a barbarian by yer measure, then dinna be soon forgettin' it. Harm Julia again, and I'll lesson ye in exactly wha' the word means, for ye'll be lastin' m' sword. 'Twill never yer hide from yer black soul in an instant, and 'tis yer lungs I'll be havin' for m' supper. The rest I'll feed tae the wolves. And rest assured, wolves still roam the Highlands in m' time, which is where I'll be takin' ye. D'ye ken?"

The Scotsman released his hold, dropping Roger straight to the floor. Roger crumpled in a heap, pain shooting through his legs, hip, elbow, and forearm, which took the weight of his fall. Roger lay upon the floor, looking up at the angry Highlander.

The Mackinnon stepped back, bracing his immense sword before him once more, and cleaving Roger with his look.

"Dunraven is a place o' mystery and shadows tha' ye little understand. But I do. Look well upon m' sword, 'tis the sword o' retribution. Bring grief tae Julia and deal wi' me."

Incredulously, the Scotsman began to dissolve for a second

time this day, and Roger found himself staring through him to the wall beyond. Still Rae Mackinnon's deep voice vibrated throughout the chamber.

"Time nor death nor aught else can pose a barrier I canna cross tae reach ye. Ye know in yer soul, 'tis true. Dinna be forgettin' it."

With that, the Scotsman disappeared completely, his sword blade flashing with firelight.

Roger tossed down another whisky. His fourth. Or was it his fifth?

Was everyone enraptured with Julia? He had to admit he'd caught the "Julia" fever long before at Asridge. Or was it Saltram? Wherever she'd been, when first he'd laid eyes on her.

His thoughts turned dark. The little witch. Lilith was cunning at manipulating men for her gain, but Julia was truly an expert.

He fingered the scab on his lower lip. Still it had not healed, the gash he'd received from Julia's ring opening it deep. Roger thought back to the night he had met Rae Mackinnon and how the Scotsman's eyes had riveted on his wound. Julia must have told him of their scuffle at the burn. Witch again. She'd gained herself a brutish protector in the Third Laird of Dunraven.

Third laird. Roger had sat now for hours in the tower library, recovering from his encounter with Mackinnon, thinking, drinking, coming to grips with the reality of the man and the possibility he had indeed stepped from the past.

Twice, now, the Scotsman had evaporated before his eyes. Though their explosive confrontation had shattered his nerves and confidence, to his own credit Roger had had the presence of mind to examine the chamber afterward. He'd found no hidden escapes or contrivances that might have feigned the effect, no evidence of deceit. He'd then climbed to the upper library and sat with his uncle's journal and bottle of Glenlivet as he read through the copious notes and data.

Unimaginably, Time—the fourth dimension—had been breached.

Roger filled his glass with more of the amber liquid and sipped it as he turned his thoughts.

So, Julia had visited the past, and, now, Rae Mackinnon had come centuries forward through something called a "time-slip." Perhaps, he could use the phenomenon to his own advantage to deal with the matter of his uncle.

Roger frowned. The Scotsman could pose an obstacle to his plans. He'd shown obvious attachment to his uncle and would likely be as protective toward him as Julia.

Roger rubbed his hand over his jaw. He couldn't allow his uncle to marry, not to a fruitful young woman who could give him a son. The situation could be remedied easily enough, the question was *how*? Given his age, the marquis's sudden demise would not be questioned overly much. On the other hand, his uncle's dabblings in the "unexplained" might provide a better solution. Rather than feigning illness, perhaps an "accident" was more the order.

Roger's gaze dropped to the journal laying open before him. He leafed through the pages to the last entry, made the day of the late-night reception in the conservatory. Running his fingers down the book's center crease, at the same time applying pressure toward the binding, he could feel the stubbled edge of pages—pages that had been carefully removed, no doubt with a razor.

The tampering had not been immediately evident, but a slight gap was visible when the book lay closed, and he could feel where the pages were missing. Why would these men of science keep meticulous records then cease their notations abruptly even while the phenomenon continued, especially with this new twist of Mackinnon coming into the future?

There must be another journal, and hopefully with it, the missing pages.

"Lord Eaton. Sorry, didn't realize you were still up and about."

Roger looked up to find Mr. Galbraith entering the room, rumpled from head to foot, his hair disheveled, his cravat hang-

ing untied about his neck, and a large green binder tucked beneath his arm.

"You're up late yourself. Or should I say early. It's nearly
dawn." Roger leaned back in his chair and contemplated the
man as he headed for the file cabinet, toward the back of the
chamber.

"I was going over some computations." Mr. Galbraith deposited the binder in the cabinet's top drawer, shut it firmly,
then turned to Roger, fingering back his glasses.

Was it his imagination, or did the man seem skittish about
something?

"Computations? Relating to the 'time-slips'?" Roger prodded.

"Yes, tonight the lunar cycle will complete itself with the arrival of the New Moon. The dynamics of the time-slip, itself,
will be in fluctuation. Or so we predict."

Roger sat forward, his spirits brightening. The time-slip had
begun with the New Moon, but then it had shifted toward the
past. It occurred to him now in a blinding flash that, for all Rae
Mackinnon's dire warnings, with the moon's new phase, the
Scotsman would no longer be able to come into the present—
at last, not until its next phase, roughly in two weeks' time.
Even then, Mackinnon could only mete out his "retribution" if
Roger remained at Dunraven. The Scotsman's sword arm
couldn't reach to England. Roger nearly grinned, but maintained a more sober aspect.

"I'd like to hear more. I've just spent the night studying the
notes in this journal here. To tell you the truth, I am enthralled.
I was thinking just now that I must join the Society myself."

Mr. Galbraith smiled at his admission and came forward.

Roger pressed on. "Here, won't you join me? You appeared
preoccupied with something when you arrived, not by your
computations I hope. The phenomena *will* reverse itself, will it
not, with the New Moon?"

Mr. Galbraith sat in the chair to his right, and adjusted his
glasses, which had slipped down his nose again. "Possibly.
Probably. We are still learning about the phenomenon. As with

the last Full Moon, there is the concern whether or not time will continue to shift at all."

Roger straightened, his brows lifting. "Do you think the time-slips might stop altogether?"

At his comment, Mr. Galbraith fidgeted with his collar, attempting to button it with fumbling fingers. "Actually, my concern is with the dynamics of the phenomenon during the critical shift itself, when the moon completes the one phase and begins the next."

Roger matched Galbraith's look of concern with his own. "I'd like to hear about that. I hope there's no danger to Julia or Mackinnon." Galbraith wouldn't meet his eyes. "What is it man?"

"Well, I haven't yet spoken to the others, but I suppose it is all right if I tell you, especially if it is your intention to join the Society."

"It is, I assure you. I should have done so long before now."

Mr. Galbraith clasped his hands before him, furrowing his brow as he detailed his concerns.

"My personal belief is that this coming night, the phenomenon will behave as it did the night of the Full Moon. According to Julia, the 'door' opened on both centuries for a period of time."

"Yes, I read that in the journal, a fascinating account—furniture appearing and disappearing from both times. Go on."

"You understand it is the stones—Julia's and Rae's—that draw them together and into one another's times. We have certain concerns about this particular time-slip tonight. Personally, I fear if Julia is not careful, she could be drawn across time and trapped in the past herself."

Roger sat back in surprise. "Is that possible?"

"Nothing can be said with surety about the time-slip. Much about it is still a mystery. I have been going over the astronomical data—the alignment of the planets, their magnetic pull upon one another and, of course, the magnetism between the sun, moon, and earth, which is even stronger. My deduction is that the time-slip at this New Moon will not behave the same as it did when the time-slip began."

Mr. Galbraith removed his glasses then scratched his head. "How can I put this simply? I do not believe, when the lunar phase is in transition, that the time door will close neatly one way and then open the other. I suspect, the phenomena will behave more as it did at the Full Moon and there will be a period when the portal will stand open to both times. Mind you, the lunar energies are at their weakest now, so that period is likely to be brief—fifteen, twenty minutes at most."

He leaned forward, replacing his spectacles, his small round eyes intense behind the glass. "If this all comes about as I predict, for a short while, Julia and Rae will be able to move in either temporal direction. But, therein also lies the danger. Should either one lose direct contact with their stone—which is their anchor to their respective times—then they might become subject to the influence of the other's stone. That is, if they are touching or their clothes brushing."

"And what would happen in such a case?"

"The one would conceivably be drawn across time with the other and trapped permanently on their side of time. However, they might not fare well in the transport. We know what happened in the case of the corset."

Roger grimaced. "I assume the results would be equally gruesome if one suddenly traveled back four hundred years."

"Exactly. They both must take care in dealing with this phenomena, particularly when the portal is bidirectional, shall we say."

Roger nodded in thought as Mr. Galbraith replaced his glasses and stood to leave.

"Well, it's all conjecture, of course."

"Of course, Mr. Galbraith. And do not worry overmuch. I'm sure both Julia and Rae Mackinnon will be careful to not remove their stones under any circumstance. It would be foolish."

Mr. Galbraith's gaze dropped away. "Mm-mm, yes, risky at very least. Well, I best be off and take this news to the others.

If they haven't considered it themselves, they'll want to make their own calculations."

Roger waited until Galbraith departed, then mulled their conversation over in his mind.

He had hoped to find a solution to his "uncle" problem. Perhaps he had—a most unique and permanent one. Should his uncle be the one inadvertently caught in a "time warp," he would tragically be dragged across the centuries, even buried in the past.

Roger smiled to himself. He liked the notion of Time doing the deed for him. What he needed now was one of the stones.

Rising, Roger perused the library shelves and looked over his uncle's desk. He then remembered the green binder Mr. Galbraith had placed in the file cabinet. Retrieving it, he glanced over the cramped lettering that appeared on the pages, some in Gaelic, others in English.

"Well, well," he muttered to himself, his interest catching fire.

He carried the binder back to the table and, settling in a chair, began to read. For the next half hour he scarcely moved a muscle, for the pages recorded a most fascinating tale, that of none other than Rae Mackinnon on the night of the New Moon.

Chapter 28

Julia paced the chamber in utter torment as she awaited time to slip, wondering, agonizing over what was transpiring across time and whether Rae even still lived.

Lord Muir and the others congregated in the Long Gallery without, no doubt wearing the carpet through to the floor. Though she knew they wished to crowd her chamber and pass these minutes with her, Julia had insisted on being left to herself. She could not bear anyone's company, not now, not without knowing what was to come.

Had Rae survived the day thus far? Or had Time already taken him from her?

Julia moved to the window and looked out toward the soaring mountains, despair threatening to rob her control.

Just as her tears welled for a hundredth time, the air grew dense and pressed in. She whirled in place to see Rae materialize before the great hooded fireplace. In the next instant, they filled each other's arm, their mouths meeting in a fierce kiss.

"You've come. You've come." Her heart sang for joy as she clasped him tight, spreading kisses over his face and lips.

"Naught could keep me from ye, *mo càran*." His mouth moved along her jaw and neck then claimed her lips once more, drawing her into a long, deep kiss.

She gasped for breath a moment later as his lips left hers and moved to her ear. "I feared what might be happening on other side, that disaster might have befallen you."

"'Tis a most joyous day at Dunraven thus far." He cheered and pulled back, fingering away a tear that had trickled down her cheek. "Donald left at dawn with his groom's escort for the Macpherson stronghold tae wed his Mairi. Iain left, too, though he was a mite late getting out o' his bed and had tae follow. He'll hae caught up wi' them by now. Beitris went along wi' Donald as did some o' the others. I took yer advice tae see the keep emptied. I'll be sendin' the rest out tae stay wi' other families and crofters in the glen. Likely, they'll think me a bit daft, but 'tis best for them, I am thinkin'."

Julia's heart plummeted. "Then you will go back?"

"Ye know I must, my heart."

She felt her heart splinter into a thousand pieces. Tears sprung to her eyes and cascaded over her cheeks. Unable to bear the thought, she buried her face against Rae's chest. His arms encircled her and held her close.

"I must see this through, *mo càran,* and do wha' e'er is required for my kinsmen's sakes. Ach, now, dinna cry. Destiny must be embraced, no' fled. I feel its pull upon me, like the moon upon the tides, and, in m' soul, I know there is aught I must do—somethin' somehow important tae the both o' us. I wouldst hae some answers o' my own as well, for a shadow hangs o'er Dunraven. Ye can tell James Edwin tae write in his books, 'tis my belief it stretches from the grave o' King James."

Rae tilted her chin to force her to look at him. "If God and Time allows, I'll come back tae ye," he vowed softly. "Ye know I will."

The minutes dwindled, their moments to share as brief as when first they met. Julia still wondered whether she should tell Rae of their child, if there was a child. Instead, she swallowed back the words. "You are with me always, in more ways than you know."

He brushed back her hair. "No matter wha' comes, 'til my last breath and beyond, I'll be lovin' ye, *mo càran,* 'til the end o' Time."

Julia felt the air thicken around them. She sank her fingers into his plaid, wishing to hold him there.

"God protect you and bring you safely back," she whispered.

His mouth covered hers in a final kiss, their lips clinging to one another's.

Suddenly, Julia found herself alone once more. Alone with her tears and a shattered heart.

Single of purpose, solemn of heart, Rae dressed with great care, pulling on his saffron shirt, pleating and belting his plaid in place. Drawing the excess over his shoulder, he fastened the material with the splendid Brooch of Glendar—the Bruce's gift, the symbol of Mackinnon lordship.

Five short months had he borne his title. Tonight would be his last hours as Third Laird of Dunraven.

Rae fixed his dirk in the front of his belt, then slipped a smaller knife under its back. Buckling his baldric across his chest, he took up his *claidheamh mor,* its freshly honed edge gleaming, and sheathed it in the scabbard at his hip.

Bracing himself, Rae quit the chamber, prepared to face the night and whatever danger lay before him.

By twos, he climbed the steps to the upper chamber. He searched its full measure, and that of each of the keep's smaller, nichelike rooms.

Earlier, he'd seen Dunraven vacated by those who resided within its walls despite more than a few protests. 'Twas done nonetheless. His kinsmen could make their complaints to Donald, who after this night would become their new laird. But Rae would not allow them to be harmed due to him.

Climbing to the roof of the keep, he gazed out over the darkened landscape. He could see naught of the distance, but 'twas quiet enough, with no sign of unrest. Of course, many hours still lay between then and dawn.

Rae descended the spiraling stairwell to ground level and stepped from the alcove. An eerie silence layered the hall. Dunraven was not meant to stand empty. 'Twas the clansmen who gave it life. But their laughter and arguments would ring out in this place no more. When the morrow came, the hall wouldst be but a smolderin' heap—like him, passed into memory in the annals of time.

Rae banked the fire on the hearth then stepped outside the door and called to Lachlan and Dugal, who stood at a short distance. As they joined him, their glances took in his fine garments and the sword at his hip.

"Och, ye are ready for reivers are ye no'?" Dugal's sober smile reflected his own expectations for this night.

"Aye, they are a canny lot," Rae retorted. "They hae been sore clever thus far. I suspect they e'en know how many men left Dunraven this morn wi' Donald. 'Tis likely they are watchin' now, ready tae help themselves tae Mackinnon cattle, thinkin' we are vulnerable."

"Weel, they'll no' be sneakin' heifers under our noses this night," Lachlan swore. "We are ready for them, wi' double the guard at Finalty Pass as ye wished."

Dugal nodded. "Aye, the thieves willna be drivin' the cattle tha' way as probably they did afore."

The three spoke several more minutes before Lachlan and Dugal began to head out to join those on watch.

"Dugal, I wouldst speak tae ye a moment aboot tha' matter we discussed several days past." Rae delayed his cousin.

As Lachlan trudged off, Dugal followed Rae into the hall. After dipping up cups of heather ale for themselves, they settled at a table near the hearth.

"Tell me again o' James Graham's movements hereaboot in the Highlands. 'Twas surprised I was tae learn o' his visits tae Dunraven. It troubles me still tae know my father kept company wi' the mon a'tall. Did my father so oppose the King?"

"Oppose?" Dugal blurted the word. "He *despised* him. Ye must understand, no sooner than ye were sent tae London wi' the hostages, James returned and called a gatherin' o' the Highland chieftains. Ye know the story—how, as the chieftains arrived at Inverness, James threw every one o' them into the dungeon pit, singin' a merry squib as he did. Yer father was among those seized, Iain, too. He accompanied yer father's tail, servin' as swordbearer.

"For months James let them rot in tha' foul place, and for a time it seemed he would hang them all. Only three o' the chiefs met tha' fate in the end, but the rest ne'er forgot the King's treachery or his contempt for the Highland clans."

Rae waited as Dugal took a long draft of beer. Wiping his mouth, his cousin continued.

"Then, heaping salt on a wound already raw, James kept the tax monies, raised tae pay the ransom price and free the hostages. He lavished it on his queen and court and filled his royal coffers. At his death—after ye and the others had languished thirteen long years in London Tower—'twas learned only a fifth o' the ransom had been paid, a pitiful sum. Year by year, as the ransom went unsettled, yer father, like many others, nursed their grievances against the king. Graham was chief amongst them. And 'twas here, in the Highlands north o' Perth, that Graham and his conspirators hid and plotted the death o' the king."

Rae dragged on his chin in thought. "How did my father come to know Graham?"

Dugal shrugged. "From Inverness, I suppose. Yer father befriended Graham for a time. Many o' us were impressed wi' the mon and shared his sympathies, Iain especially. He remembered all too well his and yer father's treatment at Inverness and it angered him that ye, his older brother, was still captive tae the *sassenach*."

"But did my father support the murder of the king?"

"Och, nae. When Graham's talk turned radical, Alasdair severed his ties wi' Graham and invited him nae more tae Dunraven. Still, Graham remained in the region, movin' aboot, receivin' help from others. 'Tis likely MacChlerich lent him aid." Dugal shook his wooly head. "But, I wouldna be surprised if some o' the Mackinnons did as well, despite yer father's instructions. Graham was a most persuasive and rivetin' mon."

Long after Dugal left, Rae continued to ponder their conversation as he waited the night out, the hall engulfed in shadows.

He considered Malcolm MacChlerich, who, if he had given aid to Graham, might yet fear retribution and wish to align himself with a larger clan. With the Mackinnon lands abutting his

own, the Laird of Dunraven must have seemed a perfect choice
for his daughter, Moira.

Rae heaved a long sigh and stretched his legs, glancing about
the hall. If a fire was to break out and consume the hall, he
could not believe 'twould be by accident. He waited alone, the
fire banked, buckets of water nearby should a spark fly out and
flame the rushes.

If Niall's record was correct, that left murder to be done this
night.

But, why? Who would wish to kill him? If Graham's con-
federates still lurked about, subsisting on a few pilfered cattle,
why would they attack the laird of Dunraven, or any other laird
in the glens, or burn the hall around him?

Again his thoughts circled. Why? Who gained by his death?
And what was it they gained?

If some in the clan wished for a more warlike leader, they
need only remove him, not kill him. Personally, he had no real
enemies. But, did his father? Did a feud boil between the Mackinnons of Glendar and another clan of which he was unaware?
Or, if there were surviving conspirators, was it possible they
blamed his father for Graham's death because his father had
withdrawn his support?

His thoughts turned to Donald. How well did he truly know
this brother—a lad of twelve when Rae left Dunraven, twenty-
five on his return? Still, 'twas inconceivable Donald would be
capable of betraying two brothers. Yet, 'twould not be the first
time greed drove a man to such perfidy. Donald, whether innocent or guilty, would in fact gain from this night.

As the hours spun out, drawing near to the lunar and temporal shift, Rae remained unsure as to what he could or should do.

As he waited, the *cailleach*'s words floated back to him.
"Seek the stone's protection. 'Twill deliver ye from harm when
naught else can."

"Deliver" him? To the future? If so, Rae realized, 'twas the
protection of Julia's stone he would need seek. But would he
even have the chance to do so?

Shouts erupted without, shattering the silence, as horses pounded into the foreyard of Dunraven Castle.

Rae thrust to his feet, his muscles tensing as he hastened toward the door. Had the reivers struck at last? Did a clansman or two ride back to give warning? But Rae saw now that more than a few horsemen filled the yard. At the distance, in the dark, he could not immediately identify them as they dismounted and moved to speak with his men who kept guard.

"What goes there?" Rae shouted out as he filled the portal, reining every impulse to race out into the midst of the men, knowing 'twas here, within the hall, fate must be played out. "Hae reivers struck?" he called out again.

At that a figure broke from the knot of the men and rushed forward. As he came into the torchlight Rae saw 'twas Iain.

Rae stepped back a pace as his brother verged on the threshold and entered the hall. His clothes were slashed, blood staining them, his cheeks and hands.

"Reivers? Nae, brother. *Camerons,*" Iain spat out, wiping the back of his hand across his forehead, leaving a smear of blood. "I warned ye, but ye wouldna listen. A party o' Camerons attacked Donald's escort. I told ye they wouldna brook this marriage. Their reiving was but a warnin'."

"What matter is it tae the Camerons who Donald weds?"

"Not tae all the Camerons, but tae one—Ronald Cameron, Lochiel's nephew. Had ye been here these last years, ye'd know o' his grievance. Ronald claims Mairi was promised tae him and vows she'll be his still and no other's."

"Why was I no' told o' this?"

Anger flashed across Iain's features and he closed a step between them, his eyes burning.

"Ye wouldna listen, brother. Ye wouldna ride down the Camerons when they reived our cattle. We could have had it oot wi' them then. D'ye leave yer spine in London Tower, brother, or will ye ride wi' me now? Now tha' Donald lays dead upon the road, by Ronald Cameron's sword."

"Donald?" Rae gasped at Iain's pronouncement, his legs near buckling beneath him. He looked at his brother aghast and found Iain choked with his own emotions, a storm of anger upon his brows, tears welling in his eyes.

"D'ye hear wha' I say?" Iain blazed, his features twisted in anguish, his voice cracking. "Donald is *dead,* and Tavis and Colm are lost, too. Come, brother. We must hurry!" Iain pivoted in place and headed for the door. "Let us cut some Cameron throats!"

Lacerated to the soul, Rae started to follow Iain out. *Donald was not to have died,* his whole being cried out. *This was not the way 'twas to be.*

Rae halted in his footsteps. "'Tis *no'* wha' happened," he muttered aloud to himself, the images of Donald's and Mairi's descendants staring at him in his mind's eye, gazing past paint and frames in Dunraven's gallery, testifying to their fore-bearer's blood passed down.

Rae lifted his eyes to Iain as his brother stayed his step and turned round.

Donald did outlive Iain and himself and ruled as Dunraven's fourth laird. The annals filling James Edwin's shelves recorded his many deeds. These things could not all be lies.

"Why d'ye tarry?" bellowed Iain, a choleric impatience replacing his look of grief. "Will ye no' avenge Donald, e'en now?" He spat in the rushes. "Och, our father wasted his tears on ye. Ye became one o' them in London's Tower, Anglicized just as James. At least he knew how tae root out his enemies."

"But, who are my enemies, Iain?" Rae took a step toward his brother, a shaft of understanding lighting his thoughts. "The Camerons? Be they mine, or yours?"

Iain's expression altered.

"Donald is no' dead, is he? Why d'ye lure me oot in tae the night? Yer clothes are rent and blooded and yet ye bear no' a mark. Is it the blood o' men, or o' cattle, ye wear, Iain?"

Iain snatched for his dirk and lunged for Rae. But Rae lurched sideways, throwing Iain off balance.

The blade arched wide, missing its mark as Iain stumbled to his knees. He started to rise again, but Rae kicked out, catching Iain's hand and sending the dirk flying through the air, tip over hilt, the blade and silver pommel flashing with firelight, as it dropped to the floor.

Iain growled, hurling himself at Rae and catching him about the waist. The two men fell, colliding with the stone floor. Muscle locked against muscle and together they rolled several times over.

Pinning Iain against the stone, Rae slogged him solidly across the jaw, then began to haul him upward.

Hurried footsteps sounded behind Rae from the direction of the hall's door. With Iain still firm in his grasp, Rae started to turn to see whether 'twas friend or foe who rushed from behind. He glimpsed a dull green plaid as pain exploded across the back of his skull and a brilliant burst of light fired behind his lids.

Rae crumpled forward, blackness closing in on him. He felt Iain shove him to one side as he rose. Rae lay unmoving, momentarily dazed, his head savaged with pain.

"This wasna our plan. He wasna tae die here."

"Shut up!" Iain barked. "What o' the others? D'ye convince them Camerons are heading wi' our cattle for Glen Darnff?"

"Aye, and they rode straight oot when I swore I'd tell the laird they'd gone after them."

"Laird," Iain snorted. "Nae, for long."

"Nae, no' for long," the other man echoed, giving a short laugh.

Pain speared Rae's side as the man kicked him with a booted toe. Rae groaned and he struggled to press upward and gain his feet.

"Iain, look, he's no' done. Shall, I finish him, for ye?"

Silence hung like a blade in the air.

"Nae," Iain responded a moment later, his tone pensive. "Just make sure he doesna get up. Then burn the hall around him."

"Aye, Iain. Will we lay it tae Camerons, too?"

"Aye, tae Ronald Cameron in particular. He's a dead mon this night, too, he and his two Cameron cousins. 'Tis wha' they deserve for breakin' wi' us and threatenin' tae reveal us as Graham's men."

"Och. If any knew we were a' Blackfriars tha' night, or our part in Jamie's death . . ."

"Quiet! None will know lest ye mean tae tell them. I promise ye, matters will change as soon as I am laird. Ye and the other lads willna need tae be livin' in the caves like animals for one."

Raw fury filled Rae at Iain's words. Ignoring his pain, he drove upward and flung himself at Iain, a roar bursting from his throat. They sprawled to the floor, but in the next instance, hands dragged him backward. Rae twisted around, catching the sight of the man's sword hilt as it came down on the side of his head.

Rae slumped to the floor, falling atop something hard that jabbed into his side as he slid toward an inky darkness.

As blackness washed over him, he heard his brother's voice.

"Torch it."

Chapter 29

Julia gazed out the narrow window of her chamber at the moonless sky. The dreaded moment closed swift upon them, the lunar phase drawing to completion before it recycled anew.

She could no longer bear to think on what might or might not be. She could only wait with hope and prayer in her heart, and will her love across Time and space to Rae.

Julia released a heavy sigh and began to move from the window when a knock sounded at the door. *Lord Muir,* she thought with a mild sense of relief. She'd sent Betty a little while ago to invite him to join her. She did not wish to pass this crucifying time alone. Though, on the other hand, she did not wish for all the others to crowd her chamber either. Should Rae not survive the night, she'd desire more privacy amidst her grief. She knew it would mean so much to Lord Muir to be present at this time, and she found she needed the dear man's support as well.

Drawing open the door, startlingly, Julia found Lilith standing there.

Her cousin swept across the threshold, not waiting to be asked in. Whisking a glance around the room, Lilith brought her jade green eyes to Julia. Her gaze touched Julia's gown for a fraction of a moment.

"Good. I see you have not retired to bed just yet. I haven't disturbed you. In truth, I'm beginning to wonder if anyone sleeps in this castle at night."

"I confess I'm surprised that you are awake at such an hour yourself, cousin. It is not quite like you."

Lilith arched a perfect brow at Julia. "No, it isn't, is it? But I have reason to be tonight." The corner of her mouth curled upward as she reached for the beaded, pouchlike purse that dangled from her wrist, and removed it.

"A note has arrived from Emmaline. It was addressed to my mother but it contains a message for you. Mother agreed you should read it and, since the castle seems awake, I thought to bring it now and take the chance you'd also be awake."

Lilith drew open the mouth of her purse and plucked out a small square of crisply folded paper the color of heather. She handed it to Julia.

Julia hesitated to open it and looked to Lilith. "Is Emmaline all right? Sir Robert? Where are they?"

"Read for yourself, Julia. You *can* read," Lilith sniped, her tone acidic as she retrieved a handkerchief from her purse.

Julia moved toward the lamp on the side table. Glancing down at the square of paper, she began to unfold it. A faint odor wafted upward. Not a light perfume, but something heavier, antiseptic. Opening the paper fully, her gaze sought Emmaline's lovely, spidery script. But the page, devoid of a single mark, stared up at her like a blank face.

Just then, Lilith's hands came from behind her, muffling a handkerchief over Julia's nose and mouth while at the same time pinning her arms to her side.

The room keeled and turned on its end. Julia felt herself falling gracelessly into oblivion.

Lilith's eyes sparkled. They could have been emeralds for their brightness, Roger thought. She smiled wide at him and help up the ring.

"Darling, you did it!" He stepped from the library chamber, closing the door behind him and gave her a sharp, swift kiss.

"What of Julia?" he asked as he relieved her of the ring and held it to the light. "Did the men arrive as they were paid to do?"

Lilith stepped into his arms and pressed her curves against him. "Don't worry, Roger. They rolled her in a blanket and

slipped out with her down the servant's stairs. By now the little tramp is on her way to Perth and back to Hampshire where
she belongs."

"I told you we'd deal with her, that she'd not cheat you out
of your title as marchioness." He gave her another kiss, then
set her aside as he placed the ring on his pinkie.

"But what of your uncle, Roger? What will you tell him?"

"Leave that to me, darling. He will be distressed, no doubt,
when he learns of your cousin's true motives. He fancies himself in love with her, and she with him. But when the truth is
out, he'll come around, you'll see. Now off with you."

He gave Lilith's backside a firm, though intimate pat.

"You need to complete your letter to your grandmother,
Lady Arabella, informing her of how Julia comported herself
with my uncle. We can trust her to deal with Julia from here
on."

Lilith started to leave, then turned back, her gaze going to
the ring on his hand.

"I don't quite understand why you desired to have my
cousin's ring, Roger. But when you're done with it, I'd like to
have it for myself. I haven't seen a transparent pink stone like
that before. It has a hint of lavender that I simply adore. Perhaps, I'll reset it into a neckpiece . . ."

"Sorry, darling, you can't have this ring. But when you are
my marchioness, I'll buy you a cartload of rings and gems.
Promise."

"I intend to hold you to that promise, Roger," Lilith warned
him with a smile, then swished down the gallery, heading for
her room.

When she disappeared from sight, Roger stepped back into
the library, where he had been sharing a decanter of port with
the men of the Society. They'd all gathered in the chamber
until it was time to reconvene below to the Long Gallery.
There, they purposed to wait with baited anticipation for the
night's events.

Well, their plans had taken an unexpected turn. Roger
smiled grimly as he passed an eye over the men, slumped in

their chairs and sprawled over their books, deep in a drug-induced sleep.

Roger wasn't precisely sure how he'd explain that. Perhaps, he could lay it to his uncle, who wished to win for himself a tad more glory than the others. Yes, that was it. Uncle had conducted an experiment of his own this night, attempting to travel through time, but not wishing the others' interference or participation, lest it dim his own prestige.

Roger looked to where his uncle slept, his chin buried in his beard.

The explanation needed refining, but no matter, when the night was through, the marquis "experiment " will have failed disastrously.

Anxious to have done with this night's dark work, Roger crossed the chamber, and after a few minutes' struggle, lifted his uncle from his chair and shouldered his weight.

Chapter 30

Roger waited in Julia's chamber for time to slip, his uncle asleep on the bed.

He was not quite certain what to expect, but then no one did this night. Of the phenomenon, he knew only what he'd culled through his readings and rereadings of the marquis's journal and the records of Niall MacMhurich, copied in the green leather binder.

Roger straightened, the hairs rising on the nape of his neck. Was it his imagination or did he feel a sudden shift, a sudden weightiness to the air? It bore down on him, an oppressive feeling. He winced as a sharp pain skimmed over his head from temple to temple.

He glanced about the chamber. For several moments nothing further happened. Then suddenly, impossibly, the trappings on the bed began to mutate in color, changing from blue to red, to blue to red, and on. An iron-bound trunk appeared and disappeared against one wall, continuing to do so time and again, as did an arched, nail-studded door on the wall to his left.

Roger realized, at once, the door opened to the age-old stairwell. He would need to exercise extreme care while passing through it, lest during its continual metamorphosis, he become trapped in the tower's wall of stone.

Going to the bed, Roger pulled his uncle upward, then hefted him onto his shoulder once more and made his way toward the door.

He concentrated on its arched dimensions as it materialized and dematerialized, counting the seconds of its duration and those between. Then, judging the moment, he opened the door and stepped through the portal.

Incredibly, he found himself standing in a narrow, spiraling stairwell, just as the records described. Though it had been sealed off long ago, it still existed unchanged, for which he was glad, the steps remaining solid beneath his feet. Torchlight flickered in brackets on the wall and, like everything else, continued to appear and disappear. But it proved enough to light his way.

With scant minutes to spare, Roger picked his way down the steps, his uncle's solid weight growing heavier to bear.

The odor of burning wood reached his nostrils and he could now see at the bottom of the stairs, tendrils of smoke curling through an open portal there—the portal itself in a constant state of flux. Roger took heart. His plan was working. With luck, Rae Mackinnon already lay dead within.

Roger's thoughts turned to the talisman Mackinnon wore about his neck. He'd need the stone to see through his plan and make it work. It would be best to physically plant the stone on his uncle, but all he must really do was to lay his uncle beside the Scotsman's body, so the two were touching and so his uncle would be dragged back in time with Mackinnon and the burning hall when the temporal shift came.

God, but he hoped the Scotsman was dead. He didn't want to attempt taking the stone from Mackinnon's neck while he lived.

Roger could feel the heat from the hall where he now stood in the alcove. Once more, he must time his movements perfectly as he passed through the stone wall. Roger coughed on the increasing smoke as he watched the wide portal, gauging its intervals of materialization. As he did, he glimpsed the fiery hall within.

The fire must have broken out a while ago for the flames climbed high to the rafters now and fed on their timber and that of the roofing overhead. Lucklessly, the roof was of wood, not of slate, as many Scots castles were. He assumed thatching covered it without, which meant he would need to be all the quicker before it collapsed.

Scanning the room, Roger spied a man laying lifeless on the floor. Mackinnon. A jubilant euphoria rippled through his veins, his plan to be so easily realized.

Making his move, Roger entered the hall without mishap. As flaming chunks of wood rained down from overhead, he quickened his pace, making his way to the Scotsman's still form.

Unencumbering himself of his uncle, Roger positioned him beside Mackinnon. He needed only the stone now to plant on his uncle and assure his success. When he was done, he would take Julia's ring far from Dunraven so the door between times would remain closed forever.

Stepping around the bodies, he squatted down and located the chain and talisman around the Scotsman's neck. Finding it, he began to draw it off.

Rae stirred, aware of a form bending over him, thieving his healing stone.

The chain rasped the skin at the back of his neck as the thief yanked and pulled at it clumsily, and began to drag it over his head. Rae forced an eye open and to his astonishment, glimpsed James Edwin, where he lay unmoving beside him. But, as the talisman and chain pulled free of him, James Edwin disappeared.

Dhia, was he dead?

Rae rolled an eye to the figure that now straightened before him, the talisman dangling from his hand. Roger Dunnington.

But how was it he could still see Dunnington, Rae wondered—here, in the hall, without the aid of his talisman?

Looking again to Roger Dunnington, Rae's thoughts cleared. Dunnington's very possession of the stone drew him to the past and made him visible to Rae, in Rae's own time. And for the brief moment Rae had seen James Edwin, the stone had still been touching Rae's person, allowing him to see into the future, the moon still on its wane.

It could only happen, though, if Time was in a state of flux.

As it must be. Before losing contact with his stone, Rae had caught sight of the hall, changing about them dramatically, from a fiery inferno to the forsaken garden of Julia's day.

Rae looked again to Dunnington, who now folded his hand around the talisman. At the gesture, a stone on Dunnington's small finger caught the light. With a start, Rae saw, 'twas Julia's ring!

Had Dunnington killed James Edwin and done harm to Julia as well to gain the ring? Rae tasted an unholy fury for a second time this day.

Fighting through the fog in his head, he started to rise upward. At once, he felt something hard beneath him, digging into his hip. Ignoring the source of his pain, he climbed unsteadily to his feet and bellowed Dunnington's name.

Even in the hall's fiery red glow, Dunnington paled to white. Rae sprang for him, stumbling as he did and catching Dunnington low about the thighs and knees, dragging him down.

Frantically, Dunnington twisted and won free. Scrambling back, he hard-booted Rae in the face.

Rae pitched back and for a moment could not focus. Dunnington seized upon the opening to make his escape. Rae rose to give chase, but just then a portion of the roof gave way and a fiery timber fell from above, knocking Dunnington to the floor and pinning him beneath.

Dunnington shrieked in agony as Rae ran forward on unstable legs. Seizing upon a nearby bench, Rae struck at the beam trapping Dunnington and sent it rolling across the floor.

Dunnington continued to scream, his clothes ablaze. Swiftly, Rae cast about for a thick wool plaid. Spying one pegged on the alcove wall, he rushed to snatch it down, then returned and smothered the flames. The shrieking stopped and Dunnington stilled. As Rae removed the charred fabric and looked on the grisly sight, he saw 'twas too late. Roger Dunnington was dead.

Rae reached for his talisman, still clutched in Dunnington's hand. But as he did, the *cailleach*'s words echoed in his ears. "Seek the stone's protection. 'Twill deliver ye from harm when naught else can."

Aye, the stone. But 'twas not his own stone he need seek, but Julia's.

Rae grimaced as he worked the ring from Dunnington's finger, one of the few portions of his body the flames had not consumed. Slipping the ring onto his own finger, the surroundings instantly began to flash around him, shifting between past and present as they had the night of the Full Moon.

Not far from where he stood, James Edwin, too, reappeared. When Rae saw his chest heave for breath, Rae himself vented an enormous sigh of relief. James Edwin lived!

Rae hastened to his side. So, this was the reason he needed to be here this night, he thought—to save James Edwin. That, too, was part of his destiny.

As hot greedy flames dropped from the roof overhead, and the heat intensified in the hall, Rae started to lift James Edwin. But as he bent to do so, he spied Iain's dirk where it lay on the floor, and upon which he'd fallen earlier, the handle biting into his hip. The distinctive grip, dotted with silver tacks, and the distinguishing knurling pattern on the blade attested to all 'twas Iain's.

Making a bold decision, Rae seized upon his brother's dirk, and hurried with it to where Dunnington lay dead. Plunging the blade into the body, he left this message to Donald and his kinsmen, identifying Iain as his would-be murderer. Justice was doubly served this day, for Roger Dunnington, attempting to murder his uncle—not to mention assaulting Julia by the burn—now lay dead as a result of his own treachery.

Going to James Edwin once more and finding him rousing, Rae helped him to his feet. Together, they started toward the hall's entrance to the outside, but as they neared it, a section of the roof gave way, collapsing in front of them and blocking their escape.

Rae drew James Edwin back, then, heeling around, headed for the back of the hall and the stairwell there. The fire forced them into the tower, but Rae took heart, knowing the keep would survive the night. Now they must, too.

With Julia's ring upon his finger, Time pulled him toward

the future. Rae exercised added precaution as he and James Edwin crossed the portal of the alcove and headed up the stairs. Reaching his chamber, again they proceeded with care as they stepped through the door and into his bedchamber.

"Rae, you must rid yourself of your talisman," James Edwin urged, then coughed the smoke from his lungs.

"I dinna hae it." Rae thought of the stone clutched in Dunnington's charred fingers, anchoring him to the past. " 'Tis lost back in time."

Just then the door burst open and Julia rushed in, followed by Angus and Tom.

Rae smiled and caught her to him. "*Mo càran,* I feared something happened tae ye. Dunnington had yer ring."

Her eyes grew large at that. "Roger? But Lilith was the one who attacked me. She took the ring."

"But how? Why?" James Edwin did not comprehend the whole of it either.

"Yer nephew hired himself some low sorts from the village, yer lordship." Angus came forward to explain. " 'Tis a bit of a long story, but Tom here alerted me to their mischief when they tried to carry off Miss Hargrove."

"Roger must have drugged the other men and me. Did he so detest me?"

"Nay, he so loved your wealth and titles," Angus said, shaking his head, though his voice was solacing.

Rae suddenly felt the air press in. He faltered a moment, under a wave of dizziness. "Julia, I . . ."

She clung to him. "No! Time can't take you. The stone, Rae, you must touch it directly."

Turning the ring around, he closed his palm tight over it.

Julia and Rae cleaved to one another, their lips meeting in a final, impassioned kiss. Tears spilled down Julia's face, and Rae braced himself for her to vanish from his arms, and for him to catapult back almost five hundred years to Dunraven's fire.

The weighted air dissolved around them and Rae waited to feel the pull of time. But long after Time had shifted, and the portal had closed, miraculously, Rae's lips continued to claim Julia's.

The arched door evaporated along with the iron-bound trunk, and the room filled with blues and creams and pale moss greens. Most spectacular of all, the trappings of the great Flemish bed ceased alternating in color, the scarlet melting to a brilliant blue, giving hope and promise to all their tomorrows.

Epilogue

Lord Muir closed the green leather binder.

"And so, according to Niall, the Third Laird of Dunraven died that fateful night, as did Iain and his accomplices, during an attack on the Cameron stronghold. It appears Ronald Cameron had anticipated the attack and had given his clan warning, which is why they were more than prepared and took no losses."

"What became of Ronald Cameron?" Julia asked, slipping forward on her chair as she swept her gaze from Lord Muir to Rae and back. "Does anyone know?"

Lord Muir pulled thoughtfully on his beard. "Ah yes, we found an oblique reference to Lochiel's nephews, living as outcasts in the Northwest Highlands. For reasons not recorded, at about the time of Rae's supposed 'death,' Lochiel himself spurned his nephews, as did the clan. The three died a couple of years later reiving Mackenzie cattle."

Rae turned to Julia. "We hae scoured the auld books and parchments tae see if anythin' is changed in the records, if we somehow altered history, after all, tha' night. 'Tis largely the same, wi' a few more explanations."

Lord Muir took up the account. "Donald averted a clan war, as Niall wrote before, but now there is an addition. Though Niall doesn't record Donald's motives, he does write that, after finding evidence that pointed to Rae's murderer, he decided to pursue a course of peace with the Camerons."

"He found Iain's knife then," Julia stated the obvious.

"'Tis wha' we are thinkin'." Rae encompassed Lord Muir

with a nod, then sent her a smile. "Donald went on tae rule as Dunraven's Fourth Laird for many years, he wrought great deeds and begat many bairns wi' his Mairi. It makes a brother proud."

Rae looked away a moment, and Julia saw a muscle flex in his jaw. There was something he was leaving left unsaid.

"What is it, darling?"

He did not meet her eyes, but dropped his gaze to the floor.

"Knowin' Donald, our deaths—mine and Iain's—must hae been devastatin' each in their own way. Niall's records still speak o' the mystery tha' persisted o'er the body taken from the ashes, tha' 'twas a man o' smaller stature than m'sel'. I only wish Donald could hae known I escaped and didna die." He reached over and caught her hands with his. "I wish he could hae known I am a happy, married mon now, and soon tae be a father."

Julia warmed at his look and smiled, knowing Rae had been more than thrilled when she could confirm her pregnancy. They had been married scarcely three weeks in a small but lovely ceremony which Lord Muir had arranged and which the gentlemen of the Society and the servants attended. Rae had teasingly, though lovingly, commented that since Dunraven—their wedding gift from Lord Muir—had grown to such proportions, they would need to fill the castle with many more bairns in the years to come.

Lord Muir cleared his throat. "Actually, speaking of Donald, I came upon something just last night, while I was going through an early Mackinnon Bible. The binding came apart, and I found this note, tucked between the two layers of leather."

Lord Muir produced what appeared to be a folded letter, its paper yellowed with age.

"I don't believe it was there before. I've examined the Bible many times. As you can see, it is written in Gaelic, which is where my capabilities end. But look at the signature, I believe it might be Donald's."

Silent, Rae accepted the paper and opened its brittle page.

His eyes traveled down the page then he lifted his gaze to Lord Muir, then Julia.

"Aye, 'tis Donald's. 'Twas written after my death, but he addresses the latter tae me."

He gave his attention again to the letter. Julia saw him take a long swallow as he read, his eyes becoming suddenly glossed with unshed tears. When he looked up, his lips formed a smile.

"Smart lad, Donald. Always was."

"Rae, what does it say?"

"'Twould seem Donald ne'er accepted my death, nor tha' 'twas my body found in the hall. He writes as if speakin' tae me right here, saying he'd known in his heart if I had died. Still, I disappeared so completely, he says he's found no reasonable explanation, though he holds his suspicions—or at least the hope—I did escape."

Julia tilted her head. "What suspicions could he have? He didn't witness any time-slips."

"He's a perceptive lad, Donald. He mentions Moira's 'green woman' in the stairwell, and certain, er, sounds in m' chamber at odd hours."

Julia flushed with warmth and avoided Lord Muir's eyes though she believed he was smiling behind that beard of his.

"Wha' most convinced him of my survival was something o' which I didna know. Once, he followed me from the hall tae speak wi' me on some matter. When he entered the chamber directly after me I'd already disappeared, as if into thin air.

"When I likewise disappeared after the fire, he writes that he has looked for me many years wi' his sons. He says he hopes I am safe in another place, wherever 'tis. He also says he kept the stone from the talisman, though the metal melted away."

Julia and Lord Muir exchanged glances. "Oh no!"

Julia placed her mother's ring in the rosewood box along with several sets of earrings, neck chokers, bracelets, and six more rings—anything with gemstones, particularly those of quartz—amethyst, citrine, agate, tiger's-eye, and more.

"Are ye done?"

"Yes these should be all."

Before she could close the box, Rae placed the large and precious Brooch of Glendar within it as well.

"We dinna know wha' the crystal in the brooch is exactly," he said by way of explanation.

Julia gazed on the lovely jewels, then with a sigh, closed the top, locked it with her small key, and accompanied Rae to the door, the box in hand. Angus waited outside.

"Ye know wha' tae do wi' these," Rae said, taking the box from Julia and giving it to Angus.

"Aye. Take them as far away as possible, t' the other side of Britain."

"London will do." Julia smiled. "His lordship has made arrangements to put them in his vault. You know it is important they stay there, and no such stones be allowed in Dunraven."

Angus nodded. "Aye. No telling what Donald did with the other one, the talisman."

"Aye, we dinna wish tae be openin' any door on the past," Rae rejoined. "Is the tower keep now completely sealed off?"

"That 'tis. Ye need not fear. And his lordship has moved his library t' below."

"Guid. Thank ye, Angus. Lady Mackinnon and I shall rest easy when the stones are far away."

"Oh, aye. I'm on my way." With that, Angus hurried off, his kilt swishing.

"'Lady Mackinnon,' I like the sound of that." Julia smiled up at Rae.

"Ye are my lady," he said simply. "And I am still laird of Dunraven, though third or twenty-eighth, I am no' sure. Still, that makes ye my lady—Lady Mackinnon o' Dunraven Castle."

Rae brushed his lips over hers, encircling her waist with one arm. Fleetingly, Julia thought of Lilith, who so coveted all the titles she might gain through the Dunnington family, including that as mistress of Dunraven and much more—that of marchioness. But Lilith had realized none of these, having returned to England in utter disgrace, Lord Muir's words ringing in her Aunt Sybil's ears.

For Lilith's collaboration with Roger and her assault upon Julia, Lord Muir forbade her to darken his door in any quarter of Britain again. As to his nephew, he avowed he had cut Roger off without a penny and disinherited him. Lord Muir further shared the "rumor" that Roger had since fled the shores ahead of his creditors and sailed for the wilds of North America. The tale was enough to satisfy any questions that might arise as to Roger's whereabouts or fate.

Julia closed her thoughts on the matter and slipped her arm around Rae's waist. Together, they returned to their spacious suite of rooms in the north wing, with its sweeping view of the Grampians. Standing before the huge windows, they took in the breathtaking sight.

"Oh, look, Rae, the moon is visible today in the sky."

"Aye, 'tis increasing like yerself."

Rae dropped a kiss to the curve of her neck and began to work upward to her ear.

"D'ye think ye can be happy here? Ye willna mind no' havin' any jewels?"

"I have you." She smiled, turning in his arms. "That is more than enough. Of course, there is gold, and silver, and pearls . . ." she teased. "But as to gemstones? No, we did what we must. We can't take the chance of permitting them within Dunraven's walls."

"'Tis truth, *mo càran*. For who can foretell if Time will slip again?"

With that, his lips closed over hers, and Time stood still as their hearts melded to one.

Dear Reader,

I hope you have enjoyed Rae and Julia's story, *A Slip in Time*, which deals with an unusual and little known phenomena called a "time slip." As time slips are still considered a theory in parapsychology circles, I have taken generous liberties in its use, particularly with the duration of the time portals' opening and the lunar connections. Otherwise, many of the details follow accounts of those who have experienced the phenomena such as a sudden heaviness coming into the air as time "shifts."

If you enjoyed *A Slip in Time*, I hope you will look for my next tale, set at a remote country manor house in the English West Midlands. Join Vanessa Wynters and the mysterious master of Sherringham, Adrian Marrable, along with a host of others—mortal and otherwise—as a haunting tale unfolds.

Just what *are* the misty forms that persistently appear in Vanessa's photographs of the old, Gothic-styled manse? And what fate really befell Adrian's first two wives?

Find out next year when *Shades of the Past* appears in your local bookstores.

—*Kathleen Kirkwood*

□ *LAIRD OF THE WIND*   0-451-40768-7/$5.99

In medieval Scotland, the warrior known as Border Hawk seizes the castle belonging to the father of the beautiful Isabel Scott, famous throughout the Lowlands for her gift of prophecy. During the battle, Isabel is injured while fighting alongside her men, and placed under Border Hawk's protection. As the border wars rage on, the warrior and prophetess engage in a more intimate conflict, discovering their love for the Scottish borderlands is surpassed only by their love for each other.

Also available:
□ THE ANGEL KNIGHT	0-451-40662-1/$5.50
□ THE BLACK THORNE'S ROSE	0-451-40544-7/$4.99
□ LADY MIRACLE	0-451-40766-0/$5.99
□ THE RAVEN'S MOON	0-451-18868-3/$5.99
□ THE RAVEN'S WISH	0-451-40545-5/$4.99

Prices slightly higher in Canada

PENGUIN PUTNAM

-------------------------------- online

Your Internet gateway to a virtual environ-
ment with hundreds of entertaining and
enlightening books from Penguin Putnam Inc.

*While you're there get the latest buzz on
the best authors and books around—*

Tom Clancy, Patricia Cornwell, W.E.B. Griffin,
Nora Roberts, William Gibson, Robin Cook,
Brian Jacques, Catherine Coulter, Stephen King,
Jacquelyn Mitchard and many more!

PenguinPutnam Online is located at
http://www.penguinputnam.com

• •

PENGUIN PUTNAM
NEWS

Every month you'll get an inside look at
our upcoming books and new features on
our site. This is an ongoing effort on our
part to provide you with the most interesting and up-to-date information about our
books and authors.

Subscribe to Penguin Putnam News at
http://www.penguinputnam.com/ClubPPI